"WHAT ARE YOU DOING HERE?" CAMILLA WHISPERED AT LAST.

"Of all the nerve! To appear in the midst of the very people you incessantly terrorize! And to let yourself be introduced as someone named John Locksley besides!"

"I could hardly let 'im intraduce me as Jason Fate," grinned the highwayman. "Not here at any rate. Devil take me but ye're more beautiful than I remembered."

"And you, sir, are just as audacious as I remembered."

They traversed the rest of the dance floor in silence making a perfect rectangle of it before either spoke again. "Have you nothing more to say?" Camilla asked then, with an edge of anger to her tone. "Does not it at all occur to you that I might at this very moment declare to the world that you are Captain Jason Fate and in less time than it takes to say it, you would be on your way to Newgate? Have you no shame? No conscience whatsoever? Not the least feeling of guilt?"

"Uh-uh," he smiled down at her, "I'm still tryin' ta figger out what 'aud-ay-tious' means. It ain't nothin' good I take it?"

CAMILLA'S FATE

Judith A. Lansdowne

Zebra Books
Kensington Publishing Corp.
http://www.zebrabooks.com

ZEBRA BOOKS are published by

Kensington Publishing Corp.
850 Third Avenue
New York, NY 10022

First Printing: July, 1997
10 9 8 7 6 5 4 3 2 1

Printed in the United States of America

*To Judy, most likely the best sister-in-law in the world
and to my brother, Joe, who never let me down—
not once—in all our lives. Thank you for always being there.*

Chapter 1

The Earl of Wheymore's second best travelling carriage lurched forward abruptly behind his four prime bays as they bolted into a wild run at the resounding explosion of two horse pistols, one to each side of them. Lady Aurora screamed as she bounced, barely awake, from the seat to the floor; Viscount Neiland saved himself from a similar fate by grabbing the hand strap in the nick of time; Miss Camilla Quinn voiced a rather unladylike exclamation, grasped the window molding beside her with both hands and stuck her head most unbecomingly out of the window to see what was happening. A chill night wind sizzled against her cheeks and drove off the lethargy that had but recently overcome her. A flash of light, a great roar, and the outrider beside her bounced sickeningly from his horse and rolled across a piece of moonlit verge. Above her on the box the groom, Malcolm, bellowed; his great blunder-buss thundered through the night. A second explosion and a third followed instantly from the rear of the coach. And then a horse the color of drizzling skies streaked toward the front of the coach. A ghost of a man in a long, drab surtout and wide-brimmed hat rode like a god-gone-mad upon its broad back. Camilla pushed herself farther through the window to watch him and gasped as he kicked free of his stirrups and flung himself onto the back of the outside wheeler. With incredible strength he pushed the beast's head downward and to the side, causing it to stumble and lurch and stumble again, slowing its pace and the pace of the rest of the team. More shots rang out. One of them sent the man's hat careening into the darkness. Beyond noticing, he struggled with the outside wheeler until, at last, he brought the coach to a dead stop. Neiland's hand came tight around Camilla's elbow and the viscount yanked her back inside.

Camilla heard John Coachman's familiar voice rumble above her and a resounding laugh answer him. "Aye, 'twas a fine chase, coachman, but 'tis time ta stand an' deliver."

Aurora squealed and huddled into her corner of the coach. Neiland clung determinedly to his swordstick and signaled Camilla to be silent. A man on horseback rode up beside the coach door; his booted foot unlatched it and swung it carefully open. Neiland flung himself into the night. There was a great thunk, a cry of pain, a curse and another thunk, and then the man in the long, drab surtout appeared in the doorway, grasped Camilla's waist in strong, lean hands, and lifted her out into the chill air. He set her firmly upon her feet and reached back inside. A moment later he lifted a struggling, sobbing Aurora from the coach as well.

"Let her be!" bellowed Neiland staring down the barrel of an extremely ugly horse pistol and holding his right arm gingerly against his chest. "Take your filthy hands off of my sister! Let her be, I tell you!"

The highwayman set Aurora safely upon the road and turned languidly toward the viscount. "Both of 'em yer sisters, Sprig?" he asked in a smooth, quiet voice. "Or only the little banshee?"

Neiland opened his mouth to voice a sardonic reply, thought better of it, and closed his mouth again without uttering a sound. His arm was probably broken, one of his men carried a pistol ball in the shoulder, a second nursed a badly bleeding leg, and a third lay, quite possibly dead, on the verge. This was not the time to reply flippantly, nor in haste.

"I asked ye if they was both yer sisters," said the highwayman softly, taking a step in Neiland's direction.

"No, I am not his sister," volunteered Camilla hurriedly, fearing for her cousin David's safety.

The highwayman turned back to look down at her and a pair of fine dark eyes sparkled from above the kerchief that had been tied to cover most of his face. "Who are ye then?"

"Cap'n," urged the only villain still on horseback whose pistol pointed directly at Neiland's heart, "quit triflin' wif the lady an' git on wif it. We ain't got all night."

The highwayman's dark eyes lit with mirth and he winked at Camilla. "We ain't got all night," he chuckled. "Ye sure—certain ain't his lor'ship's mum. Are ye 'is wife, then?"

"No, I am his cousin."

"So, welcome ta Finchley's Common, Cousin," the highwayman drawled taking her hand. He tugged the kerchief down from his face and bowed, brushing cool soft lips across the inside of Camilla's wrist. When his eyes once again met hers they shimmered with a strange perplexity in the moonlight and Camilla noted with surprise that a golden hoop glinted in his left earlobe. Most abruptly she felt the oddest stirring in the verimost pit of her stomach.

" 'Tis Jason Fate welcomes ye, darlin'." He kept hold of her hand and raised it high enough to unfasten the clasp of the diamond bracelet she wore. Removing it, he tossed it over his shoulder where it was caught by an extremely short ruffian and stuffed unceremoniously into a leather pouch. "Ye'll not miss such a trifle, eh, Cousin?" His fingers flitted like powdered moth wings against the back of her neck and her diamond necklace, too, sailed over his shoulder and took up residence in the pouch. "Will ye tell me yer name?" he whispered then, his lips so close to her ear she could feel each tiny movement of them. When she did not answer, his fingertips brushed her earlobes and her diamond eardrops entered the leather pouch as well. "Come, lass, tell me yer name. 'Tis careful

I'll be of it, I promise. I know," he murmured when Camilla did not answer, " 'tis Hortensia."

Camilla's eyes lit with mirth in the bright moonlight.

"Not Hortensia? Euphegenia then."

"N-no," breathed Camilla on a tiny giggle.

"Aw, darlin'," sighed the highwayman sweeping away the reticule that dangled from her wrist, "don't be makin' me guess. I ain't good at it—Daisy? Amaryllis? Rhododendron?"

A lovely trill of laughter swirled from between Camilla's lips. "Rhododendron?" she laughed.

"Well, ye don't never know 'bout the Quality," replied Fate with a shrug and a most engaging grin. One long, slim finger traced a gentle line down her cheek and Camilla shivered. From behind her David's cursing protest sounded merely like the groaning of the wind.

"I'd give m'life ta know yer name," breathed the highwayman. "Ye've an aura of angels about ye."

Almost mesmerized, Camilla felt his strong arms lift her back into the coach. Before he turned away she saw him draw the kerchief once again over his face. In a matter of moments a sobbing Aurora was in the coach beside her and then a muttering David. The wounded outriders and Malcolm were shoved in amongst them and to the accompaniment of shouts and shots John Coachman was springing the team toward London.

"Well, but it has been almost two weeks, and I think we should just forget about it," offered Aurora from the window seat of the Striped Saloon where she paged languidly through a recent copy of *La Belle Asemblee*. "We have come to London to enjoy the Season not to chase after highwaymen. You are certainly not to be blamed for being unable to describe him, Cammy. After all, there was only a bit of moonlight to see him by, regardless of whether he lowered his mask or not."

"Exactly so," agreed Lady Wheymore, sorting through her silks to locate the exact shade of primrose for the blossom she was presently embroidering upon a fine square of muslin. "I am sorry it happened, Cammy, but it is over and done with now and we must all set it aside."

"Yes, Aunt Mary, but he stole my mother's diamonds and I shall never get them back."

"Indeed," nodded Lady Wheymore, "but it is not as if they were heirlooms, dearest. He did not steal the Penistone rubies, or the Quinn emeralds. They were merely falderals your Mama bought once on a whim. She thought they would look nice, you know, with a new gown she'd had fashioned for the opera. And they did look quite pretty with it. But she never wore them once she tired of that particular gown."

"Well, but that does not mean some wretched highwayman may take them for his own," replied Camilla, her green eyes firing in anger. "Oh, I cannot believe how I stood there like a fool and let him take them. I did not even protest. Not once!"

"You were paralyzed with fear," suggested Aurora, setting her magazine aside. "He terrified you completely."

"Indeed," agreed Lady Wheymore. "Such a response is perfectly understandable. Though I admit I would never have expected it of you, Camilla. I should have expected you to have had a try at scratching the ruffian's eyes out."

"Yes, so should I," reflected Camilla glumly. "I cannot think what came over me." She longed to say more but bit her lower lip and stared from the window of the house in Grosvenor Square in silence. Her Uncle Ned, Earl of Wheymore, had arrived only a day after she and her cousins, and he had been most put out to discover that his sweet daughter, Aurora, and the lovely niece he had raised from childhood, had been terrified and that his son's arm had been broken. He had ranted and raged his way from Bow Street to the House of Lords, declaring that the notorious, villainous and thoroughly audacious Captain Jason Fate had ruled the High Toby quite long enough and that his brazen effrontery must be met with immediate and decisive action. The knave must be caught and hanged as quickly as possible. And Camilla had quite agreed with him—until she'd been called upon to provide Bow Street with a description of the scoundrel. Why on earth, she

wondered, had she not sat down and drawn a portrait of
the rogue? Why had she hemmed and hawed and at last
protested that most of his visage had been hidden by moon-
shadow? None of his visage had been hidden by moon-
shadow. She had seen him as clearly as if he'd stood in
the light of day.

To this very moment she could see the sparkle of his
dark eyes, the stark hollow of his cheeks, his dusky curls
dangling limp with sweat across his proud brow, and his
seductively smiling lips. But to be called upon to provide
the portrait—whether with words or sketches—that would
lead to his hanging! No, she could not! She despised him
for a miscreant, for stealing her diamonds and Aurora's
pearls and every penny in David's pockets, but not one of
their little party had been gravely injured, not even the
outrider who had lain so still upon the verge. The captain,
it seemed, was so adept at his chosen profession that no
one had ever opposed him adroitly enough to make serious
injuries a possibility. Not that that should matter, Camilla
told herself angrily. Someone might be killed at any time.
And then the man would be a murderer. And then she
would most certainly regret this unfortunate obstinacy of
hers in not revealing the austere contours of that alluring
countenance. Oh, for goodness sake, she thought, whatever in the world has come over me!

Captain Jason Fate could not think what had come over
him either as he sprawled in a worn arm chair in the parlor
of a small house in Curzon Street. Camilla's diamond
bracelet sparkled in the sunlight as he played it between
his fingers. One of his legs dangled over a chair arm. The
other stretched out toward the cold hearth. His fine, dark
eyes stared at the brightly glittering jewels as he rested his
head wearily against the chairback. Ought ta have sold off
these bloody gems weeks ago, he thought uneasily. Mad
ta keep 'em and even madder ta keep 'em always in my
pockets. Still, each time he tugged them into the open
and watched sunlight or moonlight or candlelight play
over their facets, visions of the beautiful mort sprang to his

mind. Heavenly, she'd looked, with the moonlight addin' a golden glow to the rich chestnut of her hair—standin' and starin' at him so unafraid. An' her laughter had set some odd ember in him afire, and he'd made a deuced fool of himself lettin' her see his face.

"So, Jason m'lad, have ye thought over the proposition?" A gravel-edged voice interrupted his thoughts anxiously. "I ain't pressing ye, mind, but my friend'll be needing an answer soon." A slightly built gentleman with an unruly semicircle of grey fringe around his balding pate took up a stance beside the mantle and stared down at Fate. " 'Tis a likely lay, m'boy."

"I got m'own lay, Mossie, an' a right profitable one 'tis."

"Aye, but ye cannot keep at it without pause, lad. Sure'n they'll git ye do ye not fade off from time to time. Pushing yer luck is what ye are."

"No, am I?" Fate's eyes lit with amusement at the frown line deepening between the bushy white eyebrows before him and at the odd slant to the wide red lips. "I like yer house, Mossie."

"Don't be changing of the subject."

"I'm not. Where would I live, eh, if I was ta take up this proposition ye keep mutterin' about? Not 'ere, I reckon."

"Nay, not here, Jason. At a much cushier domicile. A reg'lar palace in Grosvenor Square."

Fate chuckled and stood, stuffing the diamond bracelet unceremoniously into a pocket of his nankeen hunting jacket. He stared thoughtfully down at the scuffed toes of his riding boots. "Who is't wants m'services, Mossie? Ye kin say that. I ain't about ta be turnin' the bloke in fer a bit o' larceny, am I?" His gaze lifted to meet Moss's faded blue eyes.

"A gent by the name of Eversley. A right unhappy gent."

"Well, I reckon he'll go on bein' unhappy does he wait on me, Mossie. Ye tell 'im Jason Fate ain't no play-actor, nor ain't like ta be. I been a lotta thin's in m'day, Moss, but a knockdown, drag-out, bang up ta the mark gen'leman ain't one of 'em an' I ain't likely ever ta be taken fer one." Fate extended a hand toward the old man who dropped a leather pouch into it. "That's all?"

" 'Tis four hundred crowns in that pouch, lad."

"An' the jewels I give ye be worth three times that."

"Aye, but there's the recutting and the melting down and the resetting to be done. Ye know how it is, Jason."

Fate nodded, resigned, and tucked the pouch away inside his jacket. "An' there's yer cut an' Adderley's too, ain't there? I swear, Mossie, I don't know why I bother doin' business wi' ye. I can git a better price any one of a hunnerd other places."

"Ye love me, Jason, that's why. Like yer da I am."

Fate roared into laughter. "More like a bloody leech, Mossie. Always clingin' ta me no matter where I go. Always suckin' out m'blunt no matter how I gets it."

"Aye," cackled Elgin Moss, clapping his hands together gleefully, "just like yer da would have done, my boy. Just like yer da would have done!"

Fate shook his head, his grin wider than it had been for many a day. That was the truth certain-sure. Had his da lived, that scoundrel would've sucked the blunt out of him with as much energy an' zest as Mossie did. Still, he never much minded what Mossie took. 'Twas the cost of doin' business fer one thin' and a matter of bein' grateful fer another. He waved a farewell in Elgin Moss's direction, strolled into the hallway, out the front door, and down the four short steps to the pavement. In worn white corduroy breeches, down-at-the-heel hightop boots, his nankeen hunting jacket, and a Belcher kerchief tied loosely about his throat, he knew he looked exceeding odd as he traversed Curzon Street. The neighborhood, though not acceptable to the highest circles, still housed a number of the gentry, some younger sons of the aristocracy who were not quite so plump in the pocket as they were used to be, and many determinedly respectable members of the rising middle class. The sooner he left the vicinity, the less likely he'd be to arouse unwanted curiosity.

His stride lengthened as he reached the corner and turned in the direction of Albemarle Street and Grillon's Hotel. He tossed the little crossing sweeper a crown, grinned at the exclamation it received, and then studied the cobbles before him, looking neither to one side nor the other. His hands he kept in his jacket pockets; his mind he allowed to wander. And wander it did, back to the lady with the mirth-filled eyes and the sweet, hushed laughter that spilled so prettily from her full, enticing lips. Why'd she hafta be Quality, he sighed inwardly. A mort like that—a man would sell his soul to 'ave a mort like that jus' hold his hand. But he were foolish beyond permission ta keep conjurin' 'er up the way 'e did. He couldn't unnerstan' why he did it, or why he kep' her gems by 'im, or why, in the name o' the Princess o' Dewdrops, the flash mort hadn't run direckly ta Bow Street and told 'em what 'e looked like. He'd near as well begged 'er ta do so, droppin' his mask and kissin' her wrist like some fribbled dandy!

But she hadn't. He was certain-sure she hadn't. It'd been three weeks an' still the only notice given of the rousin' trade he an' Artie an' Harley were doin' were a poster with his name an' the price o' betrayal on't, an' not much else—certain-sure no description of 'imself.

Camilla smiled as Mr. Clarence Lilliheun assisted her onto the box of his high perch phaeton. Mr. Lilliheun, who had been chasing after her since her first appearance on the marriage mart two years before, ascended the box beside her, took the reins, and sent his tiger scrambling for a perch at the rear of the carriage as he urged the team of blacks forward.

"I am most surprised, Mr. Lilliheun, that you asked me rather than Lady Aurora to drive with you," Camilla murmured suppressing a twitch of her lips.

Lilliheun, a tall, handsome gentleman with eyes the color of an angry sea and hair like summer sunlight, grinned and shook his head. "It is your cousin's first Season, Miss Quinn. She will have so many young beaux swarming around her that she will not once be inclined to notice such a dull dog as myself."

"As I recall, Mr. Lilliheun, that possibility did not deter you from approaching me in my first Season."

"No, nothing would have kept me from doing that, my

dear. The moment I laid my eyes upon you, I knew I had to try my luck. Though why you persist in squashing my every hope, I cannot fathom. I *am* a fine catch, you know. And no," he added with a chuckle, "I will not allow you to shrug me off onto your cousin."

Camilla had the good grace to blush under the brim of her saucy green satin jockey cap. The truth was that she had tried numerous times to cool Mr. Lilliheun's ardor and would have set him onto Aurora if she could. Clare was a good-humored, handsome, and totally respectable gentleman and the heir presumptive to his uncle's dukedom. And he most assuredly was, as he teasingly suggested, a remarkably fine catch. But Camilla did not wish to catch him. She had berated herself for turning him away the very first time he had proposed to her, but when he had returned and courted her again and proposed again, she had again declined. Even her Aunt Mary could not believe that Mr. Lilliheun had returned to try a third time. "Why he might have had any one of the chicks on the marriage mart any time these past five years, Camilla," Lady Wheymore had sighed. "Why can you not see that he is determined to have you and will do anything at all to accomplish it? What more could you desire in a husband? He is handsome, wealthy, respectable, responsible and totally devoted to you. Goodness, the man is a paragon!"

"What are you thinking about so seriously, Camilla?" Lilliheun asked, his eyes laughing down at her. "You look rather as if you have just swallowed a toad."

"Oh, no, do I?" chuckled Camilla. "And to think you do not stop and set me down immediately. You are indeed a kindly and considerate companion."

"Yes, and always have been. Tell me, Camilla, what is it about me that sets your teeth on edge?"

"Oh! Oh! Nothing!" gasped Camilla. "I never, never meant to give you such an idea, Clare. You have been my true friend from the very first time we met and I cannot find anything but joy in your company, I assure you."

"But you cannot find it in your heart to marry me?"

"No," sighed Camilla, twisting her fingers together in her lap, "but that is none of your fault. It is all mine. I do not think, Clare, that I was meant to be married. I am sufficiently provided for, you know, and might exist quite comfortably on my own. And—and—I should *like* to be an independent woman."

"I see. And what will you do, my independent Miss Quinn, when you are your own keeper?"

"Write," breathed Camilla, her gaze lifting to meet his own. "I shall become an authoress like Miss Austen and everyone will wait breathlessly to read my volumes."

"And you think I would disapprove of your becoming an authoress? Is that it, Cam? Is that what keeps you from me? But it is not so. I will be proud of you!"

"No, you will not. You only think you will. In a matter of months you will be longing for a pliable, complacent wife who thinks of nothing but having your children and caring for them and ordering your household and making you comfortable, and I can never be just that, Clare. I have ambitions and hopes. I have dreams to fulfill. And they do not, truly, include a husband and children. Even the possibility of becoming a duchess someday does not appeal to me, Clare. Oh, if only I could somehow make you understand. Truly, I think you are the most remarkable gentleman, and if I could, I would fall in love with you and marry you and we would live quite happily ever after. But I cannot. I am determined to be a person in my own right and *not* dependent upon any man's consequence nor upon his charity."

Lilliheun would have replied with a number of reassurances, but his attention was abruptly drawn to his team who, startled by a sudden uproar at the curb, shied, reared, and then broke into a run. "Hold on, Camilla," he shouted. "Hold tight." And then all his concentration went to driving the fresh and frightened horses through a number of narrow gaps between farmers' wagons, costermongers' barrows, pedestrians, riders, and a number of sporting vehicles making their way along the cobbles. Camilla clung to the swaying phaeton watching with a mixture of fear and amazement the remarkable skill Clare exhibited in missing all of the targets before them.

Lips set in a grim line, his eyes taking in all possible

outcomes at once, his hands tightly entwined in the reins as he steadily and uncompromisingly pulled the great beasts back under his own control, Lilliheun displayed to Camilla's astonished eyes all the calm power and aplomb of any hero in any novel she had ever read. Her heart throbbed with excitement. Her face flushed. Her breath came in short, brisk gasps as the phaeton narrowly missed a cart of melons, swayed perilously close to a hired hack, and missed the wheel of a curricle by a hair's breadth. Just as Lilliheun appeared to have gained the upper hand and the horses began to slow their mad dash, the reins that ran to the inside wheeler snapped with a sound like a pistol shot and the horses were off again, careening down Albemarle Street.

Fate, roused from his thoughts by the sound of a ruckus, raised his eyes from the cobbles as a runaway team, iron-shod hooves sparking, bore down upon an elderly woman who stood motionless, petrified, in the middle of the street. Instantly he hurtled into the path of the brutally advancing team, thrust the woman ruthlessly toward the curb and spun about to catch the harness of the outside wheeler. His boots scrambled for a hold among the leathers as he struggled to gain the horse's back. Once there he noted the broken rein, leaped from the outside wheeler to the inside wheeler and gaining that beast's bridle began to fight the animal into a slower pace while the driver, on the box, continued to do battle with the other animal. Together they brought the horses to a stuttering halt. The tiger, his face whiter than his neckcloth, jumped from his perch and ran to the horses's heads. "Gore blimey, sir!" he gasped. "Ye's a bloody savior! I thought sure we was all o' us deaduns."

"Aye," rasped Fate, breathing hard as he slipped from the inside wheeler's back to the ground. "Thought ye was goners, m'self. Thought the whole lot of us was. 'Ere," he muttered as the driver, who had jumped hurriedly from the box, came up beside him, "someun's cut yer harness, gov. Ye kin see how clean 'tis this far through the break, eh? Bin a blade tastin' of it.''

"I'll be swaggled," exclaimed the gentleman staring, astounded, at the offending piece of leather. "Who in thunderation would think to do such a thing?"

"I'd figger out who, an' quick," muttered Fate. "Ain't discriminatin' whoever 'tis. Reckon there's a hunnerd less noticeable ways ta kill a bloke."

"Well, well, I'll look into it," sputtered the man, suddenly and inexplicably embarrassed. "Clarence Lilliheun," he said brusquely, his face, already red from exertion, turning a shade brighter. "Y'r servant, sir. Cannot thank you enough for your assistance."

"Certain-sure ye can't," grinned Fate, taking the proffered hand. "But ye done admirable, gov', at drivin' 'em, wild as they was. Naw, don't be puttin' yer hand in yer pocket. It ain't a payin' matter."

"A drink then," proposed Lilliheun, uncertain what to offer as reward for the man's quick thinking and unarguable prowess. "Or dinner? Dinner and a drink!"

Fate shook his head. "Can't. Business callin', though I thank ye fer the thought. Be bloody embarrassin' fer ye, suppin' with the likes of me at any rate."

Camilla, having managed to descend from the phaeton with the aid of a stout gentleman bystander, rushed up to the two men, took one clear, direct look at Fate's unforgettable countenance, gasped, and broke into a fit of coughing. Lilliheun turned to assist her, patted her back, told her to raise her arms in the air, patted her back again. When at last her coughing ceased and they looked back to their rescuer, Fate had disappeared from view.

"Bloke's gone off to Grillon's, sir," offered the little tiger. "Loped right off 'e did. Late fer his business I reckon."

"And I did not even get his name," murmured Lilliheun. "Tom, lead the horses back to the stable, eh? I expect Miss Quinn and I shall be forced to take a hackney coach home.

You're all right, aren't you, Camilla?" he asked solicitously. "You are not injured in any way?"

"No," Camilla replied softly. "I am fine, Clare. He did not tell you his name?"

"Never did. Not to worry, though. I shall ask about and discover who the man is and see that he is repaid somehow. If he stays at Grillon's someone will recognize his description and put me in the way of him. Most likely someone's groom or coachman or a stable hand at the hotel itself, don't you think?"

Camilla thought nothing of the sort. She had been stunned to see a man bolt into the path of the rampaging horses and extremely relieved to view the elderly lady flying rudely but safely into the hands of onlookers at the curb. Then she had been flabbergasted as the man mounted the outside wheeler and she had come totally undone to see the way he transferred himself from one mount to the other and fought the unchecked beast under control.

She had stared, wide-eyed, then closed her eyes for the longest time, then stared again. It cannot be, she had scolded herself. Come, Camilla, that villain cannot be the only man in England capable of such fearless dealings with horses. And besides, the scoundrel would not dare to show his face in London. She had convinced herself that this was indeed true. She had climbed down from the box to add her thanks to Mr. Lilliheun's. She had taken one look at Fate's rugged, austere, and thoroughly delectable face as it gazed with a charming grin back at her, and she had wanted to do nothing more than faint dead away.

Chapter 2

Elgin Moss had risen to the ranks of pseudo-respectability much as a piece of flotsam rises to the shore on an incoming tide—without thought, effort, or even desire of his own. With a slight stature, gravelly voice, reasonably high intelligence and a countenance overflowing with endearing innocence, Moss had discovered early how an urchin from the rancid, stinking warren of St. Giles's might, with proper humility, wrench at the hearts of the more socially conscious—and female—members of the upper classes. His appealing blue eyes, long golden curls, and remarkable ability to flirt angelically at an early age had won him a number of reformers' hearts, seen him to a seat in a penny school, introduced him to the rear entrances of various aristocratic households, and provided him with interesting information which he eagerly passed on to his father who was the proprietor of a thieves' kitchen called The Golden Lamb.

As a tot he had prattled out a number of likely methods and modes of prigging this or that from the gentry which his father's patrons quickly put to use, a share of their booty going to enrich the elder Moss which made Elgin's life a bit more palatable. But by the time he had reached the advanced age of thirteen and his father had succumbed to a bout of fever, Elgin Moss had learned to purloin the flimsies and the fashionables himself and eliminate the need to share anything with anyone. He'd also learned over a number of years the reasonableness of investing a certain portion of his income in likely schemes and plots involving at various times: London footpads, gentry green-horns, gullible young matrons, and blackmailers.

But never had he made so fine an investment as the evening he'd discovered a thoroughly distraught seven-year-old Jason Fate beneath the gibbet at Tyburn with two wretchedly abused bodies swinging in the breeze above him. True, Moss's first thought had been to ignore the shivering bundle of dirty rags and go on about his own business, but something exceptional had blazed at him from behind the dark eyes, a fierce passion and taunting self-assurance that had halted Moss in his tracks. He'd been all of thirty years old then; he was fifty now; in none of the intervening years had he once regretted his decision to take the boy under his own wing. Once fed and scrubbed and dressed in worn but serviceable clothes, Jason had proved his worth time and again by exhibiting an amazing ability for discovering and entering partially opened windows—no matter what floor; for removing all manner of gewgaws, coins and flimsies from people as he passed them in the streets; and for prigging ladies reticules and purloining gentlemen's pocketbooks.

He'd also displayed an overwhelming enthusiasm for any new lay Moss set before him—becoming with joyous abandonment and unbridled enthusiasm a thieves' kinchin, a gambler's shill, the bastard son of several notable gentlemen, a smugglers' signalman, and even, in a notable scheme as he approached his nineteenth year, a gypsy fortune teller. Never had Elgin Moss met with such eagerness, excitement, audacity and courage as coursed through the veins of Jason Fate.

There had been nothing the boy would not attempt at Moss's request, nothing at which he did not succeed, and no profits he ever refused to share. And the best thing of all, thought Moss straightening his cravat before the bevelled mirror at the end of the hall, the best thing of all, was that Jason had not one qualm of conscience about anything. Whoever that man and woman on the gibbet had been, they'd managed to raise a son without a smattering of knowledge of the difference between right and wrong, a son who saw good as what came to him through his own efforts and evil as what awaited him at the hands of the British government, the Bow Street Runners, and all the members of the gentry, the aristocracy and the nobility.

That perhaps was the reason Moss worried now as he turned from the mirror, took an ebony cane from the umbrella stand, popped a high-top beaver upon his head, and left the rented house in Curzon Street. Jason had never before refused to join him in a scheme, so what was it that put the lad off about the Eversley proposition? Becomin' independent, was he, 'cause of this highwayman nonsense? No. Moss shook his head sadly from side to side. Wretched brat had always been independent.

Then what? What had he said when he'd left t'other day? Never been a bang-up-to-the-mark gentleman? Well, that was true. Hadn't never even learned ta speak like one. Couldn't read nor write nor cipher neither, and he hadn't a semblance of manners—only the ability to ape someone else's. P'rhaps, after all, Jason was right. P'rhaps 'e hadn't the least chance of succeedin' and knew it directly the proposition had been made.

Still, there'd be a fortune in it for 'em. Moss sighed at the thought of the payment he'd been promised. And he was getting very nervous about Jason ridin' the High Toby. Too many good men had danced the jig at the end of a rope for that lay. Too many risks involved in't. Jus' one cove inside a coach with a pistol at the ready combined with one moment of inattention on Jason's part, and the lad's life might be speedily concluded.

The house to which Moss—resplendent in primrose pantaloons, a waistcoat of strawberry red embroidered with tiny stars of primrose silk, a cravat of deep ruby and a frock coat of blue Superfine—made his way lay at the end of a cul de sac in St. Mary's Triangle at the verimost edge of Mayfair. It was a small establishment of cream-colored brick, a mere two stories high and a scant ten room affair. Still, it was barely two-years-old and its design, though unconventional, was not to be scoffed at. The architect, a Mr. Samuel Potter, had proven in this domicile and several like it that a home might be luxurious, convenient, and exceptionally easy to heat without being grossly expensive. Moss had had thoughts of purchasing a similar establishment for himself and Jason—if the lad wished ta join 'im— with the monies promised by the generous Lord Eversley. That, however, no longer appeared likely.

One knock of Moss's ebony cane against the wide front door produced a scowling butler who divested Moss of hat and cane and without a word led him into the parlor which lay at the front of the house on the ground floor.

"Moss! I began to give up on you. Come in! Come in! Sheridan, fetch us some brandy and biscuits, eh?" A rather florid young man, respectably stout with wide blue eyes and russet hair, pointed Moss to a seat and waited impatiently for the butler to serve the brandy and biscuits and take himself off somewhere before saying anything more. When finally Sheridan left and closed the pocket doors behind him, Peter Marks, Lord Eversley, perched eagerly on the edge of a chair opposite Moss's. "I expected you days ago. Have you found the man? Are we on?"

Elgin Moss ran a finger around the inside of his collar and shook his head. "Not likely, m'lord. Won't do't."

"But why not? If he looks as you describe him, he's perfect for it."

"Aye, but he don't want ta touch it. Not a gentleman, 'e says. Never been one, never be thought one. Truth ta tell, I reckon as he's right."

"Well, but he does not need to be a gentleman," protested Eversley, sipping at his brandy. "We'll say he was raised by gypsies and I am the one discovered his true parentage. No one would expect a Romany-raised brat to go about acting and speaking properly. I certainly would not."

"Truth be, he were a gypsy brat till his mam and da met with a untimely death," Moss murmured, remembering those long ago bodies on the gibbet. " 'Twould work, I reckon, did ye not mind goin' with that type of story. But he won't do't. Got hisself a good lay an' not about ta squander 'is opportunities."

"Ah, but you've not convinced him of the opportunities available should he provide me with his services. He'd not see as much money again were he Captain Jason Fate himself."

Moss blanched and gulped the brandy. He'd not mentioned to Eversley that the man he'd petitioned to do the work actually was Captain Jason Fate.

"Go back to him, Moss. Tell him I'll increase his wages. Five thousand pounds for three month's work—and I'll foot all his bills, eh? I'll feed him; I'll house him; I'll rig him out in the best clothes money can buy. Or better yet," exclaimed the young gentleman, "you take me to him, and I'll explain the whole situation. I'll convince him of the advisability of it. I've got to have him, Moss. At least, I've got to have someone. You wouldn't happen to know of anyone else—"

"No," interrupted Moss taking the miniature of the young man Eversley had loaned him into his hands and studying it. "Not no one comes as near to this gen'leman here. 'Tis like m'lad be the cove's twin."

Eversley stood and began to pace the room with a definite bounce in his step. "You let me have a word with the fellow, eh? Whenever, wherever he wishes. I understand he is not quite on the up and up, what? I see he doesn't treasure coming here to meet me. You let him make the arrangements for a meeting, Moss, and I'll guarantee to abide by 'em. Not a villain on earth would turn down four thousand pounds for three month's work. Especially once I explain how accommodating I intend to be."

"I thought ye said five thousand," mumbled Moss and looked up to find Lord Eversley nodding his russet curls excitedly.

Ned Bedford, Earl of Wheymore, strolled into his wife's presence with a wide smile upon his face. He tugged her from her chair up into his arms, gave her a tremendous hug, and kissed her exuberantly upon her finely sculpted lips.

"My," Lady Wheymore giggled girlishly, "to what do I owe such a greeting, Ned? Have you made a fortune in the Funds?"

"No, but nearly as good, my dear. Nearly as good. I have made my point with the Regent. From this afternoon forward the militia accompanies every coach that crosses Finchley's Common. That will put an end to Captain Jason Fate, believe you me! That scoundrel will be dancing the jig at Tyburn before the week is up if he does not end dead in the dirt with a militiaman's rifle ball between his eyes!"

Lady Wheymore stared up at her husband wide-eyed. "The militia? With every coach? However did you get Prinny to order such a thing?"

"Well, I had a bit of help from Fate himself," grinned the earl. "He and his band of villains robbed the Mail last night. Can you believe it? Like slapping Prinny and every one of the Lords directly in the face. Took everything. Took it all—the strongbox, the pouches, the passengers' bags and baubles, and the deuced team too! Left the coachman, the guard and the passengers standing on the Common with nothing but an empty coach! And a broken axle on it, I hear! Prinny's flown into the boughs—ranting and raving and promising as how he'll tear that thatchgallow's heart out with his own hands. Now we'll get him, my dear. Now we'll get him!''

"Get who, Uncle Ned?" asked Camilla as she and Aurora entered the small drawing room.

"Captain Fate," Lady Wheymore replied, freeing herself from her husband's embrace and motioning the girls to join them. "The militia accompanies all coaches which propose to cross Finchley's Common from this day until the scoundrel is captured."

Aurora clapped her hands, eyes shining. "That will teach the monster," she declared. "And they will take him to Newgate and then to the Old Bailey and then to the gibbet! Oh, it serves him right, too! Just think of all the people he has robbed and in so short a time!"

"Yes, well, there is that," murmured the earl dropping down upon the brocade sopha and tugging his lady down beside him.

"There is what, Papa?"

"The fact that he has succeeded so very well in so very short a time, m'dear. Honestly, if you and Cammy and David had not been among his victims, I might even now be inclined to admire the man's prowess."

"Surely, Ned, you cannot think to admire such a ruffian?" Lady Wheymore stared at him in disbelief. "Only think of the people he has harmed—your own son walks about with his arm splinted because of the beast."

"Yes, exactly," agreed Wheymore, a glint in his eye which did not escape Camilla's notice. "But 'tis a shame such cunning and ability and courage as I hear he displays should be wasted when it might be working for England and all of Europe against Napoleon. The more thought I give it, you know, the more I wonder if I ought not propose that we send the ruffian off to the Peninsula rather than to Tyburn. He'd be of use to us there and make a degree of restitution as well. He appears to be an enterprising and dauntless individual. 'Tis doubtless that somewhere inside the reprobate are the makings of a hero."

Camilla wanted more than anything to tell her uncle

that Fate had already done something heroic, that he had saved the life of an old woman and herself and Clare on Albemarle Street, but she could not. To admit that she had recognized the man and to label him Captain Jason Fate when Mr. Lilliheun could most accurately describe him to the authorities was impossible. And now, most certainly, she could never bring herself to be responsible for anything that might lead to Fate's capture or death. Not after he had risked his life to save her own. She was no longer angry with him for stealing her jewels. He might have all her jewels, now, just for the asking.

But she would probably never see him again, never have the opportunity to thank him for his bravery or to offer him whatever he desired in repayment for his heroism. A tear formed and ran slowly down one smooth, unblemished cheek as she envisioned his strong, rugged body lying deathly cold on the Common, a trooper's ball through his heart.

"Cammy, whatever is the matter?" asked Aurora in a whisper. "You are crying."

"No, I am not," whispered Camilla back. "I—I—Oh, Rory, there is something I must tell you. It is very, very important and I need your advice most desperately."

Aurora, worried, took her cousin's hand in her own and making excuses to her parents, led Camilla from the room and upstairs into her own sitting room, where Cammy, tears now streaming from both eyes, sputtered out the whole of the tale of Jason Fate. "Oh, Rory, I cannot bear it! I cannot bear to think of him lying dead upon the Common or thrown into Newgate to await his death at Tyburn. He saved my life and Clare's! At any moment that phaeton might have tipped and sent us crashing to the cobbles! No one else made a move to do anything. Only he."

"Oh," replied Aurora, her pretty bow lips parted in amazement.

"Oh? Th-that is all you h-have to say?"

Aurora's sweet, heart-shaped face beamed and she shook her golden curls softly. "I have a good deal to say, but I do not think you wish to hear it. At least, I am positive you do not wish to hear it at present. But I shall tell you what I think we must do."

"What must we do?"

"Why send the man a warning, of course. We must warn him that the militia patrols the Common. Did you not say that he was on his way to Grillon's when he came to your rescue?"

"Yes, but Clare asked for him there and was told he had only left his mount in the stable for an hour or so, and that no one had the least idea who he was or where he stayed."

"Well, that was a lie," Aurora stated.

"A lie? But—"

"Honestly, Cammy, you are the person who wishes to write novels and anyone would think you did never read them. What hostler, I ask you, would admit to knowing Captain Jason Fate, much less to knowing where he might be found? Certainly, if the captain feels free to make use of Grillon's stable, then someone there has made it expedient for him to do so, and I highly suspect it would be one of the grooms. Go fetch your pelisse and we shall tell Mama and Papa that we are off for a stroll and instead we shall take a hackney to Grillon's."

"They will make a fuss if we do not take one of the footmen with us."

"Then we will take Gregory. He is the nicest one of the lot and he never snitches."

Camilla, busily drying her tears, looked up at that. "He does not? How do you know?"

"I just do," grinned Aurora, her pert little nose in the air. "Gregory may be trusted in anything."

The stableyard at Grillon's boiled with activity as it did all day and all night. Arrivals and departures, private coaches and public conveyances, single horses, teams of two and four, job horses, gentlemen's horses, the aristocracy's matched bays and greys and blacks and the farmers' mismatched roans and chestnuts and bobs all stamped and snorted and neighed and whinnied and shook their harness as the hostlers ran at top speed hitching one team, unhitching the next, bringing up one gentleman's mount, stabling another's.

When Gregory, the youngest, the tallest and, indeed, the nicest of the Earl of Wheymore's footmen found that Lady Aurora and Miss Camilla wished to convey a message to someone in the stables, he suggested immediately that he should be the one to do it. " 'Twouldn't be seemly,'' he declared, "for young ladies to wander about the stables, and 'twould be disaster to your skirts, if you don't mind me sayin' so. If you'll tell me the lad's name and give me the message, I'll see 'tis delivered."

"No, I think not," replied Camilla displaying a calm she did not in the least feel. "But you may procure a private parlor for Lady Aurora and see she is provided with some refreshment and remains safe until I return."

"He certainly will not," protested Aurora with a delightful pout. "I am come to support you and support you, I shall. Gregory, you may go and have a drink and meet us back here again in ten minutes."

"No, m'lady," murmured Gregory quietly. "I shan't go an' have a drink and allow you to wander 'bout a stable-yard unattended, nor Miss Camilla neither. Whither you goest, I be going too."

Camilla stared down at the embroidered toe of her half-boot thoughtfully. "Very well," she sighed at last, "we will all three of us go, though it may prove to be quite awkward. You see, Gregory, we do not exactly know to whom we wish to speak. There is someone here who knows a person to whom we wish to send a message, but we do not know who it is."

"Then you'll want to speak to the stable master," nodded Gregory with assurance. "He knows most everyone who comes and goes."

It took them almost five minutes to locate that personage and several abortive attempts before the stable master was able to remain in one place long enough to catch what they were saying to him. "Was a fella here yesterday er the day afore that were lookin' fer a gent by that description," replied the stable master his eyebrows knitting together suspiciously. "I tole 'im then that I didn't know nothin' about the bloke."

"Oh, but you must remember," pleaded Camilla, her green eyes gazing hopefully into his disturbed hazel ones. "He rides a horse the color of drizzling skies—not grey, not grey exactly, but streaky, you know. It is a large horse and very fierce looking."

"And it is imperative that we get a message to him," added Aurora determinedly.

"A matter of life or death," prodded Camilla.

" 'Ere now, whose life er death?" asked the stable master, becoming less suspicious and more bemused by the two lovely faces so eagerly turned to him.

"His," whispered Camilla. "He is in grave danger and knows nothing of it. Oh, please, sir, there must be someone here who will know how to reach him."

"An' if they was to reach 'im, m'lady, what would they say?"

"Why that he is not to go out tonight as he planned," replied Lady Aurora.

"That the militia will see to it that his—sister—crosses Finchley's Common safely. They will protect her from Captain Fate because they will be riding beside her carriage, you see."

"They will?" murmured the stable master, his eyebrows rising. "My, but he must be a big un, then, ta have the Regent's pertection fer his sister, eh?"

"Oh, no," protested Camilla as Aurora's hand squeezed hers encouragingly. "The militia has been called out to ride beside all the vehicles that traverse Finchley's Common from tonight until the villain is captured."

"Aye, there's good news, that is," grinned the stable master, "though I don't see as how 'tis life er death fer the bloke yer speakin' of. More likely 'tis life er death fer Fate."

"But he plans to guard his sister from Captain Fate or die trying," volunteered Aurora in an attempt to make the message appear pressing. "And the militia may mistake him for the Captain, you know, as dark as it will be, and he riding to meet her across the heath, which he will do."

"I wonder," mused the stable master, studying first one then the other of them carefully, "how is't ye know so much about this gen'leman's business, when ye don't know 'is name."

"Oh! Oh, he mentioned it the other day—that he was going to meet his sister—after he rescued us," spluttered Camilla, grasping at straws. "It was because he stopped our bolting team that Mr. Lilliheun came later to seek him out. The fellow was in a great rush at the time and though he gave his name, he was forced to dash off and we were both of us so upset that we forgot it."

"I see," nodded the stable master. "Well, and 'tis too bad I don't be knowin' the gen'leman neither or I'd as like as not see yer message reached 'im. Wouldn't want no honest citizen ta come ta harm at the 'ands of our own militia now, would we? But pass it around, I will, an' like as not one or t'other o' the lads will discover the gent's direction and carry it on to 'im."

The stable master smiled a gap-toothed smile at them and then excused himself and hurried off leaving them to find their own way out of the yard. "Do you think he will get our message?" Aurora asked sadly. "I wish we might speak to some of the other grooms and perhaps a stableboy or two."

"He'll see the message is passed on, m'lady," murmured Gregory from directly behind them. "Each of the hands'll hear of it and if there be one of 'em knows the gent, he'll see 'tis delivered, have no fear of that."

"Well, we have done the best we can," sighed Camilla. "I cannot think of any other way to reach him. We must just pray that one of the hostlers does know the gentleman's direction."

Garbled, twisted, tortured almost beyond belief, the message did in the end reach the extraordinarily wide ears of Master Harley Radd who was in the midst of mucking out the last of his lot of stalls. His ten-year-old frame shook with excitement. "Oooh, oooh, Danny! I gots to git home, I does. I done fergot all 'bout me own sis," he cried in a squeaky twang of a voice. "I gots ta git home ri' now. Will ye finish this fer me, eh? I'll do two o' yers termorrow, I promise. I gots ta go."

His mate shrugged, nodded, and watched as the long-legged young rascal ran full speed out of the stable, through the waiting teams, and down Albemarle Street as if all the demons of hell were on his heels. Nor did Harley cease running until he had reached the narrow opening of Basket Lane which he swung into immediately and began pounding mightily upon the first door he came to, not letting up the racket until it was opened to him by a tousled boy in short pants and a shirt stained with clay. "I gots ta see the cap'n, Tick," Harley announced breathlessly. "Does 'e be 'ere? 'E ain't gone off yet, eh? I gots ta see 'im right away!"

Fate woke, one hand quickly grasping the dagger that lay beneath his pillow, as Harley dashed madly up the skinny stairs and into the shadows of the bedchamber at the rear of the first floor. He released the blade the moment he saw the lad clearly through the shadows and raised himself on one elbow. "What's got yer dander up, Harley? Ye look like ye run all the way home."

Harley nodded, gasping for breath.

"Well, come 'ere, then," Fate smiled. He climbed from beneath the patched blanket and stood, barefoot, on the chill wooden floor beside the bed. Worn and unbrushed buckskins strained against the muscles of his thighs as he swept Harley up and deposited the boy on the edge of the enormous bed. In its day it had been an impressive, mahogany four poster, its headboard carved with cavorting nymphs, but now it boasted only three posts, one of which leaned obstinately to the left, and only one nymph had not been scratched into oblivion.

Fate poured a glass of water from the chipped pitcher beside the bed and handed it to the excited child. "Drink it slow, Harley. No, don't be talkin' until ye get yer breath back." Fate grabbed his shirt from a chairback and pulled it over his sleep-tousled curls. "Runners comin'?" he asked. "Just shake yer head, Harley, an' keep drinkin'. Ye know ye don't do nothin' but hiccup when ye been runnin' like tha'. Ye got ta get yer breathin' right first.''

Harley stared eagerly wide-eyed at him over the glass rim and kept swallowing.

"The Runners comin'?"

Harley shook his head.

"What then? Nothin' happened to yer da?"

Harley shook his head again.

"An' the childer? They ain't been carried off by Bod-kins?''

Harley shook his head again.

"Well then," grinned Fate, shrugging into his nankeen jacket, "can't be nothin' serious.''

Harley, coming to the end of the water, gasped and set the glass between his knees. '' 'Tis serious,'' he said and coughed a bit, which made Fate turn away from the tiny piece of looking glass fastened to the wall that he had just turned to in an attempt to comb his hair into some sort of order.

"You ain't comin' down ill, are ye, lad?"

"No, sir. No, Cap'n. I jus'—there were a message lef' fer ye at the stable.''

"A message? At Grillon's? Are ye certain 'twas fer me, lad?''

Harley nodded excitedly and blurted out what words he could remember, attempting to make some sense of them. "I don' know as how tha's 'sackly what were said. Didn't never knowed ye had no womenfolk. But the message come down straight out 'bout the militia bein' on the Common. I knowed ye'd wanna hear tha' part of it.''

Fate sat down on the edge of the room's only chair and began to pull on his boots. Harley watched, silent, until the job was done. "So," Fate drawled, standing again and stamping his feet into a more comfortable position inside the worn leather, "ye'll tell yer da we don't ride tonight, m'lad. You keep a eye out, Harley, while I'm gone. An' ye git the childer off the streets the first minute the sun goes down, ye hear?''

"Aye, but where ye goin', Cap'n? Ye ain't goin' ta the Common? Not with the troopers out a lookin' fer ye?''

"Nah, I figger to go an' fetch a bite ta eat, an' then ta wander about a bit. Appears we got us some free time on our hands, Harley. A bit o' a holiday, I reckon."

Fate gave the thin back a pat, pulled the dagger from beneath the pillow and slid it carefully into his boot top, then pushed aside the heavy draperies, opened the window and stepped out onto a narrow ridge of balcony. He swung himself over the side and dropped to the refuse-covered alley below. With a wave of his hand at the boy who watched, he started up the muck-strewn lane sidestepping the slops thrown from myriad windows on myriad mornings and left to rot amidst the broken cobbles. He had always hated the putrid smells and squalor of St. Giles's, but at this moment, in the slowly setting sun, neither his nose nor his eyes were engaged in passing judgement upon his environment.

Even his ears blocked out the shrieks and shouts, the raucous laughter and plaintive sobs around him. Someone'd left word at Grillon's 'bout the militia. Who? Who knew Harley were workin' for 'im? Or did they know? Sounded more like they'd lef' the message with the first cove they'd met an' merely hoped that it'd reach him sufficien'ly intack.

He'd been worritted about the militia. Knew before he did the thin' that robbin' the mail'd bring some ugly, high-'anded response from the bleedin' Fat Prince and his wretched, flush-in-the-pocket Lords. But he hadn't counted on it bein' so forthcomin'.

He cursed himself for being a fool. Thunderation, if 'e hadn't flat out brought a halt ta the best lay what he'd ever had jus' by not bein' able ta resist the urge ta thumb his nose at the gover'ment. Well, he weren't fool 'nough ta go on out ta the Common an' meet the lot of 'em head on with no un but Harley an' Artie at 'is side. Not this evenin' he weren't. No, nor the nex' either. Like as not, he'd spend the best part of his time checkin' on the truth of the matter, an' if he foun' he'd raised the wrong hackles an' they was like ta stay raised inta the summer, he'd have ta figger out another way ta keep the blunt flowin' in. Like as not if it proved out that he'd ruined his coach robbin' business, Mossie would have somethin' lyin' about what he

could do. "But not that gen'leman business," he muttered
under his breath as he turned into an even narrower alley.
"I ain't havin' nothin' ta do with bein' no gen'leman."

Chapter 3

When Captain Jason Fate did not appear on Finchley's
Common that night, nor the following, nor even the third
or fourth night after that, and the Earl of Wheymore carried word of it home to his womenfolk, Camilla's heart
soared. The captain had gotten her message! The tiny
vertical line that had taken up residence between her eyebrows disappeared entirely. By the end of the second week
of his nonappearance upon the heath, the worried glaze
deserted her eyes and they once again sparkled at the
world like living emeralds. She teased Neiland when he
arrived at Grosvenor Square to display his newly splintless
arm to his mother and dared him to dance the Quadrille
with her at the Forrester's ball that evening. And he, in
an equally exuberant mood, accepted the challenge laugh-
ingly. "But I warn you, chick," he grinned, "I don't remember all the patterns. It's been a good while since I've danced
the thing."

"Then I shall wear my riding boots, shall I, to protect
my poor little feet from your gigantic ones?"

Aurora, walking in upon them, laughed and suggested
that Camilla also carry a riding whip instead of her fan to
keep all of the gentlemen in line.

"Oh, no," giggled Cammy, "I have a much better way
to keep the gentlemen in line. I shall simply pull a few
pages of my novel from out my reticule and begin reading
aloud to them. You will be amazed to see how rapidly they
will all depart."

"Your novel?" Neiland asked, his blue eyes alight. "Have
you really begun one then, Cam? May I read it do you
think?"

"No, I do not think so. Not yet."

"What is it about?" Aurora asked. "Is that why you have

been locked up in your room for the past three afternoons and not even gone out to drive in the park with Mr. Lilliheun?"

"Precisely. And it is about—about—a highwayman."

Neiland and Aurora looked at each other and grinned.

"Is it about a specific highwayman?" Neiland asked, one eyebrow lifting slightly.

"Well, of course it is. His name is Bad Jack Pharo and he is a dreadful villain. Now, off with you, David, or Rory and I shall be ever so late for the Forrester's ball. It does take us at least four hours to dress, you know."

"So I've often thought," sighed Neiland, "especially when awaiting you at the bottom of the stairs. Do not learn from her, Rory, all the little adjustments that take forever, will you? I should like to continue to brag about my baby sister's astounding promptness. And gentlemen truly do not like to be kept waiting forever, no matter what you ladies think."

It did, in fact, take all afternoon for the girls to ready themselves for the evening. Though Aurora had already attended a number of social occasions, this was to be her first appearance at a ball and her mother had engaged a new French hairdresser who was all the rage.

There was a great debate amongst the three ladies over which of the newly fashioned gowns Aurora was to wear, and then they must decide if Cammy ought to look startlingly seductive in a satin slip of Pomona green with an overdress of Brabant lace or enchantingly demure in a Nakara muslin.

Lady Wheymore laughed when the muslin was chosen on the grounds that the pearl grey color of it was more fitting for a woman of Camilla's advanced years and asked if she, herself, as the ancient woman's aunt must attend in black or that horrid purple satin that the dowagers had taken to sporting. "Because if you must dress so colorlessly at the grand old age of twenty, Camilla, only think how I must dress! Good heavens, I am at least twice your age! More, actually. Come, wear the green, do, and the lovely little necklace of rosettes Uncle Ned gave you on your birthday. He will be so proud to see you in them."

"Oh, I had not thought! They will look wonderful with the green, will they not? Of course, I will wear them."

"Is Papa going to the Forrester's?" Aurora asked in surprise. "I thought he meant to spend the night at his club."

"Not this night, my dear. Your papa intends for you to dance your very first dance at your very first ball with him, and he is looking forward to it mightily."

"I shall never forget my very first dance at my very first ball," grinned Camilla. "Uncle Ned danced with me as well and made me laugh and sent all my jitters flying right out of the room. Your papa is the most wonderful dancer, Rory, and makes one feel so perfectly at ease."

"Indeed," confirmed Lady Wheymore with a nod as she glimpsed the doubt on her daughter's face. "And I shall take full advantage of him once he has abandoned the two of you to the younger gentlemen. He'll not sneak off to the cardroom tonight, I guarantee it. I shall keep him by my side and in my arms in spite of the present fashion. I cannot understand why a husband and wife should be expected to remain apart at public functions when they married, after all, to be together."

The ladies shared an early, light supper in Lady Wheymore's chambers with their hair still in curl papers and themselves still in dressing gowns. And when at last the French hairdresser returned to comb out their locks, and Lady Wheymore's dresser saw them neatly fitted into the decided upon gowns, and slippers were donned and fans and reticules procured, and mantles light as clouds slipped over their nearly bare shoulders, Neiland and his father were discovered to be waiting patiently for them at the bottom of the staircase both looking bang up to the mark in smart new coats by Weston, extremely conservative waistcoats, black knee breeches and neckcloths perfectly tied into Napoleons.

The night being a fine one and exceeding warm for spring, the earl had ordered up the cabriolet to carry himself and his ladies the three blocks to the Forrester's. He ordered the top left down so that he might sit comfortably with his arm about Lady Wheymore's shoulders and point out to her the constellations, all of which she had learned by heart many years ago and could easily have found with her eyes closed from the time of their engagement, but which she continued to encourage him to point out to her regardless, enjoying his self-satisfaction in doing so as much as the security of his arm so lovingly about her. Aurora and Camilla occupied the opposite seat and both young ladies watched with a certain degree of awe and wonderment the byplay between the older couple. Neiland, with a laugh and a shrug of his shoulders, jumped to the footman's perch at the back of the carriage and tilting his hat at a rakish angle waved at everyone he knew along the way.

It was while Camilla and Neiland were in the midst of the promised Quadrille and enjoying it immensely, that they both looked up to see Mr. Lilliheun, dressed to the nines in the stark black and white ensemble favoured by Beau Brummell and the dandies, cross the floor to where Wheymore stood deep in conversation with one of his cronies. A frown creased Clare's usually sanguine features, and a few words whispered in Wheymore's ear brought the earl's conversation with the others to a halt, his gaze falling full upon Lilliheun in disbelief. The two men excused themselves from the other gentlemen and made their way through a set of polished French doors out onto the ballroom balcony.

"Ten to one Clare is asking for your hand again," teased Neiland as he and Camilla came together in the dance.

"No. Why would he look so angry if it were that?"

"Because he asks and asks and you don't ever give it to him, you ninnyhammer."

"Well, but he knows I will not. I have explained it to him over and over. It must be something else."

Both of them overcome with curiosity, Neiland led his cousin out onto the balcony as soon as the music ended. Wheymore and Lilliheun were still there, so deep in conversation that neither of them noticed the arrival of the two young people.

"What is it, Father?" Neiland asked. "Lilliheun," he nodded in acknowledgement. "Is there any way that Cammy or I may be of service?"

"No, not at the moment," replied the earl with an uncharacteristic growl.

"There—that's him. It must be. Thunderation!" exclaimed Lilliheun, leaving the other three behind him and approaching the French doors.

"Him who?" Neiland queried, coming up behind the man and attempting to follow his gaze.

"My dear God!" gasped the earl on a sudden intake of breath as he stared into the ballroom in the direction in which Lilliheun pointed. "I cannot believe my eyes."

"What?" asked Camilla sneaking in between them. "Who do you see? Where?"

Lilliheun tugged her in front of himself, turned her face toward the entrance from the corridor at the other side of the room, and pointed again. Camilla's heart plunged to the very bottom of her left slipper. Beneath the portal to the ballroom—with Lord Forrester aligned on his left side and Lord Eversley on his right—hands stuffed into the pockets of a pair of kerseymere pantaloons of a dark pearl grey topped by a blindingly white double-breasted waistcoat, a bang-up-to-the-mark blue Superfine coat of Stultz's cut and a fine lawn cravat tied in, of all things, a Mailcoach, stood Captain Jason Fate. Camilla gave an almost inaudible squeak, put her hand to her mouth, took it away, put it back again.

Growing inexplicably, inordinately warm—so warm she could not believe that her entire body had not burst suddenly into flame—Camilla snapped her fan open and began to ply it rapidly, sending tendrils of soft chestnut hair swirling across her brow and wafting beside her ears. Fate's dark curls had been cropped and coaxed into a modish windblown style, a goodly portion of his tanned and hollow look appeared to have been scrubbed clean off, and his feet had been forced into an incredibly stylish pair of japanned leather shoes. Camilla's mind reeled. What was he doing here, standing as brazenly as you please in the midst of the very people he had been robbing for the past six months or more? She felt Lilliheun's hand upon her elbow and heard his voice whisper in her ear.

"Camilla, is that not the man stopped our team on Albemarle Street, or am I mistaken? He looks amazing like, but odd, you know, dressed as he is."

Cammy nodded. "It is him," she answered hoarsely and then squeaked again as the sparkling dark eyes discovered her and one of them winked audaciously.

"Well," she heard Lilliheun sigh, "that puts another crease in the muslin, don't it? Now how am I supposed to act?"

"Supposed to act about what?" Neiland queried. "What is going on, Lilliheun? Who is that gentleman?"

"Eversley claims he is my uncle's grandson, Lord Locksley's son and, therefore, my uncle's heir apparent."

"But that's impossible. Locksley died without issue. The old duke ain't got any grandsons. You are his heir presumptive, Clare."

"Aye, but not if Eversley's claim can be proved. What think you, sir?" asked Lilliheun, glancing apprehensively at the earl. "Is there any chance that it could be true?"

The Earl of Wheymore, who had not yet removed his gaze from the man under discussion, gave his head a little shake and made a sound very much like a groan. "He is the image of Lord Locksley, Lilliheun. The very image of him. 'Tis like seeing a loved one rise. Does the duke know of it as yet?"

"No, I expect not. He has been unwell and remains at Monteclaire. I gather from m'cousin, Drew, that the old gentleman does not even think of travelling to London at present. I do not expect that Eversley has taken that fellow all the way out to York to see the duke, do you? More likely they will wait for the duke to come to town. That will give Eversley more time to gather evidence to establish the claim as well. He must have some evidence besides the man himself, don't you think? I mean, my uncle will not accept that man at face value, will he?"

"No need to prove he has Locksley's blood in him," mumbled Wheymore. "That much is apparent. The question is, which side of the blanket was the scoundrel born upon? Since there never was word of John marrying, I tend to think you have nothing to worry about, Clare. Still, I hope the mere sight of that lad does not send the duke into heart failure.''

"Well, whether or not he is like to disinherit me, I owe the man a great deal of goodwill, so I expect I had best go make his acquaintance and shake his hand at least.''

"Goodwill? Why?'' Lilliheun's words had drawn both the earl's and Neiland's full attention.

"Well, because he is the chap who kept Miss Quinn and I from running even more amuck on Albemarle Street than we did. Saved our lives. I'm sure we'd have struck that old woman and overturned directly upon doing so. No way we could have avoided it. Might well both be in the grave by now were it not for him.''

"Him?'' Neiland asked incredulously.

"Him?'' echoed Wheymore, in surprise.

"Yes, him,'' declared Camilla petulantly before Lilliheun could so much as nod. "And we must go and thank him properly. He cannot be at ease, you know, amidst such a sad crush of people. He cannot possibly know anyone here but Lord Eversley.'' And snapping her fan closed, she set off with swift, determined strides across the ballroom floor, the earl, Mr. Lilliheun and Neiland trailing in her wake.

Fate's lips twitched upwards as he watched Camilla sail toward him. By thunder she was a beautiful sight! All his self-consciousness and skepticism and surliness at having to display himself thus vanished in the face of her. He bowed adequately to Wheymore, nodded on being introduced to Neiland, and welcomed Lilliheun with a handshake, but all of those gentlemen were mere distractions to be brushed aside as quickly as possible in deference to the young lady Eversley had introduced as Miss Camilla Quinn.

A discussion went on around Fate and Camilla that caught the attention and incurred the curiosity of half the room. Eversley, Wheymore, Lilliheun, Neiland, and Forrester all mumbled, all asserted, all proclaimed or declared one thing or another. Voices raised; voices lowered; bodies shifted and reshifted and then shifted again, but neither Camilla nor Jason Fate noticed.

His gaze roamed over every inch of her from top to toe; his lips parted the merest bit, as if to taste the air around her; he breathed in the faint lilac smell of her and blinked his great, dark eyes slowly, dreamily, in wonder. She, in turn, could not take her gaze from him. Her brilliant green eyes grew wistful as they traced the rugged contors of his face, wandered over the broad outline of his shoulders and discovered the narrow tapering from his chest to his waist. Her silk-gloved fingers twitched forward from moment to moment as if to touch him there or there as her eyes absorbed each bit of him. She found herself taking great, gulping breaths of him and trembled, shocked that she should do such a thing and more shocked that she should be able to distinguish, quite easily, his scent from all others. Vanilla, she thought in bewilderment. He smells like vanilla. Whyever would he? In a movement so slow as to be dreamlike he offered his arm and she placed her hand upon it. Powerful muscles rippled beneath her touch.

They said not one word. He lifted an eyebrow. She gave the faintest nod. And in moments they had left the congregation of excitable gentlemen behind and had begun a slow promenade along the verimost edge of the dance floor. A great many eyes followed them as they walked slowly around the room including Lady Wheymore's and Aurora's, but Camilla and Fate took not the least notice.

"What are you doing here?" Camilla whispered at last. "Of all the nerve! To appear in the midst of the very people you incessantly terrorize! And to let yourself be introduced as someone named John Locksley besides!"

"I could hardly let 'im intraduce me as Jason Fate," grinned the highwayman. "Not here at any rate. Devil take me but ye're more beautiful than I remembered."

"And you, sir, are just as audacious as I remembered."

They traversed the rest of the dance floor in silence making a perfect rectangle of it before either spoke again. "Have you nothing more to say?" Camilla asked then, with an edge of anger to her tone. "Does not it at all occur to you that I might at this very moment declare to the world that you are Captain Jason Fate and in less time than it takes to say it, you would be on your way to Newgate? Have you no shame? No conscience whatsoever? Not the least feeling of guilt?"

"Uh-uh," he smiled down at her, "I'm still tryin' ta figger out what 'aud-ay-tious' means. It ain't nothin' good I take it?"

Camilla studied the laughing eyes, the slightly tilted eyebrow, and the question that suffused his entire countenance, and quite overcome, she giggled like a schoolgirl. "You're incorrigible, Captain Fate."

"Whoa, hold on, Dendron. Don't be addressin' me by that monicker if ye please. I don't fancy bein' hauled off by the constab'lary at the present time. What's 'in-cor-gible?'"

"You are," replied Camilla. "And you must call me Miss Quinn if you wish to be gentlemanly."

"I don't wish ta be no such thin'. An' I'll call ye what I been a callin' of ye since first I sought a name for ye— Dendron."

"Oh," gasped Camilla, a sudden light of understanding spreading across her face and turning her cheeks an even deeper pink. "Rhododendron!"

"Aye," nodded Fate, his curls tumbling across his brow. "An' ye ain't goin' ta snitch on me now, are ye? Not af'er all this time. I waited, ye know, ta see my 'scription posted all over Lunnon, but it didn't happen."

"No, it did not. But if you are intent upon causing trouble for Mr. Lilliheun or upsetting my Uncle Ned, I shall be obliged to betray you, you know. They are very dear to me."

"I ain't set on causin' no un no trouble, Dendron. Findin' somethin' what's missin' is all I'm tryin' ta do."

"But you are lying about who you are."

"No, I ain't. I might could be this cove, Jack Locksley."

"You could be? *How* could you be?"

"Well, I know I ain't truly named Jason Fate. My mam an' da faked that name up years ago. An' I know they waren't my real mam an' da neither. They informed me of it loud enough ever' time I didn't do somethin' 'zackly right.''

Camilla wondered whether this was some Canterbury tale he was spinning, but he was looking down at her with the most confused innocence and she could not help but believe him. "Oh, you poor man. Do you mean to say that you actually have no idea who you are?''

"None. So I reckon if this cove, Eversley, says I am this Locksley fella—well, mebbe I am. Couldn't hurt none ta fine out. I reckon ye might not unnerstan' it, Dendron, but a cove'd like ta know who he really is. He'd like ta know does he got a fam'ly. It don't seem important all the time, but sometimes it gnaws at ye, the not knowin'.''

Camilla could think of nothing at all to say in reply. Her heart, which had risen from her left slipper all the way up into her throat, ached for him—for a child who knew his parents were not his parents and who lived with a pretend name, and for a man who had seized upon the slight hope that a complete stranger might provide him with his true identity and a family to accompany it. She removed her hand from his forearm and tucked it instead into the crook of his arm, giving him a reassuring squeeze. They had made, by this time, another complete circuit of the ballroom and for the very first time Camilla began to notice the attention they were drawing. "Would you like to dance, sir?'' she asked quietly. "They are about to begin a set.''

"I don't know 'ow ta dance.''

"You don't? Truly?''

"Never had no time fer dancin'.''

"Then let us go sit over there by the wall and I shall introduce to you my Aunt Mary and my Cousin Aurora who I gather are about to jump out of their chairs and come after us.''

"Yer cousin? The Banshee?''

"She is not a banshee. You frightened her.''

"I only lifted 'er out of a coach. I didn't do nothin' else. Well, I took 'er falderals—but that's what I stopped the bloody coach fer ta do, take stuff.''

Camilla took one look at his bewildered countenance as he attempted to exonerate himself and without the least thought of anything or anyone else she rose on tiptoe and brushed her lips against his cheek. In less than three seconds her Aunt Mary, Aurora, the earl, Neiland, Lilliheun, and Eversley had them surrounded. Eversley put an arm around the captain's shoulders and muttering that he must speak with the gentleman privately, urged him toward the ballroom door. Lady Wheymore and Aurora each took one of Cammy's arms and, professing they were weary beyond belief and must take their leave, escorted her toward their host and hostess. The Earl of Wheymore, Neiland, and Lilliheun followed behind the ladies, all three attempting not to scowl, and made their own farewells with gallant aplomb.

"You cannot go about kissing young ladies in public," Eversley explained seriously, all the while directing his steps and Fate's toward Forrester's study on the first floor. "It just ain't done."

"I didn't kiss 'er," mumbled Fate. "I was jus' talkin' to 'er like, an' the nex' thin' I know, wham!"

"Yes, well, don't do it again."

"Don't do what?"

"I don't know, Locksley! Whatever you did to make the gel kiss you—don't do it again! We've got off to a damned good start. Even Wheymore agrees I've a duty to bring you to my uncle, the duke's, attention. And we do want Wheymore on our side. We want to make him think favourably of you, which he won't do if you make his niece a tidbit for the scandalmongers. Wheymore's very important to us, you see. Here, come in here and sit down and I'll pour us some brandy."

Fate took a seat before the fire, accepted a glass of the golden liquid and settled back to gaze into the flames. "Why's Wheymore important ta us?"

Eversley sank into the matching chair beside him. "Because Wheymore was married to Locksley's twin sister. If he believes you to be Locksley's son, he'll support us in our battle to convince the duke. Exceeding fond of Locksley, Wheymore was. Named his own son after the man."

"I thought his son's name was David?"

"Not that one. His first son he named John Locksley Bedford."

"An' that lady what come up with 'im an' hauled Dendron away, she were this Locksley's twin? Didn't look much alike, eh?"

Eversley sighed, leaned forward in his chair, and ran his finger around the inside of his collar. "Not that you *need* to understand this, but she is his second wife. His first wife—Locksley's twin—died, and their son as well."

Fate's eyes studied Eversley's florid face in the firelight for a very long time. He watched the brandy tip from the crystal glass over Eversley's lips; watched Eversley's Adam's apple move up and down as he swallowed; watched the satisfaction appear on the man's face as the drink warmed his insides. "If ye don't mind my askin', Gov," he murmured at last, "what's in all this fer you? Sayin' they accepts me as this Locksley fella, what then?"

"Then, sir, you and I become the heirs to a dukedom," grinned Eversley, "and Lilliheun can rot in hell!"

Aurora tucked her feet under her as she settled on the sopha in the sitting room of Camilla's chambers and watched in silence as Camilla's pen moved swiftly across the paper. "But what are you writing, Cammy? Are you writing down what he said to you? Who is he? He's very handsome. Every young lady there was wishing he would cease speaking to you and ask one of them to dance. What were you discussing so seriously? Oh, do stop writing and tell me what happened!"

Camilla sighed, set her pen aside, and turned to face her cousin. "Do you know who he claims to be?"

"No, not exactly. Papa started to explain, but then— then you kissed the gentleman, you know, and the explanation went quite unfinished. Who does he claim to be?"

"Well, I should not have said that exactly. He does not claim to be anyone. Lord Eversley makes the claim that the man is Lord Locksley's son. That would make him the grandson of the Duke of Dewhurst and if he is indeed that person, he will be the heir apparent."

"How dreadful! What will Mr. Lilliheun do if it is true?"

"I have no idea. But Clare, I think, is safe on that account. Uncle Ned says that the fellow looks a great deal like the duke's deceased son, but that it is impossible he is a *legitimate* heir." Camilla yawned, placed her paper and pens back inside the escritoire, and joined her cousin on the sopha. "You will doubtless be told when you are at last introduced to him, Rory, that he is the man saved us on Albemarle Street."

Aurora's eyes opened wide. "He is—Fate!"

"Exactly. And you must *not* betray him, Aurora. Please promise me that you will not."

"Well, of course I will not, gudgeon. What a harridan I should be to tip the tale on the man my very best friend loves. Oh!" cried Aurora, both hands going hurriedly to cover her mouth. "I should not have said that. I did not mean to do so," she mumbled from between her fingers.

Camilla stared at her blankly.

"You are not angry with me are you, Cammy? I know how adverse you are to falling in love with any man, and I really, truly, did not mean to tell you that you had."

Camilla opened her mouth, closed it, ran her fingers through her long, loose hair, and then began to braid it thoughtfully. "I am not in love with him," she murmured at last. "I am simply—simply sorry for him."

"Sorry for him? But why?"

Camilla related the sad tale of his pretended name and unknown parents and lack of family and his hope that perhaps he truly was a man called John Locksley.

"I see," murmured Aurora with a tiny smile. "So the feelings he has engaged in you to this point are merely those of"—she raised one hand before her and began to tick off on her fingers as she spoke—"curiosity, merriment, pity, gratefulness, and sympathy for his upbringing. Well, that is not so very bad, then, if indeed that *is* all."

"Well, of course that's all. A woman would need to be a fool to fall in love with such a scoundrel as Jason Fate."

"Yes, but what lovely, sparkling eyes he has," murmured Aurora sweetly. "And how straight he stands. And how incredibly tempting are his curls. I wanted to jump up and run my fingers right through them."

"No, did you?" laughed Camilla.

"Me and every other young lady in the room. You didn't even notice, did you, all the jealousy flowing about you while you and he promenaded about the chamber? And oh, Cammy, his face! He has the most romantical face I have ever seen. All hollows and shadows and enticing angles. A person might get lost in the study of it."

"And he smells of vanilla," murmured Cammy somewhat dreamily, drawn in spite of herself to a pleasant recollection of her earlier discoveries.

"Vanilla? No, does he truly?"

"Vanilla. It's the most remarkable thing. I cannot for the life of me think why any man should smell of vanilla, but—but he does and it is—it is sort of wonderful."

"Well, it is a very good thing you are not in love with him, Cammy," Aurora declared with wry smile, "for loving a man who smells like vanilla could make one eternally hungry."

Chapter 4

Elgin Moss had personally inspected every room in Eversley's mansion on Grosvenor Square, established Fate in the largest guest chamber and taken for himself the second largest chamber, at the rear of the second floor. He had then taken the time to speak with every one of Eversley's staff from Mr. Glasgow, the butler, to Mrs. Daily, the housekeeper, all the way down to the little scullery maid, Becky, in the most affable and congenial manner, explaining, as best he could, the sad circumstances of Mr. Locksley's upbringing and his subsequent rescue by Lord Eversley, and gaining for Fate a remarkable amount of sympathy and goodwill and patience belowstairs. Elgin Moss was neither a totally uneducated nor an unfashionable man, and his fifty year rise from the gutters had been accompanied by a similar rise in his presentation of himself. But Jason Fate

was another matter altogether. He had never before eaten
in a dining room, much less seen a tablecloth or the new
French invention of napkins for wiping one's mouth. He
used his sleeve for that task. Nor had he the least notion
of why anyone should require the services of a valet such
as the one Eversley had provided for him—he was perfectly
capable of dressing and undressing himself; his clothes
had never been brushed or pressed or folded or carefully
kept in a clothes press or armoire before; and his boots
most certainly had never required polishing. Nor did his
living habits approach those of a true gentleman. His feet
were constantly propped upon one piece of expensive furniture or another; he slept with a dagger under his pillow
and kept a loaded horse pistol on his windowsill; he kissed
the maids, and even Mrs. Daily, whenever they looked the
least bit sad; and he betrayed a constant urge to snabble
trinkets, statuettes, and snuff boxes, and had to be stopped
and relieved of them before he left the house to keep
them from appearing on the open market. All of these
things and others the staff at Number fifteen, Grosvenor
Square looked upon with fond eyes, remarkable patience,
and a sense of humor because their thoughts had been
gently prejudiced this way or that by a perceptive Elgin
Moss. They began to value Fate's exuberant and adventur-
ous nature, his compassionate responses, and his innocent
astonishment at life in the aristocracy and to look upon
his general lack of breeding, style and refinement as insignificant beside the true value of his overwhelming character.

Eversley, who divided his time between his mistress, Mary
Ellen Hall, in St. Mary's Triangle and the house on Grosvenor Square, invested a good deal of effort teaching Fate
what would be expected of him on the Duke of Dewhurst's
arrival, devising acceptable answers to questions the old
man would certainly pose and urging Fate to further insinu-
ate himself into the good graces of Miss Quinn, since he
had apparently already made significant inroads in that
direction. "For the more we gain Miss Quinn's favor for
you, the more she'll influence the earl's favor in our direction when it comes to our claim. I've proof, Locksley, that

I think will carry the day with the duke, but it will help immensely if Wheymore is inclined to accept you beforehand.''

Fate was more than willing to continue his association with Camilla. Longed to, in fact, but had not the least notion of how to go about it. The fact that she resided in the house directly across the square had not gone beyond his notice, but he hadn't the foggiest idea how to approach her. "There's a'ways mobs o' people comin' an' goin' over there," he commented innocently one morning to Eversley's butler, Glasgow.

"Morning callers, sir," replied Glasgow. "The young people gather at one another's houses for conversation and such. A gentleman may generally call upon a young lady for fifteen minutes on the days she is receiving visitors."

"How d'ye know which days those are, though?"

"Well, generally the gentlemen are introduced to the young ladies at an entertainment and enquire if they may have permission to pay a call and when it would be convenient. Do you wish, sir, to visit one of the young ladies at Wheymore House? Is that it?"

"Aye, but I ain't like to be goin' to no entertainments, so I ain't like ta be able ta git 'er permission."

"But you attended the Forresters's ball, sir."

"That were business, Glasgow."

"I see, sir. Well, then I should think, perhaps, you might purchase a posy for the young lady and send it, along with your card, into her presence, and see if she will receive you." Glasgow noted the perplexed look on Fate's face and grinned. "Simply knock on the door, Mr. Locksley, request to see her, and Mr. Somers, the butler, who is my good friend and a very fine gentleman, will carry your card and the posy to her. You must bend your card over at the corner, you know, so she will be aware you have come in person."

Fate mulled over this advice as he cut into a cold beefsteak for breakfast. Sounded right queer to him. Still, the Quality was full o' queer starts. He worked his way through the beefsteak as quickly as possible, downed the glass of ale beside it in three gulps, wiped his sleeve across his lips, rushed from the room, pounded up the stairs to his chambers, and demanded his valet tell him was there some rules about what a gen'leman had ta wear ta pay a call on a lady.

"A morning call, sir?" asked Farmer looking up from the task of returning Locksley's shaving kit, clean, to the toilet table.

"Aye, a mornin' call."

"Why one wears morning dress, sir." Farmer enthusiastically pulled from the armoire and clothes press a splendid ensemble which included a claret, double-breasted riding coat that even Fate proclaimed was "bang up to the mark." Aware that the odd gentleman he presently served was incapable of tying a cravat in anything more than a disreputable knot, Farmer offered his assistance there as well, but Fate would not hear of it. Instead, he tied a claret and blue kerchief loosely about his neck, nodded at himself in the mirror, and allowed Farmer to help him shrug into the tightly fitting coat. Then he pulled on the glowing black Hessians, buckled on his spurs and hurried from the room. In a moment, he hurried back. "I fergot," he mumbled, crossing into his bedchamber. Farmer followed and watched with some apprehension as Fate pulled the dagger from beneath his pillow and slid it down into his boot. "Where's my huntin' jacket, Farmer? I had it on las' night. There's thin's in the pockets I got ta have."

"There are things in the pockets you must have," repeated Farmer, unable from time to time to ignore Fate's torturing of the English language.

"Aye," replied Fate, opening the armoire doors.

"No, 'tis not there, sir. I've set it here in this pile to be brushed."

Fate took the jacket from Farmer's outstretched hand, retrieved Camilla's diamond bracelet from one pocket and a tarnished silver thimble from another and a number of odd, whitish beans from a third and tossed the jacket back at the bemused valet. "I reckon that's all what I lef' stowed there. Now ye can brush it er whatever. Thank ye, Farmer, I 'preciate yer 'elp." He disappeared down the hall at a gallop, leaving Farmer behind him with a fond smile twitching at his lips.

Camilla stared in wonder at the salver that Somers had set before her on the breakfast table. Upon it lay two dew-covered daffodils and an ace of hearts with one corner carefully bent.

Somers fought heroically to maintain the noncommittal cast of his countenance, but bits of a smile kept escaping into his eyes and spilling from the sides of his mouth. He did not understand about the playing card, but he had seen Mr. Locksley pick the daffodils on his way across the square.

"B-but—" stammered Camilla. "Is it a joke, Somers?"

"No, miss, I do not believe so. The gentleman waits below and he appears quite serious."

"W-which gentleman?"

"Mr. Locksley, miss."

"Somers, is it not eight o'clock in the morning?"

"Yes, miss, and no one about as yet except yourself. What shall I tell the gentleman?"

Camilla stared again at the playing card and the daffodils and grinned. "Bring him to me here, Somers. I shall discover what this is all about."

Fate followed Somers up the staircase to the first floor and all the way to the breakfast room. Camilla had poured him a cup of hot chocolate and was setting it down as he entered. "Good morning, Mr. Locksley," she greeted him. "Please be seated."

Fate stared at the cup of chocolate. "Fer me?" he asked, slipping into the chair opposite her.

"Yes, sir. Would you like some eggs, perhaps? Or some toast? Or strawberries?"

Jason Fate shook his head, his gaze taking in her Devonshire brown riding habit and tightly braided hair, her bemused green eyes, and a tiny dimple at the corner of her mouth. "I wouldn't like nothin' else but what I see before me."

"I expect you may go then, Somers," declared Camilla,

who knew very well that Somers would go no farther than the hall beyond the open door lest someone should think Camilla compromised by meeting with this man unchaperoned. "Now, tell me, sir," she asked, as Somers exited, "to what do I owe this honor?"

" 'Tis a mornin' call."

"Yes, an eight o'clock in the morning call," smiled Camilla. "And this?"

"M'card."

"And?"

"A posy. Glasgow said I were ta take ye m'card an' a posy."

"I see," grinned Camilla, beguiled. "And who is Glasgow?"

"Eversley's butler—well, Mossie says as he's my butler fer now on accounta I be livin' there. I wanted ta see ye again, ye know, but I had ta ask how ta go about it proper."

Camilla knew she ought to explain to him that morning calls were seldom actually paid in the morning, and never before eleven. And she definitely ought to show him what a gentleman's calling card looked like, but her fingers reached to pick up the two little daffodils tenderly and she knew she could do neither. He had thought enough of her to attempt to do the thing properly, and she could not find it in her heart to embarrass him by pointing out his mistakes. "I intended to go for a ride, Mr. Locksley, after breakfast. Would you care to accompany me?"

Fate nodded at her over the rim of his cup, then set the chocolate aside and frowned.

"What?" Camilla asked.

"Don't have a horse," Fate muttered. "Had ta give Smear ta—ta somebody."

"Smear? Your horse's name is Smear?"

"Uh-huh. It's a perfeckly fittin' name. Looks like he got grey paint smeared all over 'im. But Eversley said as 'e weren't a fittin' horse fer a gen'leman ta ride an' so I had ta leave 'im with a perticuler frien' o' mine."

"Well, you shall ride one of my uncle's horses then. They are certainly fit for a gentleman. Somers," she called, "send to the stables and have Brindle saddled and brought 'round as well, will you?"

"Yes, Miss Camilla," the butler answered from beyond the portal.

Camilla had intended to exercise her little mare in Hyde Park, riding early in the morning so that Dulcette might stretch into a gallop or even a run without arousing anyone's attention or branding her mistress a hoyden—for no one rode faster than a slow trot in Rotton Row during the hours of the Promenade when all of Society went to see and be seen. Any attempt to do so was thoroughly frowned upon. But Fate ignored all of the park entrances and steered them west, taking them quite out of town and onto a very lovely plot of land with a small stream, a grove of beeches and a great many wild flowers just beginning to bud. "Aston-Croft Grove, 'tis called," he informed her with a wide, white smile. "Better than the parks fer ridin'."

"But I never knew it was here," replied Camilla. "How beautiful it is. I wonder it is not overrun with people." A glance over her shoulder showed her father's groom with a worried countenance, glancing around him in considerable distress. "What is it, Richard?"

" 'Tis this place, miss. 'Tis a haven for gypsies an' highwaymen. We ought not be here."

"Aye," chuckled Fate. "Sometimes camp in the trees, they do. But we be safe from 'em this mornin', I assure ye." He winked at Camilla, dared her to race him as far as the grove of beeches, and urged Wheymore's gelding into a run. Camilla started after him at full speed, but pulled Dulcette back into a canter as she discovered the sheer joy of watching Captain Jason Fate on horseback. Memories of him in the moonlight crossed her mind. She had known then that he was exceptional, but she had not guessed how exceptional.

When he reached the beeches and found how far behind him she was, she could see him toss back his head in laughter. He kicked free of his stirrups, bounced up to stand on Brindle's back and bowed, and then leaped to the ground and waited for her, stroking the big horse's neck. Only then did she let Dulcette have her head and they flew toward the man. When she reached him, he lifted her from the saddle and taking her hand, led her into the small woods. Richard, left to tether three horses, would not be like to catch up with them for a few moments and Camilla meant to make the most of it by interrogating the villain about his past life.

"You ride so beautifully," she said, all in a rush, "like the performers at Astley's. Where did you learn to do so? I thought you had been a street urchin in London. You could not have learned to ride like that though, in the city."

"Learned from the gypsies. I were a gypsy brat fer a long while. 'Twas only after my mam an' da—died—that I took ta livin' in Lunnon."

"How did they die?"

"You don't wanta know, Dendron. 'Tweren't pretty."

"But I do wish to know, Captain. I wish to know everything about you."

"Shhh, yer groom'll be upon us in a moment. Don't be callin' me cap'n." He grinned down at her and before she could guess what he meant to do, one gloved finger was under her chin tickling it upward and then his lips were brushing softly across hers. The kiss was finished as quickly as it had begun and it left her flustered and flushed and quite uneasy, wondering if there might be another. But then she heard her uncle's groom stomping through the woods toward them and knew there would not.

"You know," she offered, attempting composure, "gentlemen are quite fond of asking young ladies to promenade with them in Hyde Park of an afternoon. I am certain you have seen them there."

"Aye. Seen 'em often. Been among 'em from time ta time."

"Yes, well, you might ask me to drive with you there on one afternoon or another. That is a most unexceptionable way for a young lady and a gentleman to spend time alone together."

"An' ye'd not be afraid ta spend time alone with me, Dendron?"

"Of course not. I should like to do so. There are so

many things I should like to know about you that we cannot possibly discuss with Richard on our heels.''

'' 'Cept I can't drive,'' grinned Fate. ''Ain't got no carriage.''

"I am sure Lord Eversley has a curricle and will be glad to give you the loan of it. It is practically the only way that—''

"That what, Dendron?''

"That a proper young lady may be in a gentleman's company unchaperoned. Because a curricle is open, you know, and there are so many other people in the park then.''

Fate nodded and, taking her arm, steered her deeper into the woods. Richard trudged anxiously along behind them. ''Can't drive no cur'cle,'' he confessed after a moment or two. ''Can't drive no team. Only know how ta stop coaches, not make 'em go anywhere.''

"Oh,'' sighed Camilla, ''I had not thought. Gypsies do not drive curricles.''

"No, they drive wagons, but I weren't big enough ta learn ta drive ours.''

"Then I will tell you what,'' Camilla proposed. ''I shall ask my Cousin David and Mr. Lilliheun to teach you how to drive.''

Neiland and Lilliheun stared at each other in astonishment that afternoon as Camilla presented them with her request. ''You've lost your mind, cuz,'' Neiland growled. ''The man's a scoundrel, an impostor. He's attempting to steal Lilliheun's inheritance.''

"And he's attempting to steal you,'' added Lilliheun. ''I know I owe the man some consideration for having saved us, but why would I help him to steal you away from me?''

Aurora burst into laughter at the scowls on their faces but Camilla only frowned and stared down at the embroidered toes of her new jean half-boots. ''May I remind you, Clare, that I do not belong to you and therefore cannot be stolen from you? I have told you time and again that I do not wish to be your wife, nor anyone else's either. And

I cannot but think that it would be a kindness to teach
Mr. Locksley. He does not possess very many gentlemanly
skills, you know."

"I should say not," muttered Neiland. "Can't even speak
properly. It's no wonder Eversley keeps him locked away."

"He does not keep him locked away," replied Lilliheun,
studying Camilla's chestnut curls fondly. "Eversley says
Locksley has chosen on his own to stay out of Society.
Appears he does not want to be always embarrassing me.
People are gossiping enough about the possibility of his
disinheriting me without our being forced into each other's presence at any number of public functions. Do you
really wish for me to teach him to drive, Camilla?"

"Yes, I do. It is the smallest trifle after all he has done for
us. And I do not think you should be so terribly judgmental,
David. It will certainly not be Mr. Locksley's fault if he
does turn out to be the duke's grandson. He did not create
himself after all."

"I think he did," declared Neiland. "I think he did
create himself. He strikes me as a most creative person."

"You do not even know him, David!" Aurora exclaimed.
"How can you make such—such hurtful statements when
you have not even spoken above three words to the man!"

"Because I know a thatchgallows when I see one,
madame."

"Or because you are prejudiced in Mr. Lilliheun's favor
and wish to see Mr. Locksley in a bad light."

"Rory, it is all a ruse. It does not matter how much
the chap looks like Lord Locksley or that someone has
bastardized the title and given it to him for a surname.
Locksley was never married. Father says so and I believe
him."

"Father does not know everything. And if there is evidence that the man might be who he claims to be, then
it would be the honourable thing to do to examine that
evidence."

Ignoring the bickering siblings, Lilliheun slipped a hand
through Camilla's arm and walked with her to the other
side of the drawing room where they might be somewhat

58 *Judith A. Lansdowne*

private. "Are you in love with Locksley, Camilla?" Lilliheun asked quietly.

"No! Of course not! Good heavens, one would think I had asked you and my cousin to assist in an elopement! All I wish for you to do is to teach cap—Mr. Locksley to handle a curricle and two horses."

"All right, I'll do it. And Neiland will help. David only speaks as he does because he thinks he is defending me. I shall explain to him that I do not wish to be defended quite so heartily at the moment."

The driving lessons that followed that discussion were enough to freeze a man's gizzard and did almost freeze Neiland's. Having decided upon the Lichfield Road as a likely place, its being nearly deserted in the middle of the day, the two gentlemen turned up on Fate's doorstep the following morning and carried him off to learn the intricacies of becoming a capable whip. They explained to him how to splay the reins between his gloved fingers; demonstrated how one could feel the bits in the horses' mouths through the leather; instructed him how to make the horses proceed and stop and back.

When at last they thought he had got it down, they gave the reins into Fate's sole possession; Neiland stayed on the box beside him; and Lilliheun mounted to ride alongside the vehicle as they set off down the road. In less than five minutes Neiland was hanging by his hands from the box which tilted perilously over a deep ditch; the horses were rearing and plunging; Lilliheun was riding like a Bedlamite to come up with them; and Jason Fate alias Mr. John Locksley was doubled over with laughter, tears streaming from his eyes.

"Back 'em up!" Lilliheun shouted, taking his mount down into the ditch so that Neiland might let himself down gingerly onto the horse's back. "Back 'em toward the ditch enough to straighten out the curricle! Locksley! Stop laughing, man, and do't!"

"I—I c-can't," gasped Fate between whoops. "I f-fergot how. W-wait! I think I 'member!" With a much firmer hand, Fate tugged at the team, first bringing them under control and then urging them slowly backward. And he backed the vehicle directly down into the ditch rather than away from it, which set the horses into another panic, Neiland to cursing, and Lilliheun into uncontrollable chuckles.

"Get down, Neiland. We're going to have to pry the thing out of there. You take the horses' heads and I'll get behind and push," Lilliheun laughed. "Locksley, drop the reins once Neiland has gone to their heads and come back here and help me!"

It had rained the evening before and the curricle's wheels had buried themselves in the mud. Fate and Lilliheun had to throw their backs into it to return the vehicle to the road. Even with Neiland at the horses' heads, the task was exhausting.

When at last they'd got the thing back onto the roadbed, all three of them sweaty, muddy and smelling of horse, they voted unanimously to abandon driving lessons for the day. Neiland took the reins and drove to the Crown and Dragon a quarter mile down the road and ordered a pitcher of ale and three mugs which they carried outside to the front of the inn where they settled down around a weather-beaten old oak table. "You're the most cow-handed person I've ever seen," Neiland announced after two gulps of the refreshing liquid. "Even my sister could have held that team better than you. Why'd you give 'em their heads like that? Be deviled if you don't drive like a— a London footpad."

"I do, don't I?" chuckled Fate. "Like a Lunnon footpad or a cutpurse or a innkeeper's daughter."

"No," grinned Lilliheun, "you ain't anywhere near as good a driver as an innkeeper's daughter!"

Camilla was amazed to discover both her cousin and Lilliheun in excellent spirits that evening as they joined herself, Aurora, and Lord and Lady Wheymore at the opera. "You never saw anything like it," Neiland chuckled. "I must have looked a sight clinging to that box, and Locksley laughing his fool head off. And then he backs the curricle all the way down into the ditch and buries the wheels in the mud!"

"A comedy of errors," agreed Lilliheun. "You would have enjoyed it immensely, Camilla. I expect, though, that it is going to take longer to teach that scoundrel to drive than we thought. I have forgotten, you know, how long it must have taken me to learn. It seems I have always driven, but I think I began with a pony and a cart at the age of four or so and eventually grew into the rest."

"Likewise Neiland," nodded the earl. "Began driving before he was out of short coats. Not so easy to learn for a grown man who has never held a set of reins in his hands before."

"But he rides well, Uncle Ned," Camilla protested.

"But riding has little resemblance to driving, my dear. When a man rides he controls only one horse and that as much with his legs and body as with the reins. Lilliheun? Eversley says he has Lord Locksley's marriage lines— signed in his own hand. Claims John married a Romany girl shortly before he died. You will have to get your solicitor to look into it."

"A—a Romany girl?" Camilla asked. "A gypsy, Uncle Ned?"

"Aye, so Eversley says, though I have high doubts of it."

"Cap—Mr. Locksley was raised by gypsies—at least until those in charge of him died."

"He told you this?" asked the earl with sudden interest. "Why?"

"Well, we went riding, you know, and I asked him how a street urchin had learned to ride, and he told me that he had lived with gypsies as a child though he did not live with them long enough to grow into learning to drive one of the wagons."

"I don't know," sighed Wheymore, perplexed. "I just don't know. He looks so very much like John, and now it appears his background is going to match with the evidence Eversley claims to have. And Dewhurst—Dewhurst will want to believe this, Lilliheun. He will want to believe this as much as I want to believe that someday my John will be found alive. And even though I know that can never be and Dewhurst knows this has barely a possibility of being—the weight of disproving the thing will likely be on your head, Clare."

"Shhh," hissed Lady Wheymore who was one of the very few people attending the opera who actually wished to watch and listen to the performances, "they are about to begin."

Camilla pinned her gaze upon the stage but her mind could not be so easily controlled. What if Lord Eversley's tale were true? What if the remarkably handsome villain, Captain Jason Fate, were actually Lord Locksley's son, heir to the Duke of Dewhurst? She was brimming over with excitement. And what if Bad Jack Pharo, her novel's villain and the only man her heroine, Esperanza, could ever love, were truly the son of an aristocrat kidnapped by gypsies in his youth and raised to the life of the road, formed from childhood to become a practitioner of the High Toby in revenge for some hurt done the heathens by his father? And Esperanza would discover this and just as Bad Jack Pharo climbed the steps of the gibbet and the rope was placed around his fine, slender neck—"

"Cammy, whatever are you thinking?" whispered Aurora giving Camilla a dig in the side with her elbow. "It is intermission and Mr. Lilliheun has asked you to walk with him in the passageway. Oh, and here come a number of beaux to lay themselves at my feet as well," she added with a giggle. "Go. Go with him, Cammy. After all, he suffered dearly teaching your Captain to drive, and all for your sake. I only wish he would attempt to please me the way he always does you and look at me with such wonderment in those absolutely gorgeous eyes. If he even so much as noticed me as someone besides Neiland's baby sister, I would marry Mr. Lilliheun in the blink of an eye! You have not the least idea how fortunate you are."

Chapter 5

It was a week later when Andrew Borhill, Mr. Lilliheun's solicitor and his second cousin once removed, stared at the papers lying before him on his massive mahogany desk and frowned.

"What? What, Drew? Say something! They are not legitimate, are they? That cannot actually be Lord Locksley's signature? It cannot be."

"Of course it cannot be," growled the Earl of Wheymore rising from the chair next to Lilliheun's and beginning to pace the oak panelled room restlessly. "If John had married, why not tell his father or—or if there were anything unacceptable about his bride—confide in Claudia and me? He might have married a paper and pins gel and the both of them been welcomed at Whispering Winds."

"Perhaps he was not as certain of your support as you are, my lord," smiled Eversley slyly from the depths of a leather arm chair. "He did, after all, align himself with the scum of the earth. He may have doubted you would welcome a Romany into your home. He certainly knew his father would not welcome her."

"Enough!" Wheymore roared angrily. "You were nothing but a pup yourself when John died at Willemstad. You know nothing at all about him!"

"I know he married a Romany woman by the name of Constanzia Alanza Kuczenski and left her behind him in England about to give birth to the heir of the Dewhurst dukedom."

"Never!" bellowed the earl. "Never! John would never be so irresponsible as to leave his heir to the whims of gypsies. He was not a fool! He knew he went off to war. He knew he might not return. That was the cause of the split between himself and Dewhurst in the first place— that he bought himself a commission. He would have sent word to his father, would have sought Dewhurst's protection if not for his bride at least for the child."

"Perhaps he thought them safe in the cradle of his wife's own family? Or perhaps he assumed, should they meet with unexpected trouble, that his bride might present her marriage lines at Dewhurst's door and obtain protection?" Eversley's wide blue eyes glowed with mirth at the earl's sudden unease. "Wrongheaded of him, no? To expect that? Here I come to present the case on behalf of a young man who hasn't the least idea what any of this is about and you are all dead set to prove him an impostor. Imagine if instead of me a young gypsy girl with a child at her breast had come here. You would have swept her from the chambers without the least consideration—and well you know it."

"Even if the marriage lines are authentic," drawled Mr. Borhill, leaning back in the chair behind his desk, "what is there to prove that this—gentleman—is the woman's child, eh, Eversley? A notation in a beat-up old bible, a jotted note in a female's diary? Why, anyone might claim to be that child."

"Not anyone might look so much like John, though," the earl muttered. "All you need do is glance once in his direction and you will see the reincarnation of Lord Locksley, Borhill."

"Yes, but is he the legitimate heir?" murmured Lilliheun, flipping open his snuff box and helping himself to his own sort. "That's the real problem, Drew. You've sent one of your assistants to check the records at the church in the Dell in Vilxhem, ain't you? If he should find a record of the marriage there that supports the marriage lines—"

"It only proves that Locksley married, Clare," interrupted Borhill. "It gives us a day and a year, but it don't tell us if there was issue from the marriage. And the birth ain't likely to be recorded—not did it take place in some Romany encampment somewhere. Still, there might be a member of this particular Kuczenski family still alive. Personally, I am surprised, Eversley, that you did not send someone in search of them. Just one who remembers the date of the child's birth and the father's name—even if they mistake Lord Locksley's title for his surname—might support the claim. I have, in fact, sent my man, Argosy, out to look into the matter. Could take months—even years, I expect.''

"Yes, and if he finds a family member, you'll say the man or woman's a liar and a thief and not to be believed,'' grumbled Eversley angrily. "You're intending to carry this out for twenty years or more, ain't you, Borhill?''

"If that's what it takes, Eversley. If that's what it takes. After all, it cannot matter to you, eh? You have no interest in it. You have no hope at all for the dukedom. Personally, I cannot for the life of me see why you have taken up this cause. It cannot be of any benefit to you.''

"Perhaps, Borhill, I simply wish to see justice done.''

Borhill raised one weary eyebrow in speculation but deigned not to make any rejoinder. The truth of the matter was, he could not see any reason for Eversley to promote the man except to see justice done, and that bothered him more than any of the rest. Eversley's reputation had never before involved any particular love of justice.

"I think he's doing it out of pure malice,'' the solicitor muttered several minutes after Eversley had left the office. "Trying to drive you mad, Clare. Hates you. Always has. Jealous.''

"Is the signature on the marriage lines John's?'' asked Wheymore quietly.

"As near as can be divined, my lord. If 'tis a forgery, it's a remarkably fine one, but we'll not give up the fight yet, believe me. I have people all over London searching out information on this Mr. John Locksley. We may, in fact, discover a good deal more about him than Eversley wishes us to know.''

Lilliheun appeared upon the Earl of Wheymore's doorstep at precisely four o'clock that same afternoon, assisted Camilla to the box of his high perch phaeton, and took her off to the Promenade in Hyde Park.

"Look, there is Aurora with Viscount Newmont,'' Camilla exclaimed merrily. "Oh, Clare, don't you think she looks absolutely magnificent in that cherry-striped carriage dress. And her bonnet, it is positively roguish." Camilla waved as the duo passed them going in the opposite direction and Lilliheun nodded and smiled.

"She is beautiful, my dear Miss Quinn, but not near as beautiful as the young lady who sits beside me at the moment. When will you give over attempting to pawn me off upon your cousin?"

"Never," laughed Camilla, her green eyes bright. "I am determined that Rory shall have her chance with you. You would deal so well together. She thinks I take you for granted, you know, and says I must be certain to thank you for going out of your way to help Mr. Locksley."

"No, you do not need to do that," Lilliheun grinned. "Neiland and I have decided that we have not had quite so much fun in years. He is doing a great deal better, by the way. Not quite so cow-handed as at first. Determined to get the thing down, he is. Says as soon as he's sure he won't kill anyone, he shall ask you to drive with him. He is determined to become my rival for your hand, I believe, though he don't know it. Thinks we are merely friends, you and I."

"We are friends, Clare, and I am not going to marry you. I have told you so over and over."

"Are you determined to marry Locksley then?"

Camilla's face flushed a very pretty pink. "Oh, no! Never! I have explained to you over and over again that I have not the least intention of marrying anyone!"

"I beg your pardon, my dear. I thought perhaps you had changed your mind. He is, after all, handsome and no doubt charming in his own way, and he will have very, very deep pockets if his claim can be proved."

"Clare," sighed Camilla as she noted the rather forced smile upon his face, "I cannot think what to say. I know you oughtn't to be forced to associate with the man at all, but—but—he has no one. Even Lord Eversley does not seem to take any interest in helping him to better himself. And he is so ignorant about—about—how one is expected to go on in Society. I cannot help but pity him. You are a saint to take him under your wing."

Lilliheun's forced smile turned into a true grin and a

splendid chuckle. "A saint, am I, Camilla? Well, I shan't quibble over it, but methinks I'd be more acceptable in your eyes were I a rascally thatchgallows, and that's a fact! Still, you may be sure I shan't abandon your protege now you've given me charge of him. I shall do my best to turn him into a gentleman. And if I cannot manage that, at least Neiland and I shall turn him into an adequate whip."

Neiland had, in fact, been regaling both Camilla and Aurora with tales of the harrowing task of teaching Fate to drive since the very first adventure, and Camilla's eyes sparkled now with mirth at the memory of them. "I am sure you are the bravest gentleman of my acquaintance," she announced taking Lilliheun's arm. "David told me about the farmer's cart and the mail coach on the road to Portsmouth. I should have fainted dead away."

"You would have done nothing of the kind, madam. You would have taken a very deep breath, held on tightly, and encouraged the damnable man to drive faster. I know you, Camilla. You are not the least hen-hearted. And in the end, you would have fallen into whoops over the whole affair—just as he did."

"He laughed?"

"He howled. He does it all the time. I have never met a man so filled with the sheer joy of living. I swear, Camilla, I am never dull when I am with him. Nothing is ever the same as I saw it a moment before. If you could know him better, you'd be amazed at him. I vow, if he is truly Dewhurst's heir, there shall be no enmity on my part. But I cannot help but be suspicious because Eversley, you know, detests me and will do anything to stir up trouble in my life."

"Lord Eversley!" Camilla exclaimed excitedly. "Clare, would Lord Eversley have gone so far as to cut your harness? Could it have been his doing that day?"

Lilliheun's sea-grey eyes sought hers, startled. "Eversley? Cut my harness?"

"Yes! I have been thinking and thinking who might hate you enough to do such a thing and I could think of no one. But now you say that Lord Eversley detests you."

"Well, yes, but Eversley's a gentleman and my cousin

besides. He might be forever attempting to embarrass me, my dear, but I cannot imagine for a moment that he would do anything so exceptional as to attempt to murder me. No, you must put the whole episode out of your mind. I'm quite certain 'twas not an attempt on my life at all. A hostler's knife hitting the reins accidentally as he was hitching the team and he not noticing. Some purely accidental thing like that, I'm sure."

Camilla nodded and tightened her grip on Lilliheun's arm. He was truly the most wonderful gentleman. He could think evil of no one. What was wrong with her that she could not love him, could not accept his offer of marriage?

Certainly she intended to become an authoress, but a woman could do so without denying herself the joys of wedded life. Women like Mrs. Radcliffe and Madame d'Arblay had managed to succeed in both tasks after all. And besides, Lilliheun would be generous to her and supportive of her efforts.

No, she told herself abruptly, withdrawing her hand from the gentleman's arm. He will become like every other man and I like every other woman. He will expect me to spend all my time in the running of his household and the bearing of his children, and I will be drawn in to see his side of it, and my work will be pushed to the very back of both our minds. No, it would not be fair to either of us. I should grow resentful and he, all-unknowing, suffer for it.

"Camilla, look to your right," Lilliheun's voice interrupted her musings. "Can you see them? Just turning in at the gate. I'll pull over here, shall I, and wait on them?"

"Oh, it is Neiland and Mr. Locksley! And Mr. Locksley is driving!"

"Uh-huh. I expect that's why Neiland looks so pale," chuckled Lilliheun. "I'd not have brought him. Not in this crush. And there'll be the devil to pay. See if there's not. Everyone will be wanting to know who the man is."

In the crush of slow-moving carriages it took Neiland and Fate a full five minutes to cover the short distance from the gate to the place where Lilliheun had pulled aside onto the verge and even in that distance at least a dozen people had stopped to acknowledge Neiland in hopes of an introduction to the sober gentleman who handled the reins beside him. Camilla's lips twitched upward as she noted the captain's lower lip caught between dazzling white teeth.

The closer they came, the more adorable appeared the slightly askew eyebrow and the crease of concentration above the bridge of his nose. His unruly locks had been settled beneath a high crown, rust-colored beaver—a twin to Neiland's—and someone had tied a perfectly beautiful claret cravat into a Waterfall 'round his fine, long neck. The brass buttons on his coat glistened in the sunlight and his eyes glowed with determination. "Pull-up, Locksley," Camilla heard Neiland order. "Ain't you going to stand a moment and say hello to m'cousin and Lilliheun? He did not see you and I did not tell him you were up here, either," explained Neiland as the captain brought the two matched bays to a halt. "Didn't want to distract 'im, y'know. First time he has driven in a crowd."

"You're a braver man than I am, Neiland," grinned Lilliheun. "I would have made him drive another twenty years or so before letting him take the reins in Hyde Park at the height of the Promenade."

"But I made sure m'bays were tired to begin with," joked Neiland, glancing sideways to see if this provoked any response from his diligent student. What he saw was the crease disappear from above the bridge of the captain's nose, a wide smile light the austere features, and a small muscle ripple in the hollow of the closely shaved cheek next to him.

"Af'ernoon, Miz Quinn," Fate called across Neiland. He transferred the reins to his left hand, tipped his hat, and had to put both hands back on the reins almost immediately as the horses took the sudden relaxation in his grip for permission to move forward. The slight movement threw an unexpecting Neiland off-balance and he grabbed the seat with both hands. "Sorry, Neiland. Ye all right 'n tight?"

Neiland nodded and looked at Camilla with laughter in his eyes. "You wouldn't like to switch places with me for a while, would you, cuz? I've a message from m'father for Lilliheun."

"What? You're proposing to do away with the girl I intend to marry?" Lilliheun asked with the lift of a haughty eyebrow. "For shame, Neiland. And she's such a fine girl, too."

"Bosh! Cammy can drive a curricle as well as I can. She won't let Locksley run amuck, not at the going rate of speed on this lane at any rate." Neiland climbed down and handed Cammy from the phaeton and up into the curricle beside Fate. "All right then," he drawled with a brotherly growl, "off with the two of you. One time around the park and we shall meet you right here beneath this oak. And Locksley, I am entrusting the gel to you, so you must guard her with your life."

Fate nodded, gave his horses the office to start and pulled them competently out into traffic.

"You did that rather neatly," Camilla complimented him, her eyes studying his profile with something very much like pride. "And if I may be so bold as to mention it, you look amazingly handsome in your beaver and your claret cravat."

Fate glanced at her sideways and grinned. "Ye'd thought I meant fer ta murder the king when I said I wanted ta wear it, Dendron. The little valor what Eversley give me 'bout had a fit."

"Valet, you mean?"

"Aye, valor. 'Twas he what tied it. I ain't got no idea how ta go about tyin' one o' 'em. Done good, didn't he?"

"Yes," smiled Camilla, "he did very well. Captain Fate, what are you about?" she added on a gasp as horses and curricle turned up onto the edge of the verge.

"Stoppin'," the captain informed her as he stood up on the box and tied the reins to a low tree limb.

"But—but—you cannot tie the horses up like that."

"Why not? They ain't like ta hang themselves, but they ain't like ta go nowhere neither. I done it afore," he told her confidently, "with the team from the mailcoach out on the heath."

"Shhh. Someone will hear you."

"Naw, they's all too busy preenin' an' primpin'—tryin' ta impress one another. They ain't payin' the least bit o' attention ta us. Come down an' walk with me for a way." He jumped from the box, strolled around the vehicle and in a moment his strong hands were around her waist, lifting her to the ground. He took her prettily gloved hand in his own and led her up the side of a small rise and down to a rarely used dirt path that meandered along beside the Serpentine. After a bit, he stopped and took her other hand in his as well and stood staring down at her in silence for a very long moment.

He is drinking me in, thought Camilla astonished. That is just what he's doing. His eyes are gulping me down like ale. I always wondered what people meant when they wrote such things. And, oh, how thirsty he must be to let it go on so long. What will he do next? What will he say? What will I say? What would Esperanza say to Bad Jack Pharo? She felt a heat rising in her. The very roots of her hair were beginning to perspire. How on earth could he make such strange things happen to her body without a word, by touching no more than her hands?

"Ye're as beautiful as ever ye were in the moonlight on Finchley's Common," he murmured at last. "When ye're gone I'm certain-sure I've dreamed ye, ye know. But each time I see ye again, 'tis like my dream comin' true. I got somethin' ta give ye. Here, wait a mo'." He dropped one of her hands, reached into the pocket of his waistcoat, and produced four whitish little beans. "No, that ain't it," he mumbled, stuffing them back immediately. "Wrong pocket." He dropped her other hand and began to search methodically through one pocket after another. "Hold out yer hands, Dendron, will ye?" he asked and placed in them more of the whitish beans, two crumpled pound notes, a brass button, three gold crowns, and a very sorry looking thimble. "Ah, got it!" he exclaimed, his eyes sparkling as he looked at her with her hands out and piled high with his treasures. To the top of the pile, he added her diamond bracelet.

"My bracelet! Oh, I thought never to see it again!" Camilla, her hands still filled with his treasures looked up at him joyfully. "Did you buy it back from someone then? Is that how it is done?"

He shook his head and began to stuff things back into his pockets, leaving her with only the bracelet. "Let me put it on ye. 'Tis the least ye can do, Dendron. 'Tis a bit o' witchery I ain't pleased ta lose."

Camilla, perplexed, allowed him to fasten the trinket around her wrist. "What do you mean, witchery?"

He stared down at her, his eyes deadly serious, and the sheer depth of sadness and passion she saw there overwhelmed her.

"Oh," she murmured. "Oh, Jason, what is it? What can I do?"

"Nothin'," he whispered, his arms encircling her. "Nothin'."

They stood, she in his arms, for a long moment. Camilla could not think how to respond. He did not seem to expect any response. He held her softly, tenderly, and very carefully as though she were some fragile and expensive vase and then he simply released her, took her hand, and led her farther along the path in silence.

The Serpentine gurgled over small rocks beside them and the sun settled lower in the sky. A breeze began to puff and putter and brush at Camilla's heated cheeks. But Jason Fate kept his gaze straight before him and said not a word. Inside her pretty kidskin glove Camilla's hand burned with his touch and she grew breathless and excited and uncertain all at one and the same time.

As they came around a turn he stopped abruptly, tugging her to a halt beside him. Camilla followed his gaze and smiled. On the bank of the river a raggedy little boy sat very still on a big rock. Soot-streaked face, thoroughly disreputable clothes, and blonde curls made the colour of caramel by dirt, the child sat crosslegged with eyes closed. His hands rested palms up on his knees with fingers crossed. Fate gave Camilla's hand a squeeze and when she looked up at him, he put a finger to his lips and led her very quietly up beside the boy. He fished silently in a pocket, produced one of the crown pieces and set it in a tiny palm. Great blue eyes popped open and grimy little lips formed a surprised oh. The little body popped to a standing position on the top of the rock and launched itself into Fate's arms. "Cap'n! Cap'n! I knowed ye'd come!" exclaimed the child, his voice muffled in Fate's collar as he hugged the man tightly around the neck.

"Did ye now? An' how'd ye know?"

" 'Cause I prayed ye an' wished ye an' crossed m'fingers."

"An' by Jove if it didn't work!" exclaimed Fate, winking at Camilla over one small shoulder. " 'Ere now, Tick, I got a lady I want ye ta meet. No, don't be hiding yer 'ead. Turn about 'ere an' look at her. Lady Dendron," he added as the small head snuggled against his cravat and one incredibly beautiful eye stared at Camilla, "may I present to ye, Master Tick."

"Oooh, she's flash, ain't she?"

"Uh-huh. An' you must get down an' make 'er a proper bow. 'Tis 'spected."

Fate set the boy upon the ground and the child bowed at the waist.

"How do you do, Master Tick," Camilla smiled. "I am pleased to make your acquaintance."

"She soun's like angels," whispered the child up at Fate.

"Because she be a' angel, Tick. Now, tell me why ye come a prayin' an' a wishin' for me?" Without the least care for his clothing, Fate sat down on the rock and lifted the boy on to his lap. " 'Tis no one ill?"

"On'y Digger an' he no worse'n a'ways. 'Tis Da. He ain't comed home in ever so long. An' we kinnot fine 'im nowheres."

"Nowheres?"

"Uh-uh, an' ever'one has bin searchin' an' searchin'!"

"Harley been searchin'?"

"Aye, eben Harley. Ain't ye never comin' home, Cap'n? Not never? Me 'an Grig 'an Jolly 'as sweeped out yer room an' putted flowers in't, an' ever'thin'. Da would come home if ye comed. I know he would. Could I 'ave a 'niller?" The last was petitioned with a weary, plaintive little sigh and Camilla, who had settled herself beside the duo on the rock, could see tears glistening in the child's eyes.

" 'Course ye can," Fate murmured, his fingers sliding into his waistcoat pocket and producing one of the beans. " 'Ere ye go, Tick."

"Vanilla!" Camilla exclaimed. "They are vanilla beans!"

The little boy popped the bean into his mouth and began to chew pensively. "Da said as 'ow he couldn't stan' us shriekin' about no more. But we wasn't shriekin', honest Cap'n. We was quiets as li'l mouses."

"Well an' even if ye was shriekin' a bit, 'tis nothin' ta that, Tick. Childer can't a'ways be quiet. 'Tis against nature, that is. I tell ye what."

"What?"

"Ye hop off 'ome an' I shall come an' see ye tonight soon as the lamps be lit. Ye tell Harley ta be expectin' of me an' have me some tea waitin'."

"But we don't gots no tea, Cap'n. Da done drinked all what ye bringed the las' time."

"Then ye jist put the water on ta boil, Tick, an' I'll bring us some more. Ye tuck that cartwheel inta yer pocket and see Harley gits it. Now, off ye go, an' keep ta the narrows, mind. Don't be lettin' the Swells git a sight of ye."

The child planted a loud, wet kiss on Fate's cheek, wiggled down from the rock, bobbed a bow at Camilla and rushed off down the path. Fate's eyes never left the little back until it had disappeared around another turn in the lane. Then he gained his feet, helped Camilla to rise, and led her back the way they'd come. "His father is missing?" Camilla queried into the silence between them.

"Aye, but Artie Radd's ofen' missing. 'Tain't a new kind of happenin'."

"You are not worried about it then?"

"Uh-uh."

The silence descended again and Fate took her hand in his own as they walked. Camilla thought she ought to take her hand back from him but she liked how he held it and did not wish him to let it go. His silence made her anxious. Camilla had grown accustomed to gentlemen who flirted and flattered and made court promises whenever they were alone with her but never had she been alone with any gentleman so silent. Alone! For the very first time the thought occurred with a great deal of emphasis. She had allowed herself to be drawn off by this man unchaperoned and out of view of all eyes. Except, she thought, two very beautiful little blue ones in an extremely dirty, but appealing, face. "Did you know that Tick would be there?" she asked quietly. "He appeared to think he had invoked you somehow."

"Invoked?" Fate's eyebrow lifted as he smiled down at her.

"Wished you into being."

"Naw, he didn't conjure me. That there is the Trouble Rock. Mossie an' me used ta meet there did some cove twig to a lay an' the constab'lary take off af'er one of us. Ain't nobody never goes there. No Quality, I mean, or the Watch, or Runners. The childer all knows the place an' knows ta leave a token beneath the stone do there be trouble. I try ta come ever'day once or twice. Mossie comes too ever' now an' then—though not so much as he was used ta. An' there's others, as well, what come."

"Then how do you know—if others leave tokens as well—who is attempting to contact whom?"

"Ever'one 'as their own way. Does Mossie be searchin' me out, 'e leaves a 'niller with a thread run through it, an' does I be seekin' him, I leaves a 'niller skewered on a needle. 'Tis up ta ever'one ta make up their own token, ye see?"

Camilla did see and thought it a novel idea—perhaps an idea she could put in the hands of Bad Jack Pharo and Esperanza. "And if someday I should wish to contact you and could not find you anywhere, I might put a token beneath the rock and you would come to me?"

"Aye, for certain-sure."

"What would I put there?"

Fate's fingers went to his waistcoat pocket and produced a vanilla bean. "This," he said, placing it into her hand, "wrapped 'round with a rhododendron leaf. But 'tis best ta wait at the rock for as long as ye can. Mostly I come when the Quality's on the strut. There's so many people then takin' notice o' the Swells, don't no one take notice of me."

They returned to Neiland's curricle to find Lilliheun's phaeton drawn up beside it and the two gentlemen awaiting them in high dudgeon. "There, they did take a spill!" declared Lilliheun, frowning. "I knew we should not have sent them off alone!"

"Cammy, are you all right?" Neiland asked. "Locksley, you look like you've been mauled by a bear. Did the curricle tip? How did you right it again? Where have you been? You were to meet us almost a half hour ago."

Camilla, who had freed her hand from Fate's the moment they had ascended the rise, tucked the little vanilla bean into her reticule and hurried forward to assure the gentlemen that they were both perfectly fine and had merely gone for a stroll.

"Oh? And was it the act of strolling that crushed Locksley's cravat and drove it all askew and streaked his rig with dirt?" asked Lilliheun angrily. "Really, you will have to think of a better story than that, m'dear. And the back of your skirts are streaked with dirt as well. He dumped you, didn't he?"

"No, he did not," protested Camilla, a smile twitching at her lips. "He—we—I—"

"I took 'er ta look inta the Serpentine," murmured Fate, for the first time brushing at the dirt that had transferred itself from Tick to his coat. " 'Tis a magic bend in the river there, an' a person can wish upon it an'—an' toss a offerin' in."

"Never heard of such a thing," grumbled Neiland assisting Camilla up into Lilliheun's phaeton. "And how did you get so mucked-up just by making a wish?"

"Well—I went ta throw the coin, ye know, an' I lost m'balance somehow, an' Miz Quinn, she reached out ta keep me from fallin' in the water an' we both ended up on the ground."

Lilliheun gazed at Fate suspiciously. Neiland looked up at Camilla, who nodded in support of the Banbury tale.

"Well, at least you have got her back safely," muttered Lilliheun. "Come, Camilla, I'll drive you home." So saying, he nodded curtly in Fate's direction, mounted the phaeton and drove off toward the nearest gate.

"I expect Clare's jealous," mumbled Neiland climbing up onto the box of the curricle. "And I expect I'm suspicious about your walking off with m'cuz the way you did. All innocent, was it, Locksley? How the devil did you tie these horses? I never saw nothin' like it!"

Fate climbed up onto the box, released the reins from the tree limb, and handed them to Neiland. "I 'spect ye don't want me a drivin' of 'em any more, eh? Not trustin' me with yer cousin—ye likely not be trustin' me with yer team neither."

"Oh, come off it, Locksley. Doing it too brown. You ain't the least bit sensitive about my being suspicious."

"No," Fate replied, his face crinkling into a grin, "but I'm tired an' not in the mood ta be fightin' m'way through all these carriages, so I figgered ta give ye a good reason not ta let me drive for the rest o' the way."

Neiland nodded and gave the team the office to start. They drove in silence until they'd cleared the park, then Neiland glanced at the man beside him and asked outright, "Are you developing a *tendre* for Camilla, Locksley?"

"Ton-dra?"

"Yes. Are you falling in love with her? It will not do you a bit of good, you know. Cammy is determined not to marry any gentleman. She will not even accept Lilliheun, and there is not a finer gentleman in London than Clare."

"What'll she do, if she don't marry?" asked Fate, and the confusion on his face was enough to make Neiland chuckle.

"She intends to write books. She can, you know. She inherited quite enough money from her mother and father to live independently and do whatever she wishes."

"Write books?" Fate asked, his slightly tipsy eyebrow rising. "She can write books?"

"Well, I don't actually know that she can. I have not read anything she's written as yet, though m'sister says Cam has begun a novel—about a highwayman of all things!"

Fate, startled, jumped up and Neiland had to grab him with one hand to keep him from pitching head first off the box. "For heaven's sake sit down, Locksley. What's gotten into you?"

"She can't be! She can't be writin' about no highway-man! She's hoaxin' ye!"

Neiland shook his head. "No, I do not think so. We were waylaid a while back on Finchley's Common and Cammy has been writing away ever since. Why should Camilla's writing a novel about a highwayman send you into a dither, Locksley? Surely can't have anything to do with you."

"No," muttered Fate, his vivid imagination producing images of the Quality with their noses in leather-bound volumes reading all about him—and the Fat Prince, especially, deriving great glee from devoring his description.

The wee snip of a varmint, he thought. She ain't tole the law onaccounta she's savin' up ta tell ever'one at oncet. An' all along I been thinkin' her a angel. I been moonin' over 'er like a man bewitched! Naw, he thought then. She ain't doin' that. She ain't cruel. "But she be Quality," a voice whispered at the back of his mind, "an' all the Quality be cruel as devils at 'eart."

Neiland pulled up before Eversley's mansion in Grosvenor Square and deposited an amazingly pale and silent Locksley on the doorstep. "Not feeling just the thing, that's it," Neiland murmured to himself as he watched the man enter the front door. "Most likely did fall like he said and hurt himself besides."

Chapter 6

Captivated by her cousin's tale of all that had gone on in the park, Aurora's countenance changed to one of astonishment when Cammy announced her plans for the evening. "You would not dare!" she gasped. "Camilla, you cannot!"

"I will dare and you know perfectly well that I can. I shall tell your mama that I am much too tired to attend the *soirée*. You shall go on without me and as soon as I see the captain leave his house, I shall follow him. He will walk, you know, or take a hackney. He said he had to give his horse away and he has no carriage. So I shall simply walk behind him or procure a hackney myself and set it to following his."

"But surely the neighborhood will be dreadful and dangerous. Such a waif as you describe does not reside, I assure you, in the West End of London."

"Well, of course I *know* that, Rory. That is why I have borrowed Nancy's oldest round gown and her cottage cape. And I shan't wear any of my jewellery either. The people will take no more notice of me than of any other poor woman going to her home."

"Oh, I don't know, Cammy. You will be alone. It's not safe on any street in London for a woman alone, especially after dark." Aurora frowned, then pouted, then assumed a most officious glower. "I will accompany you," she declared roundly. "I shall tell mama I do not wish to attend the *soirée* either. She will go without either of us, you know, because it is Lady Mannering's entertainment and they are bosom bows. And papa proposes to dine at his club. And David has already declined to join us because he spends the evening with his cronies. I shall ask Maggie to borrow her clothes and we will go off together as a pair of chambermaids on holiday. I only hope Captain Fate does not leave before mama does." Aurora gazed down from Camilla's window which looked out upon the square and the front entrance of the Eversley mansion. "You do not suppose he will leave by the back way, do you? We will never see him then."

Dining early in Camilla's chambers, the two took turns keeping watch at the front window. They dared not don the chambermaids' dresses and capes until Lady Whey-more had gone, but they had the clothes at the ready and hurried into them the moment the Wheymore carriage departed for Lady Mannering's. When the front door of the Eversley establishment opened and the slim figure of Jason Fate strolled out to stand for a moment beneath the lamplight, the girls were ready, excited, and eager for adventure.

They rushed quietly down the servants' stairs to the side entrance, left the door on the latch, and stepped into the night. "Hurry, hurry," whispered Camilla, "we must not lose sight of him!" They scurried around the side of Wheymore House into the square just as Fate passed beneath the second lamp from the corner and both fell into step a good thirty yards behind him.

He gave no sign of seeking out a hackney cab but turned east at the corner and walked briskly toward the older parts of the city. Arm in arm, hoods of their capes pulled up to shadow their faces from view, Camilla and Aurora came near to running in order to keep Fate in sight.

"Oh, I do wish he did not take such great strides," muttered Aurora, panting. "How can any human being walk so fast without appearing to rush at all? He must have the longest legs of any man in London."

Camilla grinned, but she, too, was puffing in the effort to keep pace. He led them through the night without hesitation, turning left and then right and then left again into streets that narrowed into lanes that twisted into alleys. Streetlights became fewer and farther apart and changed from oil lamps to candle wicks. Shadows deepened and fog snaked in dirty grey tatters along gutters heaped with vile garbage.

The damp stink of poverty, neglect, and despair scalded Aurora's pert little nose and sent Camilla's aristocrat nostrils into spasms. They heard great snatches of guttural curses, shrill cries and raucous laughter. Hunched, staggering figures lurched into their path mumbling and muttering and striking out at nothing. Like demon spirits, ghostly shapes separated themselves from crumbling brick walls and floated, like the fog, off into the deep recesses of the night. "It is Hades," whispered Camilla drawing Aurora closer and clinging more tightly to her arm. "He has led us through the gates of Hell."

The captain, barely visible ahead of them, turned the corner into Basket Lane and the girls, terrified and fearing to lose sight of him, truly broke into a run and like hounds sighting the fox, fiendish forms broke from the shadows behind them to give chase howling with glee. Great heavy boots pounded and hands grabbed and tugged and slipped away from their capes which swirled enticingly behind them. Aurora screamed and Camilla gasped with fear as they rounded a corner and two powerful hands caught them up in one great bundle, swung them violently to the side and in through an open doorway. "No! No! No!" screamed Aurora, tears streaming down her cheeks. Camilla, stunned, held tightly to her cousin as they reeled across a wide plank floor and into the light of flickering tallow candles and a tiny fire. Behind them a door slammed and a heavy lock clanked shut. Tiny shadows skittered into dark corners and a deep voice bellowed, "Get m'hatchet, my darlin's. I brung ye dinner, 'deed I have!"

Camilla turned stark white; Aurora screeched; and a great pop from the fire sent them racing for the farthest corner of the little room. Camilla grabbed up a rusty poker on the way and held it in unsteady hands before them as Aurora hid behind her back.

"We don't gots no ha'chet, Cap'n," squeaked a tiny voice from behind a one-armed wing chair whose stuffing appeared reluctant to remain stuffed.

"I don' see no dinner," quaked another wee voice from under a lopsided table near the fire.

"Don' let 'er hit us; don' let her," sobbed a third voice from the shadows beside the hearth.

In the candlelight, glaring directly at her, hands on his hips, Camilla recognized through tear-bleary eyes the angry countenance of Jason Fate. The poker in her hands clattered to the floor. "Oh," she gasped. "Oh, thank heaven 'tis you! Thank heaven!" With a fluttering hand she flung back her hood.

"Oooh, 'tis Lady Dendron," sighed the voice from behind the wing chair.

"The c-cap'n's angel?" asked the voice under the table on a tiny hiccup.

"I'll be damned," growled Fate. "What're ye doin' followin' me through the streets? Are ye mad? An' who's that with ye?"

"M-me," sobbed Aurora, pushing back her own hood.

Fate's hands dropped from his hips. He unbuttoned his nankeen jacket and slipped a horse pistol from his waistband. "Harley," he called, placing the pistol on a

shelf near the door, " 'tis clear." Camilla heard steps on
the floor above them. In a moment a blond-haired boy
came down the stairs with a small bundle of blankets in
his arms. "Tick, Jolly, Grig, come out 'mediately," growled
Fate. "I've brought ye tea an' pigeon pie an' bread an'
butter." He slipped a pair of saddle bags from his shoulder.
"Leastways there were butter when I lef' the house. I hope
it ain't all gone an' melted on us."

Wiping tears from their eyes, Camilla and Aurora
watched as three tiny figures popped excitedly into view.
Two of them ran to Fate, the third crawled from behind
the armchair and came skipping toward them coming to
a stop directly in front of Camilla. "Ho! We thought ye
was the law, m'lady," grinned Tick, "er one a the Bodkins.
Ho, was we sceared! Cap'n said as 'ow someone'd been
follerin 'im ferever, an' 'e was gonna 'front 'em."

"Well, we are not the law or—Bodkins—so you are quite
safe," said Camilla quietly, stooping down before the boy
and giving him a hug. "Master Tick, may I present to you
my cousin, Lady Aurora." Tick bowed at the waist and
looked shyly up at Aurora, who looked just as shyly down
at him.

"Tick, go 'elp with tea," ordered Fate coming up behind
the boy and shoving him gently toward two very little girls
who were busily emptying the contents of his saddle bags
onto a table littered with dirty dishes. Then he seized
Camilla's wrist and tugged her toward the table, seating
her in a battered ladder-backed chair. "Ye too," he growled
at Aurora. "Come! Sit! Now!"

"Don' be sceared," breathed a tiny voice in Camilla's
ear. "The cap'n ain't neber glimflashy fer long. Not like
Da."

"Grig, fine clean cups, can't ye?" grumbled Fate, hurling
a filthy mug across the room and sending the owner of
the tiny voice scurrying away. He pointed Aurora to a seat
beside Cam, then straddled a chair himself, pounded his
fist on the chairback and muttered under his breath. He
ran his fingers through his hair sending his curls tumbling
in all directions. His darkling eyes glared angrily at Camilla.

Then he stood again and began to stomp back and forth across the room.

"Come ta colleck yer blood money, are ye?" he bellowed. "Got the Runners in yer wake? Or d'ye figger jus' ta be gatherin' more information so as ye can write in yer book where I lives an' who me chums be—so they can catch all o' us tagether at their pleasure? An' what's she doin' 'ere? Ye be needin' another witness ta send me ta the gibbet? What a bloody fool I gone an' made o' m'self! Allowin' the possibility tha' any flash mort might consider bein'—bein'—m'fren' like! Cork-brained! I bet ye had a fine laugh over tha', eh? Laughed like the devil, didn't ye? Well, but, ye ain't goin' ta laugh fer long. I'll see ye dead afore I sees these childer an' their da hauled up in the Ol' Bailey. An' I'll fine yer bloody book an' burn ever' last stinkin' page of it, if I got ta burn yer whole 'ouse down ta do it! Ain't none of yer Prim-n'-Propers ever goin' ta know m'business, not so long as I still got blood in m'body!"

Camilla sat stunned, her eyes wide, her lips parted, her face growing paler by the moment as he raged. "Are you finished?" she asked as he stopped with his hands upon the back of his chair to take a deep breath. "Are you quite finished?"

"No, I ain't!" he shouted, stomping off across the room again.

"Yes, you are!" Camilla shouted back, standing herself. "I—I—What do you mean by accusing me of treachery? How dare you accuse me of even—even thinking to betray you? Are you out of your mind? You're a madman. I see it now. A Bedlamite! After I refused to describe you to the Runners, after I refused to brand you a robber before Clare and—and everyone else, too! After I begged David and Clare to teach you to drive so that we might be alone together! After I let you kiss me!"

"He k-k-kissed you?" Aurora blurted out, amazed. "You never told me you allowed him to kiss you."

"I did not allow him to do anything!" Camilla replied, rounding upon her cousin. "He just did! Apparently he may do anything he pleases. And now—and now—it appears his pleasure is to murder us!"

Fate, who was pacing toward the door, spun on his heel and came pounding back to her. "Don't be puttin' the blame on me, darlin'! I ain't the one writin' down someone's secrets fer all the world ta read!"

"Well—of all the—who told *you* about my book in the first place? As if it were your business!"

" 'Tis my business. Ye be writin' a book about a highwayman, 'e says. An' what other highwayman do ye know, Dendron, eh? Who else's secrets can ye betray but mine? An' if ye ain't followed me 'ere ta discover me hideout an' me chums, what fer did ye follow me?"

"To—to—to—"

"Mebbe she comed ta 'elp us fine Da," Tick's hushed voice volunteered from under the table where he and Jolly and Grig had gone to huddle out of range of the captain's anger.

"Mebbe she follered ye on accounta she wants ta be cozy wif ye," offered Harley from deep in the armchair before the hearth. "I heerd as 'ow Lightfingered Lil follered Nate Button ever'where fer months—even inta the Broken Crown—on accounta she were lookin' ta be cozy wif 'im."

"She f-followed him everywhere to—to be *cozy* with him?" stuttered Camilla, the rage in her fine green eyes abruptly tinged with amusement.

"Aye," muttered Harley. "Poor Nate couldna git rid o' 'er day er night. Drove 'im blinkin' bonkers, she did."

Fate, his hand on the back of his neck, stared disbelievingly in Harley's direction.

"Went so far as ta chase 'im all the way ta the convenience at Black Will's but 'e outrunned 'er, 'e did, and slammed the door in 'er face. An' 'e din't come out fer two whole 'ours, 'cause that's 'ow long she stood there outside the door," Harley related enthusiastically. "Nobody ever seen nothin' like it. She were a one, were Lil!"

A series of muffled giggles came from beneath the table and a gurgle of mirth burst from Aurora as well. Camilla found it impossible to keep the scowl upon her face. Jason Fate walked to the door and leaned his forehead against it, turning his back on them all. His shoulders quivered suspiciously and his hands seized both sides of the door frame so tightly that his knuckles turned white.

"Well, I did not follow the remarkable Captain Jason Fate because I wished to—to get *cozy* with him," Camilla announced. Only a gulp of a giggle escaped into the affronted tone she strived to maintain. "I followed him to see where and how he lived before he came to stay in Grosvenor Square. And you are correct about one thing, sir. It was for the sake of my novel that I wished to know. But you are quite out of line to think that I would in any way betray *you*. My book is a work of fiction. Fiction, Captain Fate, not fact. You would not even recognize yourself in it."

"Yes, he would," murmured Aurora unhelpfully. "Though Camilla's given you blond hair, sir, and blue eyes and made you six feet tall."

Fate's shoulders shook more violently and he pounded a fist against the doorframe.

" 'E's gonna 'splode any minute," squeaked a voice from under the table. "Jus' ye wait." This announcement was followed by jostling, bumping, and hushed laughter.

"S-s-six foot tall?" asked Fate on a gasp of a chuckle as he turned to face Camilla. "Me? B-blond?" His fingers tugged at his dark curls; his eyes blazed with mirth; his whole body trembled; and a great roar of laughter burst into the room. "L-Lil trapped Nate in the—the—out'ouse? H-How's a bloke s'posed ta keep 'is sanity in the face o' such knowledge?"

Fate's laughter erupted into the lodging with such exhilaration, such love of life, such merry well-being, that it tugged the babes from under the table, sent Harley to rocking with glee, made Aurora bounce in her chair and clap her hands as she giggled, and set Camilla off into helpless whoops. When at last Miss Quinn caught her breath, straightened up properly, and wiped the tears of laughter from her eyes with the back of her gloves, she discovered Fate staring down at her, questioningly.

"If you were to read my manuscript, you would quite understand how it is, Captain. Bad Jack Pharo is based upon you in some ways, but it would be quite impossible for anyone to recognize you on the street as his model. And no one will recognize this place as itself either, I assure you. Only I cannot write about people and places unless I have some idea of what they are truly like—and so—and so—"

"An' so ye came snoopin'."

Camilla opened her mouth to protest but closed it again without saying a word. She stared down at the tips of her slippers in silence. A pretty pink blush crept up her neck and into her cheeks. Fate took two long strides in her direction, placed a hand upon each of her arms, and attempted to stoop low enough to look up into her face. The smell of vanilla sent her pulses racing. The slight pressure of his fingers upon her upper arms made her blood tingle and her temples pound. She looked up a smidgen and met his sparkling dark eyes.

"I reckon mebbe I spoke too hasty," he murmured. "I reckon mebbe I don' rightly unnerstan' this writin' business."

"I will let you read every word of it if you wish," said Camilla in return. "I assure you, you are not compromised in any way."

"Can't read," Fate replied.

"Not at all?"

"Nary a word. Didn't never matter—ain't nobody I know can write 'cept Mossie. Tea?" he asked, straightening and leading her back to the table from which the dirty dishes had been removed and onto which three little figures were busily setting a number of mismatched and slightly broken cups. "That there's Jolly, an' this be Grig, an' that's Harley, an' the babe in 'is arms be Digger."

Camilla was amazed to find as the taller boy settled at the table that the bundle of dirty rags he held contained a wizened little face with huge brown eyes and reddish hair.

"Good evening," she said, her eyes traveling from one

child to the next. "I am Miss Quinn and this is my cousin, Lady Aurora."

"Aw, we knows who *ye* are," Harley grinned showing a missing front tooth. "Tick ain't stopped talkin' about ye since 'e met ye. Now 'twill be Lady Dendron this an' the cap'n's angel that all the rest o' our days."

"Well, I can see that Jolly and Grig are proper young ladies," Aurora smiled, helping the children to butter slices of bread. "But I cannot for a moment guess how old any of you are—and I cannot guess if Digger is a girl or a boy. That is such an odd name for a baby, you know, Digger."

"We calls 'im Digger 'cause he's ferever diggin' out a cave under 'is covers," Harley volunteered.

"An' 'cause the cap'n wouldn't let us call 'im Rat," added Tick loudly as he cut into the pigeon pie. "I don' see as 'ow bein' called Rat be any worse'n bein' called Tick, meself, but the cap'n says as how 'tis."

"Cause ye can say as 'ow ye bin called afer' the tickin' o' a clock," explained the little girl called Jolly with a shake of lanky blond curls, "but some un called Rat gots ta be named fer a rat, don't 'e. I'm fibe," she added proudly with a shy smile for Aurora, "an' Tick be six an' Grig four. Digger, he's only 'most a year, but he ain't dead yet, so's we got hopes of 'im."

"Not great hopes, mind," announced Fate with a glance at Camilla. "Ain't likely—poorly as he be—that he'll ever 'mount to as much as Harley—Harley bein' a flat-out 'ostler at Grillon's—but we keeps a thought fer 'im, don't we childer?"

"Aye, Cap'n," the children agreed in unison, small heads nodding as Fate took the babe from Harley's arms and slid a plate of pigeon pie in front of Harley instead. Camilla was captivated as Fate balanced the babe on one knee, dunked a piece of bread into his tea and fed it to the child. That obviously being the sign, all the other little mouths around the table began to chew and drink and nibble as well.

The food disappeared to the last crumb; the tea to the last drop. Tick burped loudly and the girls giggled. Fate deserted the table for the armchair; Harley placed two more coals on the fire and moved the chairs from the table to a place nearer the hearth for Camilla and Aurora; then he took Digger from the captain's arms and sat down upon a three-legged stool close before the fire. Tick, Jolly, and Grig arranged themselves neatly in Fate's lap and within moments all of them were sailing away on the quiet tones of Fate's voice into a world of gypsies, charms, princesses and evil Bodkins in the bottom of an enchanted garden. When at last the Princess Alanda had been rescued by her brave knight and the Bodkins had left the field in disarray, Fate and Harley carried the sleepy-eyed urchins off to bed.

"Are you not going to search for their father?" Camilla asked as Fate descended the stairs.

"Aye, as soon as I get ye home. He's about some'eres, Artie is. Like as not workin' at this 'our."

"Working? In the middle of the night?" Camilla eyed the captain skeptically.

He gave her a low, cynical bow. "There be some of us, m'lady, what does our best work in the dregs of the evenin' an' the wee 'ours of the mornin'. Ye'd best be a knowin' of that for yer book, eh? Unless, o' course, this Bad Jack Pharo of yers be a most 'straordinary robber."

"Do you mean to say," murmured Aurora as she fastened her cape, "that the children's father is a thief?"

"Naw, Artie ain't no thief, Banshee. Artie's a cracksman—a prime un too. Comed in with me when I decided ta work the High Toby, but I reckon 'e's gone back ta burgl'ry by now. Prob'ly used up ever'thin' we maked on the road. 'Spensive raisin' five childer, ye know, an' him only gettin' two shares af'er 'spenses."

"I should think you and your confederates would all have a good deal of money," Camilla said as he held the door open for her, "after all of the carriages you have robbed and all the jewels you have stolen."

"Only the Quality would thin' that," muttered Fate with a shake of his head.

"And why did the children's father get two shares?"

"His share an' Harley's."

Camilla came to a dead stop on the street side of the

door. "Do you mean to tell me that you taught that child to rob coaches?"

"Didn't require much teachin'," Fate shrugged, taking her arm and Aurora's and urging them down the alley. "An' Harley ain't no child. He's near ta 'leven."

"He is only eleven years old?"

"Naw, ten—but near ta 'leven. Old 'nuff ta be earnin' his own keep."

"And were you earning your own keep when you were ten, Captain Fate?" Aurora asked, sidestepping around a particularly suspicious-looking heap of rags.

"Aye. Afore then. Me mam and da was used ta send me in through winders ta open doors for 'em when I were jus' a tyke. An' by the time I were five er six er so, I come on ta be a right good cutpurse—snibble this an' snabble that, I could, without a blink o' the eye on the part o' the party what was donatin'."

"By the time you were five or six?" Camilla's feet appeared likely to halt again. Fate tugged her forward.

"Aye. 'Twere 'spected."

"And what was expected of you by the time you were seven?" asked Camilla, the angry flash of her eyes unnoticeable in the dark.

Fate, intent upon steering them around a loud confrontation on the street ahead, did not answer at once. Camilla, her anger growing at the thought of a child forced into such a life at all—much less at the age of five!—asked the question again, louder and with a great deal more intensity—so much intensity that Fate looked down at her in surprise. Beneath the faint glow of a much abused street-lamp his eyebrows tilted and a frown line formed between them. " 'Twasn't nothin' 'spected by then, Dendron," he drawled. "By then they was dead an' I was on m'own."

Aurora gave a tiny gasp and coughed to cover it. Camilla's heart skipped a beat. From the comfortable shelter of their lives, neither had spared much thought for the lower classes or their children, had often complained of the tiny beggars, climbing boys, sweepers, and kitchen boys whose unkempt appearances and often disturbing odors offended them. The Great Unwashed, they'd learned to

call them—adults and children alike—and avoided them
like the plague. They trudged on beside the Captain in
confused silence. Neither understood the emotions suddenly loosed within them. Pity, Camilla thought, but she
was quite mistaken. It was the beginnings of guilt.

The captain led them without pause, his long stride
shortened only a bit on their behalf, back through the
labyrinth of execrable lanes and alleys, avoiding a ruckus
here and a donnybrook there, ignoring whistles and cat-
calls and all manner of affronts without batting an eyelash.
Only once did he stop, when a partially clad young woman
rushed from an open doorway and crashed straight into
him. "Oh! Oh, Jason, thank gawd 'tis you! A bloke upstairs
willn't stop beatin' upon Meggy. Foxed, 'e is an' set on
killin' 'er!"

Fate drew the pistol from his waistband, put it into the
woman's hands and, commending Camilla and Aurora to
her care, dashed into the building. In a matter of moments
a body came soaring through the second floor window
and crumbled into the street. Camilla stared long and hard
at the man who lay unmoving upon the cobbles. Even in
his shirtsleeves and stockinged feet, she could recognize
an aristocrat when she saw one. Fate came back down the
stairs and went to kneel beside the body. He felt beneath
the lace at the man's wrist, then hoisted the thoroughly
limp gentleman to his shoulder, and carried him off down
the street and into another alley.

"I reckon he ain't dead does the Watch find 'im afore
Friday," the captain muttered on his return. He took the
pistol back, leaned down and kissed the woman on the
cheek, and urged her to go look after her friend. "For
Meggy's 'urtin' an' that's a fack, Gwen. Wait. Here. Ye take
these fer a barber does ye need one," he said fishing some
coins from a pocket and placing them in her hand. "Sen'
me word ta Number fifteen, Grosvenor Square, eh, if ye
be needin' more?"

Once again he took Camilla's arm and then Aurora's,
and led them off into the damp, stinking dark of St. Giles's.
When the stench began to lessen and a goodly number
more streetlamps lit the way, when torch boys could be

seen guiding gentlemen along the streets, and chairs began to float by on the shoulders of well-muscled chairmen carrying elegantly clad ladies surrounded by well-dressed beaux on foot, the captain slackened his pace and began to look around him.

"What is it you're looking for?" Camilla asked in a very quiet little voice.

"A hack, Dendron, ta take ye home."

"Are you not going home?"

"Naw, I reckon I got ta look out Artie an' see 'e's safe. Wouldn't do for the childer ta wake up an' fine their da's bein' dragged up before the judges in the Ol' Bailey. That'd be a reg'lar depressin' thin' fer 'em ta wake up ta." He stared down at her with a very strange expression on his face and sighed.

"What?" she asked. "What is it?"

"I don't know, Dendron. I ain't easy about it."

"About what? About the children's father?"

"Naw, 'bout you an' The Banshee here. I reckon I wants ta trust ye, but—damnation, I ain't never afore met one o' the Quality what *could* be trusted. Ye ain't been lyin' ta me, eh, Dendron? Ye been tellin' me the truth?"

Camilla nodded. "The truth. I shall never betray you with so much as a wink of the eye, Captain."

"An' The Banshee?"

"Oh, no, not ever, Captain Fate," insisted Aurora before her cousin could answer for her. "Cammy has sworn me to silence."

"Well—I reckon as that'll 'ave to do—though I be a fool fer believin' it. Off with ye, then," he added as a hackney cab pulled to the curb and he opened the door and helped them inside. He gave the driver their direction and stared after them as the coach moved off. With a resolute sigh, he stuffed his hands into his pockets and turned back the way he had come.

Chapter 7

Peter Marks, Lord Eversley, waltzed Camilla gracefully across Almack's highly polished, but slightly uneven, dance floor. "It is a great pity, Miss Quinn, that Locksley cannot be here. He has formed a *tendre* for you I think. I could not put up his name for entrance, of course. No one would give him the nod at the moment."

"No, I expect not," agreed Camilla wondering what impulse had overtaken Eversley that he should ask her to waltz with him. They had never been more than casual acquaintances and he had never done more than nod in her direction since her first appearance in Society. She had thought, when first they met, that Eversley was quite handsome with his russet hair, wide blue eyes and pleasantly rounded face, but there had been a subtle air of dissipation about him even then that had made her cautious. In moments like these, in the middle of the marriage mart where gentlemen must keep to the most rigid standards of dress and decorum, the hint of the libertine that lingered upon him was well-disguised, but still, Camilla could sense it.

"I have had word that Dewhurst arrives in London on Tuesday next. Then, perhaps, Locksley's claim will be taken more seriously."

"Perhaps," murmured Camilla. "What is it, Lord Eversley, that you wish of me?"

"Why, nothing, Miss Quinn. Only your beguiling presence for the length of a waltz."

"Flummery, my lord. *You* do not find me at all beguiling."

"Oh, but I do, Miss Quinn. Exceedingly so. I have never approached you before because I knew Lilliheun was drawn to you and I, of course, stand no chance at all of securing a young lady's interest once she has come under my cousin's spell."

Camilla looked up at him with the tiniest frown. "Under

Mr. Lilliheun's spell? Me? I think you are sadly mistaken, my lord. Your cousin and I are friends, nothing more."

"And Locksley? Might he consider you *his* friend as well? What will you do, Miss Quinn, when the duke arrives and swords are drawn? On whose side will you stand?"

"Certainly it will not come to a drawing of swords, Lord Eversley. If Mr. Locksley's claim can be proved to the duke's satisfaction, why then we must all accept him as the Dewhurst heir apparent, must we not?"

"I rather think Lilliheun will not, m'dear. There will be a great rattling of sabres and perhaps years of legal rigmarole before my esteemed cousin will relinquish his claim and give Locksley the nod. A deal of Clare's consequence is involved in't, you know. He depends to a great extent upon his expectations."

Camilla wondered what she ought to say. She had not thought Lilliheun in the least dependent upon his inheritance of the Dewhurst title. Clare, after all, had inherited a considerable fortune from his father. Certainly Eversley was mistaken. "I cannot think," she sighed, "why it should be so very important to you, sir. Certainly you have nothing to gain either way. And yet, it was you who brought Mr. Locksley forward was it not? And you have searched for the proof to support his claim as well. Have you found more evidence in Mr. Locksley's favor?"

"Indeed, Miss Quinn. Quite enough to establish him in Dewhurst's eyes—though the courts will grind away at it forever if it is taken before them. It would be more pleasant, don't you think, if somehow everyone involved could be well-satisfied and a conclusion arrived at in a cordial and private manner?"

"And you wish me to convince Clare to do so," drawled Camilla.

Eversley smiled and shook his head. "It would be wonderful if you had such power, but I doubt you could, Miss Quinn. But I do ask that you not hold this nonsense against Locksley. He's an innocent in the matter. It was not he came looking for a fortune, but I who learned of him and sought him out. Once Dewhurst arrives, word of Locksley's claim will spread much farther than it has already, you know. We won't be able to contain it within the small circle of people who now share the knowledge, and Locksley will be in for some abominable treatment. I only hope that you will not join with other of Clare's friends who will do their best to make Mr. Locksley an object of suspicion, derision, and disgust. I am quite sure it would rip his heart out were you to do so."

Camilla had never given thought to what might be the captain's welcome into the *ton* if the duke were to demand his entrance. Certainly it would not be a pleasant experience for him—especially if Clare's friends continued to brand him an impostor. By the time the dance had finished and Eversley had returned her to her aunt's care, Camilla wore a worried frown. She settled beside Lady Wheymore on one of the gilt chairs set out for the chaperones, and fell into a brown study. She danced with the remainder of her partners in virtual silence and rode home in silence as well. Lady Wheymore enquired if she were not feeling quite the thing and Camilla, hoping to avoid an interrogation, sighed and said that her head was beginning to throb. She thought it would be best if she simply took herself off to bed.

Once safely tucked between the sheets she found that her head was, indeed, beginning to throb and that each throb was accompanied by an image of the captain's starkly handsome countenance. "Oh, go away, do!" she muttered into the darkness. "You have done nothing but stir up my peace since first I saw you!" For a long while she lay, her eyes closed, listening to the sounds of the night. The headache that had threatened, faded and she drifted into dreams.

She wandered through the fields and hills that surrounded her uncle's estate in Northumberland, into the home woods and down the curious, twisting path that led to the hidden garden and the fountain and the old Roman wall that divided Bedford Hill from the dense Forest of the Shrieking Specter. In her mind the curlews cried and the flowers of spring danced at her feet. The smell of pine and grass and vanilla tickled at her nostrils.

Vanilla? The smell of vanilla? Camilla's dream came to

a wrenching halt; her eyes popped open and then her mouth popped open as well at a shadowy movement beyond the door to her sitting room. She might have screamed if she had not taken another deep breath and the vanilla scent reassured her. She climbed from the bed, drew her green silk robe closely about her, slipped her feet into her slippers, and tiptoed silently across the carpet into the adjoining chamber.

His back was to her and his head bent low over the drawers of her escritoire. For a moment a flame flickered and then it was gone. She heard him sigh, was startled to hear, "Truly, Dendron, I love ye," whispered into the night.

"Perhaps so, but that is no excuse for your presence in my chamber at any hour, much less in the middle of the night," she whispered back, expecting him to jump in surprise. He merely turned slowly in her direction, and struck another of the phosphorous matches against the small, rough stone in his palm.

"Where's a candle?" he asked, and Camilla crossed to her dressing table and carried one to him. He lit it and set it on the top shelf of the escritoire. In its flickering light she could see the smile playing across his lips and the sparkle of welcome in his eyes. "I'd no 'tention of wakin' ye at first, Dendron. I'm sorry, I 'ad to."

"What are you doing here? How did you get in? What do you want?"

"Well, I come in through that window there what someone lef' open a bit. I reckon 'twas considered safe enuf, eh, bein' on the second story an' all? But there be a way up among the vines, ye see, so I took it."

"But why?" Camilla pulled her robe tighter around her. The breeze from the window which now stood wide open to the night air was chilly and giving her goose bumps.

"Yer cold, ain't ye? Come 'ere, Dendron." He put an arm around her shoulders and led her to a small armchair. "Tuck yer feet up under ye," he ordered and went into her bedchamber. He returned with a quilt which he wrapped about her shoulders and arranged to cover her in a cocoon-like warmth. Then he looked about in the dim shadows, discovered a footstool and pulled it up before her, settling down upon it and staring up at her with a mischievous grin. "I come ta steal yer book, luv."

"You what?" Camilla cried.

"Shhh, ye'll wake some un. I come ta steal yer book. It ain't that I don't be believin' of ye, but Mossie, 'e said as how I'd feel a deal happier did I know for sure what were in't. He said as how 'e'd read it ta me."

"Well of all the nerve! To sneak into my chambers like a thief in the night—"

"I *be* a thief in the night, Dendron."

"But—could you not simply ask me to see my manuscript?"

"I don't know. Could I?"

"Could you what?"

"See it?"

"But I thought you just said you stole—"

"No, I come ta steal it, darlin', but I ain't done so as yet. I can't fine it. Mossie said as how 'twas probably jus' a stack of papers with writin' on 'em an' not a reg'lar book at all. But, by gawd, Dendron, you got stacks of papers ever'where in there." He pointed at the escritoire with an exasperated shake of his head. "They can't all be yer book, can they?"

"No, of course not," Camilla giggled. "They are most of them letters from my friends and relatives and—notes that I have made to myself—and stories I have written at one time or another."

"Hunnerds o' stacks o' papers," sighed Fate with a look of long-suffering that made Camilla laugh. "An' me not able ta tell one stack from another. I thought I should be havin' ta carry 'em off an' bring 'em back one stack at a time till I fined the right one. Job like that could take the whole night—two nights mebbe—'specially havin' ta dodge the Watch on ever' climb!"

It did occur to Camilla that she was sitting in her chambers, *en dishabille,* in the middle of the night, *alone* with a thorough villain and the thought sent a shiver through her, but she could not resist his perplexed and exasperated grin and his inexplicable trust in herself. All she need do, after all, was to scream and he would be captured and taken away. Yet he trusted her not to scream. He was, in actual fact, trusting her with his life this very moment.

"Would ye give me the book?" Fate asked softly.

"Can you truly not read?"

"Uh-uh, but Mossie can."

"Then why did this Mossie person not come himself? He certainly would have known which papers to steal."

"Aye, but 'e's much too old fer climbin' vines, darlin', an' besides, I didn't treasure the thought o' Mossie stompin' about in yer chamber all on 'is own like."

"You did not?"

"No."

"But it is perfectly all right for you to do so?"

Jason Fate wrinkled his nose in thought. The tipsy eyebrow tipped even more awkwardly to the side. "Aye," he nodded at last, "fer I knows I ain't about ta do ye no harm, Dendron, even if ye was ta shoot me. Mossie, though, 'e might, ye see. Mossie don't have no feelin's fer ye."

Camilla was truly astonished at how very warm it was inside her quilt cocoon and how it grew warmer by the moment. "Does that mean that you do have feelings for me, Captain Fate?"

"Well o' course I do. I bin thinkin' 'bout it serious an' I reckon mebbe I love ye, Dendron. But I ain't sure-certain. I ain't never loved no mort afore."

His eyes met hers in the flickering candlelight with such puzzled innocence that Camilla wished nothing more than to take him into her arms and kiss him thoroughly. Of course she could not. *That* would be totally reprehensible. And besides, she was *not* in love with him—was she? No, certainly not! "Well, you cannot remain in my chambers the entire night, regardless," she muttered, slipping from the quilt and rising. "I shall give you the part of my manuscript that is completed and then you must leave immediately. There," she said placing a stack of handwritten pages into his hands. "Do not lose any of them, please. And you must return them as soon as you are finished."

Fate nodded and tucked the pages safely away inside his jacket. He placed a finger beneath her chin and planted an enthusiastic smack upon her unsuspecting lips, then took himself to the open window and departed the way he had come. Camilla stared after him nonplussed. When finally she moved to the window and pulled it closed, latching it, she could see the shadow of the man slipping in the front door of Number fifteen, Grosvenor Square.

"You are the most aggravating man," she murmured as she made her way back to her bed. "What would you have done if I had not awakened to help you?" And then she wondered just why she had awakened. Had there been a noise, some disturbance that had drawn her from her dreams? No, it had been vanilla—the smell of vanilla. And she smelled it now—more than she had when Fate had been sitting right in front of her. Camilla lit the candle upon her bedside table and lifted it in one hand, all the while sniffing in first one direction and then another. She held the candle high and a flash of red attracted her to the head of the bed.

There beside her pillow lay a Belcher neckerchief formed into a pouch and tied closed with a piece of yellow yarn. She set the candle down, bounced onto the bed, and seized the neckerchief bringing it close to her nose. It reeked of vanilla. She set it on her lap and untied the yarn. "Oh," she gasped, "whyever did he?" The opened makeshift pouch displayed a jumble of vanilla beans, cherry and apple blossoms, and rhododendron leaves, and in the midst of them, a white silk rose.

Elgin Moss snorted, chortled, and chuckled his way through Camilla's manuscript the next morning, he and Fate locked away in the first floor study with a pot of tea and a tray of cherry tarts. "It ain't all that funny," snickered the captain. "Stop laughin', Mossie."

"I—I can't, Jason. 'Tis a delightful chronicle of outlandish exploits. A pip, it is. A reg'lar spellbinder. An' ye the hero, m'lad!"

"Naw, I ain't even in it, Mossie. I been listenin'. 'Tis all about some bloke by name o' Bad Jack Pharo an' a enchantin' flash mort called Lady Esp'ranza. I 'spect it's good though, ain't it? For a book, I mean.''

'' 'Tis excellent,'' grinned Elgin Moss. ''A triumph. Yer lady-friend will be a rousin' success, b'lieve me. The Quality'll jump upon it with glee. But you *are* in here, Jason. Ye're Bad Jack.''

''Naw, ain't possible. He don't look nothin' like me.''

''Possibly not, m'lad, but he *is* you all the same. I can see the resemblance, 'specially where 'e storms inta a rage over the flash mort dressin' like a lad an' ridin' to his rescue, an' then bursts out laughin' an' takin' her up before 'im on his magnificent white stallion, Victory!''

''Aw, come off it, Mossie. She don't be writin' 'bout me. And she don't know much 'bout horses neither. A 'nificent white stallion—aye, and ye'd not git a coach robbed with that unnerneath ye. Chasin' the first mare within a mile 'twas ready for 'im is what he'd be doin', an' poor Jack stuck up upon his back blushin' from ear ta ear!''

''Still, 'tis romantic, Jason, an' the Ladies of Quality will eat it up. She has a talent has yer lady. An' see how she's gone an' changed the Trouble Rock inta a hole in a tree? Exquisite, 'tis. Charmin'.''

''An' funny,'' chuckled Fate, giving in with a shrug. ''I guess 'tis funny. An' the childer would like it.''

''Aye, indeed they would. Did ye fine Artie ever?''

The sparkle in Fate's eyes faded. ''Naw, not a sign of 'im.''

''P'rhaps he's been snabbled, Jason. P'rhaps the Runners have clapped 'im in irons.''

''An' p'rhaps he's run off like he's been threatenin' ta do since Allie died. He ain't been easy at all ever since Digger were borned.''

Elgin Moss nodded soberly. He'd never understood Artie Radd, but he, like Fate, had always had a place in his heart for Radd's commonlaw wife and Allie had always welcomed their company heartily. '' 'Twas a terr'ble night the night Digger were born. Might turn any man inta a Bedlamite,'' he conceded quietly.

''Don't be talkin' 'bout it, Mossie,'' the captain sighed. ''I don't be wantin' ta think on it. I done put it outta m'mind most of a year ago an' I ain't lettin' it back in. Ye think mebbe that's why Dendron don't be wantin' no husband? On accounta she don't wanta be 'avin' no babes?''

"It would likely keep me from takin' on a husband," Moss acknowledged. "D'ye mean ta tell me this flash mort of yers be against marryin'?''

"Aye, 'tis what her cuzin says. 'Tis why she's set on bein' a bookwriter. I 'spect 'tis how it works, eh, with the Quality? Them morts what can write books don't got ta git married?''

Elgin Moss rubbed the grey fringe behind his left ear contemplatively. "I reckon," he sighed at last. "The Quality's got all kind's a fractious rules.''

Somers, the Wheymore butler, was aware of each one of the fractious rules imposed by Society, but his ears had been filled with anecdotes of life in the Eversley household since the advent of the Locksley dynasty there and he and Glasgow had shared many a glass at the Broken Jib enjoying tales of the vagaries of Mr. John Locksley and his companion. That, perhaps, was the reason he chose to admit Elgin Moss, resplendent in carnation and pea green, into the front parlor that very afternoon without the least hesitation and sent one of the footmen rushing off to inform Miss Camilla that a gentleman wished to discuss a matter of some importance with her. He enquired after Moss's comfort, offered to relieve him of the package he carried, poured the man a glass of the earl's brandy, and left him standing before the window gazing silently out upon the square, which was exactly where Camilla found him as she hurried breathlessly into the room. "Oh," she said on a tiny gasp, "I am sorry. I thought you were—would be— Mr. Locksley.''

Elgin Moss turned to greet her, his canny blue eyes bright with curiosity. He had not as yet actually seen this beauty of Jason's and he had been longing to get a look at her for weeks. He bowed competently in her direction, openly admiring her perfect little figure, the proud set of her shoulders, the sweet openness of her heart-shaped face. "Moss," he drawled in a bemused voice. "Elgin Moss, at y'service, m'lady."

"Good afternoon, Mr. Moss. Will you not be seated?" Camilla swept the rest of the way into the room and took a seat herself upon a settee between the windows. So, this was the captain's Mossie. What an odd-looking little man he was in his carnation pink coat and pea-green knee-breeches, and how wide and bright and lively were his eyes. "Mr. Locksley has spoken of you, Mr. Moss. I am pleased at last to make your acquaintance."

"And I, yours, m'dear. I've come ta return your manuscript. May I say that both Ja-John and I were mightily entertained by it an' are hoping to read the rest."

"You are?"

"Indeed. 'Tis a wonderful talent ye possess, and so I told Jas-John. And he agreed o' course."

"Why, thank you, Mr. Moss. I am quite humbled by your kind response."

Moss waved his hand at her as if to brush away her words. "Ain't no need to be 'umble. Bein' 'umble never got nobody nowhere, if ye don't mind my sayin' it. Ye ought to be proud of yer abilities. Your goin' ta take it to a publisher when 'tis finished are ye not?"

"Yes, Mr. Moss, that is my intention."

"Good, good." Moss relaxed into the chair he'd taken and crossed one leg over the other, displaying to perfection a carnation pink shoe laced with pea-green ribbon.

What horrendous taste the man has, thought Camilla, but how bright and jaunty it makes him appear. He is like a monstrous elf or an enlarged leprechaun. "Is there something in particular that you wished to discuss, Mr. Moss? Aside from my work, that is?"

Elgin Moss nodded his balding head.

"And that would be?" Camilla asked after waiting a full minute for the man to speak.

"Well, I reckon—no, I knows—I got no business ta be askin' it of ye—"

"Asking what, Mr. Moss?"

Elgin Moss shook his head silently from side to side as

if arguing with himself, then stood and paced the floor, then turned back to Camilla with a worried frown between his brows. "All I wish to ask you, m'lady, is ta be proper careful as regards m'lad. He ain't a thing made of pen an' paper. Ye catched a deal of his soul an' put it inta your book, and ye catched a deal of his heart an' be carryin' it around in your pocket, but there's depths of heart an' soul left ta m'Jason that ye ain't got the least suspicion of and— and if ye ain't proper careful, ye could easy be the death of 'im." Elgin Moss gave a hurried bow and without raising his eyes to meet hers, left the room and presently the house while Camilla stood staring in wonder at the spot he had vacated.

Aurora came floating into the room several minutes after Moss's departure. Dressed for driving in royal blue with an outrageous bonnet covered in wax fruit and royal blue ribbons, she halted in the midst of pulling on her gloves and stared at her seemingly mesmerized cousin. "Cammy, what is it? That quaint little man did not offend you in some way? I thought to come and bear you company, but Somers mentioned that it was private business and mother thought you quite capable of handling such a personage—he is presently our neighbor, after all—without support, unless you were to solicit our intervention."

"What?" Camilla's eyes blinked uncomprehendingly into Aurora's own. "Oh! Oh! No! No, Mr. Moss did certainly not offend me. It was—I did not understand— Aurora? Will you put off your drive this afternoon? Will you go into the city with me instead? To Mr. Borhill's office?"

"Mr. Andrew Borhill?"

"Yes, there is something—there are things I wish to learn about—about Mr. Locksley and perhaps Mr. Borhill's men have already discovered some of them."

"Oh, Cammy, you do not think that Mr. Borhill's men will learn who Mr. Locksley truly is?"

"I—I don't know. I don't know what to think. Come upstairs with me while I change my dress and I shall tell you what Mr. Moss said, then you will give me your opinion of what on earth he meant to say!"

* * *

Andrew Borhill's aristocratic nostrils quivered with suppressed fury as he planted himself firmly into the chair behind his desk. "I will not under any circumstances cease my investigations, Clare! Are you mad? The man is out to disinherit you!"

Lilliheun, his sea-grey eyes weary from an excessively late evening, sighed and leaned back in the red leather armchair on the opposite side of the desk. "It don't matter, Drew."

"Of course it matters, you ninny. The man's an impostor!"

"No, he ain't."

Borhill's eyebrows rose in disbelief. "You know this for a fact?"

Lilliheun sighed again and shook his head. "No, I do not know it for fact, Drew. But—but—there is something about him. The more I know him, the more I believe in him. He has Locksley's blood in him, even Wheymore don't doubt that, and—and there are things he says—things he ain't even aware of—"

"What kinds of things?"

"The other night Neiland and I took him to Grillon's and we got foxed, and Locksley stood up and made a toast—*audentes fortuna juvat*—he says as clear as day."

"So?" Borhill's skeptical gaze never wavered.

"It is the Lilliheun family motto, Drew!"

"Eversley taught it to him."

"But he said it clear as day, in perfect Latin, and the man cannot even speak English without torturing it to death."

Borhill shook his head in exasperation. "Think, Clare. What is it that you're saying? That he learned the motto at his father's knee and it came slipping from between his lips without the least bit of thought because he was foxed?"

"Yes, I guess."

"Supposedly he was not born until after his father left the country, Clare. He could not have learned anything at his father's knee. And who else was there to teach him the motto? An ignorant gypsy girl? I rather doubt she did. The man is a fraud. He has lent himself to Eversley for one reason or another, and I have no doubt he will regret it. Peter has always been a sly one and though I cannot quite see what it is he plans to gain from this, there is something. There must be. And if I were this fellow posing as Locksley I would be very cautious because when Peter decides he has no further need of him—well, one never knows, does one?"

Lilliheun's hand went to his head and he groaned. "Enough of this Cheltenham Tragedy, Drew. Peter a threat to someone? Peter? I expect he is spoiled and sly and greedy—always was when we were children—but what you suggest is preposterous. Tell me, did your man discover anything at Vilxhelm?"

"Only that the church existed—but burned to the ground, records and all, over twenty years ago. That alone is highly suspicious. Anyone might forge marriage lines and claim they were recorded there before the fire." Borhill looked up at a light tap on his door. "Enter," he called.

Camilla and Aurora swept into Borhill's chambers before the solicitor's clerk, Mr. Dunning, had even finished announcing them. "I must beg a word with you," Camilla breathed excitedly. "I must know everything you have discovered about Mr. Locksley." She did not even notice Lilliheun until he rose to his feet. "Clare? Oh! I had no idea you were—"

"May I ask what interest you have in Borhill's investigations, Miss Quinn?" Lilliheun drawled in a tone quite unlike any she had ever heard from him before. He stared at her from beneath partially hooded eyes, an extremely cool smile barely touching his perfect lips.

Chapter 8

"Well, I think Lilliheun had every right to be angry with you," Aurora pouted prettily as she and Camilla settled back against the squabs. "He is jealous, you know. He thinks you have fallen in love with Mr. Locksley and that is why you wish to discover all you can about him. If you do not tell him the truth, Clare will fall into a serious decline."

"Oh, balderdash," sighed Camilla. "I have told Clare over and over again that I am not the least bit interested in marrying him or any other gentleman. And we cannot tell him the truth, Rory. You've vowed me a vow not to disclose Captain Fate's identity and I have vowed to Captain Fate himself not to do so."

"At least Mr. Borhill's men do not seem to have discovered who Mr. Locksley truly is. Perhaps we have mistaken Mr. Moss's words. Perhaps he meant something else entirely. What did he say exactly? Tell me again."

"He said that if I were 'not proper careful' I might be the death of Captain Fate. He said I had caught a piece of the captain's soul and put it into my book and that I carried a piece of his heart around in my pocket and that if I were 'not proper careful' I could well be the death of him. What can it mean? Surely there are no clues to the captain in my manuscript?"

"No, Mr. Moss would have said, I think, if Captain Fate could be identified because of that."

"Yes, so I think as well. And so I guessed that perhaps all this disturbance over whether or not he is Lord Locksley's son might lead Mr. Borhill to a discovery of the captain's true character and that that was what Mr. Moss referred to, but Mr. Borhill appears not to have a clue as to Mr. Locksley's being Captain Fate."

"Not a single clue," agreed Aurora.

"No, and why Clare should climb up into the boughs over my asking what Mr. Borhill may have discovered, I cannot comprehend. Oh, Clare is so very vexing. I should like to punch him directly in his high-bridged nose, let me tell you."

"That is not at all what I should like to do," murmured Aurora with a sweet smile, but her words went unnoticed as Camilla glared from the coach window at the passing buildings.

Lilliheun glared just as angrily from Borhill's window. "I swear, Drew, if she is not in love with that rogue then I am a mother hen."

"Ahh, so that's what brought about the explosion. I wondered, you know. One moment you were inclined to throw over your inheritance for the rascal and the next you were cursing the ground he walks upon."

"Well, I did not mean to do that. Curse the ground he walks upon, I mean. I cannot imagine what has gotten into me. Locksley ain't a bad sort, y'know. Never be a gentleman, of course. Much too late, I think, to hope for that. Still, if he proves to be Dewhurst's grandson the *ton* will be forced to accept him, no? Hoax him behind his back no end, of course. Never take him seriously. Still the title would lend him consequence."

"Somehow, from recent descriptions of the man," grinned Borhill, "I cannot quite see him taking his seat in Lords, Clare, can you?"

Lilliheun smiled grudgingly. "As a matter of fact, cousin, I should actually *like* to see that. That would stir the old fogeys up into a stew. You think they are upset over Prinny and his vagaries—imagine them needing to deal with a duke who speaks like a chimney sweep!"

Borhill chuckled and placed a hand on Lilliheun's shoulder. "Don't bother your head about it, Clare. He will prove to be Dewhurst's grandson or not and that will be the end to it. It ain't a problem that can go on forever."

"But if he proves to be an impostor and Camilla has fallen in love with the man, what then? What then, Drew? He is hauled off to the Old Bailey for impersonating a member of the nobility and Camilla is left to grieve her life away."

"She will turn to you for solace and discover that *you*

are truly the man she loves and everyone will live happily ever after—except for Locksley, of course."

"Balderdash," Lilliheun grinned. "Locksley will never end in the Old Bailey. He is much too savvy. First sign of trouble on the horizon and he'll be gone. And Camilla has spoken the truth—she ain't in love with me, but she does not intend to marry anyone else either, which means I may continue to hope. And everything else is in my vivid imagination."

"That's it, old chum. An excellent way to look at it."

"Right," murmured Lilliheun. "Right."

Borhill saw his cousin to the door and closed it behind him with a sigh of relief. "You can come out now, Argosy," he called. The connecting door between Borhill's office and his clerk's squeaked open. "Hinges need oiling again. Have to get Mercer on it. Did you hear all that?"

"A bit, I'm afraid," smiled the conservatively dressed young man with a shrug. "Couldn't avoid it. Some of it got mighty loud, sir. Never heard Mr. Lilliheun reach that volume before."

"Yes, well, Clare ain't usually so vehement. Actually, I cannot remember him slipping into anything near a high dudgeon since we were both in short coats. Young ladies, I fear, may make the most even tempered gentlemen into ogres from time to time. So, what've you learned about Locksley?"

Camilla set to work at a small writing desk in the morning room on the invitations for Aurora's come-out ball. Lady Wheymore had placed the list of guests into her hands the moment the girls had returned from the city and, imploring Camilla to begin addressing the cards, she had swept Rory back into the coach and off to Madame LeFaye's for a fitting. "I do not in the least expect you to do them all, Cammy, so do not think it. And we shall return as soon as may be. But Aurora must have the required gown if she is to be presented at court. You know how it is, my dear. You suffered through it yourself but two years back."

The thought of it made Camilla smile. The gown itself

would cost a fortune, and never be worn again. Her own still lingered at the very back of the armoire in the second best guest chamber. But for a space in time, she had looked like an angel in beaded white satin and Brabant lace, with wide hoops making a bell of her skirt and a luxurious headpiece of white ostrich plumes balanced elegantly upon her chestnut curls. "And what a diamond of the first water I thought myself in it, too," she whispered to herself. "I was never so pleased as when I first looked into the glass and discovered that I had somehow become a princess!" She thought that, just for moment, she would sneak off and look at the gown—no, she would not. She would address the invitations as her aunt had requested, even though the very thought of writing all those names and directions was wearying beyond belief. She gazed down the list of names. Her right eyebrow twitched just the slightest bit. She read them one by one, and the slight dimple at the corner of her mouth began to appear. "Oh, I am being sorely tempted," she complained to no one. "I wonder if I shall be able to resist?"

The more invitations she inscribed, the wider grew her mischievous smile. She paused and pondered, gave herself a little shake, and pondered again. "No, I shan't be able to resist," she giggled at last, and with a flourish set one of the engraved invitation cards before her and wrote in a fine Copperplate the names: Mr. John Locksley and Mr. Elgin Moss. I shall be in the suds now, she thought, staring down at the expensively engraved missive that invited its recipients to attend Aurora's come-out ball. "Uncle Ned will undoubtedly fly into the boughs when I confess. But he'll not embarrass the captain or Mr. Moss by doing so during the party. No, certainly he will not. He is always the most gracious of hosts under all circumstances. And—and—the captain will so enjoy being invited. I doubt he has ever in his whole life attended a Presentation Ball."

Fate was pacing madly about Eversley's drawing room and the farthest thing from his mind was a Presentation Ball. Every so often he stopped and pounded his fist upon

the back of a chair or a table top or into one of the elegantly
papered walls. Glasgow, his face ashen, stood helplessly by
without the least notion of how to calm the man.

He had sent one of the footmen off at a dash to fetch
Mr. Moss at the Broken Jib; he, himself, had taken the
crying lad with the lanky blond hair to Mrs. Daily who had
at least some idea of how to settle the boy down; and he
had sent another of the footmen to search for Lord Eversley; but he hadn't any idea what to say or do for the
thoroughly distraught gentleman presently engaged in the
total destruction of the drawing room.

He opened his mouth to propose a glass of brandy and
closed it promptly as at that very instant Fate seized upon
a china pug dog and flung it with incredible force against
the far wall. This was followed by every decorative piece
on the mantle, two of Lord Eversley's abandoned snuff
boxes and, in the end, the ormolu clock. "No, not the
clock!" shouted Glasgow in sincere grief. But his cry came
a second too late.

Fate's head turned in Glasgow's direction; the darkling
eyes flashed fire and fury; the long slender fingers of one
hand closed about a crystal brandy decanter standing innocently upon the cricket table before him; and it, too, sailed
into the wall, its contents splattering across the floral pattern of the paper and streaming slowly down to the wain-
scoting and beyond. Immediately as it hit, however, a
hoarse sob rose from Fate's throat and he turned away to
cross his arms upon the mantle and bury his head in them.

"What is it?" cried Camilla, rushing to Glasgow on the
arm of the captain's valet. "What has happened?"

"I went to fetch Miss Quinn when things began breaking," puffed Farmer. "He's a fondness for Miss Quinn,
you know. I thought her presence might calm him."

Camilla stared at the destruction in the drawing room
and inhaled deeply. Then her gaze found Fate crumpled
against the mantle and she crossed the room and put an
arm around his waist. "What is it, dearest?" she asked
softly, the sound of his sobs bringing a lump to her throat.
"Come sit with me and tell me what has happened. Perhaps
there is something I can do."

The captain let himself be led to the sopha where Camilla sat beside him smoothing the dark curls from his brow as he fought to conquer his sobs and brushed angrily at his tears with the back of his hand.

"Whatever is wrong?" Camilla asked when at last he seemed to bring himself under control. "I can see it is something dreadful."

" 'Tis Harley," responded Fate in a gruff whisper. " 'E's gone an' got hisself kilt."

"Oh, surely not!" Camilla looked for confirmation to Glasgow who had remained irresolutely in the doorway.

The butler nodded. " 'Tis what the lad said when he came pounding upon our door."

"What lad? Where is he?" Camilla asked, her fingers unconsciously playing with the curls that traveled down the back of the captain's neck.

"Oh, lord, Tick," mumbled Fate clenching his fists and digging them into his eyes. "I got ta take care o' Tick. He went plum out o' m'mind."

"Mrs. Daily is with the boy, sir," offered Glasgow with an imploring glance at Camilla. "And Farmer has gone off to fetch you some tea with brandy. 'Twill help you compose yourself before you speak with the lad."

"Yes, indeed," declared Camilla, reading the desperation in Glasgow's eyes. "You must sit for a moment or two and sip some of the tea and gather your wits about you, Mr. Locksley, or you will be of no good to Tick at all."

Fate's nod brought a sigh of relief from Glasgow, but the nod was cut short by the loud prizing of the front door knocker. The butler turned on his heel and hurried down to his post. He straightened himself as best he could and opened the door to find the usually imperturbable Lady Wheymore upon the doorstep, her face flushed, her pelisse partly unbuttoned, and the tip of her parasol pointed directly at his heart. "I have been informed that my niece has entered this establishment. You will take me to her at once, do you hear!"

"Y-yes, m'lady. She is in the drawing room at the top of the stairs, m'lady. If you will but follow me, m'lady." Glasgow climbed back up the staircase in some haste, the countess urging him on with the point of her parasol.

"Camilla! What on earth are you about!" exclaimed Lady Wheymore as she entered the room to find her niece with an arm about the captain, patting his knee and whispering to him in steadying tones. "How dare you enter a bachelor's establishment! And without a chaperone! And especially this—this—pretender's residence! Are you gone daft, girl?"

Camilla looked up to see Lady Wheymore advancing upon them with parasol raised as if to beat the captain and herself apart. Never had she seen her aunt display the least bit of temper and she was immediately filled with awe at the magnificent fire in the countess's eyes and the belligerent and terrifying trim to that lady's sails. For a long moment, Camilla truly thought the parasol would descend upon either her own head or the captain's, but then she felt Fate move beside her and lift his gaze to meet Lady Wheymore's. One look at that thoroughly distressed countenance took the wind completely out of Lady Wheymore.

"What?" she asked, a definite note of pity in her tone. "What has happened, young man? Camilla, tell me at once what has occurred." And with that she tossed her parasol to the carpet and sat down on the captain's other side, her arm going around his shoulders much as Camilla's had. And that was the moment the tea tray arrived in Mrs. Daily's own hands, Tick clinging tearfully to her skirts.

Fate opened his arms and the boy rushed into them and the two were instantly locked together, mumbled words racing from the captain's lips into one small, unwashed ear. Camilla rubbed the child's back comfortingly as Mrs. Daily herself poured the tea and Farmer added a great dollop of Eversley's brandy into Fate's cup.

"Well, you must drink this at once, Mr. Locksley," declared the countess when at last Camilla had explained, Tick had unclenched his hands from around Fate's neck and the captain had leaned back and settled the child upon his lap. "You have had a great shock and the tea will do you good. And then we shall see what must be done."

" 'Tain't nothin' ta be done,'' murmured Fate hoarsely, taking the teacup in one hand and clutching Tick tightly against his chest with the other.

"We shall see about that, sir. You must tell us, child, exactly what happened,'' she said with motherly encouragement, patting Tick's knee.

Tick buried his face in the captain's neckcloth and shook his head. "M'brother gotted tramped in Grillon's stableyard—b-by a t-team a big ol' ches'nuts. Danny come an' tole us. 'E said as 'ow Harley ain't never comin' 'ome no more. Not never.''

The shy, shocked, little voice tore at Camilla's heart. Lady Wheymore's lips pursed in thought. "You, my man,'' she said, indicating Glasgow with a jab of a finger, "will cross the square and say that Lady Wheymore requires her carriage brought around to this establishment as soon as may be. And when it arrives inform us at once. Drink your tea, Mr. Locksley. You must drink that cup and then another. You are Lord Eversley's housekeeper?'' she asked then, her eyes focussing on Mrs. Daily.

"Yes, m'lady.''

"Then you will be kind enough to take charge of this urchin. He is in need of a bath and a bed directly afterward. Lord Eversley will not deny such a small lad a bit of hospitality in such a situation as this.''

"No, ma'am, m'lady. Certainly not.''

"Certainly not,'' agreed Lady Wheymore. "You shall have him in your charge the moment my coach arrives. And then, Mr. Locksley, you and I and Camilla shall drive to Grillon's and see what may be done.''

The trip to Grillon's was a silent one. Fate slumped despairingly into one corner of the coach and Lady Wheymore and Camilla shared the seat across from him, Camilla worriedly clutching her aunt's hand. John Coachman was sent to enquire at Grillon's and came out with a thin smile upon his rugged face. "The boy ain't here, m'lady, but he ain't dead. Leastways, he waren't. Took him off to St. Mary's Hospital, they did.''

"We go to St. Mary's then,'' nodded Lady Wheymore and the coachman climbed back to his perch.

The hospital, a sooty grey building in Panton Street, tall and narrow, with a look of despair ground deeply into its stones, sent shivers down Camilla's spine. The shivers increased as she climbed the crumbling stone steps on her aunt's arm and entered through the heavy door Fate held wide for them. "Oh," she sighed, breathing in the dank, pungent air, "what a dreadful place."

" 'Tis where they send the likes o' us ta die," mumbled Fate, staring angrily about him at the darkly panelled walls.

"Oh, surely not," answered Camilla, taking one of his hands in her own. " 'Tis a place meant to save lives."

He stared down at her and shook his head. "Ye've never been," he replied gruffly. "Ye ain't the least idea. If they don't kill ye here, it ain't for lack o' tryin'. 'Tis near as bad as Bedlam in the wards."

"You were in the wards, Mr. Locksley?" Lady Wheymore successfully retrieved Camilla's hand from his as she came between them.

"Aye, oncet. Never again. I'd sooner die in the gutter. A quieter kind o' death that—wi'out people a screamin' an' wailin' all 'round ye an' prissy 'sicians pawing at ye all o' the time, worritin' ye closer an' closer ta the grave."

Lady Wheymore lifted her brows but did not contest his words and Camilla noted the martial light return to her aunt's eyes. The lady stalked toward a nurse with a wide, awkward, white starched cap and long grey skirts and immediately engaged her in conversation. That nurse, with a nod, led the three through a series of long, narrow corridors where only the dingiest light entered and tallow candles burned. Sighs and gasps, moans and shrieks and crying assaulted their ears from all directions.

Camilla kept hesitant step with her aunt in the nurse's shadow and Fate stalked angrily beside them, conspicuously holding himself in check. When at last they turned into one of the wards and discovered an ashen-faced Harley swathed in bandages on a meagre cot at the far end of a double line of cots, Fate was near to bursting. No chair anywhere available, he knelt on the hardwood floor beside the child and whispered in the boy's ear. Harley's eyes popped open.

The nurse gasped. "Why he has not once opened his eyes since they brought him in," she whispered to Lady Wheymore. "He has lain like the dead. The good doctors thought surely the wound to his head would be fatal."

One thin little hand wiggled out from beneath a dingy blanket and Fate clasped it immediately.

"If we had known the boy were—were—acquainted— with you, Lady Wheymore, or with the gentleman here, we certainly would not have brought him to the paupers' ward. I assure you, from this moment he shall receive every attention. Sir, what on earth do you think you're doing? You cannot!"

Fate, his dark eyes blazing, had already wrapped the blanket tightly about Harley and was lifting the child into his arms. His gaze met the nurse's and the ice in it appeared to freeze her, with mouth open, to the spot. He set Harley down again upon the cot, pulled a number of gold coins from his pocket and tossed them to the floor at her feet.

"That'll console yer bloody butchers," he mumbled and, picking Harley up again, he led the way down the long aisle of writhing wretches and out into the maze of corridors. Without the least hesitation he took them straight to the front door and out to the coach where he arranged Harley gently upon one of the seats, resting the boy's head in his lap. John Coachman assisted Lady Wheymore and Camilla into the vehicle and climbed to the box, urging the horses back toward Grosvenor Square.

Elgin Moss met them at the door and hurried Fate and the boy up to one of the guest rooms where he and Farmer set about getting the child to bed. "Ye must do something about the childer, Jason," Moss whispered. "Tick says as how their da be missin' still. Bring 'em here, lad. There's beds enough for 'em."

"Eversley'll turn over purple."

"I'll tend to Eversley. Ye're worth more to 'im than ye know, lad. He'll not set up a fuss. We got to git help for Harley, though. He don't look good at all."

"Lady Wheymore has sent her coachman for Dr. Sinclair," Glasgow announced from the doorway. "He'll see to the young man all right and tight. I'm pleased the boy is not dead, sir," he added with a smile at Fate. "We shall do our best for him, Mr. Locksley."

"Cap'n, Cap'n," called a pain-filled little voice from the bed. Fate was beside him in an instant, taking a flailing hand in his own.

"I be ri' here, Harley. Ri' here."

The wide blue eyes blinked open. "Murder," Harley whispered hoarsely. "They be plannin' ta murder the li'l man. I heerd 'im. Ye gotta be careful. They plannin' ta murder the li'l man an' blame you!"

Camilla and Lady Wheymore, who had just entered the room, gasped. Farmer and Moss and Glasgow stopped in their tracks and stared toward the bed. Fate tucked the thin hand back beneath the counterpane and whispered in the boy's ear, and Harley closed his eyes and breathed a bit more easily.

In the end, it was the Earl of Wheymore and Lord Neiland who traveled in a hackney to the denizens of St. Giles and Basket Lane and came home again, both a shade paler, with two little girls clinging to Neiland and a babe snuffling congestedly in the earl's arms. "What the devil she intends to do with them is beyond me," muttered Wheymore and then grinned encouragingly in spite of himself at Jolly and Grig. "Your mother, David, has not gone off on one of her crusades since you were no bigger than this monkey, but I see all the signs of one coming on. And if I'm correct, Neiland, you and I are in for a devil of a time."

"A crusade? Mama?"

"Indeed. Before we were married she was always off on one crusade or another. And the first year of our marriage we had a battle royal over the fate of a chimney sweep's climbing boy that grew into a regular campaign to save all the climbing boys in all of London. You would not believe the power she wields when she decides to involve herself. Your mother can be a hell cat for a cause, m'boy. A devil's daughter. And I believe she has somehow come upon a cause."

"These children?"

"I expect. Though what's brought them to her attention I cannot imagine."

Jolly stared at the vanilla bean she had been clutching in one tiny fist and Grig did the same, then they peered around Neiland at each other.

"What is it, children?" asked Wheymore. "Are you frightened to be taken off in a coach by two strange gentlemen? Camilla said you might well be but that the vanilla beans would reassure you. They came from Mr. Locksley."

"Uh-uh," said Jolly with a shake of her lanky curls. "They comed from the cap'n."

"Only eber from the cap'n," agreed Grig. "They's magical beans."

Wheymore gazed perplexedly at his son. "Locksley was a soldier?"

"Never said as much to me, sir. I expect he might well have been."

"Uh-huh," nodded Grig with enthusiasm. "A solcher! Wif a big 'orse an' a sword an' a pisto'!"

The earl's eyebrow lifted.

"Well, he probably was not a captain, sir," Neiland suggested. "Probably enlisted in one of the foot regiments an' now they just refer to him as captain."

"A foot soldier? With a big horse and a sword and a pistol?"

"You know how people are, sir, with children. How they tend to—embellish yarns."

"Ah, you think it's a Canterbury Tale?"

Neiland nodded. "Must be. Locksley's certainly never been an officer. Can't read or write for one thing. Comes from nowhere. No one with half a brain would sell him a commission. Enlisted or conscripted would be my guess."

"What's 'scripted?" Jolly asked, leaning her head against Neiland's arm.

"What's 'listed?" asked Grig, doing the same, her tired little eyes beginning to close. "Does it gots anythin' ta do wif the Bodkins in the bottom of the garden?"

Neiland, feeling cozily protective with a child on each side, was shocked to see his father's face grow a shade paler in the fading light. "What is it, sir?" he asked quietly. "Are you ill? Shall I call the hack to a halt for a moment?"

"No, no, 'tis nothing," mumbled the earl. "Nothing. A coincidence. The sooner we deliver these urchins into your mother's keeping, the better off we shall be. There are countless tales about fairies and gardens, no doubt. You heard them as well when you were a child, did you not?"

"Indeed. Nanny told them to us over and over again. I cannot remember most of them, but Aurora, I think, can. And Cammy, I think, makes up more and more of them even today. She's writing a novel, you know, sir."

"So I've heard," smiled the earl making an effort to adjust the infant in his arms to a more comfortable position. "I trust it ain't boring, Neiland? I shall be allowed to read the thing before she sends it off to some publisher, don't you think? It's wicked enough for a young lady of her standing to be scribbling, without it being boring scribbling on top of it. If it is boring, I shall forbid her to send it anywhere."

Neiland laughed. His father had long been enthralled with Camilla's ability to tell a story and it was he who had encouraged her throughout her childhood to read voraciously and expansively and eclectically and to adapt all she had learned to her own tales. This was hardly the gentleman to protest his cousin's bid to become an author-ess. He'd be pleased as punch to see Camilla's name upon a volume or two—provided, of course, the volumes were well-written and entertaining.

The lamps had been lit by the time the gentlemen descended with their brood before Wheymore House and Lilliheun was just lifting Aurora down from his phaeton. "Oh, my goodness, Papa, are they ours?" teased Aurora, standing on tiptoe to peer at Digger.

"They were not to begin with," sighed the earl, "though what your mother's intentions are—" he shrugged his shoulders and grinned bemusedly.

"Lilliheun, here take one," Neiland urged, a sleeping little girl in each arm. "It's a load, let me tell you."

Lilliheun, quivering on the edge of laughter to see those gentlemen so loaded with children, lifted Jolly into his own arms and followed the earl, Neiland, and Aurora into the house.

"Your mother," sighed the earl, "could never resist taking in a stray or two. It is one of the reasons she married me—I was a perfect clunch of a stray if ever there was one."

Chapter 9

Harley fluttered in and out of reality keeping Dr. Sinclair, Moss, and Farmer on edge; Tick followed Glasgow everywhere, admiration for the butler evident in every whispered "yes, sir" or "no, sir"; Jolly and Grig helped with everything at Wheymore House, from building fires to washing pots, to putting cucumber cream beneath Aurora's eyes and brushing Camilla's long chestnut curls. Little Digger crawled about the Wheymore's long abandoned nursery as if to the manor born, growing plump and less querulous from a plentiful supply of good food and constant care and numerous hugs and kisses bestowed upon him by all the women of the house—ladies and servants alike.

A clear path was emerging next to the daffodil bed on the verge that separated the Eversley side of the square from the Wheymore side and children's voices more often than not brought neighbors to their front windows at least once a day to chuckle reminiscently at a rousing game of tag or kitty wants a corner.

Lord Eversley spent most of his days engaged in subtle consultations with undoubtedly nefarious characters to further his plans for the psuedo-Locksley and all of his nights with Mary Ellen Hall in the little house in St. Mary's Triangle and took not the least notice of Harley's and Tick's presence in Grosvenor Square or anything else that went on at that residence. His attention was fixated upon proving that Moss's friend was irrefutably Lord Locksley's legitimate son—as much so as was Andrew Borhill's attention fixated upon proving the opposite.

Lady Wheymore, her head high, her chin quivering in

righteous indignation, gathered groups of highborn ladies into her morning room day after day, declaiming the horrendous state of St. Mary's Hospital and deriding the offhanded carelessness of an upper class that shirked its Christian duties and responsibilities toward those less fortunate than themselves. She caused a number of those ladies to blush, others to frown perplexedly and still others to grumble excuses and stomp angrily out to waiting carriages.

"You shall be a pariah even before you're presented," giggled Camilla as she watched Mrs. Leigh-Carr sweep angrily down the front staircase. "I mean it, Rory. If we do not stop your mama from alienating all of the most important people, no one will wish to invite you anywhere."

"Oh, pooh," Aurora replied looking up from a picture she was helping Grig to draw. "Mama is quite right to be concerned over the hospital and the lot of the poor. Don't you remember, Cammy, how terrible it was in that horrible place where we followed the captain? And everyone just ignores it. They all say the poor live in such dirt and gloom because they choose to do so—and you know as well as I that no one would *choose* to live like that. They have no choice at all that I can see so long as machines are constantly replacing them in their jobs and the Lords continue increasing the prices of foodstuffs and taxing everything from hats to horses. Only the bravest of the aristocracy will even speak up for them in Lord's. The Earl of Wright is extremely brave and persistent, I think, whenever he speaks on the matter, but he cannot succeed at bringing about the needed changes all on his own."

"No—and neither can Aunt Mary. Perhaps the two ought to join forces."

"I rather think that that may happen. Papa has invited Lord Wright to dinner and he and Lady Wright have accepted."

"And I can fairly guess what all the after dinner conversation will involve," grinned Camilla.

"What?" asked Grig. "What's it gonna inbolbe?"

"You, my little piglet!" exclaimed Aurora, pouncing

upon the child and hugging her tightly. "You and your brothers and Jolly."

"An' the cap'n?"

"Oh, most certainly the captain, though we must not call him that, remember. You must call him Uncle John the way we taught you—especially if anyone is about."

Uncle John was at that moment sitting upon the edge of Harley's bed with a spoonful of elixir balanced carefully in his hand facing stubbornly closed lips and groggy blue eyes.

"He won't take it, Mr. Locksley," Farmer murmured. "We have tried everything but holding him down and forcing it down his throat, which we can't do, his ribs being broken and his leg in a splint and all."

"Harley, open yer gubble an' swallow this stuff," growled Fate, "or I'll have nothin' more ta do with ye."

Farmer gazed admiringly as the thin lips parted and the elixir was tipped in.

"It's ashamed of ye, I am, givin' Mr. Farmer 'ere all this trouble when 'e ain't done nothin' but worrit hisself over ye fer almos' a se'enight. Barely slept, he 'as. Always at yer beck an' call. A reg'lar saint, 'e's been."

"R-really?" asked Harley in a faint voice not at all like his own.

"Aye—an' you thinkin' he was like ta poison ye! Of all the nonsense I ever heerd." Fate set the spoon aside on the night table and settled himself more comfortably on the edge of the feather ticking. "Ye'd best go get ye a bite ta eat, Farmer. I'll stay with the boy awhile."

Farmer nodded and left the bedchamber, closing the door softly behind him. "Now," Fate murmured, as he heard the valet's footsteps moving toward the staircase, "ye must tell me how yer feelin', ol' chum. Ye ain't been makin' a deal of sense, ye know, since first I found ye."

"I—I ain't?"

"No, m'dear," Fate smiled, brushing a lock of hair from the boy's brow. "Ye hurt yer noggin', Poppet, an' ye been mutterin' 'bout the oddest thin's—dragons an' castles an'—"

Harley's sleepy blue eyes popped wide open. "Murder,"

he gasped. "Goreblimey, Cap'n, they was murderers. Reg'lar cutthroats."

"Sssh, Harley. There ain't nothin' ta get all excited about. Ye tell me real quiet-like what ye heerd."

"They said as 'ow they was gonna betray ye, Cap'n. Firs' kill the li'l man, an' then blame ye fer it, an' then put the Runners onta ye."

"An' did they call me by name, lad? Do ye remember? Was it Captain Jason Fate they said flat out?"

"They said as how they were goin' ta kill the li'l man an' lay it at Fate's door. That be what they said, Cap'n. An' then they begun laughin' 'bout how they was gonna put the Runners onta ye an' collect the blood money as well. I were that scared," sighed Harley, his worried eyes growing heavy from the medicine. "I were that scared. I were muckin' out one o' the stalls, I were, when I heerd 'em talkin'. An' when I heerd what they was talkin' 'bout, I tried ta hide, but I dropped me pitchfork an' it clattered 'gainst the box."

"So ye ran away?"

"Fast as I could, only—only—they come af'er me, an' one o' the blokes, 'e shouts 'git 'im! git 'im!' an' I goes ta dodge behind one o' the coaches an all of a sudden there's horses a-stompin' all over me."

"Aye, well, ye be safe as houses, now, Harley. Ain't no cutthroats comin' ta get ye here. Sleep now. First ye get well, then we'll worrit the thin' out."

"Y-yes, sir. B-but what li'l man was they talkin' 'bout? Not Da? Why'd anybody wanta kill D-Da? He ain't never 'urt no un."

Fate stood, removed two of the pillows from behind the child, and lowered him carefully down. "Nobody'd want ta kill yer da, Harley. 'Tis some un else they were speakin' of. Sleep now, Poppet, so's ye get well quick. Ye be safe, Harley. Ain't no bully ruffians gonna come near ye again, I promise."

Lord Wright, with his unruly black curls and deep blue eyes flecked oddly with silver, fairly took Camilla's breath away. Tall, lean, and muscular, with an intriguing limp that required him to use a silver-headed cane and added to the aura of danger that flowed about him, Wright proved to be charming and remarkably amusing both at dinner and afterward.

Lady Wright was charming as well, and obviously shared his high principles and intense hunger to alleviate the sufferings of the Great Unwashed, but she was not in the least beautiful or even sophisticated and Camilla could not help but wonder what had drawn the gentleman to her at first. There is a story there, I'll wager, she thought, as she dismissed her abigail and settled herself at the escritoire wrapped in a most becoming jonquil robe, her gleaming chestnut hair brushed and foaming in curling tendrils down her back. She took pens and papers and set them upon the desktop before her. An ink pot joined them.

The adventures of Bad Jack Pharo and Esperanza had been calling to her all through dinner and late into the evening. By the time Lord and Lady Wright had departed, the urge to be writing had sent her flying up the stairs to her own chambers. It would be a mild, gentle lady of great principles and determined character, just like Lady Wright, who would come to the aid of the lovers and unearth the secret of Bad Jack's heritage and bring him and the lovely Esperanza once and for all together, never to be parted. And it would be a gentleman, much like Lord Wright who, beleaguered by a passion he could not reveal for the lady, would protect her in her efforts, join Bad Jack in his final and greatest attempt to vanquish the evil Florian, and in victory, find the courage to approach the lady just as Bad Jack approached Esperanza!

Camilla's pen fairly flew over the paper. So involved was she in the creation of these two new characters, so excited over their influence upon her plot, that she did not at first even hear the tapping. When at last the sound entered her consciousness, she thought it must be the children on the floor above playing at some game or other. But it is well after midnight, she thought at last. Certainly the babes are not up and about. She set her pen aside then, and listened more closely. The tapping came again from somewhere very close. "Oh!" she gasped when she realized. "Oh, he would not dare! Not again!"

Scraping her chair back from the escritoire, Camilla followed the sound. With an invigorating mixture of expectancy, annoyance, and exasperation, she seized one of the floral printed linen draperies and tugged it aside. From the opposite side of the window Jason Fate stared at her. Camilla fumbled hurriedly at the window latch, swung the lattice outward and nearly knocked the captain from his perch in the vines. She lunged for him, afraid he would indeed tumble, and tugged him into the chamber. He came in laughing and stumbling over the sill.

"Sssshhh!" Camilla hissed. "Are you mad? The entire house will hear you! You will be shot for a burglar!"

"Who, me?" he whispered back, straightening the set of a very well-made double-breasted jacket. "An' here I thought I looked a reg'lar dandy."

Camilla stood back and studied him. He did, indeed, look quite magnificent. He sported a gold satin waistcoat embroidered with silver threads and a cravat tied in a perfect waterfall. His buff-coloured breeches were tucked neatly into a pair of gleaming Hessians. The sight of an ivy leaf clinging to one dark curl and a streak of grime across his chin might have detracted from the image of the dandy, but only added to the sudden rush of endearment that flooded Camilla's heart. "Oh, you are such a— a—rapscallion!" she whispered, unable to keep herself from touching one closely shaven cheek with her fingertips. "Come and sit down and tell me why you've come." She led him to the small sopha beside the empty hearth and herself sat upon the edge of a chair across from him. "It is not—Harley is not worse?"

"No, much better. It ain't Harley brought me. 'Tis this." Fate's hand reached into the inside pocket of his jacket and produced an engraved card. He leaned forward and placed it into her hands. "Mossie says 'tis a invite-tation ta a ball, but I think he's tellin' me a clanker."

A secret smile played across Camilla's lips as she looked down at the invitation she had addressed herself.

"Is it?" he asked impatiently.

"Yes, indeed, sir. And addressed personally to yourself and Mr. Moss."

"Can't be. Ain't none of the Quality wants a thin' ta do with me. Don't blame 'em, mind. But they crosses the street, ye know, whenever I walk down it."

"Oh, no! How dare they!"

"Aye, an' I know they be a hoaxin' of me behind m'back. Don't be lookin' so sour-faced, Dendron. I reckon I don't mind any o' that. But why would some one a 'em send me an' Mossie a invite-tation ta anythin'?"

"Did Mr. Moss not read the invitation to you?"

"O' course."

"An' did you not understand where the ball is to be held and for whom?"

"Fer some Lady Aurora Amelia Bedford, Mossie said. At 'er home. Only we don't neither of us know no Lady Aurora Whatever, much less where the mort lives."

Camilla chuckled quietly at the perplexed look upon that austere countenance. "But you do know Lady Aurora, Captain. She is my cousin."

"What? The Banshee?"

"Yes, though you must not call her that at the ball."

"Y'mean ta say that we be invited 'ere? In full view of the public so ta speak?"

"Yes, indeed. In full view of all the Quality. And they will not turn their backs upon you in my uncle's home, I assure you. It would the outside of enough!"

"No, o' course they won't do that. Get up an' leave yer uncle's house direckly me an' Mossie turn up is what they'll do. What's wrong with The Banshee? Are 'er attics ta let?"

"Certainly not! What does that mean, exactly—attics to let?"

"It means does she be a madwoman—has 'er brains slipped out 'er ear an' lef' room fer someun else."

"Well, of all the—!"

Fate's eyes sparkled engagingly at her and Camilla, who was about to protest vehemently the observation that some-one must be out of her mind to invite the captain to a ball, found herself instead grinning mischievously at him, then lowering her eyes and confessing in a murmur that it had been she invited him and Mr. Moss. "For I did not think you would come alone," she added at the end. "But with Mr. Moss to lend you support—"

Camilla expected to hear a number of responses—a violent protest that he could not possibly attend or a muttered oath and a shake of his curly head, or even a sigh and a nod would not have surprised her. But to have him gaze deeply into her eyes, lean forward and with hesitant fingers touch a strand of her hair, surprised her no end. So did the way he stood and pulled her gently up into his arms and held her tenderly and quietly against him for a full minute, never saying a word, never making another move until at last he lowered his lips to hers and kissed her softly like the touch of flutterby wings. Then he put his cheek against her own and whispered in her ear. "I didn't never want ta be a gen'leman till now, Dendron. Never till now."

He left her chamber the way he'd entered it and she watched him all the way across the square. Surely he was the most endearing, confusing, engaging, confounding man she had ever met. Letting the drapery fall back over the latched lattice, she wandered back to the escritoire and put pens, papers, and ink away. It was much too late now to continue with Bad Jack's adventures, and besides, her mind was in a whirl. She could not seem to settle upon one thought or another, but leaped from idea to idea with incredible rapidity—the only constants were the feel of his breath on her ear and the enticing aroma of vanilla.

The very next afternoon Tick scurried across the square and in through the kitchen door of Wheymore House, his blue eyes shining with glee. Less than five minutes later he scurried out again with Jolly and Grig close on his heels, the three of them bound for the rear entrance of the Eversley mansion. "Ssshhh," he warned as together they climbed the servant's stairs to the first floor and sneaked down the long hallway to the music room. "Ye mustn't giggle er they'll 'ear ye." Hands over mouths to muffle the tiny gurgles they could not control, the three youngsters

peeked in through the doorway. Jolly's eyes grew large and
Grig's dimples deepened. Tick sat flat on the floor and
jiggled with merriment. After a few moments, seeing themselves to be totally unnoticed, they scampered on hands
and knees into the room and took cover beneath the piano,
hidden safely from view by a loosely woven piano shawl of
buff and mauve that hung most of the way to the floor.

Elgin Moss, the tails of his peacock blue morning coat
flapping energetically behind him, was singing "la-la la-
de-la-la" while hopping from one foot to another and then
spinning about with amazing gusto for a man of his age,
while Fate stood with one hand rubbing at the back of his
neck watching Moss's antics in something very near horror.

" 'Tis devilish easy, Jason. Come, try again. La-la la-de-
la-la tum-tiddy-tiddy tum-te-tum."

Fate, his face growing slowly red, shrugged and stepped
up beside Moss, then attempted to match his feet to his
mentor's.

The children beneath the piano muffled bursts of merriment and swatted at each other.

"No, Ja-John, yer left foot—lead off with yer left foot,
m'dear. Aye, that's it. An' now ye follows with yer right
like this. Ah, what we need is music, lad, actual music.
La-la-la-de-la-da—Glasgow will git us some, soon. Sent a
footman off for ta find us a caper merchant, he did. Tum-
tiddy-tiddy-tum-an' turn—ye'll see, a bit o' proper instruc-
tion an' ye'll be dancin' up a storm, ye will. Step-one-two-
three, turn-one-two-three, bow-one-two-three, an'—"

"Tell ye the truth, Mossie, I feel more like I'm stompin'
out a fire. A reg'lar clunch I be at this hippity-hoppin'
about. Don't make no bit o' sense."

"T'ain't meant to be sensical, lad. 'Tis meant to be
entertainin'. Turn-turn-la-de-de-da. Ye mayn't learn ever'one
o' the dances, but ye'll learn at least two of 'em, I promises.
That's how often ye may stand up with Miss Quinn.
Twicet."

"There's a rule?"

"Aye, lad, the Quality's got rules for ever'thin'."

Elgin Moss enthusiastically spun to his right and Fate to
his left. "Oof!" Moss cried as they came crashing together.

He grasped at Fate's lapels to keep from falling and in the process sent Fate off-balance flat onto the seat of his inexpressibles in the middle of the music room floor. The three little people under the piano could not contain themselves longer and whooped with laughter. Fate, catching sight of their gleeful little faces, roared into laughter himself.

"Spies, Mossie!" he exclaimed, springing toward the trio and tugging them out on top of himself in a giggling handful.

"We seed ye," gurgled Grig, disentangling herself from the heap of children and captain on the floor and gaining her feet to jump merrily about the room. "Dancin'! Dancin'! We seed Uncle John dancin!"

"That weren't no dancin'," squealed Tick as Fate's fingers found his ribs and tickled maddeningly, "that were hippity-hoppin' li—li—bunnies!"

"Bunnies!" cried Jolly, laughing so hard her eyes were filled with tears. "Uncle Bunny an' Mossie Bunny! Ooh you are bof so vewy funny!"

Glasgow led Mr. Poole into the midst of the chaos just as Fate rose from the floor with two giggling children clinging to him and Moss was swinging Grig around in a large circle. "Mr. Vincent Poole," Glasgow announced over the uproar, the corners of his mouth twitching upward against his will. "Your dancing master, Mr. Locksley," he added with a twinkle in his eyes.

Fate shook the children from him like a dog shakes off water droplets and bowed somewhat competently in Mr. Poole's direction. The Captain attempted to paste a serious scowl upon his face but he could not seem to cease chuckling.

"It were famous, Miss Cammy," Jolly announced some time later, waving her hands excitedly in the air. "We was hippin' an' hoppin' an' a lady what comed wif Mr. Poole was playin' the pianer, an' ever'body were laughin'. An' Uncle John was the vewy funniest of all. Mr. Poole said as 'ow he never did see anybody but Uncle John what 'ad so many feets all goin' in differen' directions at the same time! An' we maked so much noise tha' Harley wanted ta come down an' see what we was doin' an' Mr. Glasgow, 'e let 'im! He sended two footmans up ta carry Harley ri' down ta watch our lessons!''

"Do you wanna see us dance? Do you wanna?" asked Grig hopping up and down on one foot across the Persian carpet. "We kin teach you an' Lady Aurora bof. Eben Tick kin dance now. It is so vewy easy!"

" 'Cept fer Uncle John," giggled Jolly. "It ain't easy fer Uncle John. But he twied and twied and finally Mr. Poole said as 'ow 'e thoughted Uncle John might learn 'is left foot from 'is right an' become a co'peten' dancer wif another lesson er two."

"And is he going to have another lesson or two?" asked Aurora from the window seat with an amused glance at Camilla.

"Oh, yes!" exclaimed Grig. "Two at the vewy leastest. He is vewy 'termined ta do it wight, so 'e kin dance wif Miss Cammy at yer ball an' not disgwace 'er."

"At my ball?" Aurora's fine, narrow eyebrows lifted questioningly.

"Oh, yes," nodded Jolly. "Uncle John 'as got yer invitetation. We seed it. It is vewy pwetty."

Camilla had the good grace to blush as she sent the little girls off to the kitchen to request tea.

"Cammy, you never did!" exclaimed Aurora. "How could you?"

"You do not mind, truly, do you, Rory? I was sitting there addressing them, you know, and—I could not resist. I invited him and Mr. Moss to lend him support."

Aurora gazed at Camilla with a most becoming twinkle in her eyes. "It will cause a tremendous stir, you know. There are a good many people think him a fraud and an upstart for trying to disinherit Lilliheun. We shall both need to pay him a great deal of attention. And Neiland and Lilliheun had best be appealed to. If they are seen to take him up, perhaps no one will cut him."

"No one would dare to cut him in the midst of your

come-out ball. No one is so much of a rudesby. And besides—"

"Besides what, Cammy?"

"He will not care if he is cut. He has not the least desire to be accepted by Society."

"No, but I perceive that he has a great desire to be accepted by you," chuckled Aurora. "And for that reason alone he is welcome to attend my ball. And you are not to worry. I shall warn mama and papa in sufficient time—perhaps when I glimpse his unruly curls ascending the grand staircase."

Chapter 10

Aurora, in a splendid headpiece sporting a magnificent plume of ostrich feathers upon a ringlet of alternating pearls and diamonds and in a gown with three layers of skirts—one of crisp white satin, the second of Brussels lace in a floral pattern, and the third of tulle covered with seed pearls—had survived her presentation admirably. The great hoop of waxed calico over whalebone which made the yards of material in her skirts float like a graceful cloud a mere inch above the ground had not made her fall flat on her face as she had feared. Nor had the plume, incredibly beautiful but so frightfully heavy, thrown her completely off-balance. Nor had she disgraced herself in performing the extremely deep curtsy demanded of all the young ladies formally presented to Queen Charlotte and the Prince.

She and Lady Wheymore had arrived at St. James's Palace among a mad crush of aristocratic daughters and mamas in a parade of carriages all attended by liveried footmen with enormous bouquets in their lapels. The King's Cavalry in their brilliant scarlet coats and mounted upon their magnificent black horses had ridden escort the entire way and Aurora had felt incredibly like a princess.

She had felt even more princess-like when they had gathered in the tiny antechamber with the others to await the actual Presentation. The flash of jewels, the nervous chatter, the fainting of one or another of the maidens, had all added to Aurora's sense of anticipation and had brought a pretty flush to her cheeks and a brightness to her eyes.

As her turn had approached to make her curtsy before Queen Charlotte and the Prince, she'd begun to feel flustered beyond bearing. But she had pulled the thing off with admirable aplomb, had discovered herself pleased beyond belief to be acknowledged by the elderly lady and the plump gentleman, and when her father had swept her away into the crowded room of spectators, she had been exceeding proud of herself. When, later, the Prince had sought her out for a few private words of admiration and welcome, she had been so completely impressed with his condescension that her father had laughed outright.

But the entire experience of her Presentation paled next to the enormity of her come-out ball which had set Wheymore House at sixes and sevens for most of two weeks.

They sat down thirty to dinner in the formal dining room, nibbled their way through ten courses and innumerable removes including a fine Mulligatawny, *Boeuf tremblant,* a *matelot* of eels, larded guinea hens, *peu de amour,* fresh asparagus in a white cream sauce, a wonderfully trembling *blancmange* and a veritable garden of sweetmeats. Wines that had lain untouched in the Wheymore cellars for thirty years and more colored the crystal a bright red, a brilliant gold, a soft, shimmering rose. The earl toasted his daughter, his wife, his niece—and the company, delighted, raised their glasses high.

The ballroom, which had been added late in the last century and occupied the entire third floor of the establishment, gleamed in the light of three enormous chandeliers and a plethora of golden candelabras. Hung in soft, flowing swatches of gold and cream silk that billowed in the breeze from the opened French doors leading to the balcony, and decorated with thousands of wild flowers in all the colors of the rainbow, this magnificent chamber beckoned all to celebrate the sweetness and innocence of youth.

A string quintet played softly upon a small dais at the far end of the floor, all of its members dressed formally in sedate black coats and foaming white linen. Along the edge of the dance floor elaborately and delicately carved white chairs and here and there a small settee upholstered in white and gold brocade provided place for conversation and the resting of tired feet. Several of the chambers on the floor below had been emptied of their furnishings and refurnished with tables and chairs and sideboards to accommodate with wines and ratafias and lemonades, with salmon patties and liver pate's and thin slices of baked hams and roasted beefs, the palates of guests sweltering from the crush and exercise of the dance and in need of fine refreshment.

At the front entrance of Wheymore House flambeaux burned brightly against the night and a red carpet led from the cobblestones, up the front steps, into the great hall, to the very edge of the grand staircase. Footmen in livery of green and gold waited to lower carriage steps and escort ladies and gentlemen in through the open doors. Greatcoats and pelisses and capes and mantles, gloves and whips and canes and hats, all were carried by the Wheymore footmen to safe depositories on the first floor where also stood ready several antechambers and withdrawing rooms in which ladies would find servants ready to mend torn hems, to reinstate dishevelled hair, and to provide any and all assistance deemed necessary for their well-being and their fine appearance. Several young constables had been hired to keep the onlookers at bay and defend against radicals (none of whom had the audacity to appear).

The Mellon's stables had been given substantial monies to see that all carriages and teams were well looked after during the hours of the festivities. Likewise, Henry Murdoch of the Black Cock had been advanced considerable sums to see to the entertainment of the guests' coachmen and footmen and even an outrider or two.

At the spot where the grand staircase curved inward, just at the approach to the beginning of the ascent to the third floor, Aurora stood in the receiving line, flanked by mother and father, Neiland and Camilla. Name after name, title after title, Somers announced in sonorous tones and guest after guest mounted the stairs into the alcove, bowed over the ladies' hands or curtsied to the gentlemen, and were received with grace and good cheer and urged to continue on to the ballroom where music and friends awaited them. Aurora had never been introduced to such a number of persons in her entire life and the enormity of the entertainment with herself as guest of honor brought a tinge of paleness to her pretty cheeks and a slight glaze to her lovely blue eyes. It seemed forever that she stood, greeting one after another of the *ton*—persons she had known since childhood and persons she knew not at all.

The Prince Regent in a magnificent coat of scarlet with huge brass buttons and black braiding, chucked her beneath the chin and called her a pretty puss, declaring that he would be the first to lead her on to the dance floor. Mr. Brummell, following sedately in the Regent's wake, bowed conservatively over her hand and murmured that he was her servant, then grinned lazily, his fine grey eyes alight with merriment. "Do not look quite so terrified, m'dear," he drawled so that only she might hear. "You will undoubtedly take the *ton* by storm and all male hearts will tremble at your feet. Your father said so, you know, and so it must be."

The earl, overhearing, chuckled and the Beau winked.

"Never listen to that rapscallion, Aurora. I merely proclaimed to all of the Carlton House Set that you were the finest young lady ever to set foot upon the face of the earth."

"Oh, Papa, you did not!"

"Yes, actually, I think I did—but then, you are, m'dear. You must be—you're a Bedford woman after all."

Lady Jersey appeared, and Lady Castlereagh, and the Duke and Duchess of Richmond, and Sir Lionel Hurst, and an endless procession of names and faces that Aurora was certain she could never remember. Even Mr. Poodle Byng bent over her hand and smiled his most supportive smile. But it was not until the line of guests was nearly at an end and one might see an empty space or two at the bottom of the staircase, that a particular assortment of dark, unruly curls caught Aurora's eye, and she gave a little gasp.

"What is it, m'dear," the earl asked solicitously. "Something wrong?"

"Oh, no, Papa. It is nothing. It is only that—that—someone approaches whom you might think unwelcome and—"

"What? What?" The earl's head turned to glance down the stairs.

"Please, Papa," Aurora whispered standing on tiptoe to reach his ear alone. "Camilla has invited Mr. Locksley and his friend Mr. Moss, and I do so wish for you and mama to welcome them. Camilla is excessively fond of Mr. Locksley."

The Earl of Wheymore's eyes darkened, his smile diminished considerably, but he could not quite bring himself to make a scene on this night of all nights in his daughter's life. "Camilla is fond of him? Of that—that—ruffian?" he whispered back. "Surely you mistake."

"No, truly, Papa. She will not admit as much, but she has formed a *tendre* for him. Even Mr. Lilliheun sees it. Please say that Mr. Locksley is welcome here. Please, Papa."

"Well, I expect I'll not send him packing. But I will certainly not condone a relationship between your cousin and the likes of him and you must tell her so. This one night Camilla may have, but afterwards, she must remember that the man is a fraud and an imposter, even though I expect he means no harm in't."

Neiland, apprised beforehand of the likelihood of Locksley's presence was even then whispering urgently in his mama's ear and that lady, her eyes wide, was nodding in amazement and plying her fan as though she might faint dead away at any moment. But when their neighbor mounted the stairs, all of the Bedford faces were once more in check with welcoming smiles and murmuring lips.

The captain, with Moss on his left hand and Lilliheun on his right, thanked Lady and Lord Wheymore graciously for inviting him and lingered only an instant too long over Camilla's hand, his eyes sparkling up into hers with a well-contained excitement. Lilliheun gave him a subtle shove and took Camilla's hand in his own. "For you alone, m'dear, I do this thing," he murmured. "No one will cut him once they see he is on my arm. They will talk, of course, but I rather think he shall be safe for this evening."

The ball opened with a cotillion and the Prince Regent did, indeed, lead Aurora out. His pleasant smile and plump cheeks, his rotund figure and nimble feet, all combined to set the young lady at ease. Dancing with the Regent, far from a grim duty, proved to be a delight. He made her laugh; he complimented her gracefulness and beauty; he lamented that he was far too old to be her cicisbeo; and he led her from the floor amidst a round of applause that made the both of them blush.

Lilliheun, with a quirk of a smile at the corner of his lips, attempted to explain to Fate how he must place his name upon a young lady's dance card to reserve that dance for himself and was greatly taken aback by the frown that travelled over the man's countenance. "What did I say?" Lilliheun murmured to Moss as Fate moved away.

"Ye said he was to write his name."

"Yes, of course I said that. That's how it is done."

"But I never thought of it. I thought to fetch 'im a caper merchant and to be sure 'e was dressed proper and knew the right words to say when he made 'is bows, but I reckon I just didn't think of the dance cards. He can't write 'is name. He don't know how."

"Glory be!" exclaimed Lilliheun on a hoarse whisper. "Now what do we do?"

Fate, however, had not waited for the two to provide him a solution. He had wandered, instead, to the far end of the ballroom where Camilla stood amidst a group of eager young gentlemen and maneuvered his way to her side. "I expect yer dance card's filled, ain't it?" he asked quietly while her beaux looked on.

"Why, no, Mr. Locksley. It just so happens that it is not."

"Then will ye dance with me?"

"Certainly, I have the quadrille and the Roger de Coverly and the supper dance open. The supper dance is a waltz. But I thought you could not dance, Mr. Locksley?"

"I learned ta dance, Dendron, a bit. But I can't do that quadrille thin'."

"Then you shall have the Roger de Coverly and the waltz," smiled Camilla and offered him the little card which hung from her wrist by a silk riband. "Can you dance those two?"

"Uh-huh, but ye already know I can't read which ones they be. An—an' even if I could read 'em, I can't write m'name." His eyes challenged her awfully and Camilla read clearly the pride that waited to be trod upon. Several of the young men had overheard and eyed Locksley disdainfully, but Camilla simply took the little pencil in her own hand and set down his name beside the dances. "There," she said. "I shall count upon you, Mr. Locksley to make an appearance at the correct time."

"Yes, ma'am," Fate replied with a nod, and strolled off leaving Camilla's admirers staring after him.

Lilliheun and Neiland and Aurora and Camilla formed a set for one of the country dances and Lord Wheymore led his daughter out for a waltz and though a great number of curious eyes and lifted brows awaited some confrontation between Locksley and Lilliheun, or Locksley and Wheymore, or Locksley and anyone of the gentlemen of the *ton*, their expectations were not to be fulfilled. Lord Eversley, who came late, was exceeding delighted to find Locksley in attendance and drew him aside to congratulate him upon winning his way so very far into the Wheymore household.

"We are nearly there, Locksley. Just this morning Borhill's men discovered the paper that should bring an end to the controversy. A letter of credit from Lord Locksley ensuring his wife access to all his accounts. Took a deal of time to get the thing done, but I rather think it is a pretty piece of work and will stand up to even Borhill's scrutiny."

"An' yer duke? He'll accept it?"

"No reason he shouldn't. It is written on the Rossenberg Bank where Locksley was one of the main investors. Bank failed, of course, some twenty years ago, and the records have been duly misplaced. No way to disprove the thing."

Fate studied the elegantly garbed Eversley from beneath

slightly lowered lids. The man's bluff good looks and ruddy complexion made him appear a jolly good fellow. His bright eyes and forthright gaze gave no hint of the machinations of his mind. But Harley had insisted again and again that he had neither dreamed the conversation overheard in the stable nor misunderstood it. Someone had hired ruffians to kill a gentleman called the li'l man and lay the blame for it at Fate's door and then turn the captain over to the Runners for the blood money, and Fate's sense of self-preservation had kicked in full force.

Could, o' course, have nothin' ta do with this Locksley business, he told himself now, for why would Eversley wish ta send the one man who could bring 'im a share of the Dewhurst fortune ta the gibbet? Didn't make no sense as yet, but Eversley were playin' a deep game, an' Jason Fate weren't no fool. Might be any number of twists an' turns in Eversley's plots what Fate weren't privy to. Besides, he weren't prepared ta trust none o' these swells. He'd learned years ago that the Quality was dicked in the nob an' a cove couldn't go about settin' stock in 'em if 'e valued his neck.

"My, but you are scowling so fiercely," murmured a small voice beside him. "Are you not enjoying my ball at all, Mr. Locksley?"

Fate emerged from his cogitations abruptly to find Eversley had sailed off across the room and that Aurora had come up beside him on her brother's arm.

"Mr. Moss appears to be having a delightful time," continued Aurora with a smile. "See. He is about to dance with Lady Wright and she looks completely charmed by him."

"Mossie's a'ways been charmin' ta the ladies," muttered Fate. " 'Tis them wide blue eyes o' his. All innocence an' charm. A chap'd like ta black them daylights fer 'im from time ta time."

A crack of laughter exploded from between Neiland's lips.

"Naw, it ain't funny," continued Fate. " 'Tis eyes like Mossie's make life misery fer blokes like me. Ain't no mort fines me charmin' an' innocent, not with these great dark

oogles o'mine. A rogue er worse they thinks when they lay
their peepers on me—an' 'tis all because they come ta
think of eyes like Mossie's as them what is ta be trusted."

"You are blue devilled, aren't you, Locksley?" Neiland
chuckled. "I say, Rory, you ought to give the man this
dance. Lighten him up a bit. Tarkington has it, but I can
easily lure that fribble off and leave the field clear if you
like."

"Would you care to dance with me, Mr. Locksley?"
Aurora asked.

"Of course he would," urged Neiland. "Convince all
the doubters that we don't hold his claim against him for
one thing. Besides, Lilliheun dances this one with Cammy.
The four of you can form a set of your own and start all
the tongues to wagging."

"Oh, yes, let's do," Aurora grinned. "For you and Mr.
Lilliheun to share the same set would be just the thing,
Mr. Locksley. 'Tis only a country dance after all and not
very difficult. And you will feel so very much better when
you are having fun and not standing about glowering as
though you had lost your best friend."

The sight of Lilliheun and Locksley forming a set with
the cousins did indeed start tongues wagging. "I ought to
call you out, not dance with you," grinned Lilliheun as he
and Fate exchanged places in the figure. "They are all
expecting me to do as much."

"Fustian," replied Aurora as she dipped into a pretty
curtsy and rose again, "no one expects anything of the
sort. Do not keep watching your feet, Mr. Locksley. They
will do the right thing, I assure you. Not even a seven-year-
old could mistake these steps."

"Aye, but I be more than seven," explained the captain
seriously, "an' m'feet ain't near as dependable as they
was."

Camilla, overhearing, smiled encouragingly at him and
Lilliheun groaned.

"Whyever are you sighing, Clare?" she asked solicitously
as they came together.

"Because you smile at that—that rascal—in precisely

the way I wish you to smile at me. I have lost you to him, have I not?''

"Oh, of all the—I have told you over and over, my dear Clare, that I have not the least intention of giving my heart to any gentleman."

"Yes," nodded Lilliheun as they parted again, "but Locksley ain't a gentleman, m'dear, and you'd do well to remember it."

How on earth can I forget it, thought Camilla, her eyes wandering to the captain. Certainly no gentleman would insist upon calling me Dendron, or present me with daffodils stolen from the verge on the square, or come climbing through my windows in the middle of the night.

When the time came, Fate managed to acquit himself admirably in the Roger de Coverly, bringing accolades from Camilla and a sigh of relief from himself. "I heard, you know, about the dancing lessons," she confided as he escorted her back to her aunt. "Jolly and Grig could speak of nothing else for three whole days. They had the most delightful time, I think."

"Aye. The childer thought 'twas a great lark ta see such a clunch hip-hoppin' about and makin' a great gawkin' fool of hisself. 'Twas a lark," he added with a chuckle before she could feel at all sorry for him. "I enjoyed it 'mensely."

When he returned to lead her into the waltz, Camilla's eyes shone with wonder. She'd anticipated a tentative touch upon her waist and found instead a firm hand in the flat of her back. The muscles in the strong arm rippled unexpectedly and his dark eyes held a mischievous twinkle as he gazed down upon her. He swirled her into the music as if he had waltzed from the day he was born, and the solid closeness of him took her breath away. He laughed as she looked questioningly up at him. "This un ain't so worrisome, nor I can't even think 'bout m'feet with you in m'arms. 'Tis like heaven ta hold ye so."

"Oh? Is that why you do it so often? Even when there is no music?" Camilla's green eyes sparkled with mirth. "I will have you know, Captain, that never has any gentleman held me in his arms as often as you, unless it was Uncle Ned when I was a child. Even Mr. Lilliheun has not ventured to attempt it. Not that I would ever give him permission.''

"Permission? A man's got ta ask permission fer ta hold ye?" A perplexed expression made the captain's tipsy eyebrow tip even more awkwardly. "I never did hear of such a thin'. Ye be hoaxin' me, Dendron.''

"Oh? And do you hold whomever you please, whenever you please, sir?''

"Uh-huh, an' I ain't never asked no permission. No, nor had no complainin' about it.''

"Well, I expect that is because you are so experienced," Camilla replied, her eyes growing a darker green and the smile on her lips faltering for a moment. What a fool she was not to once imagine that here was a man who had held any number of women in his arms as he had held her. And Clare had probably held a number of flights of fancy in his arms as well.

"Ye're frownin'," Fate pointed out innocently. "Am I doin' somethin' wrong?''

"Oh, no, you are doing wonderfully," muttered Camilla. "I am sure you do everything wonderfully.''

The captain gave an outrageously loud guffaw and a number of heads turned in their direction. "I'm sorry, Dendron. I didn't mean ta laugh, but yer so very funny.''

"Me? I am funny?''

"Aye, an' dear to m'heart as well. Ye're thinkin' I held others like I done ye an' it's jealousy I be seein' in them beautiful daylights. Ah, but ye're wrong. There's holdin' an' there's holdin', darlin'. An' m'arms ain't never gone an' fit so proper aroun' none but ye.''

Camilla raised a disbelieving eyebrow and he laughed again, a bit more quietly, and then his hand in the small of her back brought her closer to himself and he spun her around and straight out onto the balcony. She thought he would cease to dance, but he did not, waltzing her across the small terrace and back in through the opposite doors with such a pleased expression upon his countenance that Camilla could not help but giggle. "Oh, but you are a knave, sir. And so self-satisfied.''

"Like the cat what got the cream," agreed Fate amiably.

"I ain't never before thought a actual lady might be jealous on my account."

"I am never jealous!" protested Camilla.

"No," drawled Fate, "an' I ain't never said 'stand an' deliver' neither."

Camilla went in to supper on Lilliheun's arm, Fate excusing himself from taking her on the grounds that he needed to visit the convenience—the forthright admission of which brought a smile from Camilla and a chuckle from Lilliheun. "He is the damn—ah, darndest man I have ever met," grinned Lilliheun. "I've done my best to despise him, you know. But I cannot. There are times I sit at home and kick myself for being at all interested in his welfare."

"*Are* you interested in his welfare?" Camilla asked, accepting the plate of delectables Lilliheun set before her.

"I hate to admit it, but yes, I am. He's a great gun, you know. Even Neiland says so. But what he will do should he ever become a duke, I hesitate to guess. It will not be at all pleasant for him, Camilla. Someone must take him up and teach him everything he doesn't know."

"Like how to speak properly," suggested Neiland, setting his own plate and Aurora's down across from the two. "Don't mind if we join you, do you? Rory swears she has been plagued enough by bustling beaux and needs a brief respite."

"I have not sat down once," complained Aurora, slipping into the chair her brother held for her. "I never thought how tiring it must be to be the Belle of a ball."

"And you are most certainly the belle of this ball," smiled Lilliheun, reseating himself. "I expect there will be a bevy of beaux on your doorstep every morning from this day forward. Might I hope that one day or another you will take pity upon me and allow me to drive you in the park again?"

"You, sir, may drive me in the park any day you wish," said Aurora without the least trace of hesitation. "I have met not one gentleman with whom I would rather join the Promenade."

Camilla's eyes met Aurora's and a message passed between the two that brought a wide grin to them both.

"What?" asked Neiland. "We've missed something, Lilli-heun, count upon it. The ladies share a secret in which we are not included."

"Oh, we do not, David," Aurora protested. "I have always wondered what champagne was like. This is delicious, is it not?"

"Yes, and you're not to drink more than two glasses, chick. Father's orders. Oh, my gawd!"

"What? What, David?"

But Neiland was already rising from his chair and around him other gentlemen slid their chairs back and rose as well. The Earl of Wheymore was hurrying toward the supper room door. Lady Wheymore excused herself from her table and rushed to join him. A murmur rose around the room as the object of this sudden attention stepped one foot into the chamber. Head high, shoulders square, dark eyes blazing with a bold mixture of aristocratic haughtiness and challenge beneath silvering brows and unruly silver curls brushing across his forehead, the Duke of Dewhurst struck the pose of an elderly warrior girded for battle. Wheymore stepped up before him and welcomed him.

"Didn't expect me, did you, Wheymore? Thought me too old to attend your chick's come out?"

"N-no, not at all, Your Grace. I—we—"

"We heard you were ill, Your Grace, and recuperating," inserted Lady Wheymore neatly. "And we did not wish to be a bother to you."

"Humph! No one wishes to bother me these days, but I am not in my grave as yet, young lady. And I've a wish to keep out of it for a good many years to come, though there's those as hope I'll stumble and fall in. What's this I hear, that your chick's grown so old as to be presented? And all this fuss is on her behalf, eh? Is that her, then, with Neiland? Ah, but she's come to be a beauty, Wheymore. I shouldn't wonder you'll lose her before the Season's over."

With the determined step of an old military man the duke crossed to the table where Aurora sat and bowed grandly over her hand. "Do you even remember me, my dear? I have not seen you since you came to Monteclaire for the summer with your brother and set all the staff to playing cricket. That was a good many summers ago, was it not?" There was a distinct and very familiar sparkle in the dark eyes now and Aurora noted it with a good deal of amazement. "I've brought you a gift, my girl," he continued, accepting her smile as acknowledgement that his memory was correct. His hand slipped into the inside pocket of his coat and reappeared clutching a long, thin, black velvet box. He flipped it open nonchalantly with one finger and Aurora gasped. "They were m'wife's, y'know, but she'd no granddaughter of her own to leave them to. I rather think—as fond as she was of your papa—that she would be pleased for you to have 'em."

"Oh, Your Grace, they are so very beautiful." Aurora reached out to touch the delicately wrought diamond necklace with one finger. "But you must not give them to me, sir. Certainly they ought to go to the wife of your heir."

The dark eyes glanced swiftly at Lilliheun and then back to Aurora. "No, these would have gone to Wheymore's first daughter with my Claudia, but since they had no daughter, they shall belong to you." Dewhurst bent lower to kiss the soft cheek that burned with excitement and then straightened and turned toward Lilliheun. He opened his mouth, closed it again, stared thunderstruck over Lilliheun's shoulder at the doorway where Fate leaned inelegantly with one shoulder against the door jamb, hands stuffed into the pockets of his breeches, and a series of dark curls tumbling over his brow. The entire company of guests, following the duke's gaze, inhaled at one and the same time and not a one exhaled into the silence.

Chapter 11

It was the Earl of Wheymore who exhaled first and stepped into the gap between the duke and Fate. "I apologize, Your Grace, for such an unpropitious meeting—we did not expect you, you see, and Mr. Locksley—may I introduce Mr. Lock—"

Dewhurst raised a haughty eyebrow and Camilla felt a

terrible twisting in the pit of her stomach. That the captain and the duke should be forced to confront each other in the midst of all these onlookers—it was insupportable. Her frightened gaze went instantly to Fate. Oh, she thought, he does not even suspect it is Dewhurst! The old duke will eat him alive!

Fate, noting the panic in Camilla's bright green eyes, frowned. She looked so very frightened. Whoever the ol' curmudgeon was, he thought, he hadn't no right ta be worryin' Dendron so, an' if Lilliheun and Neiland couldn't draw the cove off, Jason Fate certain-sure would. He took his hands from his pockets and straightening his shoulders, strolled to the table where Camilla sat, placed his hands on the back of her chair and raised his tipsy eyebrow questioningly in the direction of the duke. "Yer frightenin' Miz Quinn," he drawled quietly. "An' The Banshee weren't so pale when I lef' neither. An' if Lilliheun an' Neiland don't be takin' exception to't, I mean ta tell ye that I do."

"The B-Banshee?" stuttered Wheymore.

"Young man, have you the least idea who I am?" growled Dewhurst.

"No, an' I ain't much int'rested."

"Well, you had best be interested, sir," growled the duke. "And you had best find out before you say another word."

"He has not the faintest idea what he is saying, Your Grace," inserted Eversley coming at a dash to the table.

An intimidating glance from Dewhurst in Eversley's direction silenced that gentleman immediately.

"Duke, may I present Mr. John Locksley," murmured Wheymore hurriedly. "And Mr. Locksley, the Duke of Dewhurst."

"Ho!" Fate exclaimed. "So yer the cove what's s'posed ta be m'gran'father."

"So I hear," Dewhurst replied gruffly.

"Well, an' that don't excuse it. Ye've no call ta come 'ere a glarin' an' frightenin' Dendron an' The Banshee, an' that's a fack. Ye'd do best ta apologize to 'em an' take yerself off some'eres."

"Cap—Jas—Mr. Locksley, no!" exclaimed Camilla. "You do not understand. I am—it is not—it is simply that—"

"Camilla and I were both frightened at what might happen—the duke and yourself meeting for the first time in front of everyone. But nothing is going to happen, is it?" asked Aurora, her color returning along with her confidence. "Look, Mr. Locksley, at the lovely present His Grace has given me for my come-out. Is it not beautiful?"

"Dendron?" whispered Wheymore to himself. "Dendron and The Banshee? Is the man daft?"

"Aye, 'tis a pretty enough falderal," nodded Fate. "D'ye mean he ain't frightened ye, then?"

"No, he has not," said Camilla distinctly.

"How come ever'one's starin' this way like they was expectin' trouble?"

"Because they *are* expecting trouble, Locksley. They are expecting the duke to cut you down to size with a blink of his eye," drawled Lilliheun.

"Ho! I should like ta see the day I'm brought low by a crotchety ol' gent in a ugly puce waistcoat!"

"Locksley," Eversley hissed.

"What, fer gawd's sake? If ye think just because ye're determined ta prove this gent an' I be related, that I gotta kiss the cove's—ring—ye'd best fine yerself another John Locksley. I reckon I ain't like ta roll over an' let no big un walk on me like I was a molderin' carpet, gran'father er not."

Lilliheun and Neiland roared into laughter. Wheymore, beguiled into joyful memories of his late brother-in-law, succumbed to a broad grin and a few chuckles himself. Eversley sighed and rolled his eyes upward. The Duke of Dewhurst's jaw dropped; his eyes sparkled like polished onyx; and his lips twitched upward in spite of himself. "Ugly waistcoat, eh?" he managed, struggling for a sober expression. "Well, I see your taste is all in your feet as was my son's. That must add to whatever proof Eversley intends to put forward. You, sir, are a devilishly audacious brat and would be well-served if I should accept your claim and force you to study at my knee how to purport yourself like a Dewhurst.''

Camilla turned in her chair to look up and gauge Fate's reaction to this threat and found him grinning widely at the duke. Then he turned his gaze down to her, his eyes darkened considerably, and she felt the tip of a finger caress the back of her neck. "I reckon I read the sit'ation wrong, Dendron," he murmured. "But I ain't sorry fer thinkin' ta perteck ye. I expect I oughta go home. Will ye walk me ta the door, or ain't it proper-like for ye ta do so?''

"I should be pleased to walk you to the door, Mr. Locksley," she answered, and rising, took his arm and strolled with him into the hall.

"Ye'll tell The Banshee I enjoyed the thin', won't ye? I reckon I ought to of told 'er myself, but I didn't think of it," he mumbled as they descended the staircase. "Ought I to 'ave brought 'er a trinket like what the duke did? Did the res' o' the guests bring 'er somethin'? Mossie didn't say nothin' about—''

"Not at all," Camilla reassured him gently. "You did just as you ought. You came and you danced and you behaved quite properly, and I'm certain Aurora was most pleased with you.''

"An' ye, Dendron? Was ye pleased with me?" He accepted his hat and gloves from Somers's hands and led Camilla out onto the front steps through the door Somers held open.

"Most pleased," she answered.

Fate reached behind her, tugged the door from Somers's grasp and pulled it closed. His arms then came around her and he leaned down to kiss her lips softly in the gentle whisper of the night breeze. At the bottom of the steps, one of the young constables looked up and then glanced quickly away. The watchman stopped in midstride in the flickering light of the flambeaux and forgot to cry out that it was twelve o'clock and all was well and instead lowered his lantern to the ground, stared up at the captain and Camilla, and sighed.

* * *

The Earl of Wheymore paced his study with agitated steps several days later, his hands clasped behind his back, his eyes gravely studying the Persian carpet beneath his feet. In a wing-backed chair before the casement, the Duke of Dewhurst, his feet propped upon a footstool, watched silently, the papers produced in support of Mr. Locksley's claim lying undisturbed upon his lap. They had spent the entire morning in Borhill's office listening to Eversley's claims and examining the evidence. Locksley had not been present. Dewhurst, in fact, had not seen him again since the night of Aurora's come-out. "I say, Ned, 'tis not so serious a matter as to demand all this pacing about. Sit down, man, and we'll discuss it, just you and I."

Wheymore turned and stared down at the duke with a haunted look in his eyes. "What is there to discuss, sir? You've the evidence before you—and you've seen the man. Except for the roughness of his speech, I'd thought to be hearing Johnny, himself, deriding your waistcoat the night of the ball. And his eyes, and the way he has of cocking his head just so, it is all Johnny, every bit of it."

"Aye, the brat is one of us. I'd wager my fortune upon it," nodded Dewhurst. "But he ain't my heir, Ned, even should I wish him to be."

Wheymore lifted an eyebrow.

"I'd not tell ye so at the moment except I see how 'tis gnawing at your heart. There's a part of you wishes the claim to be true and a part cannot believe in spite of everything that John would marry and not commend his bride to your care and Claudia's, no matter what her heritage. And he would have, Ned. He would have come to you and Claudia and more than that—he would have come to me as well."

"But the marriage lines, the diary, the letter of credit."

"All most excellent forgeries, I'm afraid. Well done. Exceeding well done. But forgeries none the less."

"What? Are you certain, Duke? I mean, we compared them to the signatures on Johnny's letters and the handwriting appears exact."

"Indeed. The handwriting is perfectly like John's. The work of an excellent forger. But whoever is at the bottom of this lark has made one small mistake."

"What mistake?"

"Locksley's Christian name was not John William Lilliheun as it says on these marriage lines. It was Jonathan Will Lilliheun and so he would have signed it. He would never have signed with the informality of John nor added a William that he did not own, do you think?"

"But—but—I always thought—would not the forger have checked in Debrett's?"

"Most likely, but it does say John William there. I entered it so myself hoping to persuade his mama not to name the boy after me—I have always hated the name Jonathan Will and rarely use it myself, though 'tis on *my* marriage lines, you may well believe it. I always intended, you know, to go and change The Peerage to read properly, because Johnny's mama had him christened Jonathan Will whether I liked it or not. But I never quite got around to it, and then—well—he was killed at Willemstad and it seemed such a pointless thing to do. I did name Claudia Estelle," he added wistfully.

"My gawd, then the man *is* a fraud!"

"Yes, without doubt."

"Why did you not say so this morning? Why let Lilliheun and Borhill and Eversley think you were all but convinced the claim was legitimate?"

"Why because I am interested to know, Ned, who is at the bottom of this and what their next step will be. I doubt 'tis Lilliheun's plot for he's everything to lose and nothing to gain. But 'twas Borhill's man discovered the letter of credit, so Borhill might well be involved. And Eversley, though I cannot quite see what he will gain by it, discovered the man and the marriage lines. Either he and Borhill are working together or one is the dupe of the other."

"And Locksley?"

"Ah, Locksley was a lucky find for our schemer, no? Surely some one of the Lillihuen gentlemen at one time or another sowed a wild oat or two and every bit of the blood's trailed down through the years and come out in that young man.''

"You do not think him Johnny's by-blow, perhaps?"

"I doubt it. John was not one for lightskirts and opera dancers and temporary flights of fancy. He believed, I think, in love, Ned. And did he love a girl, he would have married her before he lay with her. He might assert his independence to me in any number of ways, but he would not seduce some poor maid and then abandon her. He would have seen it as an insult to his mama. No, he ain't an offshoot of mine, either,'' laughed the duke, reading Wheymore's questioning gaze correctly. "The only woman I ever bedded was my Charity, I assure you. Dull dogs, we Lillihuen men.''

"So—what are we to do, Your Grace?''

"Why, encourage the lot of them to think that both you and I, Ned, are much inclined to accept the evidence and make Locksley my heir—though we won't say so in so many words. And then we shall simply sit back and see what happens next.''

"But what will you do about Locksley? In the end, I mean. He may be transported or worse for impersonating a member of the peerage.''

"Ah, but I fail to see that Mr. Locksley impersonates anyone. 'Tis not he pushes his claim. He simply is, Ned, and a man cannot be taken to court for simply existing. From all I've heard so far, the lad don't even purport to be a gentleman, much less a peer. You like him?''

"I liked him wonderful well when he referred to you as a 'crusty ol' gent in a ugly puce waistcoat,'" smiled Wheymore. "Still, he's a problem if we're to dissemble about the claim. For if you take him under your wing, Duke, and I likewise, the *ton* will begin to acknowledge him.''

"So?''

The Earl of Wheymore rested his shoulders against the fireplace mantle and stuffed his hands into his breeches pockets. "Well, 'tis Camilla,'' he sighed. "Rory tells me that Cammy has lost her heart to the rogue. And do we make as if to accept him, Camilla will think 'tis appropriate to continue her association with him. What will I tell her? I can hardly forbid the chick to think of marrying a man who is to become a duke."

The Duke of Dewhurst rubbed a hand across his chin and arranged himself more comfortably in the chair. "Allow her to go on associating with him," he said at last. "She is as bright and independent as always, I'll wager. Turned down my nephew again, didn't she? Not wanting to be married at all. She will decide for herself whether or not Locksley deserves her interest."

"But he is not even a gentleman, and we will lead her to believe that he will be a duke!"

"Pah! If she wanted a duke, she would have jumped at Lilliheun. And if she wanted a gentleman, she'd have accepted any number of other offers—there were a good many other offers, I've no doubt. No, your Camilla will do as she sees fit and if it is this—this audacious brat she fancies, 'twill make not a whit of difference in her eyes if he is nobleman or highwayman."

"It makes a great deal of difference in Mary's eyes and in mine," grumbled Wheymore.

"Ah, well, then I shall make you a vow, Ned, eh? Does your most enchanting and deplorably self-reliant niece relinquish so much of her autonomy as to toss her cap over the rainbow for this rapscallion, I shall see Locksley is adequately and respectably established. She'll find herself quite out of Society, I expect, but she'll not give a twit for that. I will make it possible for them to live quietly in the country where Camilla may write to her heart's content— still wishing to be a novelist, is she?—and he shall be kept busily employed with his own lands. She's a fortune of her own, an' I shall match it on Locksley's behalf. I shall give him Shadow Hill, eh? It ain't entailed and Lilliheun won't quibble over it. It would not have gone to Lilliheun at any rate had things worked out differently. 'Twould have gone to Claudia and through her to your son, John."

The mention of his first wife and eldest child brought a lump to the earl's throat and he had to cough it away before he could make the least comment.

* * *

The Duke of Dewhurst's seeming acceptance of Locksley combined with the Earl of Wheymore's obvious support brought a shrug and a slight frown from Lilliheun and shouts of joy from Eversley. "We shall have it all, now," Eversley declared merrily over a glass of brandy. "See if we don't, Locksley. You shall become an outrageous and eccentric member of the nobility. Everyone will acknowledge you—no matter how much they abhor the thought of doing so—and they'll write every *faux pas* off to your whimsical upbringing. They'll declare that they knew you were of noble blood all along, that it shone through despite the neglect you suffered. And when Dewhurst dies, we shall inherit everything."

"We?" asked Locksley quietly, facing Lord Eversley over the dining table in the house on Grosvenor Square. "I thought as 'ow this job were only ta last three months at the most. Now you reckon I'm goin' ta be aroun' until the ol' gent sticks 'is spoon in the wall?"

"I guarantee you, Locksley, it will not be so very long before the old man is dead. He has a frightful weakness of the lungs and if the first of the wet weather don't take him off, he will be gone once the winter comes upon us. I have spoken to his physicians and they give him no more time than that. That's why he wishes to settle this matter of his heir as quickly as possible."

"An' what then? After the cove kicks off?"

"Why then, you inherit the title and the lands and may go about as you please, m'dear. Of course, I shall take charge of your inheritance. I trust you won't take it upon yourself to challenge my authority or my use of your money and influence, eh? I can, after all, prove that every piece of paper in support of your claim is a forgery, y'see. And I shall play the innocent in discovering 'tis so and see you off to Newgate as a wretched impostor if you cross me, sir. Though I don't mean to turn you off. Not by any means. Only if you'll not play along."

Fate's eyes sparkled as he took a long sip of the brandy, leaned back in the chair and put his boots up on the table ignoring the Irish linen cloth. "I sees it now. I'll be duke in name an' ye'll be duke in reality, eh? An' what if I have no hankerin' ta be duke at all?"

"Why then, Locksley, we shall discuss what is best to be done. Perhaps you shall decide upon a European tour for a few years or a visit to the Indies. Or perhaps you shall simply become a recluse—we'll think of some excuse to free you from it, if that's what you wish. You are not to worry about it. All will work out admirably."

"Aye, no doubt," nodded Fate. "Ye'll excuse me, won't ye, Eversley? I 'ave a 'gagement sort of. Promised ta attend somethin' er other with the old gent. Oughtn't be late."

"Of course, of course, off with you, Locksley. And give my best to dear, old, Uncle John, won't you?" Eversley snickered and reached to refill his glass.

Fate climbed the stairs to his chambers, asked Farmer to lay out whatever he ought to wear to a musicale, and then moved on down the corridor to the room where Harley, much improved, but his leg still splinted, was being entertained by Moss and Tick.

Elgin Moss, noticing immediately a familiar glint in the dark eyes, started Tick and Harley upon a game of Caution and followed Fate back out into the corridor. "What is it, Jason?" he asked. "Is Eversley gone?"

"Naw, he's down stairs drinkin' 'imself silly. I come ta remind ye, Mossie, ta step lightly. Don't be sayin' nothin' about me bein' who I am, eh? He still don't know an' there ain't no reason for 'im to, right? An' don't be encouragin' 'is nibs ta spend the night, neither."

"But Jason, 'tis the gentleman's own house. I can hardly be throwin' him outta it."

"No, but ye kin suggest as 'ow he might be better pleased ta be visitin' with his charmer like 'e has been. An' if that don't send him inta the street, ye might call upon Tick ta entertain him. That'll send 'im runnin'. I be off ta some place er other with the old gent, but then, I be goin' down inta St. Giles ta have me another look aroun' fer Artie. It ain't right he be gone this long, Mossie. I'm beginnin' ta think as 'ow somethin' bad's happened. Left a token for 'im at the rock but I ain't yet seen no answer. Been too long, Mossie. Somethin' don't be right.''

Moss nodded in agreement. "I've been tellin' the lads not to worry about their da, but they do, you know. They'll be proper glad that you're going to search fer 'im again. Got every confidence in you, they do.''

Rigged out in a coat of dark blue superfine, buff panta-loons, a gold brocade waistcoat and his neckcloth tied into a perfect Waterfall, Fate met the Duke of Dewhurst just as that gentleman descended from his coach before Number Seven Regent Street. The two of them ascended the steps together and the duke, presenting his card, let the butler precede them up the steps to the first floor where he and Locksley were announced and immediately welcomed by a stunning lady in a gown of shimmering gold and lace. "Madelane, I thank you for your consideration in sug-gesting Locksley accompany me," the duke drawled lazily. "It will be good for him to get about a bit in Society. Locksley, may I present Lady Clarence, my sister-in-law. Clare's mother.''

"Gorblimey!" exclaimed Fate in a strangled whisper.

"No, John, 'gorblimey' is not an acceptable manner of acknowledging an introduction," grinned the duke.

"I ain't acknowledgin' no interduction," mumbled Fate. "I be acknowledgin' the lady's assets an' attemptin' ta think of her as Lilliheun's mam at one an' the same time.''

Lady Clarence's lips quivered as she caught the gleeful gleam in Dewhurst's eyes. "I thank you, then, Mr. Lock-sley," she responded on a chuckle. "It has been an amaz-ingly long time since my—assets—have been so forthrightly acknowledged. Come, let me lead you to Clare. He was forced to attend, you know. I forced him. And he will be extremely grateful for your company.''

Lilliheun separated Fate from his mother and the duke immediately. "Thank the lord, I thought to be the only gentleman under fifty at this thing," he sighed taking Fate's arm. "Neiland promised to attend, but I ain't seen a whisker of him.''

"Yer still talkin' ta me?" Fate asked with a lift of the tipsy eyebrow.

"Of course, you ninny, why wouldn't I be talking to you? Obviously the duke intends to acknowledge you as his grandson and that's wonderful good luck on your part. But it makes you my cousin, you see. And it would be exceeding bad form to cease speaking to my cousin—especially as he's likely to become head of the family."

"And—and Lady Clarence would be my aunt?"

"She is your aunt, ninny. At least she will be with a mere nod of Uncle John's head and his signature on a piece of paper. Ah, there, Neiland has come thank goodness—and he's brought Camilla and Aurora as well. Neiland! You're a great gun to pop in," Lilliheun said in a rush, tugging Fate toward the new arrivals.

"M'father and mother are directly behind us," grinned Neiland. "Even had I been prevented, Rory and Cammy would have given you solace. Evenin' Locksley. All ready are you?"

"Ready for what?" asked Fate, his glance lingering upon Camilla who had expected to find him at Lady Clarence's musicale and had dressed with him in mind—her gown of Pomona green muslin clung softly and in a most complimentary way and the Quinn emeralds glittered invitingly around her lovely throat, at her ears, and around her wrist.

"Ready for the torture, Locksley. Lady Clarence thinks it her duty to torture us at least once every Season."

"I thought it was a—a—somethin' ta do with music?"

"Yes, well, it does have something to do with music—but not a great deal."

"Oh, David, you are not at all humorous," murmured Aurora, giving her brother's arm a quick and very unladylike punch. "Especially since Cammy and I must perform."

"Well, you two will do all right. It is Lady Hawthorne and Miss Clemson, and Miss Olivia Smythe I fear. I tell you, Locksley, the screeching and squalling and wailing will drive you mad."

By the time the entertainment was to begin every gilded chair in the music room was taken and a number of gentlemen found it necessary to stand at the back of the room,

A $16.47
value.
FREE!
No obligation
to buy
anything, ever.

AFFIX
STAMP
HERE

IIl..l..lll....llil.l..l..l..l.l..l.l.l..l..llii..l..l

arms crossed, their attention focussed on the tiny dais upon which the singers and musicians would perform. Fate, Neiland and Lilliheun stood among them. The captain rested his shoulders against the watered silk wallpaper and watched in wonder as one after another lady appeared upon the small stage and played the pianoforte, or the harp or the flute. Some of them sang popular tunes in lilting voices, others trilled arias from operas and one lithesome young woman performed a singularly intriguing dance to a tune played by her mama upon a harpsichord.

"What do you think, Locksley?" Lilliheun whispered.

"Some of 'em sound like cats fightin'," Fate whispered back.

Neiland, on Fate's other side, grinned. "Just wait. Aurora and Cammy are next. They will not hurt your ears at least."

Aurora and Camilla were to perform a duet upon the pianoforte—a feat normally accomplished with a minimum of fuss, for both young ladies had had lessons from the age of five and both loved to play. But Fate's presence made Camilla unaccountably nervous and she could not settle herself at the keyboard. She rose and sat a number of times before Aurora whispered, "Cammy, for goodness sake, sit! You are looking quite like a children's Jack-in-the-box." The results of this caused Miss Quinn to blush becomingly and settle next to her cousin on the bench amidst a number of titters from the other young ladies. She flexed her fingers, positioned them over the keys, and when Aurora nodded, hit three wrong chords in a row. Aurora ceased to play, gave her cousin a sidelong glance, and grinned. "Shall we begin again? I know Captain Fate is out there, but he will not bite you if you make a mistake."

"Oh, I cannot," whispered Camilla, the back of her neck burning with embarrassment. "My fingers are all a jumble. I cannot imagine what has gotten into me. I cannot play in front of the captain, Rory. I feel an absolute fool."

"Well, you are not a fool and you know perfectly well how to play the music. We shall begin again."

They began again and came to a tinkling halt as Camilla forgot where they were in the piece. Rory turned on the bench and, taking her cousin's hands into her own, looked to see tears standing in the lovely green eyes. In the audience, Lady Wheymore rose to make her way to the dais, but the earl caught her hand and tugged her back down onto the gilded chair. "Help, I think, is already on the way," he murmured in her ear, directing her attention toward the three gentlemen advancing from the rear of the room.

"Are you certain?" asked Lilliheun with a doubtful countenance. "We have not done it for years—"

"If you will, so will I," Neiland assured him, striding cockily up to the platform, his arm through Fate's. "Just follow my lead, Locksley," he hissed in a stage whisper. " 'Twill be like performing a farce at the theatre."

"I ain't never been ta no theatre," Fate announced loudly, and purposely tripped mounting the dais.

The ladies in the audience tittered and the gentlemen chuckled as Neiland tugged him to his feet, almost falling himself. "No, no, no, my dears," Lilliheun declared coming to stand over Cammy and Aurora, "that ain't the way it goes. You have got all thumbs on your fingers."

Fate, his great dark eyes sparkling encouragingly down at Camilla took both her hands in his own, winked, led her to the edge of the dais and then inspected her fingers with a slight frown. "Not this one, Mr. Lilliheun," he called over one shoulder. "She ain't got but one thumb on each hand, an' they's where they's s'posed ta be."

" 'Tis this one, then, I reckon," Neiland responded, pulling a giggling Aurora from the bench and inspecting each finger. "Aye, ten of 'em she's got!"

"Oh!" cried Aurora in the accents of a chamber maid, "I shall never play the pianoforte again! Being as I got ten thumbs—I shall be forced to play the harp!"

A bellow of laughter rose from the audience.

"A harp? A harp?" called Lilliheun, rushing behind the screens which masked the rear of the little stage and returning with a violin in hand. "I got a harp here. 'Twill be perfect for you, m'lady."

"That's not a harp, fool," declared Neiland. "That's a cello."

"No, it ain't," Fate responded with a shake of his unruly curls. " 'Tis a fiddle."

"Oh, fiddle," sighed Lilliheun, rolling his eyes at the amused audience and getting a loud groan from them *en masse.*

"Whatever shall we do?" cried Camilla, putting the back of her hand to her brow dramatically. "We are ruined! Ruined! We shall become social pariahs for we have destroyed Lady Clarence's musical evening!"

"Not yet, but we're about to," declared Neiland and Lilliheun loudly. Whereupon Neiland sat down at the pianoforte; Aurora seated herself beside him; Lilliheun tucked the violin under his chin; and Fate, placing his hands over Camilla's ears, gave them a nod to start. The cacophony was outrageous. Camilla, laughing, reached up behind her and put her hands over Fate's ears as well and both of them burst into laughter along with the rest of the room. "Enough," Fate called at last. "I reckon ye done as fine a job of wreckin' the evenin' as ye could, mates. Now 'tis my turn." With a whispered word to Camilla, he led her to the piano and saw her seated then snatched the violin from Lilliheun and tucked it under his own chin. Camilla struck the notes he had requested of her; he drew the bow across the struts and turned the screws to tune the strings. Then, with a flick of his wrist, he set the instrument aside, searched through his waistcoat pockets and produced a golden hoop which he stuck into the lobe of his left ear. He picked up the violin again and gave Camilla a wink. "I reckon ta play the one 'bout the maid of the forlorn smile," he announced to no one in particular and everyone in general.

Camilla caught her breath in disbelief as the violin began to sing. All of the audience, who had been prepared for another intended disaster, inhaled on a gasp and leaned back into their chairs, astonished. Lilliheun, Neiland, and Aurora sat down upon the edge of the dais and listened in awe as the violin mourned and cried and laughed and trilled and mourned again and then, with a quick flash of a smile from Fate to Camilla, sailed off into an Italian melody called *Zingaro,* which anyone who had ever heard

of a gypsy knew to be the very essence of the Romany love
of freedom and life.

Toes tapped, hands clapped in time, and at the rear of
the chamber, Miss Jessica Winters spun in happy circles on
the arm of her intended husband, Lord Jeffery Trevaine.

Chapter 12

Camilla, laughing, allowed Fate to escort her out onto the
balcony for a breath of fresh air. "You are impossible, sir,"
she giggled. "Do you know how roguish you look with that
gold loop in your ear?"

"Roguish? Truth? An' I thought I only looked like a
poor gypsy lad."

"Not in those clothes, my dear Captain. You look a
veritable knave. And you are a weaver of spells besides.
You have set all of Lady Clarence's guests agog, and all of
London will know of it before tomorrow has ended. Oh,
but you play so wonderfully. Why did you never tell me?"

"Ye never asked, Dendron. An' I never thought ta do
it, but Neiland an' Lilliheun said as how ye was so very
nervous an' that we 'ad a duty ta rescue ye from havin' ta
perform. An' then, well, that fiddle jumped up under
m'chin an' I couldn't resist. I love ta play the fiddle."

"Yes, 'twas obvious." Camilla stared at the shimmering
gold hoop in his left ear. One hand rose involuntarily
toward it.

"Oh, no, ye don't, m'darlin'. There's ceremonies as
mus' be observed afore ye take a earin' from a gypsy's
ear." He was laughing silently down at her in the moonlight
and Camilla could not tell whether he spoke truthfully or
not. "The golden hoop be a mystical thin' an' does a
woman touch it, 'tis fatal to 'er."

"Fatal?" asked Camilla, her green eyes wide with wonder. "How so? What can be fatal about it?"

"If ye so much as touch it in the moonlight, ye'll lose
yer 'eart to the one what wears it forever an' ever. An' do
ye take it from 'is ear, ye're a goner."

"A goner?"

"Aye. Ye'll marry 'im. Ye'll not be able ta 'elp yerself. 'Tis destiny the hoop tempts an' destiny it alters. An' ye don't want ta be marryin' no one, Dendron. So Lilliheun an' Neiland both tol' me. So does it offend ye, I'll be the one ta be removin' of it." He took her hand in his own and kissed her palm, sending little shivers up her spine, and then he reached up and popped the ring from his ear and tucked it back into his waistcoat pocket.

"But it does not offend, sir," Camilla murmured. "It dazzles and bewilders and entices a girl much as you do yourself."

"Who, me?" asked Fate, his whimsical eyebrow rising. "I reckon ye got me mixed up with yer Bad Jack Pharo, eh, Dendron? He's the one what's 'andsome an' upright an' noble an' all. I ain't none o' them thin's nor ain't never likely ta be. Or mebbe Lilliheun? I reckon he's as noble as they comes."

Camilla could not think how to reply. She could not think at all with his eyes laughing down at her and his arm slipping lightly around her waist and his slim, strong fingers tickling the back of her neck as he drew her to him.

"Oh, my goodness!" exclaimed Aurora as she came through the balcony doors. "Well, if you are going to kiss her, Captain, please do so at once because papa says we must be going and has sent me in search of Cammy. If I do not return with her almost immediately, he will come looking himself."

Camilla started and turned to look at her cousin, but Fate's hand rose to her cheek and turned her back to face him. He leaned down and kissed her softly. For a moment he nibbled at her lower lip and then he kissed her again. "I love ye, Dendron," he whispered in her ear. "Ye've got me spellbound. Ye'll remember that, won't ye, darlin', no matter what 'appens."

Fate left Lady Clarence's establishment with Neiland and Lilliheun beside him. "We'll stop for a drink at White's, eh?'' Neiland suggested. Lilliheun nodded. Fate looked from one to the other and then declined.

"Of course you'll come," Neiland protested. "You'll be our guest."

"Me? In a gen'leman's club? I think not. Besides, I got other thin's ta be about tanight."

"Like what, Locksley? Anyone would think you're embarrassed to be seen in our company."

Fate laughed. "No, but I got ta go lookin' for the childers's Da an' the places I figger ta go don't be welcomin' no swells, Neiland."

"Then you'll be hard put to get in yourself," Lilliheun suggested, looking Fate over from top to bottom. "You look as much a swell as any of us."

"Aye, but I figger ta rectify that."

Neiland looked questioningly across at Lilliheun and Lilliheun nodded. "We're going with you," Neiland declared. "An' we won't take no for an answer. You needn't think we are green heads and know nothing about the East End, Locksley. There's several gaming clubs and—and various other places lie in those environs."

"An' ye been there?" Fate asked quietly.

"Well, no, not exactly," Lilliheun muttered, "but we know people who have been there."

"Oh, ye knows people what have been there," Fate nodded. "Well, that makes the devil of a diff'rence, don't it?"

"We're coming regardless," drawled Neiland. "After all, m'mother's taking care of those children at the moment, ain't she? I expect that puts some responsibility for finding their father upon me, does it not?"

"No," answered Fate succinctly, "it don't." Nevertheless, he protested no more, not even when he turned east on New Bridge Street and they kept pace with him.

As the streetlamps grew dimmer and farther apart and the streets narrower and closer together, the quips and comments that had maintained a ragged conversation among the gentlemen faded away and the three strolled in silence down a series of rubish-strewn alleys, watching the fog flow like a white tide across the cobbles and rise around their knees. "Here," Fate murmured at last.

"Where?" Lilliheun asked, looking about him in wonder. "Lord but it smells like rotting cabbages! Worse!"

"There," Fate said pointing upward at the window to the bedchamber he had occupied in the Radd household. With a jump he reached the crumbling rail of the tiny balcony and pulled himself upward leaving Neiland and Lilliheun to stare after him. "Go 'round ta the front," he called down. "I'll git the door for ye. 'Tis the very firs' door at the beginin' o' Basket Lane."

The two gentlemen made their way cautiously to the end of the alley, came around down Waggoner's Street and turned hurriedly into Basket Lane. A door opened immediately they approached it. "There bean't no key nor nothin'," Fate explained. "Someone's got ta move the bar or ye cain't git in." He replaced the heavy bar across the door and turned to light several candles about the room.

"Do you mean to tell me that all those children lived in this—this—" Lilliheun came to a stuttering halt as he took in the tiny room with the kitchen table to the side beneath the stairs.

"Well, t'ain't near as clean as what it were when the childer were a sweepin' of it," offered Fate, climbing back up the stairs. "But there's two whole bedchambers plus the hearth an' a attic. An' it don't b'long ta no one else but Radd an' me, so as we ain't likely never ta be put out, ye know."

Lilliheun and Neiland, trailing up the stairs behind him, candles in hand, could not find words to respond.

"Unless, o' course, we both gits taken up ta the Old Bailey an' convicted of somethin'—then I reckon as yer Fat Prince an' 'is cronies'll come inta possession of it."

"You mean the government will appropriate it?" Lilliheun asked in a stunned whisper.

"Aye. Takes ever'thin' they does, oncet a man gits hisself hanged."

"But you are certainly not planning upon being hanged, Locksley," Neiland replied as he watched Fate shed his shining halfboots and replace them with a pair of scuffed and worn riding boots he'd fetched from under the three-posted bed.

"O' course I ain't plannin' on it," grinned Fate, shrugging out of the coat he'd worn to the musicale and divesting himself of neckcloth and waistcoat. He opened a brass-bound wooden trunk with a broken lock at the foot of the bed and lifted a kerseymere jacket from its depths. It was much too large for him, Lilliheun noticed, and if he were to button the thing, he might hide an entire picnic basket between it and his stomach. What he placed between it and his stomach was a horse pistol which he fetched from the top of an ancient armoire with a broken door that stood in one corner, and which he took the time to load carefully. Then he tied a yellow kerchief around his neck, fetched a wide-brimmed, low-crowned hat from inside the armoire, and returned to dig into the pockets of the waistcoat and the coat he had abandoned. Neiland and Lilliheun watched in silence as he transferred the contents of all his pockets from those abandoned to those he wore. The golden earring, a handful of vanilla beans, some folded flimsies and a few cartwheels, an enamelled snuff box, two oddly-shaped rocks and a thimble were all carefully distributed about Fate's person.

"Do ye know how ta handle a blade?" the captain asked abruptly, pulling two long and wicked weapons from the trunk. "Ye kin 'ave these. I reckon ye'll be safer do the lads see 'em at yer sides." He tossed the short swords and sheaths and belts, one to each of the men and waited while they set down their candles and buckled the weapons on. "I got ta check t'other bedchamber jus' in case," he stated. "Though I reckon Artie'd be in here were 'e in the house. 'E couldn't a helped but hear us." Lilliheun and Neiland stared after him as he strolled into the hall. He returned in a matter of moments. "Ain't there, nor in the attic. Come. I'll let ye out the door."

Lilliheun and Neiland stepped out into Basket Lane, heard the bar set across the door behind them and moments later saw Fate approaching from around the corner. "This way," he mumbled, pulling the brim of his hat lower over his brow. "An' don't be a pokin' along behin' o' me. I ain't fixin' ta tempt anyone if I kin help it. An' the two o' ye be very temptin' indeed. I 'spect I oughta warn ye—a number of blokes goin'ta be callin' me Jason. Didn't no un ever know m'name be John 'til Eversley come along an' ain't none of 'em used ta it as yet."

The trio entered and departed a score of tiny pubs, Lilliheun and Neiland drawing stares and causing lips to be licked in anticipation. But each time Locksley made it apparent that they were in his company and they both noticed how effective a deterrent that knowledge was. They accompanied him down twisting back streets and in through crumbling doorways, stepped over bodies, limp, in gutters and strolled nonchalantly through the middle of drunken brawls. They entered bawdy houses where girls as young as eleven waited shivering in the damp parlors in thin chemises, their faces painted and their hair curled in styles meant to approximate the height of fashion. And Fate, his dark eyes aware of each person and every movement asked time and time again after Artie Radd.

It was in one of the bawdy houses that a woman of small stature, with upswept hair and dark, charcoaled eyes, took Locksley's arm and led him across the room from Lilliheun and Neiland. "Ye be keepin' the strangest company these days, Cap'n," murmured Meggy. "I reckon as 'ow it got somethin' ta do with yer new lay, ain't it?"

"Aye, Meggy. 'Tis necessary ta assoc'ate with 'em fer a while. Have ye seen Radd, then?"

Meggy nodded. " 'E be upstairs. Gwen be with 'im. But 'e ain't in fine shape, Jason. Foun' 'im, we done, very early-like this mornin'. Someone done pummeled 'im good. Lef' 'im fer dead in are gutter."

"Does 'e say who done it, Meggy?"

"No, 'e don't say nothin' 'cept ta call fer ye. I reckon ye oughta go up."

Fate gave her a kiss on the cheek, collected Lilliheun and Neiland and urged them up the stairs. "Gwen!" he shouted as they reached the upstairs hall. A door opened at the very end of the corridor.

"Gawd," muttered Neiland, attempting not to breathe in the dank, strong smell of mildew that permeated the walls and bred on the falling wallpaper. Lilliheun elbowed him in the ribs and frowned him into keeping his peace.

They trailed in Locksley's wake to the open door and stepped inside to discover a woman sitting upon the edge of a very new, very elegant sleigh bed, bathing the swollen face of the man in the bed with lavender water. She rose and walked straight into Locksley's arms and leaned her head against his chest. " 'E's dyin', Jason," she murmured into his shirtfront. "I know 'e's dyin'. There ain't nothin' what even the 'pothecary kin do fer 'im."

"Aw, he ain't dyin', Gwen," murmured Fate, his breath stirring the bright gold strands of her hair. "Artie Radd be too damned obst'eprous ta die."

Lilliheun blanched at the sight of Radd, his head swathed in bandages, his eyes swollen closed, his nose broken and his cheeks and jaw covered in dark, angry bruises.

Fate placed the now sobbing Gwen into Neiland's arms and sat down upon the side of the bed. "Artie," he growled, "who done this to ye?"

"Ja-Jason?" The man on the bed rolled his head toward the sound of Fate's voice. "Ja-Jason?"

"Aye, I be 'ere, Artie."

"The childer?"

"They be safe as 'ouses, m'lad. I bin lookin' for ye forever, Artie. Where'd ye git off to? I bin ever'where. Twicet."

Disjointed, incomprehensible syllables fell from between Radd's lips and Lilliheun listened closely trying to make sense of them, as intent upon putting the man's story together as Fate himself. Neiland, distracted by the sobbing young woman in his arms, heard none of it, but only concentrated upon bringing Gwen's tears to a halt. "He be goin' ta die," sobbed Gwen, comfortably ensconced in Neiland's strong arms. "Oh, them poor childers, ta be left wi'out mam or da!"

Neiland had not the least idea what to say or do other than hold the buxom young woman and allow her to thoroughly dampen his exquisite neckcloth which was coming to look much more like an artist's rag. The paint from her face rubbed off upon it; the charcoal from her lashes painted black spots here and there, and he was exceeding grateful when Locksley approached and coaxed the pretty little watering pot away from him. "Hush, Gwen," Fate murmured, taking his handkerchief from his pocket and dabbing at her eyes and cheeks and chin. "Artie ain't goin' ta die, m'darlin'. I'm goin' ta fetch a coach, I am, an' take 'im where 'e'll be well looked af'er. Ye done splendid, Gwennie, ta take 'im in like ye did, an' now ye musn't worry no more, eh?" Neiland watched the stack of flimsies Locksley carried pass into the young woman's hands and from there down into the lace bodice of her gown.

"Ye're a dear 'un, Jason, that ye are," sobbed Gwen. "An' we prays fer ye ever'day, that there's not a constable'll fine ye, nor a Runner what'll discover ye about yer business."

Fate planted a wet kiss upon her cheek and with Lilliheun and Neiland at his side made his way back down the stairs and out onto the street. His stride quickened as he made his way back through the alleys and narrow twisting lanes and slowed only as he came at last into the more acceptable parts of town, where he procured a hackney with the intention of going back to remove Artie Radd from the bawdy house and carry the man to Grosvenor Square.

Lilliheun protested loudly, much to Neiland's astonishment. "You cannot possibly take the man to Grosvenor Square, Locksley. You've a young invalid there already and the rascal's brother—and three more children stowed across the way who are constantly running to you for one thing or another. Do you think Eversley will not notice a new addition? Do you think he will not protest your turning his house into a nursery and hospital? You are lucky beyond belief that he has not booted you all out."

"Not lucky," mused Fate. "We been workin' at keepin' 'is lor'ship outta the childer's way and visa verci."

"Yes, well, it will be three times as difficult if you take Radd there. The man's devilish hurt and raving as well. And think how merely the sight of their father in such a case will frighten the children. No, you cannot take him to Grosvenor Square. He shall come to my chambers on Regent Street. My man, Cammet, and I will look after him."

Neiland, recognizing a familiar tone in Lilliheun's voice, put in his oar, advising Locksley that since Dewhurst was in town and had shown signs of accepting his claim, he would likely not have a moment's peace until the duke had departed again. "And Dewhurst, you know, is not like to accept any excuses from you. You will not be able to keep much of an eye upon your friend, I assure you, Locksley. Better to take him to Lilliheun's. Cammet's got no one else to look after but Clare."

It took them the entire ride to the bawdy house and half the ride back to convince Fate, but in the end, the two combined to achieve a victory and the hackney driver was directed to turn the coach toward Regent Street and Lilliheun's chambers.

"Now, tell me why you wanted this fellow in your keeping, Lilliheun," Neiland sighed after Radd had been attended by a hurriedly-summoned physician and Fate sent uneasily on his way home. "I heard it in your voice or else I'd not have supported you against Locksley. 'Tis his friend after all."

"Yes, exactly. And there is something havey-cavey going on."

"No, do you think so?"

"I do. First the boy is trampled, then his father is found beaten mercilessly and both of them are hand in glove with Locksley."

"And you think—what?" asked Neiland, collapsing onto the chaise longue with a glass of porter in his hand.

"I don't know—but I find it suspicious."

"You do?"

"Yes, I do," nodded Lilliheun, settling into the wing chair and stretching his long legs out before him. "And I intend to discover exactly what is going on."

Grig could not contain her four-year-old ardor for a moment and came hopping and twirling with joy into the breakfast room at Wheymore House. "Da is founded! Da is founded!" she chanted enthusiastically.

"Oh, how wonderful!" Camilla exclaimed with a grin. "I am sure you are very happy, my dear."

"Uh-huh! Eber'body's 'appy as larkses! I be dancin' wif joys!"

"Yes, we can see that, dearest," laughed Aurora. "Was it your Uncle John found him?"

" 'Twas Uncle John an' Lor' Neilan' an' mister what's got such pwerty hairs like the sunshine."

Camilla could not think for a moment of whom 'mister' might be and looked at Aurora questioningly.

"Clare, I believe," Aurora said around a bite of toast. "Is it Mr. Lilliheun you mean, Grig?"

"Aye, Mr. Lil'un. 'E be the pwertiest cove in all the whole worl', ain't 'e?"

Camilla motioned the little girl to her and lifted her on to her lap. "Indeed, sweet one, he is very handsome—and good and kind as well."

"Yes, the kindestest, mostest best cove in the whole worl'. Uncle John tole Tick as 'ow Da weren't feelin' jus' the thin' an' 'ow Mr. Lil'un done said as Da mus' stay wif 'im until he be better agin," declared Grig in an excited rush. "Oh, I am so berimost happy, I could gibble!"

"My goodness," the Earl of Wheymore smiled as he strolled into the room and began to serve himself from the sideboard, "how incredibly lucky I am this morning to be able to break my fast with three such lovely ladies— and one of them about to gibble!"

Aurora and Camilla smiled widely and Grig slipped from Cammy's lap to run to the earl and curtsy with a little hop and a dip before him. "G'morin', yer lor'ship."

"Good morning, young lady. And may I ask who taught you to gibble?"

"No one. I a'ways knowed, since I was li'l. Eber'time Uncle John tickled me I gibbled—from the bery firstest time."

"Ah, I see. And may I ask why you feel as though you are about to gibble now?"

"Becuz my da is founded!" shouted Grig exultantly and began to dance around and around the earl. "My da is founded! My da is founded!"

The Earl of Wheymore laughed, set his well-filled plate upon the table and scooped Grig up into his arms. He planted a kiss upon one ear, told her he was delighted that her father was no longer missing, and sent her, with a pat on her bottom, off to the nursery to rejoin Jolly and little Digger. "Do you know," he said softly, opening an eggshell with a tap of his knife, "I cannot help but think of Johnny whenever those little ones are about."

Camilla and Aurora eyed each other worriedly. For as long as they could remember the subject of the earl's first born son had been a forbidden topic in the household. The tragedy that had taken both him and his mother from Wheymore's life had never once been spoken of in their presence.

"It is the things they say," Wheymore murmured, spooning a bit of egg into his mouth and smiling softly. "Like gibbled. 'Twas Johnny's word for giggling as well. I do not believe any of you children ever used it. Claudia enjoyed so much to hear Johnny mispronounce things that she encouraged him in it. He was no more than an infant after all. It made no difference and it delighted her. Your mother, on the other hand," he continued with a smile at Aurora, "was always very particular that her children learn to speak correctly from the beginning. She dismissed at least one nurse that I remember because the poor woman would talk baby-talk to Neiland despite several warnings. I used to fear being dismissed myself on that count."

"Oh, Papa, no," Aurora grinned. "Mama would never have sent you packing for such a thing."

"You think not? Well, perhaps you're right, but I dared not do anything to upset her, you know. I was so very aware of the prize I'd won that I dreaded even a frown upon her brow."

"What—what was Aunt Claudia like?" Camilla asked hesitantly, her hands playing with the napkin on her lap.

"Well, she would not have been your aunt, my dear, for our family should never have been linked with the Quinn's at all if I had not married your Aunt Mary. But had you somehow come tumbling into Claudia's life as you did ours, why, I believe she would have enjoyed every moment of it. Yes, indeed she would have. I have never again met a woman who loved life so well as Claudia. Not even your mama," he said reminiscently with a glance at Aurora. "For though your mama is most kind and has a charitable heart and a great propensity for taking in strays, she is also most practical and cautious and looks a great deal to the future on her own behalf and on her children's. Claudia never looked to the future at all that I could tell. She revelled in the present. Each day was to her a new beginning, the start of an excellent adventure. She was very fanciful, too," he chuckled softly, his gaze going directly to Camilla. "She invented the most wonderful stories. Most of them," he added with a small sigh, "were about Bedford Hill and the hidden garden and—"

"And what, Uncle Ned?"

"And the Bodkins in the bottom of the garden," the earl added quietly with a look of wonder on his face. "I had always thought they belonged to us alone—those Bodkins. 'Twas a shock to hear Grig and Jolly speak of them when Neiland and I went to fetch the babes, for I thought Claudia invented Bodkins herself. But there, shows how much a stuffy old earl knows about children's tales. Still, Claudia had Johnny convinced that the Bodkins truly existed. Even saw them once, he did. How we were used to laugh, she and I, over such charming *naivete* as the boy possessed. He could ride, you know," the earl added proudly on an afterthought. "Merely a pony, of course, but he could ride it well by the time he was two. Not at all afraid. A great deal of bottom, like his mother, and a heart and soul like hers as well."

"I expect you were very proud of him, Papa," Aurora offered, her blue eyes bright with wonder that after all these years her father should finally speak of the boy.

"Very proud," nodded Wheymore. "Equally as proud as I am of you and David and Camilla. I have been blessed beyond deserving," he added in a hoarse whisper, "to have had the honor to raise you three rascals after I thought I had lost all. And that is quite enough sentimental drivel for this morning. I have promised to accompany Dewhurst to Tattersall's and I shall be abominably late.''

"Oh, Cammy," sighed Aurora once her father had left the room, "after all these years—to hear papa speak of Claudia and Johnny—it is like a miracle. I must tell mama at once. Do you think it means the terrible wound to his heart has healed at last?''

"Scarred over and safe to touch now, I should think," nodded Camilla with a sense of dreaming in her eyes. For a man to have mourned the loss of his wife and son so deeply that he could not bear to speak of them for over twenty years and then that he should suddenly be healed by an urchin with golden fluffs of hair who gibbled—what a grand tale to tell. How romantic it would be to set it down for all the world to read. Of course, she could not use Uncle Ned's real name, nor Claudia's, nor Johnny's, but even still, she could feel the passion, the sensitivity, the sheer power of the story rising within her. I will, she thought. I will weave a story around it that will not in the least suggest Uncle Ned, but I will keep the core of it exactly the same. Only, she thought with a hint of tears mounting to her eyes, only I will discover some way to bring the child back to his father in my tale. There must be some way to do that. Some way. But first, she reminded herself with a tiny shake of her head, I must finish the story of Bad Jack Pharo. Oh, I can hardly wait to see him and Esperanza happily married and raising a parcel of children!

Chapter 13

Vauxhall Gardens had not changed much at all since last Camilla had visited them, but this night they seemed somehow mystical and intriguing and potentially dangerous. The Duke of Dewhurst, whose party it was, had procured for them a box decorated with paintings by Francis Hayman of a country dance and a fair, and Aurora, who had never before been to Vauxhall, delighted in touching them and pointing out this particular smile upon the face of a maiden or that particular style of a gentleman's shoe.

Lilliheun did much to encourage her in this, adding his own comments as to the ability of the artist and the number of times the paintings had had to be retouched because of all the curious fingers constantly trailing over them. Neiland, his gaze roaming over the Grove beside them, paid little attention to his sister and a great deal of attention to the damsels in the other boxes and those who strolled the Grand Cross Walk, the Grand Walk, and the South Walk which bounded the Grove. In the Grove Mr. James Hook, organist and composer, was presently performing a number of his own compositions, though later the orchestra would appear to strike up the music to which couples would dance happily beneath the stars.

The Duke saw his young guests were kept well-supplied with the nearly invisible shavings of ham, the tiny roast fowl, and pastries and biscuits and cheese cakes for which the Gardens were famous, and glasses were filled again and again with arrack to wash the viands down. His great, dark eyes, Camilla noticed, glanced constantly at Fate who sat across from him, an arm resting along the front rail of the box. "You are unimpressed, Mr. Locksley?" Dewhurst queried at last.

"With what?" Fate asked, his gaze meeting the duke's directly.

"With Vauxhall, boy. There're a good many people think it the best entertainment in all of London."

"Aye, so I've heard," replied Fate in a slow drawl quite unlike any of his own garbled but always enthusiastic tones. "I expect it is a fine entertainment, sir."

Camilla's own gaze flew to Fate so quickly and obviously that Neiland burst into laughter and Lilliheun was forced to shush him with a well-aimed kick to the shin.

"What is it, my dear?" asked Dewhurst, also noticing. "Is there perhaps something you wish to say?"

"Oh, oh, no, Your Grace. Only that everything is quite wonderful. And—and particularly the little chickens." Camilla's face felt quite warm as she heard the words emerge from between her lips and she discovered that she could not take them back. Good heavens, she had never spoken such drivel in her life. Who cared anything at all about tiny chickens? Not she. She wished to know where Fate had developed such a drawl and who had taught him suddenly to pronounce heard with an h and entertainment with all of its syllables audible.

From across the table, Lilliheun raised an eyebrow at her and then shook his head. Not me, he seemed to say. I had nothing to do with it. "Perhaps you would care for a short promenade, Miss Quinn," he suggested. "If Neiland and Lady Aurora will join us, we shall be adequately chaperoned, eh?"

"But that will leave the duke and Mr. Locksley all alone," protested Aurora. "Perhaps we ought to wait just a little, until mama and papa arrive. They did say they intended to join us as soon as they left Lady Saveage's rout."

"Yes, but that will be a while yet, I expect," Neiland offered. "Come, Rory, let's do walk a bit. Perhaps the duke and Locksley wish to be private, gudgeon," he added in a whisper as he helped her to rise.

"Oh, I had not thought. Of course, you are correct, David. I am certain they have a great deal to discuss."

"Do we have a great deal to discuss?" probed the duke thoughtfully as the quartet of young people departed. "I know not a bit more about you than I knew the day we met, Mr. Locksley. Except, of course, that somewhere you have learned to play the violin like a virtuoso. Otherwise, you appear to have nothing at all to say for yourself. Are you my grandson?"

Fate's gaze roamed the table and came to settle upon the remains of one of Camilla's acclaimed fowl.

"Look at me, lad. Are you my grandson or not?"

"I have not the least idea," drawled Fate. "That is something must be settled between you and the solicitors, no? How much does it cost?"

"What? The solicitors?"

Fate's eyes lit with laughter, but still he kept them lowered upon the carcass of the fowl. "No, that bird, sir."

"I have not the least—"

Fate lifted a tipsy brow at the duke and that gentleman stopped in midsentence and began again.

"Three shillings or thereabouts."

"What? For one?"

"Yes, for one."

"What s'preme gudgeons ye all are. 'Tis a wonder there's a one of ye got so much as a tuppence to yer name. Three shillin's'd feed the childer for a fortnite. An' them ain't chickens neither. Sparrows, I reckon. God didn't never make so tiny, pathetic a chicken in all of eternity."

Dewhurst's lips twitched at the corners, but he merely eyed Fate innocently and shrugged. "You are upset with our style of life, I assume," he said after a long pause. "But then, we of the Quality are quite complacent, you see. When one has the funds, one spends them."

"Tosses 'em away fer nothin'."

"No, Locksley, for enjoyment, entertainment, the finer things in life. You ought to accustom yourself to the idea. If you prove to be my grandson, you shall inherit a veritable fortune, you know."

"An' need ta take lessons on how ta throw it away?"

"Hardly," the duke laughed. "But you will not bother about a few shillings here and there, certainly. Not that I think you are truly bothered about them at the moment. 'Tis something other than the price of Vauxhall chickens on your mind, Locksley. Will you discuss it with me? No, do not attempt to recreate that bored drawl," he added as Fate took a deep breath and frowned thoughtfully. "I accept that you can pronounce an h now and again, and that you know some words have a number of syllables you generally dispose of, but to attempt to speak properly for the entire length of a conversation is like to prove inhibiting for you.''

"In-hib-iting?''

"Yes,'' grinned the duke. "It means that it will slow you down and make you think too much about how you say things, and so you will grow distracted and leave out a great deal of what you would normally say.''

"Oh. Well, I ain't a beetle-brain, ye know. Mossie said as how ye'd think me a beetle-brain the way I talks.''

Dewhurst placed his elbows on the table and rested his chin on his fists as he studied Fate intently. "I think you many things, Mr. Locksley, but I assure you, a beetle-brain is not one of them. Now, what's put you in the sulks?''

"I ain't in the sulks. I'm fidgeted.''

"Fidgeted? Over what? Have the gentlemen of the *ton* been giving you a bad time? Inclined to consider ourselves superior, you know. Unless I acknowledge you formally, the others will be inclined to doubt your antecedents. Will not let you into any of their clubs. Think you're an impostor.''

"Naw, ain't got nothin' ta do with none o' that. Got ta do with some friends o' mine, an' some strange thin's happenin' to 'em ever since I—''

"Ever since you what, Locksley?''

"Ever since I begun associatin' with swells. I always been a dangerous cove ta know, but I ain't never been this dangerous.''

Dewhurst's thick grey eyebrows rose and he leaned closer to Fate with undisguised curiosity animating his countenance. "Tell me,'' he urged quietly. "What is it that's been happening? You may trust me, my boy, I assure you. Grandson or not, you have Lilliheun blood somewhere in your veins and I have taken a liking to you as well. You'll do no better than to confide in me.''

Fate, who had never confided in anyone except Elgin Moss and from time to time Artie Radd, leaned back in his chair and studied the Duke of Dewhurst for a considerably long time.

Camilla and Aurora listened in horror as Lilliheun and Neiland described their odyssey into St. Giles and the recovery of Artie Radd. There were not yet a great number of people traversing the Grand Walk and the four were uninterrupted in their conversation by the need to acknowledge friends and acquaintances. This lack of interruption brought the hideousness of what they all assumed must always have been Fate's life home to them more intimately than any had intended. "And now it seems someone dogs his tracks and has taken it in mind to injure those closest to him," Lilliheun concluded on a near whisper. "We have some responsibility, I think, to help protect Radd and his children—and more than likely Locksley himself—for 'tis possible his coming forward to claim his inheritance brought these attacks about. If we had none of us taken him up, perhaps he and the Radds would be safe even now—at least from the particular ruffians who seem to be after them at the moment."

Camilla's hand tightened on Lilliheun's arm. "Oh, Clare, we knew only that Mr. Radd had been discovered. The children were not told, I think, that he was so terribly injured. They have been so very happy the past three days, singing and laughing, because Mr. Locksley had found their father for them. Most likely that is why he seems so very different this evening."

"Indeed. He has been at my digs every free moment, though there is not much he may do but sit with Radd and attempt to break into his ravings. Radd recognizes his voice, you see, and rests easier when he hears it. I doubt between Radd and the boy at Grosvenor Square that Locksley has had a bit of time to himself and he is quite likely exhausted. I'm amazed he makes a member of our party tonight."

"But he must. Dewhurst invited him and it would be sheer idiocy to turn down the man you wish to acknowledge you," Neiland offered. "Have you discovered anything at all, Lilliheun?"

"Discovered anything?" Aurora asked, tugging her brother to a standstill and turning to confront Clare who strolled behind them with Camilla. "What have you to discover, Mr. Lilliheun? Surely you are not become involved in this gruesome business?"

"Certainly I am become involved," replied Lilliheun immediately. "Do you expect me to stand by and do nothing? I rather think the man has become my friend and I am not like to allow a friend to suffer under such threats."

"But if what you fear is true—if—if—these ruffians are truly after Mr. Locksley, they will not stop at harming you."

"I should like to see the day that I am turned coward by some bully-ruffians," snorted Lilliheun angrily. "Whoever it is threatens Locksley and the Radds, they shall find their reign of terror brought to a halt, you may believe me."

Camilla was surprised to see how pale Aurora grew beneath the pretty Chinese lanterns strung along the path amidst the elms. She relinquished Lilliheun's arm and went to support her cousin. "Clare is quite capable of dealing with such heathens as these men must be," she said encouragingly. "And I am sure he will be very, very careful, won't you, Clare?"

"Of course we shall be careful," offered Neiland nonchalantly.

"Oh, not you as well, David," sighed Aurora. "You are not become involved?"

"What, Rory? Do you look to see me cry craven when I might be of help to Locksley and Lilliheun? I think not. Besides, m'dear, we shan't take on a passel of thieves and villains all on our own, you know. We shall simply look into the matter and drop a word at Bow Street when we discover what is going on."

That comment drew the blood from Camilla's face and Aurora took one look at her and gasped. "B-Bow Street? Oh, no! You cannot!"

"Hush, Rory, you promised," Camilla hissed. "You gave me your solemn vow."

"What solemn vow?" asked Lilliheun, placing Aurora's hand upon his arm and beginning to stroll again. "Do not look so fearful, my dear. The only ones who will be harmed, I assure you, will be the villains in this piece of work."

"B-but you are wrong to think that—that Mr. Locksley cannot protect himself and Mr. Radd. He is quite competent. It is merely that he did not once suspect Mr. Radd to be in danger. Now that he knows, he will take the matter into his own hands. He will not like for you and David to be involved."

"Then we will not tell him," offered Neiland from over her shoulder. "There is a mystery here, Rory, and I do not intend to be left out of it."

Camilla tugged on her cousin's arm angrily. "Cannot you see you are making things worse," she whispered hurriedly. "Honestly, David, you are such a gudgeon sometimes. Aurora is afraid for you and Lilliheun and you are increasing her fear by sounding so—so—enthusiastic."

By the time they returned to their box, the four had settled between them little more than not to speak of the matter for the remainder of the evening. Lord and Lady Wheymore had joined Dewhurst and Locksley and welcomed the quartet of young people with wide smiles and tales of Lady Saveage's rout that set them all to laughing. When at nine o'clock the great bell sounded and they all went to view the amazing magic of the Cascade with its miller's house and a rippling waterfall that turned the miller's wheel and frothed as though it was a real and a roaring spring, Camilla had all but decided that her perceptions upon the earlier stroll had been correct. Aurora was deeply smitten with Mr. Lilliheun, and Clare was in the midst of developing a *tendre* for the girl. The thought made Camilla rather nervous. Of course she had always known that the two would be perfectly matched, but in this first realization of a dawning relationship between them came a sense of loss.

"Why such ponderin'?" a voice whispered in her ear. " 'Tis fair magic how it flows, but 'tain't near as magical as other thin's I've seen. Smile, Dendron, please? I ain't askin' for myself, ye understand."

Camilla turned to meet Fate's eyes sparkling down at her and the corners of her mouth veered upward without the least thought. "Who for then, if not yourself, sir?"

"Why for this whole assembly. 'Twill make 'em sad do they see the prettiest gel here lookin' so sorrowful. Ye've been promenadin' with Lilliheun; will ye walk with me awhile? Or be ye too tired?"

"I am not in the least tired," replied Camilla taking his arm. "Where shall we walk?"

"There," he answered, pointing.

"No, I do not think so," smiled Camilla. "That is the Dark Walk and a young lady would be thoroughly compromised by parading there with a gentleman unchaperoned."

"I keep forgettin' about them thin's," mumbled Fate, running nervous fingers through his curls.

"What things, Mr. Locksley?"

"Them chaperones an' all. Ye got too many rules, Dendron. They's enough ta drive a man ta Bedlam. Does a chaperon gotta be anybody in perticular?"

"Why, no. Just someone extra."

"Good, 'cause then I knows just the person. Stanny," he called, reaching into the crowd and pulling out a short, wiry figure bedecked in rose pantaloons, a buff jacket, and a very natty catskin vest. "I needs ye for a bit, Stanny. Would ye mine helpin' me out?"

"Cap'n?"

"Aye."

"B'gad but I didn't almost rekernize ye all done up like a reg'lar swell! Anythin' ye want, m'dear. Ye name it an' 'tis done."

"I want ye ta come walkin' with us, Stanny."

Camilla watched as a number of gold coins made their way from Fate's pockets into Stanny's hands. "That's 'bout all I got at the moment. Is it enough?"

"More'n enough. Do it fer free, I would."

"I know, but it ain't right. Ye got a livin' ta make an' I be pullin' ye away from it. I reckon we must tell some'un as we're goin', eh, Dendron? I reckon tha's prob'ly a rule too."

Camilla grinned and nodded and led the way to Lady Wheymore's side. "Mr. Locksley and I are going for a stroll along the South Walk, Aunt Mary. I wish to show him the painting."

"Very well, my dear, but take Neiland or Aurora with you."

"But we have a chaperon, Aunt Mary. The man in the catskin vest. He is a bosom beau of Mr. Locksley's."

Lady Wheymore's brows came together in a disbelieving frown, but the earl, beside her, whispered in her ear and she gave a nod and sent Camilla on her way. "What makes you so positive, Ned, that Mr. Locksley's friend may be trusted?"

" 'Tis not his friend in whom I place my trust, Mary. 'Tis in Locksley himself. Fond of our Cammy, he is. He'd no more force his attentions upon the girl than plant himself before a runaway team, so it does not actually matter whom they take along to play propriety."

The South Walk down which they strolled followed at a good ten paces by the personage known as Stanny, was well-known for the remarkable painting of the ruins of Palmyra that stood at the far end of the path. Seen from afar, one might almost think the ruins were real. Fate, however, paid not the least bit of attention to what stood in the lights beyond, his eyes were all for Camilla and she felt herself begin to blush under his unguarded gaze. She advised him to look about and notice the beauty of the arches under which they passed, and began a discourse upon the history of the Gardens.

"I knows all 'bout 'em," Fate interrupted. "I been 'ere any number o' times. It ain't only swells allowed inta Vauxhall. I been 'ere ta a masquerade even—me an' Gwen. Weren't much fun, but profitable."

"Oh," replied Camilla stumped for a moment. "Oh!" she said again as his meaning dawned upon her. "You came here to steal!"

"Well, ta filch a cartwheel er two from unsuspectin' pockets, aye. 'Tis why Stanny's 'ere tonight."

"Do you know that for a fact, Captain?"

"Not if ye were the Watch, I wouldn't, no. Wouldn't

have no least idea why Stanny come—except ta see the magic. But 'e don't know how ta do nothin' else, Stanny don't. 'E didn't 'ave the benefits of a proper edjucation like Mossie give me."

"I see."

"Do ye, Dendron?"

"What?"

"Do ye see? When ye look at me, do ye see what I am? I saw 'ow ye jumped at the table when I come out with proper words. Near ta took yer breath away, it did. Scared ye."

"It did not. I was merely surprised to hear you speak so—so properly."

"I can, ye know, if I put m'mind to it. I ain't no ignorant cove what can't learn nothin' more'n what 'e knows already."

"Of course you are not."

"No, an' I ain't no fearsome villain neither, nor no bully–ruffian."

Camilla could not fathom where in the world this conversation of his was meant to lead, but she nodded supportively. He came to a halt on that nod beneath the second of the archways and looked around him, then led her aside to a small stone bench that sat just a bit off the pathway in the midst of some rose bushes.

He searched through his pockets rapidly, muttered under his breath, and searched again. "Damnation, but I fergot m'handkerchief jus' like Mossie said I would!" He began to struggle out of his coat and was spreading it on the bench before Camilla could think of a word to say. "There, that's the ticket. Now yer skirts won't take no damp ner nothin'." He urged her to a seat and then began to pace silently back and forth before her.

The man called Stanny came up to them, grinned a gaptoothed grin at Camilla and took himself silently to lean against the arch and stare off in the opposite direction. In a matter of nine or ten paces, the captain spun himself down beside her. His legs stretched out before him, his hands clasped together between his knees, he leaned slightly forward and stared at the grass beneath his feet.

"I ain't no bully–ruffian," he repeated very quietly. "I been lots of things what ye wouldn't be proud ta know of, but I never did kilt no un, nor took part in the beatin' of a cove senseless fer ta earn a wage, nor took no freedoms with no morts what weren't willin' of it. I reckon I done shot a bloke er two on the High Toby, but I didn't never shot 'em dead. I a'ways made sure I didn't."

"I am certain you were most careful," murmured Camilla, a great sadness welling up about her heart and giving it a distinct and painful twist. "I am certain you have always done the best you could not to harm anyone."

"Aye, that's the truth, Dendron. Course I been forced ta do a bit of harm now an' agin—like that flash cove what I throwed out o' Gwennie's window that night ye an' The Banshee was with me—but it were a necessary thin', that. An' he didn't die."

"I am pleased to hear that."

"Aye. But—but—" His great dark eyes flashed at her suddenly and what she thought she saw there took her breath away. "Dendron, I ain't sure-certain what ye see when ye look at me. That's what I'm sayin'. I'm sayin' what I am, so ye can't be mistakin' me for some un else—for some un like that Bad Jack Pharo what's in yer book—or—or this Locksley bloke. I ain't honorable nor courageous nor none of that sentimen'al swill—nor I ain't some lost heir of some righteous duke with all the flimsies in the worl' jus' fallin' outta 'is pockets. I ain't no more them than I be a bully-ruffian. I just be me, Jason Fate. I don't even be a captain truly. That part's maked up. An' all my life I just done whatever I figgered I could ta stay alive. An' I ain't never in my life thought ta see the day when a—a *angel* like yerself would come upon me."

He shifted beside her and a strong, tense arm went carefully around her shoulders and a sturdy, but somehow gracefully elegant, hand took hers, and Camilla thought that even in the shadows of the lanterns she could see his very soul rising to meet her in his eyes. "I ain't no gen'leman, Dendron, an' I ain't got no right ta be sayin' of these thin's to ye. No, nor I didn't never expect ta be a sayin' of 'em ta any swell lady. But I reckon as how I love ye beyond

anythin'. An' I reckon as how ye ought ta be knowin' it.
An' I don't oncet think I be good enough or smart enough
or proper enough for ye to look at twicet, but ye own
m'soul, Dendron. I give it to ye here an' now, freely an'
without no plottin' or plannin' involved in't. 'Tis yers ta
do with what ye wish, now an' forever."

Camilla shivered and wrapped her arms tightly about
him in the night. She buried her face in the fine white
linen of his cravat and inhaled deeply the scent of vanilla
that rose from it. She felt his arms go around her as well
and her heart beat rapidly as they held her possessively to
him. His lips brushed her hair and tasted tentatively of
her brow.

She looked up at him and his lips came gently down
upon her own, but they did not part from her as they
had before. Instead their pressure increased and then his
tongue whispered across her lips and she felt the most
horrendous aching in the very pit of her stomach and she
pulled him even more tightly to her, longing to be one
with him, to somehow melt straight into him and never
be separated from him again, and she kissed him back—
over and over—her passions rising until she thought she
must shatter. It was he who pulled free of the maelstrom
first and eased her back to a realization of where they were.
" 'Tis time ta return ta the others," he murmured in her
ear. "I reckon they'll be worried about ye. I would not
trust ye with a cove like me for much longer, m'self."

He stood and helped her up, retrieving his coat and
shrugging into the form-fitting garment as best he could
without the help of his valet. Then he grinned and made
an attempt to straighten the little circlet of flowers in her
hair and the rumpled silk scarf about her shoulders.
"There, I reckon ye'll do," he whispered glancing over
his shoulder at Stanny whose gaze remained steadily away
from them. "Don't be forgettin' what I said, Dendron.
Don't be thinkin' 'twas some pretty speech like what the
Quality bucks be spoutin' at the drop of a lady's 'kerchief.
Ye been ownin' me heart for near a month, an' from this
night on, ye be the keeper of Jason Fate's soul as well."

Chapter 14

On the entire drive back from Vauxhall, Fate huddled in the far corner of Lilliheun's coach across from Clare and Neiland, replied only sparingly to their sallies, and spent most of his time gazing in silence out into the darkness. "You are exhausted, Locksley," Lilliheun proclaimed at last. "I told Miss Quinn so and I was correct. What you ought to do is take yourself straight to bed and—"

"I'd like ta look in on Radd firs'."

"I rather think he'll do fine without you," Neiland offered. "It's nearing one o'clock, and you truly do look as if you haven't slept for weeks. We'll drop you at Grosvenor Square, no?"

"If Radd is greatly improved or—or otherwise—I shall send you word immediately," Lilliheun assured. "I expect he will be asleep and we'll have not a word out of him until daylight. The tonic Dr. Snoresmore left with us appears to be doing him a great deal of good. Cammert got some down him just before we left tonight and he drifted right off to sleep. I rather think you ought to do the same."

Fate nodded. He *was* tired, more tired than he could ever remember being in his entire life. And his mind would not stay upon Artie Radd or Harley or even the conversation inside the coach. It seemed all cushioned about with the softness of Dendron and lit with fuzzy fireworks inside his brain. He descended the steps in front of the Eversley mansion, bid Neiland and Lilliheun goodnight, and nearly stumbled as he climbed the front steps and opened the door.

"He's about had it, eh, Neiland? I think I have too. Let you off at your digs or are you bound for one of the clubs?"

"No, Great Russell Street will do nicely, thank you," sighed Neiland. "I shall make an early night of it and tomorrow you and I, my dearest Clare, will be off in search of villains."

"I ought not let you join in, Neiland. Your sister will lay

anything that happens to you at my door and I rather think I should hate for that to happen.''

A small smile crept over Neiland's countenance in the darkness of the coach. ''Becoming attracted to Rory, Lilliheun? I never would have believed it. Thought you would carry the willow for Cammy all the way to your grave.''

''Camilla wants merely to be my friend,'' groaned Lilliheun, ''and she means it, I fear. I don't know how it is, Neiland, but she cannot think we shall suit. She has told me again and again, and finally, I think, I must believe her. And your sister—''

''My sister is a minx with a mind of her own and she's trampled a number of hearts already. Turned down an offer from Farview only two days ago. Father says as how she has set her cap for a certain gentleman and will have him come hell or high water.''

''Who?'' Lilliheun asked, startled. ''Which gentleman? It ain't that rascal, Donleavy? He's been near living in her pocket the last fortnight. Or Raspberry? No, don't tell me it's Raspberry! If it's that fribble, I don't want to know.''

Neiland chuckled. ''No, Clare, it ain't Raspberry or Donleavy. Someone else entirely. Quiet gentleman, steady, dependable, you know the type.''

''A dead bore,'' declared Lilliheun irascibly.

''No, really Clare, he ain't all that bad. A bit thick when it comes to the ladies. Stiff-rumped, too, from time to time,'' grinned Neiland, ''though he's not nearly as high a stickler as he once was—been seen driving about the town with the most outrageous character of late. And I happen to know that he's lowered his standards so much as to welcome one of the Great Unwashed into his own digs.''

''M-me?'' stuttered Lilliheun in such innocent surprise that it sent Neiland off into gales of laughter. ''No, really Neiland, you ain't hoaxing me?''

''I shouldn't think of it, you beetle-brain. Rory has had her eye on you since first I brought you home from school with me when we were twelve. She hoped that as soon as she was out of the schoolroom, you might take notice of her.''

"W-well, I have. I have noticed her. Only I always thought of her as a child. But she is not so much a child now. She's grown, ain't she?"

"I rather think she has, Clare. Grown quite a bit. Why do you think Cammy has been forever throwing you in Rory's way?"

"To get rid of me," grinned Lilliheun.

"Well, Cam knows perfectly well that Rory has developed a *tendre* for you—more than a *tendre*. The chit's determined to bring you up to scratch. And knowing m'sister, she'll succeed."

Lilliheun could not stop grinning. He bid Neiland goodnight at that gentleman's lodgings, sent the coachman off to the stables when he reached his own digs, and was still grinning as he let himself into his chambers. It was not until he looked up to discover a grim and pale-faced Cammert seated stiffly upon the edge of the chintz sopha that the grin faded. "Cammert, what is it, man? Radd has not—"

"No, no, sir. He is not dead. He has, in fact, been sleeping peacefully ever since you left."

"Then what's got you upset, Cammert? Obviously you've suffered some shock."

"Yes, sir. Oh, I—would you care for anything, sir, brandy perhaps?" Cammert, suddenly realizing he sat immobile in the presence of his master, rose quickly.

Lilliheun pushed the little man back down. "I know where the brandy is, Cammert, and I shall pour us both a glass, eh? And then you will confide in me what has got you so visibly upset." Lilliheun filled two glasses, carried one to Cammert, and settled himself into a well-worn wing chair with the other. "Now, what's got you fidgeted?" he asked solicitously, crossing one leg over the other. "You look like you have seen a ghost."

Cammert, who had been valet to Lilliheun's father before his death and whose allegiance to the son was beyond question, shook his head slowly from side to side and took a sizeable swallow of the golden liquid. "Not a ghost, y'lordship. Nay, not any sort of spirit whatever."

"What then?"

"This," sighed the man, opening his palm and displaying a crumpled piece of paper. Lilliheun took the thing, set it upon his knee, and attempted to press some of the creases out of it to make it more readable. "Where? Who?" mumbled Lilliheun as he stared at the scribbled words. "How did this come to be here, Cammert? 'Tis a hoax of some kind surely."

"It came through the window of the second bedchamber, sir, tied around a rock."

"The window was open?"

"No, sir, the window was closed. 'Tis open now until I can contact a glazier in the morning. Called Mr. Grims, I did, from downstairs, and he and I managed to secure a board across it, but 'twill not hold should anyone care to try a hand at breaking in."

"Someone threw a rock through my window?"

"Yes, sir, with that infamous note attached."

"But—" Lilliheun eyed the scribbling again.

"It barely missed my head. Looking to Mr. Radd, I was, at the time. I thought someone had fired a pistol at us."

ye be a dedman rad an yer fren fate to does ye bring um inta it

Lilliheun read the thing aloud and then read it again. "Then the men who beat Radd have traced him here. But how? Surely there is no possible connection between— your friend, Fate?—No, that cannot mean Captain Jason Fate. Radd cannot be a highwayman. Locksley would have known if he were. Locksley is practically one of the Radd family." Lilliheun's eyes grew dark with anger at the thought of the villains daring to invade his own chambers and cursed under his breath as he crumpled the note and tossed it toward the empty grate. " 'Tis not worth the time it takes to read it, Cammert. I shall have the Watch around in the morning and the Runners as well if necessary. Mr. Radd is safe here and you as well, old fellow. I shall see to your protection myself. These rock-throwers are nothing more than cowards, afraid to come upon Mr. Radd's protectors face to face."

Cammert choked down another swallow of brandy and

Lilliheun was quick to notice how the glass shook in the valet's hand.

"No, really, Cammert. You've nothing to fear. I vow it."

"I—I—you don't fully under—understand, sir," stuttered the valet.

"What don't I understand, Cammert?"

"I—I—Mr. Radd awakened when the rock entered, sir, and called out."

"Called out?"

"Yes, sir. 'Jason!' he called. 'Pistols!'"

Lilliheun frowned. "Well, but you said the window breaking sounded like a pistol shot."

"It did, sir. But 'twas 'Jason' he called to, and—"

"And what, Cammert? Out with it!"

"'Tis what he calls Mr. Locksley, sir, when he's wandering in his mind," murmured the valet quietly.

Lilliheun's eyebrows raised and he stared at Cammert as he lifted the glass of brandy to his lips. When he had taken a sip and rested the glass back upon his knee, the corners of his mouth were turning upward in a disbelieving smile. "You think that Locksley is Captain Jason Fate, Cammert? Is that it? Locksley?"

"Yes, I expect 'tis exactly what sprang to my mind."

"Yes, well, you may dispose of that idea, Cammert. Mr. Locksley's given name *was* Jason. He told me, in fact, that he had not the least idea he was born John until Eversley tracked him down and informed him of it. It was Eversley, I expect, told him he must answer to John Locksley and not the name he had grown accustomed to. But he is most certainly not the nefarious Captain Jason Fate, Cammert. Why there ain't a dastardly quality attaches to the man! I expect the villains who scribbled that message have made a mistake in regard to Radd as well."

"But—but how can you be so certain, sir, as to Mr. Locksley, I mean."

"Because Miss Quinn's coach was stopped by this villain, Fate, on the moor. Do you not remember, Cammert? And she saw Captain Fate face to face. Though she could not describe him for Bow Street, most surely she would recognize him again were they to meet, and she and Mr. Locksley have met time and time again."

The color had slowly been seeping back into the little valet's face and he gave a great sigh of relief at Lilliheun's explanation. "Well, then," he said with a tentative smile, " 'tis all some great misunderstanding—and I as guilty of it as the rapscallions who tossed that stone. I have every confidence that no young lady of Quality would think to equivocate about such a great matter as the identity of a highwayman, sir—especially not your young lady. I am most greatly relieved. And I shall trust you as to our continued safety."

"Thank you, Cammert. I assure you, your trust is not misplaced. Now, might we both retire do you think? It has been a long evening, Cammert, and my eyes are refusing to remain open any longer."

Camilla and Aurora were to be found sitting prettily in the long drawing room the next day entertaining a number of morning callers while Lady Wheymore played chaperon. The group of young people were busily discussing the likelihood of an excursion to the Tower, Mr. Dunleavy and Miss Diana Appleby proposing that they hire a boat of some sort and enter by the Traitor's Gate. "It would be the most exciting thing," urged Miss Appleby in a quiet, well-bred voice tinged with enthusiasm. "Think of all the villains who were carried to imprisonment in just such a way!"

"I prefer not to think of it," smiled Mr. Jonathan Gale, who was a robust young man with the deadliest shirt points Camilla had ever seen. "It is a deal more pleasant to think of the crown jewels and how wonderful they would look upon such lovely ladies as are now assembled."

"Doing it too brown, Gale," laughed Dunleavy. "Besides, ladies are intrigued with villains."

"Oh, yes," agreed Aurora with a gleam in her eye for Cammy, "especially the handsome, athletic sort who are not truly evil, but merely misguided. Those with fearsome reputations but golden hearts."

"Do you not remember that exquisite villain in *The Intrepid Heart?*" offered Lady Daphne Neuman with a sigh. "I am certain that were I the heroine, I should have been quite capable of reforming him and I should have run off with him to Gretna Green in a moment if only he had asked me."

"Oh?" murmured Captain Harry Walker of the Horse Guards. "Then perhaps we must all run off and become villains, gentlemen. I shall become Captain Jason Fate, of course, because I have spent the major part of my time the last thirty days riding back and forth across Finchley's Common in aimless pursuit of that rapscallion—who, by the way, appears to have vanished from the face of the earth."

"What, not a sign of him, Walker?" asked Dunleavy with a sudden scowl. "Frightened him off for good do you think?"

"I don't think we have frightened him off at all, Dunleavy. I rather think he was warned somehow and has gone off on holiday until he has word we have given up the chase. Never had one sighting of him—not even the first night."

"Possibly he is a good deal more intelligent than you give him credit for, gentlemen," offered a low voice from behind Walker's shoulder. Captain Walker spun around and blinked in amazement. "Your Grace, I did not see you enter."

"No, by George, you did not, nor any of the rest of you young scamps. But here I am nonetheless and about to write *fine* to your plotting and planning for one morning. Lady Aurora, Miss Quinn, I have Lady Wheymore's permission to spirit the two of you away with me. Run get your bonnets or whatever lovely damsels wear these days. My coach awaits us at the front steps." So saying, the Duke of Dewhurst bowed politely to the assemblage, bestowed a kiss upon Lady Wheymore's hand, and strolled from the room to await the girls in the hall. "And do not dawdle, my dears, for the horses are fresh and eager to be off," he added as Camilla and Aurora hurried up the staircase to fetch hats and pelisses and gloves.

"Where are we bound, Your Grace?" Camilla asked, as she settled herself into the crested coach beside Aurora. "Would you rather not sit facing the horses, sir? It is often uncomfortable to ride facing the rear."

"For we elderly people do you mean?" grinned Dewhurst as the vehicle began to jolt over the cobbles. "No, I am only teasing, Miss Quinn. And I am quite comfortable where I am, thank you. Besides, we are not going far."

"Where are we going, Your Grace?" Aurora queried gazing about at the powder blue upholstery and the fine cut-glass vases that held a rosebud beside each door.

"Only for a ride in the park, my dear. Tell me, what was all this talk of Captain Jason Fate? I have heard, of course, who he is, but why is his name being bantered about in your drawing room?"

"Oh, it was only Captain Walker funning us about becoming a villain to ensnare the ladies."

"I see. Well, he will need to change himself a good bit to become Captain Fate, won't he? Have to swap his golden curls for dark and whittle himself down a bit, and change his speech entirely of course. And even then it will take a great wrenching of his dignity to come anywhere near Locksley's insouciance, will it not? Walker has always been rather proper. No, I cannot for the life of me see him making the change. Can you, Miss Quinn?"

Camilla stared wide-eyed at the duke, her lips parted, a tinge of pink heightened the color of her cheeks. Aurora gave a little squeak. Her hands flew to cover her mouth.

"Yes, m'dears, I am very well aware that Mr. Locksley and Captain Jason Fate are one and the same. And I am also aware that you have kept this fact from everyone, including your father, Aurora."

"But—but—how?" cried Aurora. "Was it Mr. Borhill? Oh, dear, I knew he should discover it with all his minions probing about!"

"Oh, Your Grace," pleaded Camilla reaching across to take his aging hands into her own. "Please do not betray him. He is not truly a villain. I vow he is not. And he shall never rob a coach again—or—or—anything of that nature. And—and—I shall repay whatever he has stolen from the funds mama and papa left me. I promise I will. Please, sir, he is a good man at heart. It is only that he does not truly understand how wrong he is to do such—such things.''

'' 'Tis only that he cares not in the least how he takes the *ton*'s money, as long as he takes it,'' replied Dewhurst. ''Look how he sets himself up to be my grandson. Do you not find that in the least despicable? And the two of you—such properly raised young women—to go along with him in such a scheme!''

''Cammy is fond of him,'' declared Aurora, her bright blue eyes meeting the duke's directly, ''and I am fond of him as well.''

''And he *could be* your grandson,'' Camilla added imploringly. ''He does not at all *know* who he truly is. He was raised by gypsies and made to steal for them and when they died, he knew not who he really was or any other way to go on.''

''The gypsies, my dear, did not just die,'' drawled Dewhurst, allowing Camilla to keep hold of his hands. ''They were hanged at Tyburn before the lad's eyes, and he has despised both the Government and Polite Society ever since, for he blames the entire Upper Class for their deaths and for the misery and poverty that has always surrounded him. At least he did until one night upon Finchley's Common when his opinion of at least one of our numbers began to undergo a decided change.''

''H-how do you know all this?'' Camilla asked in wonder, releasing the duke's hands and leaning back against the squabs. ''Has Mr. Borhill discovered everything about him, then?''

''Borhill, as far as I know, has discovered nothing, m'dear.'' Dewhurst with a quick smile reached upward to tap at the little trap door above his head. When the coachman opened it, the duke instructed him to circle Hyde Park and to continue to do so until further notice. ''Andrew Borhill has not thought to ask the right person about our Mr. Locksley. I, on the other hand, have.''

''Whom? Whom did you ask, Your Grace?''

''Why, I asked Locksley, Miss Quinn. Or should I say,

Captain Fate? He is an intelligent young man, regardless of his obvious shortcomings, and brave as he can stare. For all he knew I might have summoned the Watch immediately he began to speak truth to me at Vauxhall, but he was more concerned for your and Lady Aurora's safety than for his own neck."

"For our safety?" whispered Aurora, puzzled. "But why should he fear for our safety?"

"It seems that some associates of the captain's have been seriously harmed of late and though he is not certain what it is all about, he has come to think that 'twould be better to err on the side of security and arrange for the protection of those close to him—you and Camilla and some children named Radd especially, though he is anxious over Lilliheun's and Neiland's safety as well. He has sought my advice and assistance in the matter and I intend to give it to him. That, m'dears, is why Lord and Lady Wheymore, the two of you, these children and Neiland and Lilliheun will accompany me to my estate at Longbourne. I expect I shall invite Eversley as well. We shall call it a house party, I think."

"And the captain, Your Grace?" asked Camilla quietly.

"The captain will remain in London and attempt to discover the source of the threat. If it turns out to be beyond his power to bring the thing to a close, then he will ride to Longbourne and seek my help. 'Tis a matter of a half-day's ride at the most that will separate us, and the lad thinks he will deal more easily with the problem once he knows the lot of you are safe. Marshall," he added, tapping at the trap, "take us to Gunter's."

"Yes, Yer Grace," the coachman called back.

Neiland stared at the window that the glazier was rapidly repairing and then back at the crumpled note that Lilliheun had retrieved from the parlor grate. "Has Locksley seen it?"

"No, not as yet. Ought I show it to him do you think? I convinced Cammert it is all some misunderstanding—the part where Fate is mentioned, I mean, but—"

"But the fact that it was tied to a rock thrown through your window was not a mistake, old fellow, and must be attended to. Have you called in the Runners? Spoken to the Watch?"

"No, Neiland, I ain't done nothing yet," growled Lilliheun. "I have just tumbled from the clothmarket. Do I look like a man ready to meet the public, much less anyone from Bow Street?" Lilliheun rubbed sleepily at uncombed hair and wandered from the room where Radd still slept under the influence of another dose of tonic back into his own bedchamber. Cammert had just set out his shaving kit and was busily stropping an ebony-handled straight razor. Neiland bounced down onto the unmade bed and watched as Cammert covered Clare's face with lather and began to shave him. By the time the morning shadow had been removed from cheeks and chin and Lilliheun had donned suitable morning dress, Radd was stirring in the adjoining chamber, Cammert had gone off to procure them some breakfast, and Jason Fate was climbing the stairs to Lilliheun's apartments.

"Come in, Locksley," Neiland urged, opening the door at Fate's knock. "Radd is just beginning to wake. The fever has gone completely, we think."

Fate nodded, raised a hand in Lilliheun's direction, and strolled through the parlor into the bedchamber where Radd lay and the glazier was just gathering up his gear.

"What 'appened?" Fate asked and received a disbelieving stare from the craftsman for having dropped his h.

" 'Twas a rock thrown through the window, my lord."

Fate's grin set the man back a moment. "A rock, eh? Done a fine job o' fixin' it, ain't ye? Can't tell a thin'."

"N-no, my lord."

"I ain't no lord. Just done up like un, which I can see yer suspectin' an' which is the truth o' it. Won 'erful queer, ain't it, ta see me in this rig-out an' then 'ear me talk? I reckon 'tis 'bout the best joke in all o' Lunnon."

The glazier laughed and left the room and Fate pulled a straight-backed chair up beside Radd's bed and placed the back of his hand against the man's cheek. "Ye're cooler," he muttered.

"Jason?" Radd's eyes opened wearily as far as they were able.

"Aye, Artie, 'tis me."

"I be home then? I can't be stayin' home, Jason, they'll fine me and the childer'll be in danger."

"Naw, ye ain't home, Artie, an' the childer be safe as 'ouses. Ye be in the chambers of a fren of mine. Ye been here for days, an' this be the first time ye made a bit of sense. What 'appened?"

"I—I—" Radd groaned and Fate, abandoning the chair, settled himself on the edge of the bed where the man might see him easily. "Talk ta me, Artie," he urged quietly, "before one of the others comes walkin' in 'pon us. Who done this to ye?"

"Dan'l Peace an' 'is lot."

"S'blood," cursed Fate under his breath. "What was ye doin' with them, Artie? That lot'd pull yer fingernails out with a pliers jus' for a evenin's en'ertainment. Ye know better'n ta git involved with Dan'l Peace."

"I didn't mean ta, Jason," groaned Radd, "but he come ta the 'ouse a lookin' fer ye an' when I telled 'im ye was gone an' not like ta be back, he an' them blokes a his said as 'ow they had a propersition fer me." Pain was evident in Radd's eyes, but he fought his way through it to explain. "Said as 'ow they wanted me jus' ta teach 'em how ta waylay a coach like we done an' they was willin' ta pay a 'stravagant amount. I reckon I shoulda knowed better'n ta b'lieve 'em. They wanta waylay a coach, arright, but only 'cause they wanta kill the bloke what's gonna be a ridin' in't. An' then they wanta lay the whole thin' at yer door."

Chapter 15

Fate did his best to reassure Radd, guaranteed him that Daniel Peace hadn't the least chance of laying anything at his doorstep and that from that moment on Peace had little chance at all of avoiding the beating of his life. But the truth was that Fate knew it imperative to Radd's health that he hold his own emotions in check and he strove mightily to keep the man from divining both the depth of his anger and the extent of his fear. It was a great relief to the captain, in fact, when Cammert appeared at the chamber door with a tray and inquired whether or not Mr. Radd might be able to eat a bit. Fate gratefully gave up his place to Lilliheun's valet and wandered down the hall to the small dining room where Lilliheun and Neiland confronted him with China tea and a plate piled high with beefsteak and shirred eggs. "I'll wager you have not eaten a thing as yet, you're here so early," Lilliheun drawled.

"And you ate barely enough to choke a sparrow at Vauxhall last evening," contributed Neiland. "Sit down, Locksley, and dig in."

Fate's tipsy eyebrow rose as his glance roamed between the two of them. " 'Tis some'at of a trap, ain't it?" he murmured, pulling a chair up to the table.

"A trap?" Neiland stopped with a forkful of beefsteak half way to his mouth. "What makes you say that, Locksley?"

"I see it in yer eyes, m'dear. 'Ave ye talked ta Artie? Is that it?"

"No, we have not spoken with Radd as yet," offered Lilliheun around a mouthful of biscuit. "Is he making sense this morning?"

"Aye. If it ain't Artie gots ye fidgety, what is it then?"

"Nothing," drawled Neiland with a quick look at Lilliheun. "We are not a bit fidgety, are we Clare?"

"Not a bit of it, David. We are quite composed, Locksley.

Simply enjoying a pleasant breakfast and pleased to have you join us. Like some jam on that biscuit?''

"No. I reckon there's enough of somethin' else bein' spread about here without addin' jam to't.''

Neiland's lips twitched upward and Lilliheun laughed outright. "I swear, Locksley, you're impossible!'' Neiland protested. "We thought to set the thing aside until you'd gotten some decent food into you and were feeling outright complacent.''

"What I'm feelin' is outright s'picious.''

"You've a sixth sense about such matters, obviously,'' chuckled Lilliheun, fishing about in his pockets and producing the note which had arrived so ignominiously the evening before. "Here. This is what we wish to discuss with you,'' he said, handing the crumpled paper across the table to Fate. "Came through Radd's bedchamber window last night attached to a rock.''

Fate unfolded the note, stared down at it, turned it over, stared down at it again. "What's it say?'' he mumbled, and held it up before his eyes.

"I know it ain't particularly well-written, Locksley,'' chuckled Neiland, "but it ain't that hard to—''

Lilliheun made hushing gestures in Neiland's direction then stood and strolled over to stand behind Fate's chair. "'Ye be a dedman rad an yer fren fate to does ye bring um inta it,''' he read aloud, haltingly. "Badly scribbled. Wouldn't be able to read it myself if I did not have a cousin wrote just as badly. Frightened Cammert near to death, let me tell you, when it came crashing through that pane.'' Lilliheun took the note from Fate's hands and stuffed it back into a pocket and went back to his own chair.

"Soun's like somethin' Peace'd write,'' muttered the captain, leaning back and sipping at his tea.

"Peace?''

"Aye, Dan'l Peace. 'Tis the cove what's af'er Artie.''

"How on earth—Lilliheun, do you *know* anyone called Daniel Peace?'' asked Neiland.

"Not a soul. Why?''

"Well, how did he find Radd then? I will swear that no one followed us here that night.''

"Naw, they didn't," murmured Fate. "If they'd a been followin' of us, they'd 'ave attacked us, an' we'd all be deadmen. Peace be a reg'lar thatchgallows, an' not like ta quibble over a few extra coves lyin' at his feet. He might done been lookin' fer Artie all this time an' one a his cronies seen me comin' in here an' looked inta it so ta speak."

"I expect that's possible," mused Lilliheun. "Do you think this Daniel Peace responsible for Harley's accident?"

"Might could a been some of 'is chums. Wouldn't a been Dan'l. Harley woulda rekernized Dan'l."

"That's it then," muttered Neiland. "We shall call in the Runners and put them onto this man's scent. Unless— Radd is not truly acquainted with Captain Jason Fate, is he, Locksley? The note mentioned Fate, and if the Runners think him involved with the man, they'll arrest Radd as well as Peace."

"Ye bean't settin' no Runners onta nobody!" exclaimed Fate, rising from his chair and stomping off into the parlor, followed cautiously by the other two gentlemen. "There ain't no case fer ta be bringin' them cowardly snitches inta it! I be the one what'll deal with Peace, an' in m'own way."

"But, Locksley, they've beaten your friend near to death," Lilliheun pointed out quietly as he watched Fate's hands tighten into fists, relax, and tighten again. "Like as not they'll do the same to you."

"I should like ta see the day!" shouted Fate, slamming his fist into the top of a wing chair. "They be nothin' but cowards an' crows, an' I should like ta see the day I don't be holdin' m'own against 'em."

"Yes, but, they have threatened to kill Radd and—and Fate—you never did say if Radd is acquainted with Fate, you know—and I expect they'll extend the threat to you should you go after them." Neiland stood with one arm along the fireplace mantle, absorbed with Locksley's reaction to the situation. He had witnessed anger many times in his life—from his father's imperious bellows to his friends' silent, haughty stares to the sharp-tongued assassinations of several good fellows by certain jealous snakes among the *ton*. But he had never seen such incredibly controlled anger as Locksley displayed before him now. He had the distinct notion that were this Peace fellow to enter the room at that very moment, Locksley would explode like a cannonade and the chamber be filled with flying shell casings and deadly shot. Yet aside from pounding once on Lilliheun's chair, and raising his voice a bit, Locksley remained outwardly exceeding calm. "Does Radd know Fate, Locksley?"

" 'Course Artie knows Fate. Most ever'body in St. Giles knows Fate. I knows Fate—that don't got nothin' ta do with it!"

"You know Fate?" Lilliheun queried with a glance at Neiland. "Broke David's arm, he did."

"Prob'ly didn't stand an' deliver like he tole ye, eh, Neiland? Goed af'er 'im with somethin' most like. Fate don't stand around lettin' the Quality pound on 'im, ye know."

"No, I can certainly vouch for that," nodded Neiland. "He knocked the swordstick from my hand with one blow and twisted my arm enough to break it before I knew what had happened."

"I expect he didn't mean for ta break it," Fate mumbled with a rather shamefaced expression that set Lilliheun to pondering. "He don't reg'larly go about hurtin' people."

"Just steals from them," offered Lilliheun quietly.

"Aye, same as all them bar'sters, an' bankers, an' swells, an' the Fat Prince an' his mates an' the whole bloody government. He just does it more personal like."

Somers, with a splendidly blank look upon his face which hid a great deal of pride for the accomplishments of his friend, Glasgow, across the square, entered the morning room and to the accompaniment of a series of delighted exclamations from Lady Wheymore and Lady Aurora and a visiting Miss Amanda Potts and her mother Mrs. Potts, presented Camilla with a small silver vase filled with iris, sweet williams, candytufts and forget-me-nots, surrounded by cuttings of rosemary and thyme and lavender. Beside it, on the salver, lay a gentleman's calling card with one corner discreetly folded.

Camilla's eyes lit as she read the imprinted name. "Oh, how lovely," she smiled, sniffing at the blooms. "You must send Mr. Locksley up at once, Somers." Camilla's eyes sparkled into the butler's with the shared secret of the first posey and the first morning call Mr. Locksley had paid her, and they were both for a moment very close to laughter.

"Mr. Locksley begs to be excused, miss, knowing there's company, and asks if perhaps you will join him for a stroll in Green Park whenever convenient. Shall I tell him yes, Miss Camilla? He plans to take the children as well, if you are amenable."

"An excellent idea. Tell him, Somers, that the girls and I shall await him at two o'clock, if that is all right with you, Aunt," she added with a smile at Lady Wheymore.

"Quite acceptable, m'dear, but you must take one of the footmen with you and perhaps Annie."

Annie, no more than a child herself, was a little kitchen maid whose experience with myriad brothers and sisters had made her a favourite with Jolly and Grig and she had been given a transfer of duties because of it, released from the kitchen and sent to the nursery. She delighted in this respite from pots and pans and being a most intelligent and creative child, could be counted upon to keep the younger ones out from under foot while they remained at Wheymore House.

Camilla agreed eagerly, certain that Annie would enjoy the outing as much as the other children.

"And Gregory, Mama," Aurora suggested. "Let Gregory be the footman who attends. He is marvelous with the children."

Lady Wheymore chuckled. "Indeed, and do not think that I am unaware of Gregory's other attributes."

Mrs. Potts raised a questioning eyebrow as all of the girls, including her own Amanda, giggled.

"He is," Lady Wheymore explained, "the most conformable young man and not like to oppose a bit of high spirits. The girls are fond of him on that account. I have, in fact, never once heard Gregory grumble. I do not believe there is a churlish bone in his body."

"And he is very handsome in his livery and exceeding tall and straight and imposing," offered Aurora. "Everyone envies us when Gregory trails in our wake."

"Enough," chuckled Lady Wheymore. "Off with all of you. I am certain Camilla needs your help to decide upon which walking dress she shall wear and I know Amanda will enjoy helping the little girls—I do believe that Mrs. Dailey has sewn new dresses for them both and sent them over only yesterday. Lord Eversley's housekeeper has been magnificent through this whole episode," she added to Mrs. Potts as the girls hurried upstairs to Camilla's chambers. "She has both little boys under her charge across the square and still finds time to provide clothes and treats for the girls and the baby. Now they have found the children's father, of course, we have all begun to dread the day he will be well enough to take them from us."

Mrs. Potts, who was one of the few ladies thoroughly inculcated with the zeal for reform propagated by Lady Wheymore of late, nodded thoughtfully. "But is it not possible to discover a position for the father? Surely the man will be shown to possess some abilities."

"Oh, Wheymore is set upon it. He has given me his word that none of them shall go back to that dreadful place from which they came if he needs must put their father to work as his own valet—which, of course, would be most unsuitable and he would never dispense with Connie, but you understand what he meant."

"Indeed. His lordship is the kindest and most understanding gentleman. You are so fortunate in your husband, my dear."

"I am," smiled Lady Wheymore proudly. "I most certainly am."

The gentleman in whom Lady Wheymore was so fortunate was at the moment deep in thought in the comfort of a large wing chair in a back parlor of White's. He had just been exiting the club after placing a bet on the outcome of a mill between Jed Thomas, known to many as The Grim Reaper, and a relative newcomer, Harry Spring, when he had walked directly into his son and Lilliheun who had each taken an arm, spun him about, and escorted him back inside. "The thing of it is, we cannot possibly call in Bow Street, Father," Neiland ended his explanation with a sigh. "They both of them know Fate—Locksley knows him as well as Radd."

"Yes, and they more than know him, I think," murmured Lilliheun. "My guess is they are friends of the villain, sir."

The earl harrumphed and made a steeple of his hands.

"Well, you see how it is, Father. We cannot possibly let Locksley go after this Daniel Peace on his own."

"I rather think Lilliheun might let him," drawled Wheymore. "Locksley's been nothing but a sword in his side from the first."

"No, sir, he ain't," protested Lilliheun. "I don't know how it comes to be, but I'm fond of the rogue and though I ain't pleased to think I've lost Miss Quinn to him, still, I never truly possessed her heart, did I?"

Wheymore shook his head sadly. "I fear not, Lilliheun, though I interceded for you as best I could. Told her I did not know a finer young gentleman in all of Britain— next to her scurvy cousin, David, of course."

Neiland laughed. "No, really Father, you must not go about calling me scurvy."

"I expect not," grinned the earl, "but at the time you were putting on dandified airs and I was annoyed with you."

"An entire year ago!" protested Neiland.

"Shirt points so high they'd poke your eyes out if you turned your head and not your body," chuckled Wheymore. "Do you remember, Clare? And twenty fobs at least on his waistcoat."

"And shoes with heels so high as to make him mince when he walked," laughed Lilliheun. "And a beaver with a plume! Do you remember that dreadful hat, sir?"

"Indeed. I have had it stuffed and shall show it to my grandson as proof of his father's folly," drawled Whey-

more, taking a good deal of delight in the blush that rose
to Neiland's cheeks. "No, no, boy, don't be embarrassed.
These are exactly the memories a man holds dear—memories of his son making a damned fool of himself. I believe
my own father had just as many memories of me as I have
of you, David. And I expect you are not nearly as hilarious
as Johnny might have been."

Lilliheun's eyebrows rose suddenly and he set them back
in place as quickly as possible before the earl should notice.
Neiland did likewise. "Do you think Johnny would have
been—amusing—Father? Truly?"

"You must not think badly of me, Neiland, but yes, I
think the boy would have grown to be an endless entertainment—full of whimsies and larks and vagaries enough to
keep us all in whoops from morning until night. You would
have liked him," he added a bit soberly. "He would have
made you an excellent brother. But enough—I have not
spoken of Johnny for years and now his name is on my
lips twice in less than a fortnight. Claudia would call it a
portent. So, you wish my advice, do you, on this Daniel
Peace business?"

"Indeed, sir," nodded Lilliheun.

"I say 'tis best both you and Neiland keep out of it. If
you cannot," he added, raising his hand to silence the
protests he could see about to erupt from both, "then you
must offer Locksley your services and if he accepts, follow
his instructions. Radd is *his* friend, after all, and Daniel
Peace *his* enemy, and I've no doubt our Mr. Locksley is
quite capable of dealing with the situation. He keeps a
knife, you know, under his pillow and a horse pistol on
his window sill—no, it is not on his window sill any longer,
but on top of the armoire now that little Tick has joined
the household."

"How do you know?" Neiland asked, amazed.

"Somers told me," grinned Wheymore. "He tells me a
great many interesting things of late—he and Glasgow,
Eversley's butler, have become bosom bows since the
advent of Locksley at Grosvenor Square. At any rate, I
suspect our Mr. Locksley is not a stranger to violence and
handles himself well. If you feel obliged to help him, be

certain that is exactly what you do. Do nothing to hinder
him or make his task more difficult. A man likes to have
friends, but he does not like seeing them harmed, and he
does not like putting one friend in jeopardy to save
another, and that's a fact."

Camilla, in a walking dress of blue-sprigged muslin, with
matching blue gloves, blue kid shoes, a whimsical straw
hat covered with blue forget-me-nots and a pretty parasol
of blue silk trimmed in white, stood in the open doorway
of Wheymore House laughing quietly as on the step below
her a young gentleman dressed to the nines in a scarlet
cut-away and buff pantaloons and small, but perfect, Hessians was seriously engaged in pinning rosebuds—one
each—upon Jolly's and Grig's matching white lawn
dresses. Below them, on the walk, a bang up to the mark
Corinthian was holding a third rosebud and when Tick
had gotten the first two pinned, handed it to the young
gentleman to bestow upon Annie. "Oh, sir, Mr. Locksley,
I cannot," protested that young lady, blushing. "I ain't
naught but a maid."

"Without who we'd be forced ta put the childer in the
zoo," drawled Locksley lazily. "Be gracious, Miss Annie,
and accept Tick's offerin'. He's fond o' you, I think."

That observation brought a giggle from all of the children and a quickly hushed chuckle from Gregory. As soon
as Annie's rosebud was fastened and she had Digger settled
in her arms, Fate climbed the steps, offered his arm to
Camilla and escorted her safely to the cobbles. "Now," he
said, "our trek begins in earnest. Onward, Tick. Ye an' the
girls lead an' Greg'ry will guard are rears." This statement
brought a guffaw from Gregory and Tick and a giggle from
all of the ladies. Fate, himself, merely raised the whimsical
eyebrow and smiled laconically. "Somethin' I said?" he
asked Camilla innocently.

"Oh, no, Mr. Locksley," she chuckled looking up into
the dark eyes that sparkled down at her. "We are all of us
being silly."

"So I thought," he said, sticking his nose into the air

with a haughtiness that set Camilla to laughing outright. "What? Have I not got it correct?"

"G-got what correct, Mr. Locksley?"

"The nose, m'dear. Ain't that how Dewhurst sets 'is nose when 'e's bein' priggy?"

"Priggy? What, sir, is priggy?"

"Dewhurst in a s'perior mood."

"Oh," laughed Camilla. "Oh, I see. You are mimicking the duke now, are you?"

"Uh-huh. If 'e's ta be m'gran'father, I figger I ought ta learn the best parts of 'im, no?"

The little company of strollers drew a number of glances along the route to Green Park and even more within the park itself. Most of them, Camilla noted with a certain amount of pride, were approving and some even envious. The children did look wonderful and were behaving wonderfully as well, and the handsome man beside her, she knew, was bringing sighs from a number of lovely lips. If only he were truly John Locksley, truly the Duke of Dewhurst's grandson, what a miracle could come of it!

"What're ye thinkin', Dendron?"

"Only how beautiful we all look and how many people must think us a perfect young family."

The eyebrow raised. "Fam'ly? Us?"

"Only a thought, Mr. Locksley. You needn't panic."

"I ain't panickin', Dendron. I jus' thought as how ye didn't never want no fam'ly—no 'usband nor no childer, I mean. Neiland and Lilliheun, they said as how ye didn't want ta be married."

"I do not," Camilla replied. "I wish to remain independent and—"

"Be a auther-ress."

"Yes, exactly. But how sweet the girls look with Tick beside them and Annie tending Digger so seriously as if he were the next Prince of the Realm."

Fate hissed as though he had been burned and she turned to look up at him, startled. "What is it?"

"Don't never speak o' Digger an' Royalty in the same breath."

"Why not?"

"Ye'll curse 'im. He gots enough trouble wi'out bein' cursed. Ever'thin's against 'im already for bein' borned in St. Giles an' havin' Artie fer a da an' no better connections than me an' Mossie."

"But there are no such things as curses," Camilla said, waiting for the gleam in his eyes that would tell her he was teasing. The gleam did not appear. "There are not, Mr. Locksley. You *do* know there are not?"

"Sure as there's witches, there's curses, Dendron."

"There are no witches either."

"Aye, there are. I knows one er two of 'em."

"No, you cannot," murmured Camilla giving his arm a shake. "Witches are only pretend and curses as well."

Fate shook his head soberly.

"Come, sit with me on that bench for a moment or two," Camilla suggested, tugging at him. "I must speak with you seriously. Gregory," she called to the footman, "will you be so kind as to take the children to the little farm and show them the animals?"

"Yes, miss," Gregory acknowledged with a tug of his forelock and swept the children off before him.

"Now," said Camilla, sitting down on the very edge of the ornate little bench and tugging Fate down beside her, "you must tell me why you think that witches and curses are real."

" 'Cause the Princess of Dewdrops tole me so," he replied. "She be magical an' use ta come ta me when I was little. But I reckon I done somethin' terr'ble, on accounta one day she went away an' never come back agin."

Camilla heard the yearning and admiration in his voice and recognized from his eyes how a swift vision flitted through his mind. For a moment she felt the oddest twinge of jealousy for this woman, whoever she might have been. But whoever she might have been, she had most certainly done Jason Fate a great disservice, filling the child's innocent mind with talk of witches and curses. Still, she, too, had been audience to many a story of magical beings and spells and fairies, but *she* had had the good grace to grow up and realize that such tales were just that—tales. "How can you—how can you have grown up to think that the tales some lady spun for you as a child are true, sir? Certainly you must realize that magic—"

"Nay, Dendron, don't be sayin' nothin' 'bout magic. 'Tis ye what don't know the truth. There be pow'ful magic all about us. Some of it be good an' some evil, but all of it beyond imaginin'. The Princess of Dewdrops were beyond imaginin', but she comed ta me—ta me," he repeated in the most disbelieving tone, "an' she give me a token ta pertect me."

"A token? What sort of token?"

" 'Tis just a token," he said, his eyes focussing upon the gravel path at his feet, his lips beginning to turn upward.

"Do you carry it with you? May I see it?"

"I a'ways carries it, Dendron. An' ye already seen it oncet. Ye jus' did not rekernize it for what it was."

"Please let me see it."

"No. Why? Ye don't b'lieve in magic. Ye as much as said so."

"Oh, you are being obstinate—and on purpose too. I can see you are longing to laugh, you wretched man!"

Fate chuckled and placed his arm along the back of the bench. "I can't help but ta laugh when I see ye growin' so pertickler curious, Dendron. I never did see the like of ye. Ye always be wantin' ta know what ye cannot an' see what's not offered for ye ta see. Ye got ta know, don't ye? Ye got ta know ever'thin'. It pokes an' prods at ye some'ere inside."

Camilla had the good grace to blush at the accuracy of his remarks and bowed her head in mock despair. "Alas, I am infamous for my curiosity, sir, and you have found me out."

One of his long fingers touched her shoulder blade and she could feel him drawing soft circles upon it through the thinness of her gown. But the impropriety of such a thing was nothing compared to the glow those little circles seemed to build within her and she hoped he would go on drawing them forever. Oh, what a totally improper thing to wish, she told herself, glancing to the side to see a most enchanted smile upon that Spartan and somehow very dear face. He was gazing, not at her, but off into the distance.

"Did Dewhurst have a word with ye?" he asked softly, as if speaking to her through a dense fog. "Will ye an' The Banshee go with the childer to this house of 'is in the country? 'Tis only until I've dealt with the matter of Dan'l Peace."

"Daniel Peace?"

"Aye, the cove what near kilt Artie. Oncet 'e be settled, 'twill be safe, I reckon, for ye ta come back."

"Jason, how could you tell the Duke of Dewhurst that you were Captain Fate? What made you think to do such a thing?"

His gaze came back to her directly and he put a finger under her chin, tilting her head back until she must stare directly into his eyes. " 'Tis because I love ye, Dendron, an' I could not bear for nothin' ta happen to ye on accounta me. An' I knew, did I tell 'im the truth, he'd not think twicet about pertectin' ye."

"But he might well have turned you in to Bow Street."

"No, not that un. I can't be explainin' it, sweetings, but 'tis in his eyes an' in the way 'e stands an' speaks an' even in the way he lis'ens ta me. I didn't never felt so much like I could trust some un like I felt I could trust 'im. An' I trust ye," he added, bringing his lips temptingly close to hers. "I trust ye, sweet thing, an' a'ways will."

Camilla's conscience sprang abruptly into action and she pulled back before Fate could kiss her. "Not here," she said with great determination. "Someone will see and my reputation will be in tatters. You have the most dreadful influence upon me. I cannot believe how far from propriety I have strayed—over and over again—on your account. My aunt and uncle would ship me off to the country immediately if they knew of it."

"I be shippin' ye off to the country, myself," grinned Fate, "an' ye don't seem ta mind."

"Uncle John!" came a breathless shout and both Camilla and Fate looked up to see Tick darting toward them across the grass, a huge animal closing fast at his heels.

"My heavens!" Camilla exclaimed, jumping to her feet. "The creature will eat him!"

Fate leaped to his feet as well, but not soon enough. The enormous beast hurtled wildly into the air and came down directly upon Tick, knocking him roughly to the grass. Camilla squealed and dashed toward the child, only to find herself caught up in strong arms and set aside as she reached the thrashing pile of fur and flailing boy. "Stay, Dendron," Fate ordered, and bending over the pile, he scooped Tick up by the waistband of his inexpressibles and lifted him to his shoulders, well out of the great brute's reach. "An' ye, sor," she heard him say sternly, "cease this nonsense 'mediately. Sit down, sor! Sit!"

Camilla squeaked as the monstrous creature sprang at Fate, but then she heard the captain chuckle as he pushed the shaggy beast down, wiping at his face with the sleeve of his coat. From the little bundle of scarlet and buff on Fate's shoulders Camilla heard a gurgle of laughter and from farther across the lawn came a chorus of excited voices. Jolly, Grig and Annie were running toward them as fast as they could while Gregory followed more slowly, carrying Digger.

Chapter 16

"No," the captain said quietly, and Camilla's smile widened. He was once again seated on the bench. Beside him on his left stood Grig and on his right, Jolly. Behind him, Tick straddled the bench back as if it were a horse. Gregory, standing beside Camilla, chuckled and shook his head.

"Pwease?" Jolly murmured, her arm around Fate's neck, her head resting on his shoulder. "Oh, pwease?"

"We will be bery, bery good, foreber an' eber," assured Grig, planting a kiss on his ear then snuggling her cheek against his and twisting the curls on the back of his neck gently around her tiny finger.

"An' Harley'll feel so much bedder!" put in Tick, popping Fate's curly-brimmed beaver on to his own head. "I knows 'e will. An' ye'll be the finestest gen'lemun in the how worl' do ye let us. Finer even than—than—Mr. Glasgow!''

Camilla could not take her eyes from them, not even to check and see that the object of this overt cajolery was present and behaving. What a wonderful picture they made, the four of them—the three children so intent upon Fate, and he delighting in their wheedling while attempting to appear sternly immovable. What a splendid father he will make, she thought, as his arms went gently about the two little minxes who were practicing their budding feminine wiles upon him and presently whispering promises in his ears. Other strollers passing by gazed at them and the enormous dog panting at Fate's feet with quiet smiles.

"But we ain't got no place for such a monster, darlin's, an' yer da will 'ave a proper fit."

"There's lots a room unner my bed," offered Tick, wide-eyed with hope.

"Dere's rooms unner are beds too!" squeaked Jolly, fairly shaking with excitement because the captain had said something besides "no".

"An' we will take care o' 'im all by areselfs," Grig added coaxingly, her arms going around Fate's neck.

"Well, I doubt that, Grig. It'll take all o' ye jus' ta walk that critter."

" 'E's brave an' will perteck us when Harley an' da an' you is workin'," cried Tick, reading approaching acceptance into the captain's words. "An' 'e will perteck Lady Dendron, too."

Fate's eyes raised to search for Camilla and found her smiling at him with Gregory to one side of her and Annie and Digger to the other. "If you please, Mr. Locksley," Annie said, making the captain a curtsy, "Master Tick did pay for the dog, sir. A whole shilling an' three pence and a han'ful of 'nilla beans."

Camilla's hand went to her lips to smother a giggle.

"A shillin' an' thruppence an' a han'ful of 'nilla beans?" Fate repeated in a dazed tone. "Tick, who'd sell ye a brute li' this for so little?"

"I reckon the cove what owned 'im," declared Tick with offended authority, the captain's hat slipping down over his eyes. "Even gived us 'is lead, 'e did. Wanted more, but I said as 'ow a shillin' thruppence be all I 'ad. I throwed in the 'nilla beans extra-like. 'Is name be Trouble."

"Rrrr-arf!" inserted the beast at the sound of his name.

The stern countenance that had been threatening to dissolve under the onslaught of childish coaxing gave way completely and Fate roared into whoops of laughter. "T-trouble," he gasped between whoops. "Aye, now there's a rec'mendation for ta own 'im! Greg'ry, did ye see the cove what sold 'im ta the childer? Be it likely the cur were snabbled?"

"Highly unlikely, Mr. Locksley. 'Twas young Lord Dennis who resides in St. James's Square. I expect the dog was indeed his own. At the time Master Tick approached him with the offer, the lad was beating at the creature with a stick. Apparently, it had gone off after the sheep."

"Ah, a sheep dog, is 'e?" laughed Fate. "An' bein' beaten fer follerin' his nat'ral inclinations? Well, I reckon this Lord Dennis be'd at his wit's end—prob'ly embarrassed an' out o' breath, eh?"

"Certainly red, Mr. Locksley—and panting."

"Do ye know this Lord Dennis, Dendron?"

"Indeed," Camilla replied, suppressing her own laughter. "He is quite reputable, I assure you—and at least nine by now."

"I expect we'll be hearin' from 'is da, then, wantin' the beast back."

"Oh, no, I do not think you will escape that way, Mr. Locksley. Lord Dennis is quite spoilt and if he does not want the brute, his father will not pursue the matter. It's likely had the boy not sold him to Tick, the animal would have been shipped off to one of the farms or—if he truly harasses the other animals—" Camilla had the good grace to wonder if she ought to throw this in on the children's side, but since it was possible, she thought it best to make it clear to Fate"—he may well have the beast destroyed."

Gregory turned his gaze to her, but Camilla shook her head slightly, admonishing him to hold his peace.

Fate looked down at the great clunch of a dog lying adoringly at his feet. Then he looked at Jolly and Grig and Tick. Then he sighed and shrugged his shoulders. "Do ye got the lead what the lad gived ye, Tick? Well, put it on 'im then. I ain't about ta walk down the street wi'out he's got somethin' ta keep 'im from dashin' out af'er someun's team."

A rowdy cheer went up from the children and Annie and Gregory and Camilla as well.

"I ain't got the least notion where we're goin' ta put the thin'," Fate murmured as the dog was suitably leashed. The captain offered Camilla his arm and herded the little group of smiling faces toward home. "Eversley's bound ta notice one day er another that 'is house is gittin' crowded."

"Has he not remarked upon Harley and Tick already?"

"No, we been keepin' the lads under wraps so ta speak. 'Tain't hard. 'E don't come aroun' of'en. But dogs makes noise, ye know, an' comes runnin' in, even when ye tells 'em not ta. They ain't near as 'bedient as boys."

Camilla grinned. "In my experience, boys are not always obedient either."

"More 'bedient than dogs," sighed Fate. "Ye can reason with lads, an' ye can threaten 'em wi' dire consequences. But dogs only looks at ye wi' them big eyes, an' does what they likes."

The Earl of Wheymore stalked into the Duke of Dewhurst's study with a scowl upon his handsome face and words of protest on his lips. "You must bring an end to it, Dewhurst. You know the man ain't your grandson and you must say so before this drama gets any farther out of hand."

Dewhurst looked up from the papers upon his desk, sent his butler scurrying off with a quick glance, and invited Wheymore to take a seat. "I have not the vaguest idea to what you refer, Ned. How has it gotten out of hand? Take a deep breath and then speak clearly as you used to do when I was your dreaded father-in-law."

That remark brought a quick a smile from Wheymore

and he did indeed take a deep breath, but the scowl reappeared and the look in his eyes sent a twinge of worry across the duke's shoulders. "I'm sorry, Duke. I have had the most disturbing afternoon. There is a mill brewing between Locksley and some foul villain who threatens the life of his friend, and David and Lilliheun are determined to become involved in't."

Dewhurst sat back and listened to the tale of the window, the rock, the note, and Locksley's response. "And the boys are prepared to fight beside him," Wheymore finished.

"I find that admirable in them," drawled the Duke, accepting a glass of Madeira from the hands of the butler who had come quietly into the chamber with a tray of refreshments.

"But Locksley and Radd know Jason Fate," Wheymore protested once the butler had disappeared again. "Friends with him, Lilliheun thinks. I cannot have Neiland involved with such a villain as Fate—imagine should it come to light that my son has fought in defense of that scoundrel's friends—not to mention that Neiland has never in his life fought with anyone outside of Jackson's saloon or Angelo's Haymarket fencing school."

"None of which you said to Neiland and Lilliheun?"

"I—what could I say? They know, after all, what Jason Fate is and they think not to hold such an association against Locksley. They say he is their friend and 'tis their duty to stand by him in defense of Radd."

"Of course they would see it that way. You did not raise Neiland, my boy, to abandon a friend in need. You would expect him to behave honorably and I would expect the same of Clare. It is not Locksley's association with Fate that rattles you."

"It is not?"

"No, 'tis the part about Neiland's never having fought before. You know as well as I that the sort of fight that will ensue between Locksley and this Daniel Peace will include nothing of honor or fairness or any sort of rules. You're afraid Neiland's inexperience of such savagery will lead to his being killed, Ned. A man who's lost one son holds the other much more dear, and to risk the chance of losing him to a person who must be numbered amongst the scum of the earth cannot be in any way acceptable. You were wise not to make a great breeze over it with Neiland, though. But 'tis expected you should wish the whole thing at the devil.''

"I do wish the whole thing at the devil."

"Well, 'tain't going to go to the devil—but Locksley has already proposed that I remove those two young gentlemen from harm's way. Plans are already laid to draw them into the country for a week or more. Perhaps they had best be implemented sooner than intended."

"Plans?"

"Aye. A house party at Longbourne which you and Mary will not refuse to attend—neither will Aurora nor Camilla nor Neiland nor Lilliheun, I assure you. And you will bring the children you have stowed somewhere about Wheymore House and the two boys who stay with Locksley. My secretary is even now preparing the invitations. I shall speak with Locksley and we shall attempt to adjust the date so that your David and Lilliheun are out of town well before Locksley deals with this Daniel Peace. They'll protest, of course, but I shall override them. I am, after all, a formidable gentleman to cross—even in such a small thing as a house party."

"It ain't that David cannot hold his own in a mill," Wheymore murmured. "He ain't a poltroon, my son."

"Of course Neiland ain't a coward!" agreed Dewhurst hastily. "Nor are you for worrying over him. But what passes for fighting amongst gentlemen, Ned, is not at all what will happen when Locksley and this Peace meet and even Locksley won't want the lads involved in't. I can assure you that Locksley will not discover Daniel Peace's whereabouts until after Neiland and Lilliheun have left town."

Wheymore sighed. "I had no idea that Locksley meant to look out for Neiland's welfare. Did he know of the threat, then, before the boys did?"

"He feared such a thing was in the offing the moment they discovered Radd. He sought my advice as to everyone's safety and we have devised this house party as the answer. Don't worry, Ned. Locksley may not be my grandson, but he is far from the slime with whom he's forced to contend, and there's an honor about him despite all his shortcomings.''

The Earl of Wheymore departed the duke's residence with a sense of both relief and puzzlement only moments before Fate arrived. The captain was greatly relieved to hear that he had missed a meeting with that gentleman. '' 'Cause I wouldn't want ta be explainin' to 'im about this muddle,'' he sighed, settling into the chair Wheymore had recently vacated. "I reckon 'e's worritted about Neiland.'' He stretched his long legs out before him and the heels of the polished Hessians found a place on the glowing top of the Duke of Dewhurst's mahogany table. "Dan'l Peace ain't a cove what boys oughta be playin' with.''

"You,'' proclaimed Dewhurst, his brows drawing together in a scowl at the offending boots, "are little more than a boy yourself, scoundrel, and incredibly audacious. Remove your boots from my table this instant. Gentlemen do not go about putting their feet up on the furniture.''

"They don't?'' asked Fate. "Where do they put 'em?''

"On the floor, sir!''

"Well, but then I ain't no gen'leman,'' mused the captain, his feet remaining on the table. "An' it don't matter how old I be—I knows 'ow ta fight Dan'l Peace an' 'is chums.''

"Yes, so I imagined. Is he very dangerous?''

'' 'Stremely.''

"Is there someone will help you?''

"In St. Giles? Naw, I wouldn't think so. Ever'body's 'fraid of him—'cept me—oh, an' Dibs!'' he added with a sudden grin that Dewhurst found charming despite his chagrin over the boots.

"Dibs?''

"Aye, but come ta think of it, he's in Newgate an' ain't like ta git out soon, if at all.''

"Why's he in Newgate?''

"On accounta he got catched,'' replied Fate, astounded at Dewhurst's apparent stupidity.

The incredulity on the captain's face set the duke off into a bellow of laughter. "What did he get caught doing is what I wished to know," chuckled Dewhurst finally. "He is not a highwayman?"

"Dibs? Naw. 'E be too big for ridin'. Ain't no 'orse willin' ta carry 'im in the whole of Lunnon. Catched an' tucked away for thrashin' a Runner—well, three o' 'em—which 'e shouldn't a done, but they is the most annoyin' snitches, I swears they are."

The Duke of Dewhurst's dark eyes widened. "Three of them? He thrashed three Bow Street Runners? At one and the same time?"

"Aye."

"How large is this person, Jason?"

" 'Stremely. Like what a mountain would be could it walk."

"And would he help you fight this Peace and his cronies if he were free?"

"Aye," nodded Fate. "Dibs be m'fren an' not feared o' nothin'."

"Then I shall have him released."

"Huh?"

"I'll set Borhill to it, and if he cannot succeed, I'll see to it myself."

"Huh?"

"I am a duke, Jason. With that title comes a great deal of influence and power. You'll see. Lilliheun and Neiland and the girls and the children will be out of town by Tuesday, and your friend—Dibs?—on your doorstep by Wednesday."

The captain spread his feet apart to get a clearer look at Dewhurst. "Damme but I wished ye *was* m'gran'father."

"Perhaps I am, Jason, eh? They are still searching about for proof, you know."

"Aye, but I'd not wager upon it," sighed the captain, his chin resting upon his fist. "Ain't at all likely."

"You have my eyes, boy, and a face so like my son's as to be his twin. Somewhere inside you there's a bit of me at least."

"But it ain't the crim'nal part, I reckon. I 'preciate yer not turnin' me over ta Bow Street, ye know. I reckon I'll be out o' yer hair afore ye need ta do't."

Dewhurst searched the starkly drawn face intently. "You are not proposing to go back to the High Toby, Jason?"

"Naw, I reckon I have done wi' that. I gots ta fine some better lay what with Artie all broken up like 'e is. Mebbe I'll take ta bein' a footpad."

Dewhurst would have exploded had he not noticed the dancing diamonds in the captain's eyes and the slight quivering of his lips. "You are hoaxing me. What is it you would like to do, Jason?"

"For true?"

"Yes."

"Marry Dendron an' live like a blasted lord, raisin' a castle full o' childer what all looked like 'er. An' I'd be likin' ta be able ta read 'er books all by m'self, an' mebbe even learn ta write. An' I'd like ta talk the way ye do, too, an' empress the hell out of 'er. But it ain't bloody likely. 'Specially the marryin' part."

"I had the distinct impression that the two of you were smitten with each other."

"She don't want ta be married. 'Sides there ain't no way a actual lady like her could ever marry a cove like me. 'Twouldn't be 'ceptable. Ruin 'er it would—wouldn't it?" he asked, a sudden light of hope in his eyes.

"Quite possibly," nodded the duke. "Society would certainly be aghast at it."

"Aye, tha's what I thought," muttered the captain, the light of hope quickly extinguished. "So I reckon I ain't goin' ta bother 'er no more. I reckon oncet I takes care o' Dan'l Peace an' she be safe, I best fade off inta the night so ta speak."

"And drop your claim, Jason, to inherit my title?"

"I reckon. Ye 'cided already I ain't this John Locksley. I knowed it when we talked at Vauxhall. I could see it in yer eyes. An' even if I was," he added, standing, "ye wouldn't admit it. Ain't no stiff-rumped flash cove in the whole world what would wanta be related to a thatchgallows like me."

Dewhurst accompanied him to the front door and watched him stroll off, hands in his pockets, down the street. "He is the most compelling young man," the duke murmured under his breath. "Hanks!" he shouted, summoning his secretary out into the downstairs hall. "Send 'round to the City for Borhill. I want him as soon as possible!"

Elgin Moss was busily calming Mrs. Daily as Fate tramped into the kitchen through the kitchen garden door and slumped down into a chair by the table. The captain folded his arms on the bleached oak and, disposing of his curly-brimmed beaver by dropping it upon the polished tiles, lay his head on his arms and closed his eyes. The high drama of such an entrance without so much as a word out of him brought both Moss and Mrs. Daily to instant attention.

"Mr. Locksley, whatever is wrong?" asked Mrs. Daily solicitously. "Are you not feeling just the thing, sir?"

"What is it, lad? Be ye in queer stirrups?"

Fate raised his head with obvious effort and stared up at them. "I be right sorry," he sighed.

"About what, boy?"

"About what, Mr. Locksley?"

"Ever'thin'. 'Specially fillin' yer fine 'ouse with a couple o' rapscallions an' a brute like I brought 'ome this af'er-noon, Mrs. Daily. I reckon I didn't have no right ta do that to ye, but I didn't know what else ta do with the monster. Dendron said as 'ow they'd be like ta—ta destroy 'im. I couldn't do nothin' then but bring 'im 'ere, 'specially seein' the childer's faces. But we be outta yer way soon, I promise," he added with only a hint of sadness touching his voice, though the housekeeper could well read the depths of it in his clear, fine eyes.

"Oh, Mr. Locksley, an' I'm certain 'tis no trouble at all. I'm pleased to have you and the boys and the little darling girls running in and out. It's life you've brought to this dull old place, and that's a fact. I admit I was a bit nonplussed at the sight of such a great beast as that Trouble bounding into my kitchen all unexpected, but if Cook had not fainted dead away and the little scullery maid run screaming out into the garden, why I should have made no fuss whatsoever."

"Thank ye, ma'am," replied Fate softly with a slight nod of his head, "but I know that ain't truth. I been a sore han'ful to ye all ever sincet I come, an' I 'pologize for it. Mossie, does Harley be all right?"

"Fine, lad. Tick be with him right this very minute showin' him what entertainin' tricks Trouble be capable of."

"Good. That's good. Will ye come an' talk ta me, Mossie, when ye has the time? In that big room with all the windows?"

"The sun room, 'tis called."

"Aye, the sun room. Will ye come? I got thin's ta tell ye an' I needs yer advice." With what appeared to be great effort, Fate wrenched himself to his feet, and leaving his hat where he had dropped it, he wandered off into the corridor beyond the green baize door.

"Well, I never!" exclaimed Mrs. Daily, bending down to retrieve the beaver. "There is something terrible wrong, Mr. Moss. He is always so light-hearted and filled with energy. Surely something dreadful has happened. You must go to him at once. I shall send tea and cakes after you."

Moss nodded and, taking the hat from her, hurried off after the captain. He found him sitting with one knee crossed over the other in the corner of the black and gold striped sopha which stood with its back to the sun room windows. Fate was chewing on a vanilla bean and running his fingers through his curls.

"Jason?"

"Aye?"

"What's this all about? I never did see such a Cheltenham Tragedy as ye played out before that poor lady. Practically tore 'er heart from her bosom."

"Beg yer pardon I'm sure, Mossie. I didn't mean for ta do that, but I cannot seem ta help m'self. I be so tired."

"Tired?"

"Aye. I cannot even want ta see the childer."

"Are ye ill, lad?" Moss stalked across the room and

laid a hand on Fate's brow. The captain pushed it away impatiently.

"Ye are warm, Jason."

"Naw. 'Tis warm in 'ere. Me an' the childer be goin', Mossie. 'Tis over an' done with."

Elgin Moss stared disbelievingly at his protege, then flopped down upon the sopha beside him. "Eversley has called a halt to't? I saw him but yeste'day an' he said nothin' of abandoning the scheme."

"I be abandonin' the scheme. I cannot abide it no longer, Mossie. 'Twill be blood now an' the Runners on m'heels an' me climbin' them steps ta the gibbet in front of ever'body. Oh, Gawd, but I cannot bear the thought of 'er seein' me like that. Dan'l Peace be in't, Mossie, an' I obliged ta put a end to 'im."

"Peace?" Elgin Moss came near to choking on the name. He coughed, cleared his throat, and attempted to sort out in his mind what on earth Fate was mumbling about. "I don't be follerin' ye, Jason. Ye got ta tell me from the beginnin'."

When at last Fate's dulled drone came to an end, Elgin Moss was frozen upon the sopha, his face drained of all color, his eyes glazed with fear. "Peace and his chums means ta murder this little man and lay it at yer doorstep, an' they're prepared ta turn ye over to the Runners and murder Artie, an' ye're planning on joinin' up with Dibs and stoppin' Peace afore he can manage any of it? And this duke, he knows as how ye not only be a imposter, but Captain Jason Fate? And them lordships, Neiland an' Lilliheun, they be willing ta fight fer ye and ye got ta keep 'em from getting kilt? And mebbe Peace will go after the childer an' Miss Quinn?"

The Captain nodded wearily.

One of the footmen entered with a tray, glanced at the two of them and set the tea and cakes before them without a word and departed hurriedly.

Moss poured out and then took a strawberry tart and stuffed it silently into his mouth. He chewed thoughtfully, swallowed, took another. " 'Tain't no wonder ye be comin' down ill," he murmured at last. " 'Tis enough ta make anyone's brain turn feverish. It cannot all be true, Jason," he added. "It makes no more sense than the ravings of a lunatic. There be somethin' ye're misreading er somethin' ye're imagining."

"Don't matter," sighed Fate, staring down into a cup of China tea. "The scheme be ended. I figger ta stick Dan'l Peace's spoon in the wall. I didn't never kilt nobody afore, Mossie. But I cannot let 'im kill Artie, an' he will. An' from the moment me an' Dibs takes 'im on, I'm catched, for his chums'll turn me inta Bow Street in a flash, an' the Fat Prince'll have me hung afore the sun goes down. Only—only—"

"Only what, my boy?"

"I—I—ye'll watch over 'em, won't ye, Mossie, when I'm dead? The childer, I means, an' Artie, an'—an' Dendron? There ain't gonna be much blunt, on accounta I figger Eversley ain't gonna pay up, not gettin' at all what 'e bargained for, is 'e?"

"I doubt it."

"No, so I thought. Aw, damme Mossie, I wished I was this Locksley cove! I wished I was borned a swell an'—an' I met Dendron somehow elset from 'ow I done, an' she didn't mine bein' married so much like she does, an' her an' me could go off tagether an'—" Fate's voice trailed off into silence.

Elgin Moss, the color returning to his face, set his empty cup upon the tray, took the untouched tea from Fate's hand and set it aside as well. Then he urged him to stand and led him, unprotesting, to his bedchamber. Between them, he and Farmer undressed the unresisting captain and tucked him into bed, fending off attempts by both Tick and Trouble to advance upon the man and explaining in quiet tones that the boys and the dog must be less noisy, because Mr. Locksley was feeling devilish queer.

Chapter 17

The following Monday the street before Wheymore House seemed to overflow with carriages though there were, in fact, only the earl's newest drag, his second best travelling carriage, the Duke of Dewhurst's landau and stanhope, Neiland's curricle and Lord Eversley's barouche. Lilliheun, who had delivered Radd quickly and quietly at one o'clock that morning into Fate's care, stood next to Fate now on the steps of the Eversley mansion and laughed at the harried looks on the other gentlemen's faces as they attempted to divide passengers and luggage among the vehicles. "I expect I'll be forced to send for my curricle as well," he chuckled, "if only to carry the overflow. You are positive you will not join us, Locksley? I can well leave Cammert behind to look after your friend."

"Naw, got other thin's need doin', Lilliheun."

"But nothing concerning this Daniel Peace, eh? You'll wait for Neiland and me before you tackle that villain. We've vowed to assist you in't, Locksley, and we will. It's just that Neiland and I cannot rightly turn down m' uncle's invitation. Extremely bad *ton*—not to mention the breeze it would raise."

"Nothin' concernin' Dan'l Peace," Fate lied nonchalantly. "Ye won't be gone longer than 'til nex' Monday. Peace'll wait till then."

"Yes, so Neiland and I thought. Especially since now the man will not have the least idea where Radd is. I am certain no one saw us move him last night."

Fate nodded, his attention caught by a lovely lady in a *capucine* carriage dress who waved gaily in his direction. He waved back, but did not move from his position on the steps.

"Locksley," called Neiland, jogging easily across the square and coming up beside them. "Father says we are ready for your boys. Do you need help carrying Harley down?"

Obviously he did not for he turned on his heel and strolled back into the house returning in a few minutes with Harley, leg still splinted, in his arms, Tick struggling with a carpet bag beside him and a footman carrying two more portmanteaux bringing up the rear.

"In the landau, Locksley, on the seat facing the horses," instructed the Duke of Dewhurst as they reached the conglomeration of conveyances. "We'll leave the top down, shall we, young man?" Dewhurst asked with an encouraging grin at Harley. "And your brother will not mind sharing the backward facing seat with me—even if I am a rather stodgy old gentleman. There are some pillows there to prop the lad up with and help protect that leg, Ja-John."

"Aye, I reckon ye're goin' ta like this 'scursion, Harley," offered Fate with a determined attempt at jolliness. "Think of it—ridin' off inta the country in the comp'ny of a duke! You an' Tick!"

"An' Trouble?" asked Harley as Fate set him gently down upon the deeply padded seat and began to adjust the pillows about him to help him sit properly and to protect his leg from jarring.

"Trouble?" echoed Neiland, leaning in through the open door to give Fate a hand. "What sort of trouble are you afraid of, Harley? The duke's coachman will not spill you out if that is what worries you."

"Aw, lor'," mumbled Fate, bestowing a quick kiss upon Harley's head, climbing down, and tossing Tick up into the open carriage, "I fergot all 'bout Trouble. I don't reckon he's been invited, Harley."

"Yes, he has, Mr. Locksley," contradicted a sweet voice beside him. "But there is no room for him in the landau, Harley, so he must ride in my Uncle Ned's second best carriage with the girls and Digger and Annie," Camilla explained. "Oh, and here he comes now," she chuckled. "The girls have been playing with him, I'm afraid. You must tell him how wonderful he looks," she added with an amused glance at Fate. "And you must not laugh at him, sir. He is very proud of himself at the moment, I think."

A surprised snort escaped Neiland and Fate's lips turned

upward though the smile did not reach his eyes as Gregory approached with Trouble prancing on the end of his leash. The great brute had been combed and brushed and two pink bows decorated his ears while a third had been used to gather the fur from out his eyes and tie it up in the center of his head. At sight of Fate, the dog leaned eagerly into his collar and dragged Gregory straight toward the landau. In a moment two giant paws were propped upon Fate's chest, and a long, pink tongue was striving to reach his nose. "Enough," murmured Fate, burying his face in the shaggy fur, tugging at the floppy ears, and raking his fingers up and down the brawny back. "Get down now, ye rascal. Whew, Harley," he added forcing a wide smile for that young man, "be 'appy he's ridin' with the little 'uns. 'E smells somethin' horrible."

"He does not," protested Camilla. "I will have you know that he is wearing Essence of Jasmine—which is all the crack, believe me! Unfortunately, the girls emptied the whole bottle upon him."

Tick and Harley both giggled.

"What a magnificent bear!" exclaimed Lilliheun with a wink for both boys as he came up beside Fate. "To whom does he belong?"

"All o' us!" cried Tick, standing up upon the seat and leaning over the side of the carriage for a closer look at his dog. "Trouble 'longs ta ever'body!"

"Are ye certain ye wish ta take 'im?" Fate asked Camilla.

"Don't you wish us to do so, Mr. Locksley? I thought he would be good company for the children, and he will enjoy running about Longbourne with them."

"But 'e won't be no trouble?"

"Trouble? He cannot help but be Trouble," gurgled Camilla. "It is his name after all. Come and discuss it with me," she found herself saying. She took his arm and drew him out of earshot of the others. "What is it, Captain? You look so—so—sad. Did you wish to come with us? I am certain the duke would be—"

"Naw, I might come later—"

"If you are in need of the duke's assistance? He has confided in Aurora and me about the purpose of this house party, and I think it is admirable of you, Jason, to wish to protect us, but you will not put yourself in danger, will you? True danger, I mean. Once you discover who it was harmed Mr. Radd and where they may be found, you will set the Runners on them, will you not?"

Every word that fell from those extremely kissable lips drove like a spear into Fate's heart and he found it hard going to maintain a confident countenance. She was at once the most independent and the most innocent woman he had ever met and though he longed to rail against the innocence that believed that Bow Street would come to the aid of Jason Fate and to protest the independence that even now forced him to give up all dreams of marrying her, he could not find it in his heart to do so. They were part of the reason he loved her after all. So he simply shrugged his shoulders, assured her that should he require assistance those at Longbourne would hear from him immediately, and escorted her to the earl's second best travelling carriage where he bid Jolly and Grig and Digger a fond farewell and helped Gregory and Annie to settle Trouble into the vehicle amongst the children. Then he wandered with her on his arm to Eversley's barouche and handed her into Eversley's care.

"It's a shame you are not coming with us, Locksley," Eversley said. "I cannot think why you are not."

"I reckon it be jus' for family-like," mumbled Fate in reply. "An' a treat for the childer. I reckon I don't be no family ta the duke jus' yet."

"But you will be," whispered Eversley low enough to keep Aurora and Camilla from overhearing. "I assure you, the thing is all but done. I expect that upon our return, you shall be heir to a dukedom, m'lad. Farewell, Locksley," he called as the captain stepped away.

The little entourage, once the ladies' abigails and the gentlemen's valets had been alloted seats, moved regally down Grosvenor Square with Lilliheun and Wheymore riding beside. Fate stared after them until they disappeared 'round the corner then trudged back to Eversley's mansion and sat down upon the front stoop. His heart had stuttered with hope for a brief moment at Eversley's words, but he told himself he weren't no dolt nor no cork-brain an' he knowed 'e probably weren't never goin' to see any of 'em again except from the back of a wagon what were carryin' him ta the gibbet.

Glasgow, who had watched the entire proceedings from the long window beside the front entrance, opened the door, came quietly down the first two steps, and without the least deference to the cleanliness of his well-cut inexpressibles, lowered himself to the stoop beside the captain. In less than another minute Elgin Moss had taken up position on Fate's left side. Somers wandered over from across the street and stood with one foot on the bottom step and his hand clutching the rail. And though each one of the men wished in some way to wipe the forlorn cast from Fate's countenance, not one of them could think of a word to say.

On Tuesday morning, a bewildered, suspicious, and somewhat cantankerous Andrew Borhill made his way into Fate's breakfast room with a genuine mountain of a man in tow. "I'm blessed if I can understand what's going on here, or what any of it has to do with his grace," he muttered tartly, "but I was told to deliver this person into your care, Locksley."

The captain looked up from a plate of ham and eggs, registered the surprised look upon the giant's face and the scowl upon Borhill's, and invited them both to join him in breaking his fast. Borhill declined with a snort and stomped out, but the scoundrel known as Dibs grinned widely, heaped a plate full at the sideboard to which Fate pointed and, straddling a chair, began to breakfast heartily. The captain requested politely that Glasgow see they were not disturbed and once the butler had closed the door, sat back in his chair and grinned widely. "Ye done growed bigger still, Dibs. Don't ye never gonna stop? I reckon as 'ow yer tall as two men already an' wide as three."

"An' ye still ain't no bigger'n a burp," chuckled Dibs around a mouthful of beefsteak. 'Ow'd ye come to lan' in this cushy 'stablishment? I be fair struck down ta see 'twas ye I been summoned ta.''

"It ain't nothin' but a snibble, Dibs. Me an' Mossie come in handy ta some swell for a bit is all. We be outta 'ere afore ye can count ta ten.''

Dibs laughed and gulped half a glass of ale. "Ye knows 'ow long it takes me ta count ta ten, don't ye, Cap'n? Ye could fair raise a fambly an' gran'childer afore I'd git it done correck like. So, what're ye be wantin' ol' Dibs fer? Ye got yerself in the briars some'ow, ain't ye?''

Fate nodded, took a long swallow of coffee and, resting his elbows upon the table and his chin on his fists, began to explain. Dibs's eyes which were wide-set and almost colorless grew an amazing shade of aquamarine as the captain rambled through his tale. The large, thrice-broken nose appeared to twitch. The plump, bewhiskered cheeks puffed to an even more magnificent size and the strong, stubborn chin stiffened.

"Damned if Dan'l Peace ain't about ta meet 'is maker,'' growled Dibs around three slices of bacon. "We be af'er 'im soons I finish this bit o' sust'nence, Jason. 'E ain't 'bout ta be killin' Artie—no, nor layin' ev'dence against ye, neither. See if 'e does oncet I git m'hands upon 'im.''

Elgin Moss entered the chamber at that moment, greeted Dibs, and poured himself a cup of tea. "I'm goin' with ye,'' he announced, taking a bite of strawberry tart. "No slight on ye, Dibs, but I ain't about ta stand aside while m'lad takes on the likes of Dan'l Peace—not even with you at his side. Nor I am not about ta see the two of ye bound for the gallows. At the very least I shall stand witness 'twas Peace attacked ye an' not t'other way about. And they'll believe me, too. Ye see if they doesn't. An' I be swearin' on the bible that ye ain't Jason Fate as well,'' he added with a scowl at the captain, " 'cause that'll be their cry if ye wins. But ain't nobody in St. Giles's will support 'em. We'll keep ye safe, lad. Ye may be assured of't. Artie, he be wantin' ta come with us, ye know, but he can't stand as yet wi'out he topples over.''

"Kin I see 'im?'' asked Dibs, one large hand dwarfing

a muffin. "I ain't seed Artie since afore Jason come lookin' fer 'im them few weeks back."

"Aye, he's upstairs, Dibs. Ye can come up an' talk ta 'im while Jason an' I changes our gear. Ye ain't plannin' on wearin' them breeches an' such about the neighborhood, be ye Jason?"

"Naw, I reckon not," smiled Fate tentatively. "Wouldn't wanta be 'ssassinated fer bein' a swell. D'ye truly think we can settle this thing without I git m'self gibbeted, Mossie?"

"Indeed I do, m'boy. Indeed I do. While ye been walkin' about in the gloom, I been thinkin' on it in perticuler, an' Sunday af'ernoon while ye was sleepin', his grace come knockin' on the door an' suggested as how we oughta ponder tagether, he an' I. A fine gen'leman, that Dewhurst. I reckon mebbe he does think ye be 'is gran'son. Asked me all 'bout how I found ye an' what I knowed about yer mam an' da. Then he sat thinkin' real serious-like, give a shake of 'is head an' said as how we had ta figger a way ta keep ye from the gallows. Said as 'ow he'd handle the Fat Prince an' his cronies easy enough, an' so long as I was ta fine as many people'd swear ye wasn't Jason Fate as were threatenin' ta swear ye were, why he'd take on Bow Street an' the Bigwigs as well."

For the first time in days Fate's eyes sparkled. "He said that? The old gent?"

"Aye. Fond of ye, I think, Jason. Says ye got more bottom than any man 'e's ever met an' are brave as ye can stare, an' he ain't about ta let no hangman lay 'is hands upon ye does 'e got ta lift 'is own sword in yer defense."

"Me neither," chimed in Dibs around a mouthful of strawberries. "I ain't about ta let no gentry-law put a end ta ye, nor let no 'angman git 'is paws upon me neither. Don't be frettin' it, Cap'n. 'Twill all turn out proper fine in the end."

St. Giles in daylight was as daunting as St. Giles in darkness though only Elgin Moss—who had abandoned the place years before—noticed. Nearly naked children played lethargically amidst the filth-strewn gutters; half-starved dogs and flea-ridden cats sniffed and pawed and scuttered amongst piles of garbage; an enormous grey body and long hairless tail waddled out of view at the end of one alley, though not soon enough to keep Moss's heart from stuttering. He had forgotten about the rats. Shrill cries and drunken curses rattled about them and the smells of moldering cabbages, boiled potatoes and scalded milk hung heavy in the hot air. Fate sidestepped an elderly woman in worn black bombazine, nearly lifting her from the pavement to keep from knocking her down. He planted a kiss on the wispy grey hair that fluttered across her brow, fished three coins from one of his pockets, placed them in her hand, and took three apples from the basket on her arm. "G'day ta ye, Miss Lizbeth," he said then, bowing at the waist. "I swear ye be lookin' a pure vision this af'ernoon."

"Go away wi' ye, Cap'n," she replied, bestowing upon him the same toothless smile he had known for years. "We bin a'missin' o' ye 'ere abouts."

"I been a missin' ye, Lizbeth. Ye knows Dibs, don't ye, an' Mossie?"

"Oh!" she gasped on an intake of breath. "Elgin Moss, hisself! I thought 'e done died by now."

"Well I ain't," replied Moss, taking an apple from Fate's hand and biting into it.

"Mus' be on the edge o' it," mused Lizbeth, watching him chew. "Elset ye'd not be back 'ere wanderin' about. Ye a'ways did 'ate this place."

"Naw, he ain't fixin' ta die," Fate grinned. "We just come lookin' for Dan'l Peace."

"Are fixin' ta die then, all three o' ye," nodded the woman sagely. "Peace be holdin' court at The Painted Swan. Been gettin' right uppity since ye been gone, Cap'n. Been stirrin' up trouble ever' night."

"Gonna cease stirrin' shortly," murmured Dibs, taking one of the apples from Fate, biting into it, and chewing energetically.

"I thank ye, Lizbeth, for the information," Fate said, pressing another coin into the woman's hand. "Ye take care, darlin', an' God bless ye."

The Painted Swan was a stinking little thieves' kitchen

buried deep at the end of a narrow, twisting lane called
Blithe Street. A nondescript, crumbling building amongst
a row of other crumbling buildings, no sign marked its
presence nor encouraged patronage. Those who fre-
quented The Painted Swan did so for reasons other than
drink and good fellowship. Murderers, cracksmen, footpads and blackmailers gathered within the dingy walls and
mumbled plans and plots amongst themselves. Evil straddled the chairs at every table and depravity was served up
with the blue ruin. Eyes snapped to the doorway; voices
ceased and chairs scraped aside; knives clacked to table
tops and horse pistols rose from waistbands as Jason Fate's
shadow flowed before him into the dismal chambers.

"Well, I'll be damned if it ain't the Cap'n," growled a
husky and amused voice from the farthest, darkest corner.
"Be ye lookin' fer someun, Fate? Me, fer instance?" Daniel
Peace was a compact man of medium build with shoulders
the width of an axe handle, forearms twisted thick with
muscle, hands wide and heavy with the long, strong fingers
of a strangler, sultry hazel eyes and hair the color of chestnuts. "Come," he urged standing, hands on hips, feet
widespread. "I been expectin' ye."

The captain made his way between chairs and around
tables with an insouciance that belied the whirling of his
mind and the almost unnoticeable darting of his eyes as
he appraised the men and weapons around him. Dibs and
Moss followed in his wake, looking neither to left nor right.

"So, m'dear, will ye join us in a glass? Or do ye prefer
settin' straight down ta business, eh?" Peace's rather inso-
lent smile wavered a bit as Dibs walked up behind the
captain, but it regained its superiority as his eyes fell upon
Elgin Moss. "I thought as how ye was visitin' with Bow
Street, Dibs, an' I never did think ta see ye saunterin' inta
sich a despicable tavern as The Painted Swan. Who's ye're
fren? Archie, move yerself an' give the Cap'n a chair."

Fate ignored the mouse-like little man who scurried away
and instead of accepting that seat, rounded the table until
his back was to the far wall, whereupon he hooked the
chair from under another fast-rising crony of Peace's with
the toe of his boot, turned its back to the table and strad-

dled it, resting his arms along the chairback. Dibs strolled over to stand behind him on one side and Moss on the other.

"This be Mr. Elgin Moss, Dan'l," said Fate with a nod toward Mossie. "I reckon as mebbe ye heerd of 'im sometime er 'nother. 'E be a fren of mine an' Artie's."

"Ah, yes, Radd," grinned Peace, lowering himself back into his chair. "I do 'pologize 'bout Radd. But business be business, Cap'n."

"Aye," nodded Fate, his eyes growing hard as stone in the gloomy light, "an' 'tis business I come ta speak with ye about. Ye threatened Artie's life, didn't ye? An' mine as well."

"I did, Cap'n. I did. But 'twas merely ta remind Radd ta keep 'is gabster shut. I ain't about ta make good on't."

"Ye ain't?" Fate's tipsy eyebrow rose slightly. "An' ye ain't about ta snitch on me ta the Runner's, Dan'l? Or lay a murder at m'feet? 'Cause that's what I heerd, y'know," he added, leaning back a bit, removing the horse pistol from the waistband beneath his jacket, and setting it gently upon the table. "I tends ta b'lieve what Artie tells me, y'know, 'specially when someun's beat 'im proper ta keep 'im from tellin' me."

Peace glanced to the pistol and back to Fate. "Ye ain't foolish enough ta think ta use that here an' now, Cap'n?"

"I reckon I am, Dan'l, should I hafta. I ain't like ta miss with it. I expect ye knows that as well as anybody. Nor Dibs ain't like ta miss snappin' at least two necks afore someun takes 'im down. An' Mossie—well, I'd be more leery o' Mossie than either one o' us. 'E's fast, Mossie is, so fast a cove don't never see 'im move afore the bloke be down 'n' dead."

Elgin Moss smiled coolly to give confident credence to this out and out clanker. It never ceased to amaze him how Jason could look a man straight in the eye and tell the most outrageous Banbury tales.

Daniel Peace gazed calmly about the room. At least twenty sets of eyes surreptitiously flashed him a message of ready support. "Ye're a fool, Fate," he growled quietly.

"I a'ways thought ye were. Now I'm certain-sure. A fool or a Bedlamite."

"A Bedlamite," mumbled Dibs, "an' more dangerous fer it."

"Oh, I ain't got no doubts 'bout Cap'n Fate's bein' dangerous," hissed Peace. "I know as 'ow he's dangerous. What?" he growled angrily as a tall, cadaverous-looking man burst through the door, began to rush toward him and then halted. "What's up, Grimball?"

"M-message fer ye, Dan'l."

"Bring it."

The man came cautiously to the table and offered Peace a twisted skew of paper. Peace spread it open and studied the writing, then folded it and stuffed it unceremoniously into his waistcoat pocket. "I reckon that settles it," he sighed. " 'Twas kind of ye ta come at sich an opportune time, Cap'n."

Peace placed both hands on the table top, pushed himself to his feet and sent the table skidding across the room. He did not manage it quickly enough, however, to keep Fate from seizing the pistol and firing. Peace slammed back into two of his cronies as the ball caught him in the shoulder. Three bodies came flying over the table at Fate. Dibs caught two of them and sent them soaring in the opposite direction. Mossie, with a groan of anticipation of pain, ducked the third and sent a fist pounding upward into the man's unguarded stomach.

And then the entire tavern exploded. Knives flashed; cudgels cracked; shouts and moans and the sound of stumbling, scraping boots filled the air. A chair slammed down over Fate's shoulder; a cudgel caught him in the midsection; but the knife in his boot was suddenly in his hand and then soaring end over end and burying itself with a thunk into the middle of a broad chest.

Dibs shook bodies from him like a dog shaking off fleas. Bones snapped in his hands; men shrieked and scuttled away; gun powder flashed. Mossie dove through the melee, landed on top of Peace, rolled off and was caught by an uncountable number of hands. A fist cracked against his chin. Another thumped into his stomach. A third smashed

into his nose. And then his arm was jerked to the side and
he was catapulted from their grasps back toward the far
wall and Fate, bleeding lips set in a grim line was in his
place, fists pummeling brutally against faces, stomachs,
ribs; boots kicking into groins and knees; spurs raking
against unprotected calves and thighs. Dibs waded through
writhing bodies toward Moss, and Mossie was up again and
prying Fate's bloodied knife from a chest that no longer
rose or fell. Together he and Dibs turned back into the
fray, but not soon enough.

Daniel Peace had regained his feet; his own pistol
pointed directly at Fate's back; the powder flashed; the
gun roared; and Fate fell limply forward into waiting arms.
Dibs's surprised gasp was cut off by a heavy cudgel bashing
into the side of his head and Moss was felled by a like
blow, though Fate's knife bit sharply up beneath a ribcage
as Moss went down. In the far corner of the room, a pale-
faced, sweating cutthroat in a striped catskin vest gasped
just as loudly as had Dibs and then stuck a bleeding fist
into his mouth to stifle the sound.

"Tie 'em up," growled Peace, bending over the inert
Fate, "and toss 'em all in the cellar. If we're lucky they
won't none o' 'em die till we turn 'em over ta the Runners
fer the dire deed they be 'bout ta perform this very night."
Despite the blood soaking his shoulder, Peace laughed
and several other tired voices joined with him.

Chapter 18

Camilla had not meant to eavesdrop upon Eversley and
Lilliheun. She had simply dozed off in the duke's wonderfully comfortable wing chair in the library while perusing
one of His Grace's volumes on the geographical highlights
of Northumberland, some of which she wished to use in
the conclusion of her tale of Bad Jack Pharo. Had she not
spent the entire morning tramping about the grounds of
Longbourne with Tick, Jolly, Grig, and Trouble, chasing
them at a run most of the time, or had she not eaten such

a delicious nuncheon—which had added extremely to her sense of peace and lethargy—her eyes would never have drifted closed over the volume. But they had drifted closed and had not opened until Lilliheun's voice had waked her.

It was the tone of his voice that startled her, the seriousness and worry she heard in it. Her first thought had been to spring to her feet and announce her presence, but then Eversley had mentioned the name Locksley in a tone of equal seriousness and she had waited to see what Fate's patron might wish to say to Clare about him. What she heard convinced her to make herself even smaller and more insignificant in the depths of the chair so that neither gentleman would take the least note of her.

"I cannot possibly accompany you, Lilliheun. I wish I could, but I would only slow you down as ill as I feel at the moment. What you ought to do, I think, is take Dewhurst's landau. That's the fastest of the equippages, especially with his greys in the traces. And you might trade teams at Newhope. I have a team of chestnuts stabled at the Newhope Inn that will carry you like the wind the rest of the way to London. I shall send Neiland after you on your own bay as soon as he returns from the village."

"You'll be sure to do so," Lilliheun replied soberly. "Though the message does not ask for him, Neiland's assistance may well be necessary."

"Yes, of course, though I don't understand what can possibly have occurred."

"Nothing to concern yourself about, Eversley. Neiland and I shall handle it. You'll be sure to tell the duke what has happened?"

"Of course, cuz. Immediately he comes in from his ride."

Camilla remained huddled in the chair until the sounds of both gentlemen's footsteps had faded and then she hurried from the library herself and fled up the servants' staircase to her bedchamber. Flustered that Aurora and her Aunt Mary should be off riding with the duke and her Uncle Ned, she wrote a hurried note and went to prop it upon Aurora's pillow. She then returned to her own chamber, donned bonnet and pelisse and rushed back down the servants' staircase, out the kitchen door, and through the vegetable garden to the stable where she watched for her chance to enter the closed carriage unnoticed by the grooms who were even then busily hitching up the horses. She knew such behavior was highly exceptionable and that she ought not attempt to play such a trick upon Lilliheun, but panic, very deep in her heart, urged her on. If Jason was in such dire circumstances as to send all the way to Longbourne for help, then she must be with him and she must be with him as soon as possible. She had no wish to waste time arguing with Clare who would be dead set against taking her.

It was the cheeriest sound Elgin Moss had ever thought to hear—Fate's quiet groan in the dank, blinding darkness of The Painted Swan's cellar. "Jason," he called quietly in the direction from which the groan had come. "Jason, can ye hear me?"

"M-Mossie?"

"Aye, lad. No, don't be thrashin' about, Jason. Ye've been shot, m'boy. Jus' lie still."

"B-but I can't see ye, Mossie," mumbled Fate anxiously. "An' I can't hardly move."

"It's 'cause we be tied up, Jason, somewheres in the dark."

"Oh, good," replied Fate, a hint of mirth mixing with the pain in his voice. "I thought mebbe I'd gone blind an' par'lyzed or somethin'. Wh-where's Dibs?"

"Right 'ere, Cap'n," muttered the man-mountain angrily. "Trussed up like a pig fer butcherin'. Ye lay quiet now an' I'll see can't I git over ta ye."

"Can ye see 'im, Dibs?" asked Moss.

"Naw, but I figger 'e ain't too far off. 'E don't soun' real well, Mossie."

Moss listened as Dibs attempted to slide and thump his way across the hard-packed dirt floor they could not see, to the place they supposed Fate to lie.

"Cap'n," Dibs said after a few moments of twisting and scuttling. "Say somethin'. I reckon I lost ye."

"Shhh," Moss hissed. "There's steps. I hear someun comin' down some steps."

It was a great credit to Moss's sense of hearing that he heard even the least tapping of a boot heel, for the man in the striped catskin vest was doing his utmost to make no noise at all and succeeding quite nicely as far as he could make out. At the bottom of the cellar stairs he held the lantern higher, looking for the door behind which the three men had been locked. He sighed in relief to see only two chambers, one of which stood open and the second of which was held closed only by a heavy wooden bar across the door.

Setting the lantern at his feet, he lifted the bar and slid it aside, then retrieved the light and held it up before him as he entered the cellar chamber in which Dibs, Moss, and Fate were held captive. "Thank God," he sighed as the light showed him all three men staring up at him. "I feared they'd harmed you so badly you would not even yet be conscious."

"Who the devil are you?" asked Moss suspiciously.

"M'name's Argosy," murmured the man setting the lantern on the dirt floor and beginning to saw at Moss's bonds with a small blade. "I'm in the employ of Mr. Andrew Borhill."

"Borhill? Borhill the solicitor?"

"Exactly. I have been loitering about St. Giles's attempting to discover Mr. Locksley's history since first Eversley brought him to our attention, and you will be amazed to know that not until the moment the three of you walked through that door did I receive any hint at all that he might be Captain Jason Fate." Moss's bindings snapped and Argosy left him to untie his own ankles, moving on to free Dibs. "Peace and his cronies have gone now. There's only a few villains left in the barroom. I think we might easily sneak out through the rear door. They did not bother to set a guard at the top of the stairs."

"And once we're out?" asked Moss, free and crossing to help Fate sit up. Argosy joined him and began slicing at the ropes that held the Captain. "No, don't be wigglin' about, Jason,'' Moss ordered. "Ye be shot an' we don't know where.''

"In the back somewhere," whispered Argosy as the ropes gave way. "Here, hold this lantern and let me have a look." Argosy inhaled a gasp as Moss raised the lantern. "We need to get him to a surgeon," he muttered stripping the wide black cravat from about his neck and tugging a handkerchief from his pocket. "Here, hold these a moment and let me see where all this blood has come from." Argosy's fingers probed the back of Fate's head where the dark curls were matted with blood. "Damn," he mumbled, "it's a wonder you're not dead."

"Well, I ain't dead," pouted Fate. "Ow!"

"Ye lost a bit o' ear, Jason," Moss announced. "Ri' at the top."

"And you've acquired a wide grove along your skull," added Argosy. "Hold still and let me bind it up for you."

Fate held as still as he could manage, but his head ached and his legs were jumping from having been tied, and he was anxious to get out of the cellar. And it hurt exquisitely when Argosy pressed the folded handkerchief against the groove and over the injured ear and Mossie tied the cravat tightly around his head to keep the pad in place. He tried to ignore their clumsy ministrations by watching Dibs investigate the contents of the cellar, but he found his eyes growing blurry the longer he stared into the semi-darkness and gave up trying to follow the big man's movements.

"There," announced Argosy, "that'll have to do for the moment. What about you two?"

"Ain't nothin' but a nick," mumbled Dibs, stuffing a bottle of blue ruin into the inside pocket of his coat.

"Bit of a headache is all," muttered Moss, busily searching his own pockets. "Ah, here it be."

"What, Mossie?"

" 'Tis the note what that cove brought Dan'l. Snabbled it from Dan'l's pocket, I did, in the midst o' the fray."

"What's it say?" Fate attempted to turn and look at Moss, but the chamber began to swirl around him and he ceased to move. "Whew, I reckon I be a bit dizzy. Read the thin' ta us, Mossie."

Elgin Moss bent closer to the lantern and stared at the elegant copperplate that covered the paper. "It don't say nothin' much," he murmured at last. "Best get outta 'ere, Jason, before someone thinks ta come check on us."

"But what's it say, Mossie?"

"Nothin', Jason. It don't say nothin' won't wait till ye get yer poor head looked after. Dibs, be helpin' the lad, will ye? Mr. Argosy an' I will go ahead an' check that the way be clear."

Camilla grunted as the landau bounced over a particularly deep rut in the high road. Lilliheun, as she had guessed he would, had dispensed with the services of a coachman and chosen to drive the team himself. Still, she did not want to crawl out from under the rug on the floor of the vehicle where she'd hidden herself quite so early in the journey. It was possible Clare might look back through the little isinglass window and see her within, and as they were not yet terribly far from Longbourne, he might very well turn the team about and carry her back to the house. But he was driving at a spanking pace and she was being tossed about like so much loose baggage. And it was terribly hot and mucky on the floor under the rug, too.

At last a mighty jarring of the wheels over another rugged spot in the road decided her. Cautiously she peeped out from under the robe. She could see the merest bit of Lilliheun's back through the tiny window set into the retractable roof of the carriage. What on earth am I afraid of, she asked herself with a great deal of asperity. I will simply huddle in the far corner of the seat with my back to him and he will see nothing, even if he should for some unaccountable reason turn to look. I am all at sixes and sevens, that's what it is. I am so very worried about Jason that I'm not thinking properly at all.

The long skirts of her apricot walking dress made climbing from beneath the rug and gaining a safe position on the seat a more difficult task than Camilla had expected, catching as they did beneath the covering and about her ankles and taking a strangle-hold 'round her knees as the landau continued to bounce mercilessly over the rough track, but at last she succeeded and leaned thankfully against the squabs. It will not be too much longer, she thought, and we will be on the main road to Newhope. That will be much smoother and a great deal more comfortable. And then, she told herself even more cheerfully, we will gain the Newhope-London road and we will fly like the wind without the least bit of jogging about.

With a tiny sigh her thoughts turned from the road to the man for whose deliverance they made the journey. Certainly Jason was in serious difficulty. Perhaps the man who had injured his friend, Mr. Radd, had come after Jason as well.

Or perhaps someone had discovered—discovered that he was Jason Fate and—and the Runners were—"Oh, please," she whispered plaintively in the confines of the coach, "please don't let them catch him, dearest God. He's a good person; truly he is; he does not deserve to be—to be—gibbeted." The sting of tears in her eyes forced her to search hastily for her reticule. She found it on the floor beneath the rug, jerked it to her and took her handkerchief from it.

A vanilla bean, caught in the folds of the fine linen, popped out onto her lap. She dabbed at her eyes, then caught the little bean and clasped it tightly in one hand. "Don't be afraid, my dearest," she murmured. "Whatever 'tis that threatens, I shall save you, even if it is Bow Street or—or Prinny's infamous militia. I shall not let anyone harm you, not ever." Visions of his austerely drawn countenance forcing a smile for the children at their departure came with astounding clarity to her mind.

He was worried even then, she thought. Something was dreadfully wrong even on Monday morning and I was so conceited as to think him merely pouting because he was to be left behind. What a fool I am. Certainly I should have known. He feared a threat to us so much as to confess himself to the duke and beg him take us to Longbourne for safety's sake. Certainly he was threatened as well.

"Oh, Jason, why did you send us all away? What was in your mind to remain in London without a friend to help

you?'' The landau turned sharply to the left and sent
Camilla spilling across the seat in a most unladylike fashion,
forcing a breathless "oof!" from between her lips. She
pushed herself upward again hurriedly and muttered some
scathing phrases concerning Lilliheun's driving prowess
until she noticed that the road beneath them seemed
smoother and that the landau seemed to travel forward at
a much increased pace. We've turned onto the Newhope
road, she thought then. We have already reached the
Newhope road! Oh, Clare, bless you. You are the finest
whip in the entire world. No one else could have carried
us so far so fast! Neiland will have to ride like a demon to
catch us.

Neiland, however, was not riding at all, but stretching
out his long legs on a footstool in the back parlor at Longbourne and sipping at a glass of port while digesting the
latest tidbits in the copy of the *Gazette* he'd procured from
Adderley's in the village. Eversley, confident that his plans
for Lilliheun would not be discovered until it was much
too late for anyone to ride to that gentleman's rescue,
flashed a victorious smirk in Neiland's direction and pretended to peruse a volume of the collected works of Dr.
Samuel Johnson. It was not until after the duke's riding
party had returned that either of the gentlemen stirred,
and then they did so languidly. "Enjoy your ride, Father?"
Neiland queried, setting the paper aside as the earl
entered.

"Indeed. Longbourne is the most interesting estate.
Constantly changing. Dewhurst's raising beef cattle now,
out on the western edge, and thinking of draining the
little marsh and making a park of it. Discovered some sort
of ruin as well when they were turning over the old sheep
pasture. Roman, perhaps. He has men digging it up. A
pity Lilliheun did not see it. We shall have to send him in
that direction tomorrow. He will be more than interested."

"Lilliheun did not ride out with you?" Neiland asked.

"No. Thought he had gone into the village with you,
David.''

"Well, he said he might follow, but when he did not, I assumed he had joined your party."

"Saw him lounging about the library earlier in the day," Eversley inserted with a devious innocence, closing his volume. "Did not mention his intention of doing anything in particular. I expect he's gone off for a sleep or a stroll through the gardens or some such." That will hold them at least until dinner, he thought with a feeling of deep satisfaction. And by dinner that officious, overbearing prig will be beyond Newhope with no danger at all of anyone from here riding to his assistance.

"Well, I'd best be getting out of all my dirt," muttered Wheymore. "Duke will expect us dressed for dinner in an hour or so. Intends to keep country hours from now on, he says. Grown accustomed to dining early." The earl laughed at the look on Eversley's face. "I know, Eversley. He allowed us to dine late last evening, but he announced as we were returning that country hours would hold sway from now on. He cannot abide the rumbling of his stomach when his dinner is not before him by six o'clock. Neiland, I would suggest you do something about what you are wearing. Don't like Hessians in the dining room, Dewhurst don't. Right formal old gentleman."

Neiland was just in the midst of gaining his feet when a loud wail echoed down to them from the second floor and then another. "Mama! Papa!" And in a moment the sound of small feet pattering down the stairs and hurrying along the corridor held all three gentlemen spellbound.

Argosy stared at the note for an extraordinarily long time. He read it over again and again while Elgin Moss fidgeted and paced and fidgeted about the front of the apothecary's shop. When at last Argosy looked up, Moss was staring at him through a bottle of red-tinted liquid.

"This cannot possibly mean what I think it means," Argosy murmured.

"Why not?" Moss set the bottle aside and snatched a mortar and pestle from a counter. Nervously tossing first one then the other into the air, he turned his back on

Argosy and began pacing again. " 'Tis so plain even Dibs could not mistake the meanin' of it. Peace an' 'is villains are off ta stop a coach somewhere between London an' Newhope, an' kill some cove. And I happen ta know that then they plan ta lay it on Jason's doorstep an' turn him over ta the Runners. An' me an' Dibs with 'im most like, seeing as they had us already secured in their cellar." Moss came to a sudden halt and turned sharply to face Argosy. "Ye're not plannin' ta turn Jason over ta the Runners, are ye? Ye are," he muttered, recognizing a flash of guilt as it flitted across Argosy's countenance. "Why'd ye bring 'im here, then, ye fiend? Did ye think he could not survive Newgate lest 'is head were stitched up proper? Ye were afraid he'd not live ta see the hangman? A pox on ye, ye devil!"

"No, no, no, no!" sputtered Argosy angrily. "I was not even looking for Jason Fate. I told you already that I was sent to discover what I might about Mr. John Locksley. Borhill needed proof he was not Dewhurst's heir and it was my task to find it. It was never my task to find and capture Captain Fate."

"But ye found 'im anyway, didn't ye? An' now ye be thinkin' about collectin' the blood money."

"I am not thinking about any such thing, Mr. Moss."

"Yes, ye are."

"Well, perhaps the thought did cross my mind a moment ago, but it has since been overshadowed by other matters. Even if Locksley and Fate are one and the same, that don't prove that he is not the Duke of Dewhurst's grandson, and I should be as good as hung myself were I responsible for the execution or transportation of Dewhurst's heir, believe me."

"Aye, that I believe," nodded Moss. "Jason," he added, as Fate walked tentatively into the front of the shop followed by a clucking apothecary and Dibs. "Ye ought not be walkin' about."

"An' so I told him. But would he listen? No! He must be up and off as soon as I set the last stitch. If Mr. Dibs had not sat upon him, he would not even have a bandage 'round his brow!" exclaimed the frustrated apothecary.

"I'll not be responsible does he fall down and die in the street, I assure you of that."

"Ain't gonna die in no street," mumbled Fate. "Got other thin's ta do. Dibs, will ye hail a hackney fer ta take us back ta Grosvenor Square?"

The apothecary's eyes grew to three times their normal size at the expressed destination. He looked all of them up and down, from head to toe, one after the other. "Grosvenor Square?"

"Well, one can't dress too gaudily, my good man, when one goes slumming, you know," Argosy replied haughtily. "A fellow would be a fool to wander about St. Giles in anything but the worst of rags. Shall we be off then, Locksley?" he added, producing a number of flimsies from the pocket of his coat and counting them out into the apothecary's hand.

"I thought ye done that wi' actu'l style," grinned Fate, settling back against the dirty squabs of the hired coach. "'Bout as 'igh an' mighty as the duke hisself."

Argosy nodded, smiling. "I thought so too. Haven't worked with Borhill for so long without learning the, uh, attitude, so to speak."

"No, but ye ain't worked with 'im long enough ta learn 'ow ta sufficiently distract me from m'intentions though," returned Fate with a quick scowl. "I reckon I got a right ta know what were in that note, Mossie. Spill it."

Elgin Moss did not, however, spill it, holding out until the four of them had reached the Eversley mansion and made their way at Fate's insistence into the chamber where Radd was being tended. Fate gave a great sigh as he stepped into the room and Artie's eyes—as clear and bright as ever they had been—met his own. "Thank Gawd," he murmured, dropping down on the edge of the mattress. "I thought they'd come ta do away with ye, Artie. 'Twas all I could think about, 'specially as Mossie wouldn't say what was writ in the note."

This brought a look of guilt to Moss's face and he stuttered and sputtered about how he would gladly have revealed the contents of the note had he known what Fate imagined.

"No, ye wouldn't, Mossie. Ye're stubborn as they comes. Ye would just 'ave said it ain't so an' lef' me ta wonder. But I reckon it's got ta do with this business o' murder what Artie heard about, and that's got ta do with me. I got a right, Mossie, ta know what I be up against." Fate listened in silence as Moss read the missive. Dibs, filching a cold piece of toast from a tray beside Radd's bed and munching it thoughtfully, slumped into a chair at the foot end of the bed and listened with equal intensity. Artie Radd inhaled a gasp as he caught the gist of it and tugged at the Captain's sleeve.

"Now? Taday? They's goin' af'er the cove taday, Jason?"

"I reckon they be half way there b'now, Artie. Wherever 'tis."

"Newhope is southwest of London," offered Argosy. "I have only stopped there once, but 'tis just off the main highway to Longbourne—Dewhurst's estate."

"Ye're hoaxin' me," Fate said with a hint of exasperation in his tone.

Argosy shook his head slowly. "Truth," he drawled.

"Well, damnation! If I'd a knowed all this yesterday, I coulda gone along with the rest a 'em, an' pr'aps me an' Lilliheun an' Neiland coulda—"

"Lilliheun?" gasped Artie Radd, snatching at Fate's arm.

"Aye, Artie. 'Twas his digs ye was stayin' at afore we moved ye 'ere. Ye know, the flash cove what 'elped me carry ye ta the carriage Sun'ay night."

"The one what that Camme't fella was always sirrin?"

"Aye."

"Arrgh!" Radd's face turned several shades of pale.

"Artie, what is it?" asked Moss solicitously, crossing to put a hand on the man's shoulder. "Are ye ill again?"

"Lilliheun," Radd muttered, brushing the hand aside. "That be the name what Peace were throwin' about. Lilliheun. That be the cove what they plan ta kill!"

Radd's words spilled into a shocked silence and settled uneasily there.

" 'Sblood," hissed Argosy at last.

"Lilliheun," muttered Fate. "Lilliheun—li'l man—Harley thought they was sayin' about a li'l man. Devil take it! Whyn't that boy learn ta speak the King's English!''

Chapter 19

Lord Eversley felt a distinct trembling in the pit of his stomach as he sat immobile amidst the increasingly violent storm that raged around him. "Totally out of the question!" Wheymore roared. "Unimaginable! Camilla would never pull such a stunt, nor Lilliheun neither! Damnation, but someone shall answer for this! They have been duped somehow, the both of them!"

"Ned, hush," urged Lady Wheymore with a sense of hopelessness, for she knew he would not be hushed, not once his face had reached that particular shade of red. "There is some mistake, that's all. Camilla did not take the time to explain fully."

"No, she most certainly did not!"

"Oh!" wailed Aurora plaintively from within her brother's supportive embrace. "Cammy will be thoroughly ruined and Clare will be forced to marry her. A young lady cannot go jauntering off about the country in a gentleman's company, all alone, and so very far, without—without—and Clare was just beginning to like me! Now I have lost him—to Cammy who does not want him in the first place." Aurora buried her face in Neiland's neckcloth and burst into tears.

"Lilliheun's taken the landau though James does not recall seeing your niece anywhere about," bellowed Dewhurst stomping into the library. "Let me see Camilla's note again, Ned. There is something havey-cavey here and if 'tis Lilliheun's idea of a joke, I shall have the lad's head on a plate!"

Wheymore passed Camilla's hastily scrawled missive into the duke's hand. "Dearest Rory, I have gone with Clare to London. Do not fear. All will be well," read the duke gruffly. "Humph! What kind of a message is that? Have gone to London. Why? Are you certain the gel has her wits about her, Ned? For a person who wishes to be a writer, she don't write enough to fill a thimble! They are not eloping?"

"Heavens, no!" exclaimed Lady Wheymore. "Why on earth would they suddenly elope when Clare has asked her very properly at least three times to marry him? It makes no sense."

"Besides," Neiland offered as his sister burst into a fresh round of tears, "one does not elope *to* London, Duke. One elopes *from* London *to* Gretna Green."

Dewhurst nodded curtly in acknowledgement of the truth of Neiland's observation then swung around to scowl pensively at Eversley. "Do you know anything at all about this, Eversley? You were here, were you not, all afternoon?"

Eversley stirred uneasily on the sopha. He crossed one knee over the other, then uncrossed them, then crossed them in the opposite direction. The fool gel had somehow overheard his words to Lilliheun—or Lilliheun had been stupid enough to confide in her. Whatever, Lilliheun must be close to Newhope by this time. He'd left near two hours ago. If I am lucky, Eversley thought, they will waylay him in less than another hour and Peace and his cronies will have the good sense to kill the interfering Miss Quinn as well. Of course they will kill the gel, he told himself. They are not so stupid as to leave behind a witness! And since she will be dead, she cannot point a finger at me. A triumphant smile slipped onto Eversley's thin lips as he contemplated the outcome of his plan but he subdued it as he looked up into the duke's eyes. "I know nothing at all about it, Uncle. Cousin Clare did not see fit to confide in me. We are not the best of friends, you know. Though why, if he must do something so foolish as to run off with Miss Quinn, he could not give me at least one opportunity to dissuade him, I know not. I would have counselled him otherwise had he come to me."

"Well, he did not," muttered Neiland. "I'm going after them, Father."

"We are both going after them," the earl declared. "Dewhurst, we require the loan of your fastest horses if we are to have even a hope of reaching them before they reach London.''

"But what good will that do?" sobbed Aurora as Neiland passed her into her mother's arms.

"If they are seen to arrive in Town in the company of your father and brother, dearest," murmured Lady Wheymore encouragingly, "not one eyebrow will be raised. What better chaperones might Cammy have than Uncle Ned and David?"

"Indeed," grumbled the earl, already stalking toward the hallway. "And once we are in London, I shall box Lilliheun's ears for him. See if I don't!"

The long morning spent traipsing about and playing with the children and the long journey the day before and an almost sleepless night spent in contemplating the highlights and depths of Jason Fate's starkly handsome face had combined with the smoothness of the road and the lulling movement of the landau to send Camilla into a deep slumber from which she did not awaken until the carriage door slammed open and Lilliheun's voice roared a most improper but unmistakable oath. "Oh!" she cried, startled. "Oh, Clare! Are we in London already?"

"London?" stormed Lilliheun, struggling to bring his temper under control lest someone in the inn yard take undue notice of them. "No, madam, we are not in London. We are in the yard of The Newhope Inn."

"Oh, yes, you are having Lord Eversley's chestnuts put to. It will not take long, will it, Clare? We must hurry."

"We, Miss Quinn, are not going to hurry," growled Lilliheun, climbing into the landau and sitting on the seat opposite her. "What are you doing here, Camilla? When did you climb into the landau? Why? And how do you know I am bound for London?"

"I—I know everything, Clare," stuttered Camilla, for the first time intimidated by the irate light in Lilliheun's eyes. "I overheard, you see, in the library. I had—had fallen asleep in the wing chair and woke to hear your conversation with Lord Eversley."

"Wonderful! And since you had not the least confidence in my ability to help your friend, you sneaked into the landau and—"

"No! No, Clare, that is not it at all!" cried Camilla. "I have every confidence in your ability!"

"Oh? Then why are you here?"

Camilla had not the least idea how to answer him. This was a gentleman in whom she had always trusted, whose good opinion she valued, and whose friendship she deeply wished to preserve. And it did seem as if she had no confidence in him—the fact that she had stowed away as she had. How could she explain her feelings? Tears started to her eyes and she dashed them angrily away with the back of her hand. "I—I—oh, Clare, I don't know what to say! I was so very frightened, you see, for Jason. I had no idea what awful thing had happened and I thought—I thought—I must be with him, Clare. Truly I must be. I cannot bear the thought that something dreadful will happen to him and I shall not be at his side to help him! What if he is gravely injured—or—or—killed! Or what if—if he is taken prisoner and thrown into Newgate!"

"Newgate," muttered Lilliheun, offering the young lady his handkerchief. "Why on earth would he be thrown into Newgate? And why do you call him Jason? Radd calls him Jason, but you did never know him before Eversley introduced him to us as John Locksley."

"It is because—because I did know him before we were introduced, Clare," murmured Camilla, refusing to meet Lilliheun's gaze. "He is Jason Fate."

"Captain Jason Fate? Locksley? Camilla, you are mistaken!"

"No. I recognized him when first he halted our runaway carriage on Albemarle Street, but I could not—I could not condemn him to the gibbet, Clare. Can you understand? He saved our lives. How could I betray him after that? And he has never done anything truly dreadful, you know. Not really."

"Ho, no!" exclaimed Lilliheun. "Just waylaid innumerable coaches, stolen jewels and money and even the mail!"

"Oh!" Camilla burst into the sobs she had been struggling against all along. "Oh, n-now I h-have ruined every-every-thing. N-now you w-will n-not wish to h-help him at all!"

Every last vestige of anger shriveled away inside of Lilli-heun as he stared helplessly at Camilla. Hesitantly he rose from his seat and moved across beside her. Tentatively he put an arm about her trembling shoulders and eased her gently against himself. "Do not, Camilla," he whispered, feeling her quake in his arms. "No, do not cry so. I am fond of Locksley—Jason Fate or not. I promise you, I am, and I shall not desert him. I haven't the vaguest notion what I shall do if he is caught by the Runners, my dear, but I shall not let him go to the gibbet—nor will Neiland, I promise you."

"You—you won't?"

"No. You're in love with the man, ain't you, Camilla?"

"Y-yes."

"So in love that you would marry him?"

"Y-yes."

Lilliheun sighed.

"Oh, Clare, I am so very sorry. I did not in the least intend to fall in love with him. I did not mean to fall in love with any man—not ever. But he is so very kind and courageous and whimsical."

"And lucky," added Lilliheun in an undertone. "Come, m'dear, dry your eyes. The team has been hitched this last ten minutes, and every moment more we delay may put Locksley in greater danger. I cannot imagine why Neiland has not come up with us by now, but we can wait no longer. Locksley—I mean, Fate—would never have sent for assis-tance if his situation were not dire."

"And—and—I may accompany you?"

"I ought to make you remain right here at this inn and send word to your uncle to come and fetch you," muttered Lilliheun. "If I had a bit of sense, that's exactly what I would do."

"But you haven't the least bit of sense?"

"No. I expect I have been associating with that rascal you love for much too long. I understand what you feel, m'dear. But you must do exactly as I and Neiland say or as Locksley says if indeed there is trouble. You will do him not the least bit of good, you know, if you come to harm."

Argosy had never ridden at such a spanking pace in his life and still he was far behind Fate. It had taken at least a quarter hour for the horses to arrive at Grosvenor Square and he had been impatient with Fate's insistence that no other mounts would carry them as far and as fast. Fate, however, was proved correct. The horse beneath Argosy was not even breathing hard, yet his hooves flew over the road barely touching the ground. That the animal could possibly maintain such a pace as far as Newhope was doubtful. That Fate's mount could maintain its pace for one more mile, Argosy could not believe. He was not surprised then when he rounded a bend and found Fate stopped dead in the middle of the road ahead. "What? Has he gone lame?" Argosy asked, gasping for air as he pulled up beside the Captain.

"Smear? Naw. He ain't never come up lame yet. Got the feet o' a ballet dancer, 'e does. I reckoned just ta wait on ye so's ye wouldn't get lost."

"Lost? How could I get lost?"

" 'Cause we be leavin' the road."

"No, Fate, really, the toll road will take us directly to the London-Newhope road. It's the fastest way."

"No, but I rekernize this place. I been 'ere afore. I don't 'member no place called Newhope, but I can get from 'ere ta the old Lunnon road in less'n a 'alf hour. Can this road get us there that fast?"

Argosy stared. "N-no," he stuttered at last, "not that f-fast. How—?"

"This way then," Fate urged, giving Smear a nudge and directing her off the main highway and onto a low track. "C'mon, Tuggle," he added, reaching across to give Argosy's mount a pat. Ye got ta keep up, m'dear. 'Tis a 'mergency."

Once again they were off. They rode hard and in silence, leaving the track to leap a fence and cut across a large pasture, to ford a stream and rumble single file through a small wood. They traversed a marsh, skirted the edge of a bluff and in less than a half hour they were pushing through a hedgerow onto the London-Newhope road. Argosy pulled up, amazed. "How did you do that? We've covered near twenty miles in less than ten."

"Aye, 'twas a shortcut."

"Yes, but how—"

" 'Tis always shorter ridin' 'cross country. Don't ask no more, Argosy. There be a gypsy curse on any what tells a outsider how the paths be marked."

"There are paths? And they're marked?"

"Aye, plain as daylight. We got ta be careful from 'ere on. No tellin' where 'zactly Peace an' his cronies be waitin' fer Lilliheun."

Fate, who wore once again the long, drab surtout he had abandoned when he had left the High Toby, produced two horse pistols from the deep pockets. He loaded them carefully and handed one to Argosy.

"I'm afraid I am not a very good shot, Captain. And I have never used such a pistol as this in all my life."

"Jus' be careful," grinned Fate. "That un b'long's ta Artie an' it ain't trustworthy. As like ta go off while yer ridin' as not. Keep it in yer hand an' pointed away from ye—an' away from me. Do ye got a blade? 'Tis likely we're gonna need ta fight 'em hand ta hand. Peace ain't gonna turn tail an' run. Leastways, I don't think 'e will. Are ye all right, Argosy? Ye look a bit—"

"I'm fine, Captain. I am just nervous. I shall shoot as best I can and I shall use my fists to the best of my ability, but I cannot, I think, wield a knife."

"Ye take this un anyways, Argosy. I got another. Maybe ye won't be needin' of it, but ye keep it in yer belt jus' in case." Argosy took the knife and then watched, somewhat agog, as Fate fished a gold earring from his waistcoat pocket and put it in his earlobe. " 'Tis for luck," smiled the captain, and with a nod of his curly head which now sported a silk kerchief that covered the bandage circling his brow, he took Argosy's hand in his own, shook it, and then tapped a spur against Smear's side.

* * *

Neiland was amazed at the speed and certainty with which his father rode straight at fences and hedges and streams. He, himself, was hard pressed to keep pace. Somehow he'd never noticed the strength and prowess and courage of the man. Where was I, he wondered, not to have seen him like this before? He has always been just my father—dignified and stiff-rumped and a stickler for propriety. By Gawd, but he's a regular nonesuch on horseback. He flies. He fears nothing. We shall come up with Lilliheun in no time.

They did, in fact, reach Newhope only a half hour after Lilliheun and Camilla had finally departed the inn. The earl stalked impatiently across the yard as the hostlers ran to saddle fresh mounts. "Thank goodness Dewhurst boards some stock here," he mumbled as Neiland came up with him. "We should never catch them were we forced to ride any of the stable hacks."

"I don't expect any of the stable hacks could go at such a pace as you demand, sir," replied Neiland. "They would be more like to drop in their tracks."

"And you?" Wheymore asked, coming to a halt and turning to smile at his son. "You are not like to drop in your tracks, David?"

"No, sir. Not hardly."

"Good. I worried about you, you know. I rather think you have never been forced to throw your heart over so very many obstacles at such speed before. Still, I knew you would be directly behind me. I could never have sired a faint-hearted son. We shall hold to the road the rest of the way. We do not want to chance overshooting them."

"No, sir. You are very worried about Cammy, aren't you father? Lilliheun is a perfect gentleman, you know. He may be trusted to see that Cam does not come to any harm."

"Indeed," murmured Wheymore. "Which is why I cannot understand any of this. There is something distinctly havey-cavey here, David. Dewhurst thinks so too. He told me as much before we left. Come, the horses are ready."

The two gentlemen quickly crossed the yard, mounted, and were instantly racing up the London-Newhope road.

Camilla had begged to join Lilliheun on the box, but he had forbidden her. "Only think," he reminded her, "any gabblemonger who chanced to see us might dine out on the tidbit for weeks. Besides, it is much too dangerous, Camilla. At such a rate of speed as we are travelling, you are like to fly off at the first great bump." He'd grinned at her, but he would hear no more arguments from her and had closed her inside the conveyance.

The sun was lowering in the sky and the small watch on her lapel read five minutes of six when the first explosion of gunpowder drew her to the window. A second pistol shot sent her dodging to the far side of the seat as a ball splintered the side of the landau and lodged just beneath the isinglass. Of a sudden came the pounding of hooves against the hard-packed earth and the jerking of the carriage as Lilliheun laid the whip across the team's backs urging them to even longer and somewhat panicked strides.

Camilla turned hastily to stare out the little window between herself and the box and gasped as another gunshot sounded and Lilliheun wrenched forward, losing the whip, but struggling to hold the reins. Even in the growing dusk, Camilla could see the blood that erupted from his shoulder. Along both sides of the landau riders flashed into her sight and out of it again, and then there were more shots, a horrendous screaming of horses, a tremendous jolt that sent the landau careening forward and down until the back wheels of the carriage were in the air, and a screech which Camilla knew came from between her own lips.

Turned upside down and tangled in her skirts, her head and arm and side feeling distinctly odd, she struggled angrily to free herself from the tipped conveyance. Clare, she thought, cannot have survived such a crash. There can be nothing left of the box at all. He will have been smashed to pieces along with it.

All around her shouts and curses lashed the air but she paid them not the least heed and in the end pried open the splintered door of the landau and tumbled out onto the road, a bundle of torn skirts and petticoats. She fought her way to her knees only to be tugged immediately to the ground. "No, don't, Cammy. Wriggle back under here as far as you can—up between the wheels."

"Clare! Oh, Clare, I thought they had killed you!"

"Not yet, m'dear. A bit bruised an' bloodied is all. Farther back, Camilla. Right up against what remains of the box. That's m'girl."

No sooner did Camilla reach the small nook into which Lilliheun had directed her than he turned and rolled, short sword in hand, from under the coach. "No!" she cried. "Clare, do not!" She searched hurriedly about her for some sort of weapon, seized upon a splintered length of wood from the broken box and crawled frantically after him. A countless number of men swarmed over Lilliheun as Camilla threw herself into the fray swinging the bit of broken lumber with all her strength first at one head and then another. Huge, rough hands attempted to grab the wood from her, but she hung on, jabbing it into the chest that the hands left unprotected.

She heard Lilliheun grunt, saw him stumble and quickly right himself then stumble again and go down. She ran to him and, standing over him, screamed and struck out again and again and again until the sharp, splintered stick was finally wrenched from her grasp and a powerful set of hands came about her waist, lifted her into the air and flung her toward the far side of the road.

She landed on the thick, soft grass of the verge and, sobbing, pulled herself to her feet to dash back into the fight only to see a ghost of a man in a long, drab surtout hurtle from the back of a horse the color of drizzling skies and into the midst of the villains attacking Lilliheun. In a moment, a second man fell upon them as well. As if in a dream she heard Fate's voice shouting over and over again, "Get 'im out! Get 'im out! Argosy, get 'im out!" More gun powder flashed and more, but she could not hear any explosions. She could hear nothing but the captain's voice.

And then the oddest sort of man was stumbling toward her across the road, and she had to shake herself to realize that it was not one man, but two—one half-supporting, half-dragging the other.

Argosy eased Lilliheun to the grass at her feet and bent over him a moment. "He is not dead, Miss Quinn," he said then, looking up and quickly undoing his neckcloth. "Bind this 'round his shoulder as tightly as you can and use his cravat to bind the wound on his head. And take this to protect yourself," he added, gently placing the knife Fate had given him into her palm. "I have appropriated Lilliheun's short sword." And then he was gone, racing back across the road toward the weaving, staggering mass of arms and legs and bodies beside the ruined landau.

Just as Camilla bent hurriedly over Lilliheun two more horses came flashing from the direction of Newhope and in an instant both came to a rearing halt and spilled two more men into the fray.

She forced herself not to look anymore, but set the knife on the ground beside her and concentrated upon binding Clare's wounds. She refused to listen for the sound of Jason's voice amidst the uproar and tugged the neckcloth as tightly as she could 'round Lilliheun's shoulder and fastened the cravat clumsily, but firmly, about his head. And then she could look away no longer and she peered into the deepening dusk. The mass of arms and legs and bodies was no longer writhing. A strong, tall gentleman was walking toward her. She reached unconsciously for the knife and then recognized the sober face in what remained of the daylight. "Uncle Ned!" she cried and ran to him, her dress torn and shredded and covered with blood. "Oh, Uncle Ned!"

He wrapped her in his arms and held her very tightly for a long moment and then whispered in her ear. "Locksley is greatly injured, m'dear, and asking for you. 'Tis you he calls Dendron; is it not?"

Camilla's heart, which had pounded and soared and railed and wrenched through the agonizing attack, seemed to stutter to a stop. What little was left of the world fluttered and grew dim before her eyes. And then she caught herself up and stiffened considerably in her uncle's arms. He nodded at the feel of her and led her across the road to where a number of bodies lay motionless. One man lay with his head in Neiland's lap, and Camilla bent hurriedly down, her uncle with her, unwilling to release her from his grasp.

"Jason," she said, fighting to keep a sob from her voice.

"Dendron?" His hand reached toward the sound of her voice and it was then she saw the dark stains across the front of his shirt as his coat fell open.

"I am here, Jason. You are going to be all right. I know you are. You must only rest now, and we will take care of you."

"D-Dendron? I c-can't see ye."

She grasped his hand quickly, kissed the palm of it—bloody as his chest—and held it tenderly against her cheek.

His other hand fumbled at one of his waistcoat pockets and then at the other. He groaned, and his fingers fished inside the pocket anxiously, and then he was grasping something tightly in his fist. "I w-want ye t-ta have m'token, D-Dendron. It'll—it'll keep ye safe yer whole—whole—life. The P-Princess of D-Dewdrops p-promised. It'll k-keep ye s-safe—an'—an'—" Fate's voice was failing and Camilla leaned closer. Oddly, she could feel her uncle leaning closer with her. "—an' perteck ye from the—B-Bodkins—in the bottom o' the gard—" Fate's voice rattled meaninglessly in his throat, his arm moved toward Camilla and his fist unclenched. A tarnished thimble rolled to a stop at her knees. Her Uncle Ned's arms tightened around her and a wail of despair broke from Wheymore's throat and echoed into the evening air like a lost soul seeking its Maker.

Chapter 20

The Earl of Wheymore, one leg competently bandaged by
Lord Wright's physician and a lump of court plaster covering a long cut across his grizzled jaw, sat silently upon
a ladder-backed chair in the green saloon of Kimberly,
the Earl of Wright's southernmost estate. His entire body
shuddered uncontrollably from time to time and then just
as abruptly ceased all movement whatsoever.

His eyes, Camilla noticed fearfully, did not meet either
her own or his son's, but stared, sightless into the corridor.
Neiland, much too silent himself, placed one of Lady
Wright's woolen shawls around his father's shoulders.
"Please, Father, cannot you tell us what has shaken you
so terribly?" Neiland asked, kneeling down before the earl,
and placing his own strong hands on his father's knees.
"What made you shout so to the heavens and then go
silent? You have seen death before, Father. I know you
have. 'Twas not that."

Camilla, bruised from head to toe but clean and warmly
wrapped in one of Lady Wright's elegant dressing gowns,
opened her fist to stare down at the tarnished silver thimble
which she had been loathe to set aside even to bathe.
Dulled and scratched, it flickered only weakly in the soft
lights of the candelabras. Thank God, she thought, that
Mr. Argosy had come upon the Earl of Wright so soon in
his search for help and that Kimberly should be so close
to where the landau had been waylaid. Surely both Jason
and Clare would have died had help not come so quickly
or had there been no place so near to carry them. The
thought brought tears again to her eyes and she dashed
them away with the back of the hand that did not cradle
the thimble. As she did so, her glance found the Earl of
Wheymore's eyes resting upon her. "What is it, Uncle Ned?
Is there something I can do for you? What do you see?"

"It's that thing in your hand, Cammy," murmured Neiland. "The token Locksley gave you."

" 'Tis a thimble," groaned the earl heavily. " 'Tis a very old and dented thimble."

"Yes, indeed it is," agreed Camilla softly. "Would you like to see it, Uncle Ned?"

"I should like to hold it."

Camilla rose and carried it across the room to him. Her eyes met Neiland's questioningly as she placed the thimble gently in the earl's palm and his large, trembling hand closed tightly over it. His eyes closed then too and his lips began to move silently.

"What, Father? What are you saying?" asked Neiland in a whisper. Camilla had never seen such deep concern before upon her cousin's brow and even in her own sorrow, she could not help but pity Neiland.

"I am praying, David," murmured the earl. "I am praying God against all odds to spare your brother's life. Where is Wright?" he growled then in tones more like his own. "Where is that damnable surgeon? What are they all about up there that they cannot send someone to tell us how the boy does?"

"My b-brother?" Neiland rocked back on his heels and stared pleadingly up at Camilla. My father has lost his mind, his eyes told her fearfully. "There—we—no, it is Lilliheun they tend to upstairs, Father. Lilliheun and—and Locksley."

The earl's fist tightened around the tiny thimble and with a great sigh he heaved himself from the chair and stalked toward the doorway. He paused and looked out into the hall and up the staircase. "By God, but I will go up there and find out for myself how things stand," he roared.

"No, no, Uncle Ned, you cannot!" Camilla and Neiland both hurried after him and each taking an arm, they tugged him back into the saloon and down onto a sopha between them. "Dr. Soames has forbidden everyone except Lady Wright and the servants who are helping him. Lord Wright is waiting in the upstairs corridor and will come directly there is any news. As hard as it is for us, we must all keep out of the way, Uncle Ned, or Clare and—and—Mr. Locksley might well die."

"He is not Mr. Locksley," said the earl quite as calmly and sanely as either Neiland or Camilla could wish.

"Well, no, perhaps he is not," murmured Camilla.

Wright's careful gait upon the stairs and the tap of his cane as he crossed the parquet at the bottom of the staircase drew all their eyes to the doorway once again. Camilla could feel the sheer power of the man as he entered the saloon. It was as though the air itself began to whirr with his energy. "So you're feeling better, are you, Wheymore? Heard your bellow all the way at the top of the stairs. Lilliheun will survive nicely Soames thinks, though he won't be up and around very soon." His brooding blue-black eyes with the silver flecks fell upon Camilla and then Neiland and then flicked back to Wheymore.

"And J-Jason? Mr. Locksley?" Camilla's voice wavered slightly as she asked. Why must she ask? Why did Wright not simply tell them how the captain did as he had with Clare?

Wright shook his head, looked down at the Aubusson carpet beneath his feet, looked up at her. "Soames says he will be dead by dawn—but Ellie says not," he added hastily. "My money lies on Ellie. She wouldn't let me die, you know, and I rather think she will not let that young man do so either. She says he is both courageous and obdurate and that he will not yield to death. And they have managed to stop his wounds bleeding at last."

"I must go to him," gasped Camilla.

"No, you must not," Wright declared, the sheer power of his gaze pinning her to the sopha. "You, Miss Quinn, must go with Jane, who will appear in a moment, and be put to bed yourself. Ellie says you will be of no use to either of the gentlemen if you do not. They are both of them beyond knowing who attends them this moment, but tomorrow, she says, you must be prepared, because both of them will be calling for you."

"But—but—if she is mistaken and Jason should—"

"If my wife is mistaken, Miss Quinn, you will be summoned immediately, no matter what the hour. But I assure you, she is a better judge of what a man may survive than any physician. And you, sir," he drawled, his gaze falling upon Neiland, "are also commanded to take to your bed. Mr. Argosy has already sought his. No, I shall not discuss it with you," he said with an upraised hand as Neiland sought to protest. "My valet awaits you in the second chamber on the left in the south corridor. Ellie says Dr. Soames did not bind your shoulder and ribs so that you could sit in the parlor and aggravate both injuries. I will see to your father's comfort, Neiland. Allow my valet to see to yours."

Thus dismissed Camilla and Neiland each bestowed a kiss upon Wheymore's cheek and left the room to be met in the corridor by a middle-aged woman who introduced herself as Jane, her ladyship's abigail, and escorted them up the staircase, directing Neiland which way he must go and then taking Camilla to the bedchamber prepared for her.

In the green saloon Wright lowered himself into a wing chair facing the sopha and directed his unsettling glare upon Wheymore. A footstep behind him was greeted by a request for Madeira, which the butler fetched immediately, pouring each of the gentlemen a glass and leaving the decanter upon a small cherrywood cricket table beside Wright. "Now, we shall discuss, you and I, what's turned you into a mound of quivering pudding, Wheymore," scowled Wright. "And then we shall decide what to do about the matter."

"I am not a mound of quivering pudding," growled Wheymore. "And you, sir—"

"What's that in your fist, Ned?" interrupted Wright without the least attempt at politeness.

Wheymore's fist opened and he looked down at the thimble.

"Tell me," urged Wright. "I ain't your best friend, but at the moment I am the only confidante available and you will feel more the thing do you confide in someone. It's to do with Locksley, ain't it? *Is* he Dewhurst's grandson? Is that it? Have you discovered a nephew only to come within a hairsbreadth of losing him?"

"You—you think he will not die?" Wheymore's fist

closed over the thimble again and his weary eyes sought truth in Wright's.

"I think he'll live if we all do as Ellie says we must. Soames is a competent physician, but he knows nothing of how much a man's mind and spirit are involved in the battle against death. My Eleanor, on the other hand, has good reason to know exactly that and I trust her judgement implicitly. He'll not die, Wheymore. We shall all see to it. Now, answer my question. Is he Dewhurst's grandson?"

"Yes," murmured the earl, "but not a Lilliheun."

"Not a—? Then who—?"

"He is John Locksley Bedford—my elder son, Wright."

"Oh, m'god," whispered Wright and could think of nothing more to say. Though they were not closely acquainted, Wright, like most of the gentlemen of the *ton*, had heard the tale of the tragic death of Wheymore's first wife and the subsquent loss of his son. The lady had been killed in a carriage accident and the boy supposedly wandered off into the forest along the lane. A great search had been mounted for the child but to no avail. And though a less stubborn man would have been forced to concede that a boy numbering only a few months beyond the age of two and probably injured as well could never survive beyond a night in the wilds of Northumberland, Wheymore had continued to search for months afterward.

" 'Twas years before I could give him up for dead. Even after David was born I hoped to find Johnny somehow, somewhere. And now—now—If he dies, Wright, after I have just discovered him, I shall die as well."

"Are you certain 'tis him?"

The Earl of Wheymore's fist opened once more and he leaned forward to place the thimble in Wright's hand. "I know the feel of it like the back of my hand. I know the dent just below the rim from when I stepped on it. You look, Wright. The top bears initials, does it not?"

Wright stood and carried the thimble closer to the light of one of the candelabras and stared down at it. He rubbed the top against the sleeve of his coat and stared again. Deeply engraved and barely legible beneath the tarnish, the scripted letters came into focus. "C.E.B." he said quietly.

"Claudia Estelle Bedford," murmured Wheymore. " 'Twas a trinket I brought her from London the final month of her confinement with Johnny. She was busy sewing baby things, you know."

"But how did the boy come by it?"

"She gave it him as a token to ward off the evil Bodkins! We laughed about it for days afterward. She was accustomed to take him with her to the hidden garden and tell him stories, and she would pretend to be Clarissa, the Princess of Dewdrops, and she named him Sir Jason, Knight of the Forests Wild. And the stories were always about evil little beings called Bodkins who lived in the bottom of the garden. We laughed because he believed in them, you know. He even imagined he saw one once—a Bodkin! And—and—this evening when he thought he was d-dying, he fished the thing from his waistcoat pocket and attempted to give it to Camilla. A token, he told her. From the P-Princess of Dewdrops. To protect her all her life. Esp-pecially from the Bodkins in the bottom—" Wheymore's voice broke completely and he buried his head in his hands. When he looked up again, Wright was taking a seat beside him and putting an arm around his shoulders.

Camilla woke, screaming, from a nightmare and sat straight up in bed only to be taken instantly into a pair of waiting arms and hugged against a caring breast. "Do not, dearest," whispered Lady Wheymore, smoothing soft, chestnut curls behind a shell-like ear. "It was a bad dream. But it is all at an end and you are perfectly safe."

"Aunt Mary? Oh, Aunt Mary, the most dreadful thing has happened!"

"I know, my dear. We have only now arrived from Longbourne to have the entire tale poured into our ears. Lord Wright's messenger did not know the whole of it, you see, and we were all terrified lest you or your uncle or Neiland or Lilliheun be fatally injured. Thank heaven you are not."

"But Jason—Mr. Locksley—Oh, Aunt Mary, I must dress and go to him at once."

"Indeed you must not," declared Lady Wheymore solemnly. "First you must drink your morning chocolate and wash your face and let me fix your hair and then you must go downstairs and break your fast as any young lady might be expected to do. And when you have finished breakfasting, you will join myself and Aurora in a pleasant stroll through Lady Wright's rose garden. And then we shall join your Uncle Ned and Neiland and the duke in Lord Wright's study."

"But—but—"

The grimly determined look upon her aunt's usually cheerful visage sent waves of apprehension through Camilla. She began immediately to imagine the worst. Dr. Soames had been correct. Jason had not survived the night and no one had come to fetch her as they had promised to do.

Oh, how horrible, to die alone in a strange house with not a familiar face anywhere near, not a loving hand to hold or a recognizable voice to ease one into that nonending sleep! Tears rose to her eyes and though she fought against them, she could not force them back and they overflowed in silence down her pale cheeks. It was her own fault. She had been so hideously proud, so provokingly independent. Never had she admitted to anyone except Lilliheun that the captain owned her heart—that she loved him beyond all reason. And what good to tell Lilliheun, who was himself so gravely injured that he could not intervene for her and insist upon her right to be at Jason's side.

And Jason—she had not even admitted to Jason that she loved him—loved him so much as to be willing to bear the condemnation of all of Society to be with him. "I— I would have gladly m-married you, m-my darling," she whispered, sobbing. "Without a s-second thought, I w-would have d-done."

"Cammy, what on earth are you mumbling?" asked her aunt, placing a little lawn handkerchief into Camilla's palm. "And why are you crying? Do you hurt somewhere, child? Tell me, where is the pain?"

"I am c-crying," declared Camilla, forcing herself to look directly into her aunt's worried eyes, "because—because the m-man I l-love was let to die alone amongst s-s-strangers!"

"Oh, good heavens, is that all. And here I thought you had been injured more severely than anyone knew." Lady Wheymore, seeing Camilla's chin tilt and a blazing light mount to the brilliant green eyes, smiled softly. "The man you love is not at all dead, my dear. Mr. Locksley is holding on to life quite tightly and with both hands."

"He is?"

"Indeed, and has quite astounded Dr. Soames. Your Uncle Ned is even now seated beside that young rogue's bed bathing his brow with lavender water and responding to the rascal's mutterings with equally incomprehensible mutterings of his own."

"But—but—how did you know that I meant Mr. Locksley, Aunt? I th-thought I had never—"

"Goodness, we have all known you loved him since the moment he appeared at Aurora's come-out ball. Rory and David, I think, knew even before then. The thing is, we did none of us know if you knew, my dear, or how you would feel about it if it were pointed out to you, so we none of us did. Come now, drink your chocolate before it is frigid and let me help you to dress. Your Mr. Locksley is being competently attended to and you shall see him soon enough."

When at last Camilla, Aurora, and Lady Wheymore entered Wright's study, Neiland and the duke were both pacing the pretty Persian carpet and the Earl of Wheymore standing by Wright's desk fiddling with the wax jack. He turned immediately they entered and taking his wife's arm, escorted her to the comfort of a deep wing chair upholstered in dark red leather. Then he settled on the arm of the chair and urged the others to light some place or he would be certain to break his neck attempting to keep all of them in view.

"For I have something extremely important to say to the lot of you," he continued as the younger members of the group pulled footstools and chairs about him and the duke took possession of the most comfortable chair. "A veritable miracle has happened and it concerns us all. Camilla," he said, leaning forward and offering her the tarnished thimble he had taken from her the evening before. "I thank you with all my heart for the loan of this token, but you must take it back now. 'Twas given to you with a great deal of love and much as I wish to have it, I shall not deprive you of it." And then, putting his arm gently around his wife's shoulders, the Earl of Wheymore related to them the tragedy of his first wife's death, the loss of his first son and the incredible reappearance of Sir Jason, Knight of the Forests Wild.

"It *is* Johnny!" cried Dewhurst ecstatically, his face wreathed in smiles. "I had hoped as much! I have been praying for a way to prove it! The rapscallion *is* my grandson!"

"Indeed, sir, and though he ain't your heir, I thought you might be pleased to own him."

"More than pleased, Ned. Thankful and joyous and—and—delighted! But I'll teach him to keep his boots off my tables from now on, the audacious brat!"

"And you, David?" Wheymore gazed intently at Neiland. "His return makes you a younger son. If I acknowledge him, he will be the next Earl of Wheymore and not you, David."

"*If* you acknowledge him? *If,* Father? How can you not? How dare you not?"

"Well, he has not the least notion who he is, and he is not at all capable at the moment of understanding should I attempt to tell him. So I have decided that unless you are all of you willing to accept him, I shan't say the truth, but shall think of some other way to keep him by me and provide for him."

"Well, of all the stupid stuff I have ever heard," protested Lady Wheymore with a small tear glistening in the corner of one eye. "To think that any one of us would begrudge you the joy of welcoming your Johnny back home! You are a total ninnyhammer, sir, and that's a fact!"

"Neiland?" The earl gave his wife's shoulder a grateful squeeze, but his eyes never left his younger son's face.

"Well, it will take me a moment or two to grow accustomed to the idea, Father. He is likely to prove a particularly awesome elder brother to have, you know. But I rather think you have a duty to tell him the truth of the matter. And I don't think I shall fall into despair over losing the title. In fact, I shall most likely fall into an endless bout of giggles watching him wield it." The wide grin that sprang to David's face and the laughter that flashed in his eyes brought a relieved sigh from the earl.

"That's it then," he said quietly. "I shall explain to him directly he is able to understand. Aurora," he added with a smile in that young lady's direction. "You will not mind so much to be teased by two brothers, will you?"

"No, Papa," she replied with a tiny gurgle. "But will you please, when you have explained to him that you are his papa, tell him he may *not* refer to me as The Banshee ever again? He will *have* to listen to you, will he not?"

"I am sure 'tis merely a fond nickname," murmured the earl, not at all sure that his newly restored son would accept the least bit of ordering about at his hands. "Camilla," he said abruptly, "is there anything else you have a wish to know?"

"M-me, Uncle Ned?"

"Yes, you, Camilla. I hope to forestall your imagination—wonderful as it is—from running off in eight different directions at once. Your thatchgallows has just gone from being thoroughly unacceptable to being a respectable fellow with a title in his future. He will not lose standing in your eyes because of it, eh?"

"L-lose standing?"

"Well, he'll not be such an underdog anymore, my dear. Can you give your heart to a viscount, do you think?"

Camilla blushed at his words and he laughed and reached out to pinch one brightly pink cheek. "I see that you can. That settles it then. All he must do is have the good grace not to die on us and we shall all have a new Bedford to plague to our heart's content. Run along, Cammy. Lord Wright is with Johnny at the moment, but you have my permission to replace him. Stop and see Lilliheun first, my dear," he added. "I have assured him that you are well, but his mind will be more at ease does he see you for himself."

Lilliheun smiled up at her when she entered and reached to take her hand. "You *are* all right," he said softly as if to himself. "I never thought to see the day a young lady came so fearlessly to my aid. You were magnificent, m'dear, and I thank you heartily for it."

"But Jason—I mean, Johnny—and Mr. Argosy saved you in the end, Clare. I am so very grateful they came along. I could not believe when I saw him flash by me on Smear."

"Smear? His horse? Naturally he could not have a horse with an ordinary name. Is there nothing ordinary about him, Camilla?"

"Nothing."

"Then you must go to him. I know he fights a great battle at the moment. He cannot lose, you know, with you beside him."

"I—oh, Clare—I love you. Truly I do, but it is—it is not the same sort of love I feel for him."

"I know," sighed Lilliheun. "It is because I *am* ordinary."

"You are not!" cried Aurora from the chamber doorway. "You are the most extraordinary man I have ever met— next to my new brother, of course. But brothers are not to be taken into account."

"New b-brother?" asked Lilliheun uncomprehendingly.

"Go away, Cammy, do, so I may tell Clare all our news," urged Aurora with a pretty little smile and a wink of one blue eye. "He will not pay me the least attention while you are in the chamber."

"I rather think he will," replied Camilla as Lilliheun gave her hand a squeeze and grinned up at her. "You will be all right, won't you, Clare? You will not go and die on us or anything evil like that?"

"Hardly," said Lilliheun. "Go away, miss, and leave me to Lady Aurora's tender mercies."

Camilla bestowed a kiss upon Clare's bruised cheek, left him with her little cousin, and hurried down the long corridor in search of the chamber where the captain lay.

She found him buried deep beneath a pile of quilts in a great canopied bed of ancient lineage guarded by Lord Wright. That gentleman welcomed her with a wide smile and leaning toward the man in the bed announced with some hope of being understood that the angel-lady had come at last to lead him back to the safety of the garden.

"I don't claim, Miss Quinn," whispered Wright, "to understand exactly what it is he mumbles, but it concerns you and Bodkins, and he has been defending you from them for the longest time. He's exceeding improved though," added Wright quietly as he abandoned his chair next to the bed and settled Camilla there in his stead. "When they carried him in last evening, he'd not even the strength to mumble, and now he is at it continuously. I shall leave you alone with him, shall I? If you require the least assistance, you've only to ring and someone will come."

Camilla stared for a very long moment at the abused face upon the pillow. That, and part of his dark curly head and one hand, the arm above it wrapped about with bandages, were all that could be seen of him. She left the chair and climbed up onto the edge of the mattress taking the slim-fingered hand into her own and giving it a gentle squeeze. "Jason," she said quietly, "can you hear me, dearest one? You are safe now and I shall keep you safe forever and ever."

His eyes did not open at the sound of her voice. She doubted they could open even did he wish them to do so. Never before had she seen a face so thoroughly battered, eyes so swollen, a nose so competently broken.

"Jason," she said again as his bruised lips moved awkwardly. "It's me. It's Dendron. We are safe now, dearest."

For a moment the poor abused lips ceased their movement and the dark head ceased to stir uneasily.

"Captain Fate," said Camilla more loudly, " 'tis me, Dendron. I love you."

The hand she held attempted to clench around her own, but could not and fell open again. "Dendron," murmured the lips painfully. "Dendron—look out!—Bodkins!"

Chapter 21

It was a full three days later that the Duke of Dewhurst scowled over the note Argosy handed him. "So, you did not just happen to be riding down the road?"

"No, Your Grace."

"Sit down, Argosy. You look positively dreadful. Are you certain you ought to be up and about?"

"I am fine, Your Grace. Captain Fate did most of the fighting and took most of the punishment."

"Yes. You will not refer to him by that name again, will you, Argosy?"

"No, sir. No, Your Grace. I—"

"You did not think. From this point onward, Captain Jason Fate no longer exists. He was killed in an attempt to waylay Mr. Lilliheun along the London-Newhope road. You and my grandson, Mr. Argosy, with assistance from Wheymore and David, did away with the villain. Do you understand?"

"Perfectly, Your Grace. You have decided to acknowledge Locksley."

"As my grandson, yes—as my heir, no. He is Claudia and Wheymore's boy and so you will tell Borhill. He may cease any further inquiries into Mr. Locksley's antecedents. We have proof positive of his identity." Dewhurst missed the look of amazement on Argosy's face as he stared down once again at the note in his hand. "You have no idea who sent this message to—what was his name?—Peace?"

"None."

"Well, but it must have been someone who knew when Lilliheun would set out for London—and, devil it, that he would be driving my landau! How such information—" Dewhurst walked to the bellpull in the corner of the morning room and tugged it once. Within a matter of moments a footman appeared. "Discover if Miss Quinn is up and about and if she is, convey my greetings and request that she join me here without delay."

"Yes, Your Grace," murmured the footman, bowing and then turning upon his heel and hurrying off down the corridor.

Camilla was astounded to be summoned by Dewhurst and left her breakfast instantly in response. "What is it? What may I do for you, Your Grace?" she asked immediately she entered the morning room. "Has it something to do with—with—Johnny?"

"Indeed, m'dear. Sit down, please, and tell me why it was that you and Lilliheun set out so precipitously for London."

Camilla, settling herself upon a bright chintz settee, looked up at the old duke in wonder. "But I thought you knew. Certainly Lord Eversley passed the message on to David as he said. He must have done, for David and Uncle Ned came after us full-tilt, did they not?"

"They rode after you, my dear, because Aurora discovered your note and we feared your reputation would be compromised travelling to London unchaperoned."

"But—but—Lord Eversley did not tell David of the message from Jason—I mean, Johnny?"

"What message, m'dear?"

Camilla, mystified, revealed all she had overheard in the library at Longbourne and explained that she had sneaked into the landau without Lilliheun's knowledge and that, when he discovered her, Lilliheun's compassion had overruled his common sense and he had allowed her to continue on with him.

"Damnation!" exclaimed the duke at the end of her recital. "Argosy, had my grandson sent anyone off to Longbourne that you know of?"

"No, sir, not that I know of. I understood that the note I gave you was the first knowledge he had of Mr. Lilliheun's intent to drive back to London. Had Mr. Moss not so deftly snabbled the thing from Peace's pocket, I expect we'd not have had a clue of what was about to happen."

"No, of course not. Eversley never had a message from Johnny. 'Twas fabricated. Was it Eversley suggested that Clare take the landau, Camilla?"

"Y-yes, sir."

"And he assured Lilliheun that he would send your cousin, David, after him?"

"Yes, sir, he did. He said Clare would do best to take the landau and leave his mount for David to ride, because David would catch up with him faster that way."

The Duke of Dewhurst's frown deepened and the dark eyes that reminded Camilla so very much of the captain lost all their sparkle. "And I have left the fiend in charge of the children," he muttered angrily, with a shake of his head.

"I—I do not understand, Your Grace." Camilla's mind whirled in an attempt to follow the Duke's train of thought.

"Eversley," hissed Argosy on an indrawn breath.

"Indeed," responded the duke gruffly. "Eversley did not send David after you, Camilla. He made no mention whatsoever of a message from Locksley or of Lilliheun's having gone to London. Had you not written those few lines to Aurora, we'd none of us have taken note of your absences until dinner, and by then, of course, aid could not have reached you in time to prevent your deaths. 'Twas all a most ingenious plot, m'dear, for Eversley to dispose of Lilliheun without the least suspicion falling upon himself. Who would suspect that my own sister's son, a gentleman who has no claim at all to the title, could have devised such a dastardly plot? Eversley likely paid Johnny to come forward and meant to control him and the title and fortune after my death. Control Johnny or confine him somewhere in the country under threat of exposing him. I understand the greed. Peter has always been greedy. But that he should be so jealous of Clare as to wish to murder his cousin—"

Dewhurst tugged the bellpull. "Pen, paper, and one of the grooms in my presence and ready to ride as soon as possible," he bellowed at the footman who answered. "I shall send a message to Longbourne at once and instruct my staff that Eversley is to be kept under guard until my return. Argosy, can you ride?"

"Yes, Your Grace."

"Then you will go to London and inform Borhill of what has occurred."

"And you will tell Mr. Moss, won't you please, what has

happened?" inserted Camilla quietly. "He will be in a panic not to have heard a word from Jason in all this time."

"I will stop and inform him of all that has occurred, Miss Quinn," promised Argosy, and bowing, he rushed out into the hall and in a moment or two pounded down the stairs as if the devil himself were at his heels. Camilla excused herself from the duke's presence and hurried up the stairs and into Fate's bedchamber.

Lord Eversley, his blue eyes blazing and his red-gold locks falling in disarray across his brow, was wishing above all things that he had not had the outrageous idea of taking the Radd children back to London with him. It had seemed, at the time, a practical thing to do. It would not take the duke long, he knew, to unravel the plot once he had spoken to Lilliheun or Miss Quinn. So Eversley had, since the majority of the duke's staff were far too old to handle such a task, offered to remain at Longbourne to explain to the children why the adults had departed so hastily for Kimberly and to console and entertain them until someone had decided what was to be done with them.

But as soon as they had all risen and breakfasted the next morning, he had informed the head groom that he intended to take them on a short excursion and packed all of them except the infant into the Earl of Wheymore's second best travelling carriage and mounted the box himself, insisting that he had not driven four-in-hand for a while and would enjoy the experience immensely. And he would have enjoyed the experience too, if the coach had not been filled to the hilt with children, if they had not insisted upon taking that noisome dog with them, if Harley had not just two days before received from Dewhurst a set of crutches, and if little girls were not always finding it necessary to locate a convenience.

Nevertheless, he had headed the horses toward London, hoping to trade the children's safety for his own safe passage to the continent. He had not driven to the mansion on Grosvenor Square, where he expected Locksley and Moss to be still in residence, but had drawn up instead before the house he shared with his mistress in St. Mary's Triangle, where the children had piled out of the coach in a tangle of arms and legs and wooden crutches, making a great deal of noise and demanding to know if Uncle John was there. Mary Ellen Hall, aghast, had sent immediately for Eversley's little tiger, who had taken the team in hand, freeing Eversley to chase after the little urchins and the enormous dog who had scampered enthusiastically everywhere and gather them into the house.

Mary Ellen Hall had been Eversley's mistress for almost two years. She had lingered for less than two hours after the children arrived, and then had departed in a nervous flurry, saying she could not abide them for another moment—not even for all of Eversley's money.

Somehow Eversley had survived that first night and the two days following, but now he was close to the end of his tether. He had convinced the children that Locksley would soon come to collect them and he wished to heaven it were the truth. He was beginning to debate just how much of a risk it might be for him to lure Locksley to the house and hold him captive as well just so he would manage the urchins. Holding Locksley captive, however, seemed an impossible thing to do, so he abandoned that idea and tore at his hair while he attempted to think of another possibility.

He was in the midst of these cogitations when a great to-do erupted on the first floor landing. There was a great clatter and bang, an ear-piercing shriek, a series of frightened dog yelps, the clamour of young male voices and the click-clack of tiny running feet across the parquet. "Mister Eberley! Mister Eberley! Come quick!" piped Jolly, dashing into the parlour and jumping up and down excitedly before him flailing her hands with a good deal of enthusiasm. "Harley 'as twied ta slippy-slide down yer bamister an' his crutch gotted stuckeded in the railin'!"

"Oh, no," Eversley groaned.

"Yes!" cried Jolly, now tugging insistently at his sleeve in an attempt to pull him up from his chair. "An' it spinned away an' flewed against the wall an' hitted Tick right smack in the 'ead. An' Tick bumpeded inta Grig an' knocked 'er down the stairs an' she ploppeded ri' on toppa Trouble! Oh, it is the most awfullest accident! Hurry! Hurry!"

Eversley forced himself to follow the anxious little girl out into the corridor where various and sundry appendages—some human, some dog and one wooden—thrashed about on the floor at the bottom of the staircase. Apparently Tick and Harley had both flung themselves atop Trouble as well, and the big dog's frightened yelps had turned to rapturous barks as he deduced it to be a game of rough-house and he playfully attacked first one then another of the children.

Eversley reached tentatively into the undulating pile, caught a piece of sprigged muslin skirt and lifted a wiggling, giggling little Grig up into the air. He swung her into his arms then deposited her behind him upon the parquet next to Jolly. "And you stay right there, missy," he ordered reaching into the pile again and seizing upon a coat tail that proved to be attached to Tick.

The butler he employed at this residence appeared just in time to have Trouble's collar thrust at him. "Take this animal into the rear yard and do *not* let him back into the house until I say!" bellowed Eversley at the man. "And you, sir," he added, lifting Harley to his feet and tucking one crutch beneath his arm while Tick ran to fetch the other. "You will do me the courtesy to take your brother and sisters to the morning room and find something quiet to occupy the lot of you! You are not to be running about and sliding down my bannisters! You've got a broken leg for God's sake!"

" 'Tis a'most mended, sor!" declared Harley joyously. "It don't even 'urt no more!"

"No, well I am pleased for you. Now go! All of you! Out of my sight! And not another sound until tea-time!"

Eversley watched them traverse the corridor to the rear of the house then took himself back to the parlor. Of all the fool things he'd ever done this had to be the most foolish. What on earth did he know about children? Maybe he'd be better off to tie the brats up and toss them into one of the bedchambers. No—someone of the small staff of servants would be bound to notice that. Why the deuce did he not hear from the duke?

Certainly when the old man's minions did not discover him at Grosvenor Square they would come nosing around the house in St. Mary's Triangle. Everyone knew that he kept Mary Ellen here. Like as not, his note containing his demands for the children's release had not yet reached Kimberly. That was it. But, Lord, how much longer would it be? From the rear of the house came a great sobbing howl and then another and another.

Eversley's hands went over his ears, as he tried to think. If Lilliheun and Miss Quinn were not dead—if they were not dead—perhaps he would stand a chance of straightening things out with the duke. He would protest he'd been out of his mind with envy and that Lilliheun had goaded him into it by lording it over him all of the time. Perhaps the old man would listen. No, the old man would not listen at all. Hated sobbers and whiners. He'd have more respect for Eversley's abducting the children the way he'd done than for Eversley's approaching him with a bunch of stupid excuses. But he will not turn me over to the Runners, Eversley thought hopefully. So long as I have the brats, he will bargain. Locksley's fond of 'em, after all, and the wretched duke has apparently grown fond of Locksley. "Oh, shut that beast up!" he shouted abruptly at the top of his lungs. "Where am I living, in Bedlam?"

Camilla, who had been exiled from Fate's chamber by Lady Wright in order that she might change the captain's bandages and cleanse the deep knife wounds in his side and thigh and the enormous crease across his rib cage made by an errant pistol ball, as well as the channel cut through his right forearm and the old wound to his head, was wandering aimlessly along the drive path when the rider appeared. "This Kimberly?" the man asked, pulling his horse to a stop beside her.

"Indeed it is."

"Then I've a message to be delivered here for the Duke of Dewhurst."

"Oh. I'll carry it to him if you like," smiled Camilla raising her hand to take the paper. "If you ride around back I am certain that Cook will see you have some refreshment. Must you wait for an answer?"

"So I've been instructed," nodded the man. "I shall wait in the kitchen, shall I?" And he took his horse at a walk the rest of the way up the drive and around toward the stables.

Camilla turned her footsteps back toward the house and had just reached the front entrance when another man on horseback appeared. This man she recognized instantly as Dewhurst's own head groom and welcomed him with a ready smile. "His Grace," she said as a stableboy came running to take the man's mount, "is in the morning parlor." She waited for the groom to climb the steps and together they entered the house and followed Wright's butler up the broad staircase to the first floor.

Dewhurst rose as Camilla entered the room, nodded to his groom, and inquired as to what Miss Quinn wished of him. " 'Tis only a missive I deliver. I met the messenger in the drive and offered to carry it to you for him. He awaits any reply in the kitchen, Your Grace."

"Wait, don't go, Camilla," murmured the duke, opening the sealed page and scanning the elegant copperplate lines. "Well, I'll be da—devilled! You say the man who delivered this is in the kitchen?"

"Yes, Your Grace," nodded Camilla wondering at the sudden frown upon his aging visage.

"And Colly, you have come to tell me that Eversley and all of the children except the baby are missing from Longbourne, eh?"

"Y-yes, sir," answered the groom, awed by the duke's prescience.

Camilla gasped involuntarily, but the duke waved a calming hand at her and shook his head.

"They are all perfectly safe, Colly. Once you have rested a bit, you will return to Longbourne, will you, and tell Mr. Ridgely to ignore the missive I sent this morning and assure him that Eversley and the children have simply gone upon an unexpected but perfectly unexceptional holiday."

"Your Grace," he replied backing out of the room, his hat in hand.

"Camilla, m'dear, will you fetch your uncle and David for me? They are with Lilliheun, I believe. And perhaps Lord Wright's advice might be worth having. If you should happen to see him anywhere about you might—"

"No," said Camilla and then blushed quite becomingly. "Oh, I am so sorry. I did not mean to—yes, yes, I did mean it. The truth is that I have been left out of things quite enough, Your Grace, and I do not mean to be left out again."

"Eh?" asked the duke, an eyebrow cocking in her direction. "What's this, m'dear? Rebellion?"

"If that is how you wish to see it, yes, sir. I and my opinion have been dispensed with very politely over and over again and I shall be dispensed with no more. I perfectly understand that all of you wish to shield me from unpleasantness, but I am *not* a child."

"Of course you are not," mumbled Dewhurst, unconsciously rubbing the back of his neck.

"No, and that I should be shoved from the room when Jason's wounds must be tended to, or hurried off the moment any sort of emergency presents itself, I find abhorrent. You will tell me, sir, what you know of Lord Eversley and the children and you will request my opinion in the matter, or I shall—"

"What?" asked Dewhurst suppressing a distinct tendency of his lip to quiver upward.

"Well, I do not exactly know. But I shall think of something."

The duke strolled to the corner of the morning room, gave the braided silk cord of the bellpull a tug, and waited in patient silence until Wright's butler appeared. He sent that solemn gentleman off in search of David, Wheymore and Wright and a tea tray, and then urged Camilla to a seat and sat down across from her. "Eversley," he said, leaning back and crossing one leg over the other, "has kidnapped the children and is holding them for ransom."

Camilla's hand fluttered to her breast.

"The ransom he wishes to collect, m'dear, is his freedom. He hopes I will see things his way and agree to let him traipse off to the continent unhampered rather than place public charges against him. I must give him my word that he shall be allowed to leave England, with his fortune, and without any spectre attached to him whatsoever. His messenger awaits my answer, as you know, in Wright's kitchen. What, my dear, would you advise me to do?''

"I—I—"

The Duke raised a hand to silence her as the tea tray arrived, then urged her to continue as the footman departed.

"You were about to say, m'dear?"

"I should refuse to bargain with Lord Eversley at all," stated Camilla with a defiant tilt to her chin.

"Not even to save the children, Camilla?"

"Save them from what? From threats? Never once in all of this has Lord Eversley raised his hand against anyone. *He* did not attack Clare. No, he must hire some ruffians to do so. And *he* did not harm Harley either, nor Mr. Radd. 'Twas all done by hired ruffians. And now that his fiendish hirelings are killed or gaoled who will he get to carry out his high-blown threats? No one, I think, for he will not have time to make arrangements and he will not harm anyone himself. He obviously has not the stomach for it."

"Who hasn't the stomach for what?" asked David. "What goes on, Duke?"

"Yes, I should like to know as well," added Lord Wheymore entering the room behind his son and immediately followed by the Earl of Wright. "Who is it, Camilla, you call a coward so diplomatically?"

"I have word from Eversley," the duke informed them as each of the gentlemen helped himself to a cup of tea and a few pastries and took seats close to Camilla and Dewhurst. "He has kidnapped the Radd children in hopes of escaping to the continent unhindered. I should appreciate your advice, gentlemen, just as I appreciate Miss Quinn's."

Eyebrows rose as it became apparent that Camilla was to be allowed to remain—except for Lord Wright's, Camilla noticed, somewhat amazed. That gentleman simply gazed mirthfully at her with his silver-flecked eyes and then winked.

"Well, but you're accustomed to consulting women, Wright," muttered Wheymore as a chuckle escaped the Earl of Wright's lips. "You do it ceaselessly."

"Only because, being continually surrounded by them, I have come to appreciate their wisdom. This is the first chance I have had to escape it in years—except for Ellie—and now I find I have not escaped at all. No, do not frown, Miss Quinn. I am not hoaxing you. I have a deep respect for the considered opinion of a number of ladies, and I am certain *your* considered opinion will not disappoint me either."

Camilla did not know what to make of the gentleman, but then the duke began to discuss what was to be done and her attention was drawn quickly away from him.

When at last a plan of action was decided upon and Dewhurst was in the midst of penning an answer to be carried back to Eversley by the messenger, Camilla excused herself and rushed off to the chamber in which the captain lay. She popped in along the way to greet Lilliheun, discovered Aurora sitting beside the bed reading aloud and waved at Clare from the doorway. He grinned widely up at her and put a finger to his lips so she blew him a kiss and hurried away.

No one was with Fate when she entered his chamber. She walked quietly to the head of the bed and looked down to find him sleeping peacefully. "Lady Wright has undoubtedly dosed you again with her magic tonic," Camilla whispered, smiling fondly upon him. "And I am extremely grateful, dearest, for she has saved your life and given me a second chance."

"A secon' chance at what, Dendron?"

"Jason? You are awake? And—and—you know me?"

"Well, o' course I know ye, darlin'. I been 'alf out o' my mind, ain't I? I knew it. I done that oncet afore when I got kicked in the 'ead by a great clod of a 'orse. But I knowed ye was some'eres about 'cause I heerd ye call ta me and I felt ye holdin' m'hand. Don't say that weren't ye, Dendron, 'cause I knowed the feel of ye."

"Oh! Oh, Captain, I am so glad you are all right!" With uninhibited exultation Camilla climbed up upon the bed, threw her arms around him, and pressed a decidedly enthusiastic kiss upon a tiny space of his brow, the tip of his nose, the corner of one unshaven cheek, and the exact center of his chin, which were the only places that he appeared not to be severely bruised. When at last she sat back and surveyed him, he was smiling lopsidedly up at her, tempting the cuts on his lips to pop open. She was about to order him to cease smiling immediately lest they did when he caught her hand in his own and asked quietly, "Second chance fer what, Dendron?"

"To—to say the correct things," she answered, blushing. "I have never ever said exactly the correct things to you. It is because I am so exceedingly stubborn, of course."

"Camilla, what on earth do you think you are doing? Get down at once," growled a voice from the doorway. "Ain't it enough he's near dead from attempting to rescue you and Lilliheun, without you bouncing around upon the mattress making every inch of him smart the more?" Lord Wheymore fixed her with a most suspiciously gleaming eye. "Get down now, my girl. Awake, are you, Johnny? And about time I should think. Tough breed, we Bedfords. Don't hold with lying around dazed once we decide we are not going to die."

Camilla slid demurely from the bed as her uncle approached and took the chair beside it. He pulled her down upon his lap, which he'd not done since she was twelve years old. "Cammy and I, John, have a thing or two to straighten out with you."

"My name ain't John. 'Twas all a fudge. M'name be Jason—"

"Yes," interrupted the earl, nodding gravely. "I know. Sir Jason, Knight of the Forests Wild."

Chapter 22

Camilla smiled and bestowed a kiss upon her cousin's pert little nose. "You are entirely too excited, Aurora," she chuckled. "Not only have you inherited a new brother, but Clare is becoming most infatuated with you. How will you ever sleep a wink?"

"I shan't," declared Aurora happily. "I am walking in dreams right this very moment. Oh, Cammy, has it not been the most wonderful day?"

"Yes, indeed," laughed Camilla, "but the day is long over and the entire household has settled down for the night. We must do so as well, gudgeon. Off to bed now."

Lady Aurora pouted prettily but then kissed her cousin back and skipped off down the corridor to her own chambers.

Camilla felt like skipping herself. She could not believe all that had happened. She was a bit apprehensive about the children, of course, but when her Uncle Ned had laid their plan out before the captain, Jason had expressed great confidence in it, and that had given her more confidence as well. And he had seemed so much improved. She had visited him often during the afternoon and evening and each time there had been noticeable improvements.

His color was returning. He had eaten a great deal. True, it had been little more than broths and gruel, but his appetite had definitely been present and there had been not the least sign of fever when she had stopped to bid him goodnight only an hour or so earlier. And he had been so very pleased—astounded, but pleased—to learn that the Earl of Wheymore was his father and Lady Wheymore his stepmother and David and Aurora his half-brother and half-sister. Almost, she thought, he had not believed it. But her Uncle Ned had laid one after another of his doubts to rest until the captain had had to accept that he was, indeed, John Locksley Bedford. Though she would never think of him as such. No, to her he would always be

Captain Jason Fate, the man she loved—the man who needed her and desired her and loved her and whom she needed and desired and loved in return.

She felt an overwhelming need at the moment, in fact, to kiss that wretchedly abused face just once more before she retired for the night, and not stopping to think of the sheer impropriety of it, she wandered out into the hall in her nightrail and made her way quietly to the captain's chambers. Silently she slipped through the darkened dressing room and into the bedchamber that was lit only by a single candle flickering its feeble light on the washstand far from the bed. With tiny steps she approached the jumble of covers where the captain lay, intending merely to bestow a chaste and tender kiss upon his brow and gasped to find the bed empty.

"Sshhh," whispered a voice behind her, "ye'll wake someun."

Camilla spun around to discover Fate, attired in a borrowed nightshirt, leaning quietly against the door frame through which she had just passed. "What, sir, do you think you are doing?" she asked on a quiet little intake of breath. "You must get back into bed immediately."

"Uh-uh."

"No, Jason, truly you must. You cannot possibly go walking about."

"Well, but I ain't walkin' about. I'm standin'."

Camilla took a deep, exasperated breath. "Why are you standing?"

"Because I meant ta fine m'clothes, but ye come in off the hall jus' as I were about ta light some candles. Ye tramped ri' by me without so much as a by yer leave."

"Well, you will not find your clothes in that dressing room, sir. They no longer exist. Burned, I think."

"Burned? Someun burned m'clothes?"

"They were all torn and bloody and dirty. I expect no one could have made them wearable again. Why did you want them? All of the things from your pockets are in this little table here beside the bed, your earring as well. Jason, do come over here, won't you?"

"Uh-uh. Ye'll make me get back in tha' bed."

"How could I possibly make you? You are a good deal larger than I."

"An' ye're smarter an' better at persuadin' like—ye'd 'ave me under them covers in a blink. Ye come 'ere, Dendron." He held out his arms to her. She could not help but notice that he did so with some degree of caution and a snatch of pain. She crossed the room and walked into them carefully and they closed around her. His lips kissed the top of her head and then her brow and then the tip of her nose and finally touched her own lips very softly, very tenderly, and very, very gingerly. She thought to kiss him back, passion rising in her, then remembered how bruised and battered were those lips and did not. "Jason," she whispered up at him. "What are you about? Tell me."

"I be plannin' ta ride ta Lunnon."

"London!"

"Shhh, Dendron. Ye'll wake whatever of m'keeper's sleepin' in the nex' room down."

"But—but you certainly cannot ride to London," she declared in a much quieter voice. "You will tear all your wounds open again and bleed to death before you gain the high road."

"No—"

"Yes!" hissed Camilla. "Dearest, you cannot even hold me without distressing yourself. Think what should happen to you upon horseback! Why do you wish to ride to London?"

"To—to get the childer from Eversley."

"But we *shall* get the children from Eversley, Jason. We have a plan. You said yourself that it was a proper good one."

"I know, but I've been thinkin' an' there be a much simpler way. Only I mus' 'ave some clothes ta wear an' a way ta get ta Lunnon afore mornin'."

Reluctantly Fate released her from his arms, moved back into the dressing room and began to light the candles. An unwilling groan escaped him as he reached to hold the taper to the wicks of the candles upon the mantle and immediately Camilla was beside him, taking the taper from his hand and completing the task for him. "There, sir," she whispered, "all alight. Now what do you wish to do?"

"See if there's anythin' in 'ere I can wear," mumbled Fate, opening the doors of an enchanting armoire lacquered in black and decorated in the Chinese style.

Camilla thought she must surely have lost her mind. It was not as if she could not stop his nonsense in a moment. Someone was asleep in the very next chamber to this and had been sent to sleep there just to be near should Fate require assistance in the night. All she need do was call for that person. Instead, she helped Jason to search through what were obviously some of the Earl of Wright's older country clothes until they found some that might fit. Once they were laid out, however, Fate collapsed into a wing chair near the fireplace rather than hurrying to climb into them.

"You see," said Camilla, turning to stare at him. "I am correct. You are much too weak to be thinking of going to London. You are exhausted from just looking through an armoire."

"I ain't 'shausted," sighed the captain.

"Oh. Then what are you?"

"Tired."

"Jason, do give over."

"No."

"I cannot allow you to harm yourself. I shall call someone to come and put you back to bed. Jason, there is nothing else I can do."

"Dendron?"

"What?"

"Ye could help me."

Camilla attempted not to see the pleading deep in his blackened eyes, or the sheer stubborness, or the trust. "No, I will not—h-help you to—to—further injure yourself. Oh, you are a supreme mule!"

"Ssshhh."

"Ssshh yourself! You cannot even get out of the nightshirt, can you?"

"I could if ye helped me. An' I could get ta Lunnon if

ye helped me, too. I reckon I could do anythin' in the world if ye helped me, Dendron.''

And that was how they *both* came to be dressed in Wright's old clothes, moving quietly about his stable hitching one of his bays to his stanhope. Camilla demanded that Fate mount to the seat and she led the horse far down the drive path at an impossibly slow pace in order not to wake anyone in the stables or the house. When she judged they were clearly beyond anyone's hearing, she mounted to the seat herself, took the reins into her hands and urged the bay to a trot.

She felt Fate's eyes upon her and turned to him with an eyebrow cocked beneath the low-crowned, wide-brimmed hat under which she had stuffed her chestnut curls. "No," she said with a determinedly steady tone, "you may not drive even part of the way. The cut on your arm will rip right open if you should need to pull hard upon the reins. And I shall not drive any faster. You will be jiggled about entirely too much and the wound in your side will open and you will bleed to death. Then what will I do? I cannot live without you, you know.''

"Ye can't, Dendron?"

"No."

"But I thought ye intended ta live wi'out any man. I thought ye was determined ta be a auth'ress.''

"Oh, I shall be an authoress, sir. I rather think I shall never run out of tales to tell so long as you are with me. You—you do wish to be with me?" Her gaze became so abruptly apprehensive that Fate was forced to put his arm around her waist and caress her cheek with the tip of one finger.

"I never thought ta see the day," he murmured. "Are ye meanin' ta ask if I want ye ta marry me, Dendron?"

"Y-yes," gulped Camilla around a great lump that had risen in the middle of her throat. "I l-love you, Jason, and I want to be your w-wife.''

" 'Sblood!'' exclaimed the captain in a hoarse whisper. "If that don't beat ever'thin'. I thought as I was lucky when the earl comed ta start explainin' about 'ow I was 'is own son, an' how they all wanted for me ta be one o' their fam'ly. But now I reckon I mus' be the luckiest cove in the whole world!''

It was shortly after dawn when Camilla halted the stanhope before Eversley's house in St. Mary's Triangle. Her eyes were gritty from the dust of the road and her face smudged. Her hands ached from the long bout with the reins. Fate studied the house for a very long time, then gave her a soft kiss on the cheek and climbed gingerly to the ground. He took the reins from her hands and tied them to the hitching post. Camilla climbed to the ground herself, and hand in hand in the grey mist of morning they walked silently around the side of the house to the rear yard. Fate looked upward and pointed at an open window on the second floor. ''Ye wait right 'ere, darlin'. I won't be but a minute er two.''

''Jason, you cannot. There must be a lower window open.''

''No, this un's fine. There be a reg'lar path straight up the wall to't. Keep yer daylights peeled fer the Watch, m'lad,'' he chuckled, two fingers knocking the brim of Camilla's cap down over her eyes, ''an' whistle loud does ye see 'em comin'.''

He is out of his mind, thought Camilla wearily. The man is completely out of his mind. And I am out of mine as well to let him talk me into such a thing. He will kill himself. I know he will. His wounds, which I bound so tightly for him before we left, but which have not even begun to heal, will come tearing open and he will fall down at my feet and bleed to death. And how I will ever explain it—standing here in the Earl of Wright's breeches and jacket and hat with Captain Jason Fate dead at my feet! They will toss me into Bedlam without the least hesitation.

Anxiously Camilla ceased to gaze about for any sign of the Watch and raised her eyes upward instead. She thought to see Fate clinging desperately to the vines, exhausted. She saw nothing but a wide open window. Heavens, she thought, he is in already? How does the man do it? She returned her gaze to the area around her, stuffed her hands into the pockets of her breeches and rested her shoulders against the damp brick of the house. A smile twitched at her lips as she remembered helping Fate to doff his nightshirt, wrapping his wounds as he instructed, and then helping him to don breeches, shirt, and jacket. And the boots—both of them had had terrible trouble with the boots they'd found in the bottom of the clothes press. Jason's feet had been too big and hers much too small. He had told her how to stuff the toes of her boots with crumpled paper enough to keep them on, but there had been no answer for him until they had discovered his own boots in one corner of the bedchamber.

But she did not truly wish to think about boots. What she wished to think about was the bruised and battered, but thoroughly beautiful, body he had displayed to her without the least hesitation. *What would you think, my Jason, if you knew I had never seen a man before, except he was made of marble and resided in some dusty museum?*

Something very tiny fell upon the brim of her hat. Something else fell upon it. She stepped away from the bricks and looked upward. Jolly, in what appeared to be a gentleman's shirt with her pelisse buttoned crookedly over the top of it, sat on the edge of the window sill, a length of linen tied firmly around her middle. Behind her Jason Fate grinned and threw Camilla a salute. And then he lowered the child carefully down the side of the building and into Camilla's arms. Quickly Camilla untied the length of sheet and Fate pulled it back up, this time attaching it to a tired but thoroughly trusting Grig who descended with one hand holding to the vines and the other rubbing at tired eyes.

Tick, who had managed to don his breeches and shirt, had the sheet tied around him, but only as a precaution, as he climbed down the vines entirely on his own. "The cap'n's hurted," he explained as Camilla quickly undid the knot, "an' I be too big fer 'im ta lower proper. 'Sides, I knows 'ow ta climb. He says fer ta tell ye, Miz Dendron, that 'im an' Harley an' Trouble is goin' down the fron' stairs an' will meet us at the fron' door."

Camilla looked back up at the window fearfully. The

length of linen was disappearing through it and then a
hand lowered the window back to its original setting.

"C'mon, Miss Cammy," Jolly urged, tugging on her
sleeve. "The cap'n be 'spectin' us 'roun' front."

"Was we real, actual kidnapped?" asked Tick in a hushed
voice tugging Grig by the hand around the side of the
house. "The cap'n said as 'ow we was kidnapped. Ye look
real like a 'ostler in them duds, Miz Dendron, but purty,
though."

Camilla smiled at him distractedly. Harley. She had never
once given thought to Harley, nor that enormous dog.
When Jason had suggested how simple it would be for him
to remove the children from right beneath Eversley's nose,
she had thought only of his lowering Tick, Jolly, and Grig
to safety. She had not once thought of Harley. How on
earth did he expect to get a crippled boy and a dog the
size of a small pony quietly down the front staircase and
out onto the street? Someone inside would surely wake
and shoot him for a burglar!

The lot of them were just stepping cautiously around
the front corner of the house when the front door opened
and Harley, fully crutched and almost fully dressed, hob-
bled out onto the front steps, Trouble beside him and
Fate immediately at his back. "Quickly now, childer," Fate
whispered as the little ones ran to him. "Tick, an' Jolly
an' Grig, ye must all sniggle onta the seat of that carriage
there, an' Miz Dendron will drive ye ta Grosvenor Square.
An' when ye gets there, ye must wake up ol' Mossie immedi-
ate-like an' tell 'im what 'as 'appened."

Camilla, glancing at the children as they rushed to the
stanhope and attempted to climb to the seat, looked back
to Fate worriedly. "But what will you and Harley do?" she
asked. "You cannot just wait here until I return for you."

"We be goin' for a stroll, Harley an' Trouble an' me,
in tha' direction," he said, pointing. "Come back quick
as ye can, darlin', an' ride directly pass the 'ouse an' take
notice if any un be stirrin' about. I don't reckon as Eversley
be gonna raise any alarm over the missin' childer, but 'e
might well come a lookin' fer 'em." He raised the brim

of her hat and planted a kiss upon her lips and sent her off to drive the children to Grosvenor Square.

Glasgow, rapidly pulling on his breeches and attempting to stuff the tail of his nightshirt into them, raced for the front door muttering curses beneath his breath. That anyone should have the audacity to be ringing the bell at such an hour! Certainly 'twas some buck in his cups come to the wrong establishment! He swung into the front hall, his slippers skidding across the parquet, himself nearly coming up flat against the entryway wall, and with a disgusted scowl wrenched open the door. His jaw dropped.

"May we enter, Glasgow?" asked Camilla politely, a smile threatening at the corners of her mouth. "I realize it is deplorably early for a morning call, but there is a slight emergency."

"Miss Quinn?"

The awe-filled tone in which the man said her name brought home to Camilla immediately a fact she had forgotten several hours ago—that she was dressed in men's clothes—very dirty men's clothes at this point she suspected.

"Ah, yes, Glasgow. The children and I—"

"Come in! Come in!" The frazzled butler leaned down and scooped a sleep-bewildered Grig up into one arm and Jolly into the other. "Tick, be off an' knock upon Cook's door, an' say we be needin' a bit of breakfast, lad. He will have heard the bell and be rising at any rate. Miss Quinn, if you will follow me?"

Camilla trailed in Glasgow's wake up the staircase and into the morning room.

"There shall be coffee or tea or—or chocolate—yes, chocolate would be good, would it not?" murmured Glasgow disjointedly, setting the little girls down upon a long sopha. "I expect the children will like some chocolate."

Camilla smiled wearily and kneeling, began to unbutton Jolly's pelisse. "I must speak to Mr. Moss, Glasgow, as quickly as possible. Please tell him not to dress. Mr. Locksley and Harley await me even now."

"Yes, ma'am," nodded Glasgow and exited the room, his long legs carrying him rapidly up the staircase to the second floor and Elgin Moss's chambers. Camilla had gotten no farther than to divest both girls of their pelisses, lay them down with pillows at opposite ends of the sopha and cover them with the pelisses, when Elgin Moss appeared in the doorway, stuffing his shirttail into his breeches, a robed Farmer trailing in his wake carrying a pair of boots.

"What is it, m'dear?" asked Moss, seating himself upon a Chippendale chair and reaching for one of his boots. "Is it m'lad? He's not gone and taken a turn fer the worse? That upset we all were to hear Mr. Argosy's tale, but relieved as how Jason weren't no worse off than 'e were." Moss stopped in the midst of pulling on his second boot to cock an eyebrow at Camilla. "He's talked ye inta doing somethin' foolish, ain't he? Ye'd not be here at dawn dressed like that for no other reason."

Harley, wielding his crutches energetically, made his way to a small bench in the little park that lay at the very tip of St. Mary's Triangle. "We bes' jus' sit 'ere, Cap'n, eh?" He plopped himself down upon the bench and patted the place beside him. "Yer hurtin', ain't ye?"

"No," replied Fate, lowering himself carefully down beside the boy.

"Well, it ain't 'ard ta see ye got yerself beat upon. An' ye're bleedin' besides."

"No, I ain't."

"Uh-huh! It be comin' ri' through yer jacket. I kin see it."

"Damn," mumbled Fate looking down at himself. There were two small dark stains spreading across his jacket, one where his forearm had been bandaged and the other at his side.

"Who been cuttin' upon ye, Cap'n?"

"Dan'l Peace an' 'is cronies," mumbled Fate and, patting Trouble who had nestled up against his leg, he explained to Harley all that had happened since the children had been carried off to Longbourne.

"Whew!" exclaimed Harley. "I wished I'd been there, Cap'n. I'd of 'elped ye good."

"Ye did 'elp me good, Harley. Ye looked after the childer, an' ye 'elped me ta git the lot of 'em out that window rig   ick like. Yer a fine lad, an' tha's a fact."

"An' a   ily a—a—"

"Viscou.   e, tha's what they says."

"Then   on as how we ain't goin' ta be ridin' the High Toby no more. I don't 'spect as 'ow Da will go an' do it on his own. 'E won't will 'e? I'd be scared did we keep doin' it wi'out ye, Cap'n."

Fate's arm, despite the bleeding, went supportively about Harley's shoulders. "Naw, yer da won't think ta go on the High Toby, jus' ye an' him. 'Sides, I be goin' ta 'ave a bit o' money, an' a bit o' land some'eres. That's what they says. I reckon as 'ow mebbe we can all of us git by on that if we be careful. Ye'd like ta live in the country some'eres, wouldn't ye, Harley?"

"Aye," breathed Harley, nodding excitedly. "I liked the country!"

"Aye," grinned Fate. "I thought ye might 'ave. An' the childer liked it as well, didn't they?"

"Better'n anythin'! Be ye goin' ta marry tha' lady, Cap'n?"

"Dendron?" Fate smiled softly. "I reckon, Harley."

"I reckon ye better," agreed Harley solemnly. "She be set upon 'avin' ye."

"She does?"

"Aye, Cap'n. First she comed all the way ta Basket Lane af'er ye. Then she 'vited ye ta 'er party. An' now she come drivin' ye here all the way from the country—an' dressed like a boy, too. I reckon she be *dead-set* on 'avin' ye."

Directly before them a hackney pulled to a halt and Camilla and Elgin Moss hurriedly emerged. Camilla took one good look at the captain and felt her heart sink. He had grown very pale in just the little time it had taken her to return, and she could see, just as clearly as had Harley, the blood staining his jacket. "Oh, Jason," she sighed, on the verge of tears. "I was right all along. Your wounds have come open again. You are so very, very stubborn! Why would you not listen to me? Why could we not have waited for the others to rescue the children as they planned? Why did I ever let you convince me to—to—"

Elgin Moss, without ceremony, lifted Harley from the bench, stuffed him into the hackney and tossed his crutches in after him. Then he took Fate by the arm and assisted him into the coach as well. Trouble leaped in after Fate without the least urging. "I reckon as 'ow ye've a good deal to rail at the lad about, Miss Quinn," he murmured, "but now ain't a good time for it. In ye go," he concluded, helping her inside as well. Moss climbed up beside the driver and the hackney turned and started back the way it had come.

Camilla, on the seat beside Fate, placed a hand upon his brow. He pushed it away. "I ain't feverish," he mumbled. "I jus' be bleedin' a bit."

"Ye be bleedin' a lot," observed Harley casually from the seat across the way that he and Trouble shared. "She only be meanin' ta care fer ye, Cap'n."

Above them the trap opened and Moss's face appeared. "We're stoppin'," he announced with a grim visage. In a moment the coach door opened and Moss was lowering the steps. "I reckon as how ye might like ta join me, Miss Quinn," he said quietly.

"Oh, but we must get Jason to a doctor, Mr. Moss."

"Jason, ye goin' ta die anytime soon?"

"Naw, Mossie. I 'spect not fer a while."

"Good. Ye'll understand that I cannot allow ye ta damage yerself farther, m'lad, so ye'll remain in this carriage. Miss Quinn, I know as 'ow ye'd like ta join me. Come along."

Puzzled, Camilla descended the steps and discovered that they had stopped immediately before Eversley's little house. Elgin Moss took her arm, marched her to the door and twisted the bell. The door was opened by a rather confused looking butler and coming down the hall behind him Camilla spied Eversley.

"Who the devil is it, Hornby? Has someone found those blasted urchins?"

The butler stepped aside. His master strolled into the doorway. And Elgin Moss, his lips set in a grim line, threw a punishing right directly into Eversley's midsection. Eversley, the breath taken completely out of him, doubled over. Elgin Moss stepped aside and with a flourish presented the gasping lord to Camilla. "I should suspect, wi' them boots, miss, ye might like a knee," he said politely.

Camilla, all the fear, the horror, the trauma of the past few days coming to the fore, hesitated not at all and kicked Eversley in the knee with all her might and then slapped his face as well.

"That will teach ye ta harm *our* lad," hissed Moss lowly and turning, he offered Camilla his arm and escorted her back to the hackney where Trouble was barking excitedly, Harley applauding, and Fate resting against the squabs in the far corner, a wide smile on his battered, weary countenance.

Chapter 23

Almost six months to the day following, Andrew Borhill watched with a quiet smile as Mr. Lilliheun inspected a perspiring Fate, strolling around him with quizzing glass in hand and a somber countenance. "I think not," murmured Lilliheun. "Much too gauche. What do you think, chaps?"

"I think 'tis the waistcoat throws it off," declared David resting one shoulder against the unadorned stone wall of the tiny chamber. "Are you certain you cannot find the other one, Moss?"

"T'ain't here," replied Elgin Moss. "Got lef' behind I reckon."

"What's wrong with this un—one?" asked Fate, tugging agitatedly at his neckcloth.

"Well," sighed Lilliheun with a twinkle of mirth in his grey-blue eyes, "nothing, m'lord, if you actually want to get married looking like a—a—Bartholomew baby."

"What? What? Who looks like a Bartholomew—

'sblood!'' grinned Wheymore as he came to a halt just inside the chamber door. "Lilliheun, what have you done to my boy?''

"Me? I ain't done nothing—I mean—I have not done anything to him, my lord.''

"Ain't it vexing to have to watch your language whenever you're around him?'' chuckled David.

"Ye don't,'' mumbled Fate. "Ye only do't when ye've a mind to plague me.''

"Oh, most certainly not,'' offered Borhill innocently. "The Duke of Dewhurst has requested that even I keep a lock upon my cant. 'Twill make it easier, he says, for you to learn to sound like a gentleman.''

"Well, I ain't no gentleman!''

"You most certainly are,'' said Wheymore, standing before Fate and making minor adjustments to the immaculate linen neckcloth. "You are a gentleman, a viscount, and will one day be the Earl of Wheymore and take your place in the House of Lords.''

"Not in *that* waistcoat I hope,'' snickered Lilliheun.

"And there is not a thing wrong with your waistcoat, Johnny. They are only having you on, m'boy, because you're so very nervous. You oughtn't be nervous, you know. Reverend Mr. Jolnes will not bite you.''

"No, but this pretty li'l chapel mi' git struck by lightnin''' offered Artie Radd from the doorway. "I niver thought ta see Cap'n Jason Fate inside a chapel, lessin' he be dead.''

"Well, he ain't dead,'' growled Moss, running an impatient hand through the greying fringe around his ear. "Which ain't ta say that all of ye ain't gonna be exackly that if ye persist in hecklin' the lad. Be they ready, Artie?''

"Aye. All ready an' waitin' on 'is nibs an' t'other gen'lemen.''

A solemn scowl from Wheymore sent all of the kibitzers hurrying from the antechamber and into the chapel. "Pay none of them any mind, Johnny,'' he said then, putting an arm around Fate's shoulders. "You are not wishing to back out of this marriage, are you, m'boy? A gentleman don't, you know. Ain't done. Just not the thing.''

"N-no, sir, I mean ta—to—marry Dendron all right. I

reckon I meant ta—to—marry 'er right from the first time I laid m'daylights on 'er. But I never thought 'twas more'n a dream. I never thought could truly 'appen—happen. Is this waistcoat very dreadful?''

The Earl of Wheymore could not believe that this remarkably handsome son of his did not know how extraordinary he looked in the elegant black and white wear that Camilla had requested he don for the ceremony. "It's exactly what it should be, John. Camilla will think you perfect, and there is no one else you need please in the matter."

"I reckon I'd like ta—to—please you, Father," mumbled the captain in nearly inaudible tones.

Wheymore's eyes sparked with delight. He gave his son a resounding slap on the back, steered him through the doorway into the little chapel of St. Mary of the Angels, and dashed away to escort his niece up the aisle.

Lilliheun and David stood grinning beside Fate as the pipe organ began to twiddle and hum and finally burst into a sweet symphony. Two beguiling little girls in matching dresses of whispering blue silk laden with seed pearls and overlaid with dainty pinafores of Brussels lace came carefully down the aisle scattering tiny handfuls of pink rose petals energetically about them. The captain almost did not recognize Jolly and Grig, but as they approached the altar where he stood both of them wiggled white-gloved little fingers secretively at him and smiled widely and he could not help but smile in return. Behind them a young gentleman carried a blue velvet pillow cautiously before him in both hands, his bottom lip caught between his teeth as he concentrated on the ring he balanced thereon.

Tick was so intent upon not dropping the thing that he never once looked up to see where he was going and might well have fallen right up the altar step if Harley had not reached out quickly from the front pew and steered him to the side. The captain's lips began to quiver. Behind Tick, a lady of enthralling beauty in a gown of blue silk the exact color of her eyes stepped gracefully forward, a bouquet of red and white roses and baby's breath in her hands and a pretty pink blush to her glowing cheeks. The captain felt Lilliheun wiggle uneasily beside him, heard him exhale abruptly, and then saw David surreptitiously poke the besotted gentleman in the ribs. "M'sister, The Banshee, is practicing for the future," David whispered. Fate could not help himself. He laughed.

And that was how Camilla beheld him as she entered the chapel on her uncle's arm—laughing—his dark eyes asparkle. She gasped at the pure exuberance and elegance of him and engraved the image upon her memory. Wheymore pressed her hand gently and Camilla returned the pressure in a tacit acknowledgement of the glowing embers that the glorious, exceptional Captain Jason Fate, Sir Jason, Knight of the Forests Wild, John Locksley Bedford, Viscount Neiland even now fanned into a fierce blaze of love within them both.

Camilla, in a high-waisted, gently flowing gown of white satin, deceptive in its simplicity, and carrying a bouquet of white roses intermixed with bright yellow daffodils that had not been picked from the green in the center of Grosvenor Square only because it was much too late in the season for those particular blooms to have survived, with a circlet of daisies in her chestnut curls and a small pearl necklace at her throat, advanced up the aisle at a most graceful and stately pace.

From the front of the chapel, Fate watched, enraptured. "There be no way so beautiful a lady can be wantin' ta b'long ta me," he whispered as he took her hand. "Are ye sure-certain ye wish ta—to—do this, Dendron?" Camilla did indeed wish to do precisely that to which he referred and proved it to him then and there.

There were festivities, of course, after the fact, and a good deal of merrymaking. But since Camilla had wished to be married in the little chapel near the earl's estate in Northumberland not as many members of the *ton* shuffled about on the ballroom floor or wandered through the gardens as might have been expected had they been wed from the house in London. The wedding unwittingly became a select and exclusive affair that would be speculated upon for a goodly number of weeks and those who had not made the foray into the wilds of the north would be envious of those who had for a long while to come.

One particular gentleman, however, did arrive, though late, on the arm of the Duke of Dewhurst and surrounded by a retinue of gay and charming aristocrats. He entered the ballroom with a light step and an engaging smile which only faltered for a moment when he came face to face with Lord Wright who had so often taken great joy in plaguing the life out of him. But Wright was in such good humor that not one pun, one witticism, one unwanted comment passed his lips. He bowed with an elegant flourish, offered the gentleman a resounding compliment upon the manner in which he had resolved the fate of one Lord Eversley, late of London, presently of Calcutta, and strolled off to send someone in search of the bride and groom.

It was David who discovered them deep in the shadows beneath the ballroom balcony and rousted them out with threats of dire consequences. "For he is determined to make m'brother's acquaintance. There is no avoiding it. And you must stand beside Johnny, Cam, and see he does not go taking a swipe at the man."

"But what man?" asked Camilla giggling. "Who is this paragon?"

"Oh, no, I ain't saying," laughed David tugging at the both of them. "Wright's gone off to find father so he can make the introductions properly."

And make them properly, Wheymore did. True, the smile upon his face was somewhat enigmatic as he took his son's arm and led both Jason and Camilla to stand before the gentleman. But no one could doubt the pride that beamed across his visage as he pronounced the words: "Your Royal Highness, you know, I believe, my new daughter-in-law, Camilla, and may I present my elder son, John Locksley Bedford, Viscount Neiland."

With near a hundred pairs of eyes watching, Captain Jason Fate failed to bow, or even nod, but instead looked the Fat Prince up and down as if that royal gentleman were an Elgin Marble. Camilla held her breath. The Earl of Wheymore chewed his lower lip. Across the ballroom Elgin Moss and Artie Radd stood frozen. The Duke of

Dewhurst winked audaciously at Camilla from behind the Prince Regent's back and Lord Wright stared up expectantly at the ceiling, obviously waiting for it to come crashing down upon their heads.

"M'Father 'as—has—spoken to me about ye," Fate said at last. "I reckon I don't b'lieve but half of it."

It was as much as anyone could expect from him, Camilla thought, taking hold of his arm with both hands. All his life he had despised the Royals and the aristocrats and lay blame upon them for the misery and deprivation of his world. Surely someone had explained his previous circumstances to Prinny. Surely the Regent would not have come here expecting obeisance from such a man as Jason Fate.

The Prince Regent's slightly protuberant eyes blinked as though he had been struck. And then one corner of his mouth began to twitch upward. And then the other corner followed. "I choose not to believe but half of what I have heard of you either, m'boy," he responded softly, extending his hand. "I am pleased at Wheymore's extreme good fortune in recovering a most beloved son and congratulate you upon equal good fortune in obtaining the hand of the beautiful and beguiling Miss Quinn."

"You were astounded. Admit it," Camilla teased later that evening as the two sat side by side before the fire in the parlor of the snug little dower house that Wheymore had made available to them. "You expected the Prince Regent to be some sort of ogre, didn't you?"

"I don't wish ta be speakin' about no Prince Regent," murmured Fate, holding her more tightly against him and bestowing a kiss upon the top of her head as it rested pleasantly against his shoulder. "Nor I don't wish ta—to—be discussin' the weddin' or the ball or none of the people what attended."

"You do not, sir?"

"No, Dendron, I don't."

"What would you care to discuss then?"

"Nothin'," he said, setting her aside and rising from

the sopha. ''There be somethin' we need to be doin', not discussin'.''

Camilla looked up at him, her emerald eyes all innocence. ''And what might that be, my darling husband?''

''Ye stay right there,'' he ordered soberly and left the room. She heard him climb the stairs, heard his footsteps cross the room above, heard the opening and closing of several doors and then he was descending the staircase again. In a moment he was in the parlor doorway. His jacket, neckcloth, and shirt collars were gone, his waistcoat hung open, his shoes and stockings were missing, but about his brow was tied a red silk bandanna and from his earlobe hung a golden hoop. He came and tugged her from the sopha and led her through a set of French doors out onto a tiny balcony. '' 'Tis a full moon,'' he said, holding her an arm's length away from him.

It was indeed a full moon and very bright and across the grounds the orchestra still played and the sounds of partying carried to them on the breeze. Camilla stared up into his sparkling eyes and remembered another night and another moon and the glint of gold beside a starkly handsome face. Her hand rose to touch his cheek and then moved softly to the dark curls that near covered the ear from which the earring hung.

''Ye'll be certain to remember what it was I told ye about touchin' it an' such, won't ye?'' grinned Fate with a most seductively lifted eyebrow. ''Ye be doin' so at your peril, m'pretty.''

'' 'Tis a mystical thing,'' Camilla whispered. ''Do I touch it, like so, I shall be fated to love you forever and ever.''

''Aye,'' laughed the captain quietly as her finger sent the hoop swinging. He gathered her into his arms while she played with it and nibbled a bit at her eyebrow to distract her.

''Oh, no,'' Camilla protested. ''You have come awearin' of it to tempt me, sir, and you shall not distract me now. If I do remember aright, 'tis a thing of destiny an' should I be removin' of it from where it now clings, I shall be forced to marry you.''

''Uh-huh.''

"Of course, we are already married, so this cannot be seen as quite so great a threat."

"There's somewhat I didn't mention," mumbled Fate cheerily.

"Oh? And may I ask what that might be, your roguishness?"

"If ye take it from a gypsy's ear what ye be already married to, yer soul will be his for eternity."

"Well, that does not seem too bad a bargain, dearest."

"An' one thin' else."

"Oh?"

"Ye'll be bearin' his child afore a year is out."

"Oh, you think so, do you?" giggled Camilla snatching the shining hoop from his ear and tucking it provocatively into the bodice of her gown.

Fate laughed and lifted her into his arms. Her skirts swishing at his knees, he carried her through the parlor, up the staircase and into her bedchamber where he deposited her upon a glorious new sleighbed as soft as clouds. And in a moment he was beside her, pulling her into his arms and kissing her with a passion that swept her breath away.

The modish young matron who turned to stare so steadily into the elegant bow window of Hatchard's bookshop in Piccadilly attracted a good deal of attention. It might have been because of the way the whimsical confection of cream straw and cherry silk ribands sat upon her chestnut curls, or because of the exquisite fit of her Parisienne-styled forest green walking dress decorated with cherry braid, or because of the adorable pink blush upon her cheeks and the merry gleam in her bright emerald eyes, but it was none of these things. It was not even because of the enormous dog with matching cherry ribands on its ears which sat patiently beside her, tongue lolling. Rather, it was the sudden recognition of *who* the matron was that brought all to a standstill.

"Lady Neiland," sighed Allegra, Lady LaRoquette, herself a young matron, newly married. "She is everything beautiful and elegant and—and—"

"Romantic," provided her younger sister, Fiona. "And it is her second novel she stares at so raptly in Hatchard's window. Did you not love *The Earnest Heart,* Allegra? And this one is even more enticing. It's called *M'Lord Mysterious.* They say both are written about her husband though she won't admit it. I began the second yesterday, and I have already near finished the first volume. Oh! Oh! Allegra! It's him. I am certain it's Viscount Neiland just coming across the street!"

Indeed it was Viscount Neiland, dressed to the nines in a coat of dark blue Superfine and buff pantaloons, his glossy dark curls in disarray, his eyes sparkling with enthusiasm, with a babe of indeterminate age cradled in one arm contentedly sucking upon the nether corner of his dishevelled neckcloth, who came bouncing across the cobbles to join Camilla at Hatchard's window.

"Well, and where have the two of you been?" asked Camilla with a twinkle in her eyes. "Not cavorting about Tattersall's I should hope. Little Ned is really much too young to be buying his own horseflesh, my dear."

"I doubt they've been to Tat's," replied a familiar voice from over her shoulder. "Gone to stir up trouble in the House of Lords, I should think. Spied the both of them conversing with Wheymore and Wright in the entry way only an hour ago."

"Oh, no," laughed Camilla, turning to take both of Lilliheun's hands in her own. "Don't say so, Clare. The Lords are still reeling from the ruckus those hooligans raised over the orphanages and the hospitals."

"Yes, well, your husband does tend to encourage reformation and rebellion in Wheymore and Wright, y'know. Hullo, Johnny. Might I have a try at holding my godson do you think?"

"Only if ye be willing to sacrifice yer neckcloth. He's about to sport a new ivory," grinned Fate, handing the babe over. "Have ye seen it, Lilliheun? Dendron's new book?"

"Indeed. Aurora brought all three volumes home near

a week ago and fell into raptures over it immediately. I think she particularly likes the young woman referred to as The Banshee. Now, why do you think that is?"

"Well, but it is not Rory precisely," Camilla protested.

"It's close enough for those of us who know the wench," laughed Lilliheun, offering his neckcloth up in sacrifice to Master Ned's sprouting teeth.

"M'lord Mys-ter-ious'," murmured Fate, staring into Hatchard's window and putting an arm about Camilla's waist. " 'Another as-toun-ding romance from the pen of the Viscountess Neiland.' Why do they not call ye Dendron?" he asked then, his eyes meeting hers teasingly. " 'Tis yer name is it not?"

"Jason?" Camilla stared at him, her eyes wide. "Jason, you *read* that notice! You did! You read it perfectly!"

"And ain't ye been teaching me to do just that for months and months?"

"Yes, but—but—you never have read anything correctly until now. I thought you would never understand—"

Fate's face crinkled into laughter. "I didn't want ye to know, Dendron, how well ye taught me. I like the way ye teach an' I didn't want ye to stop."

"So why betray yourself now, old chap?" asked a thoroughly amused Lilliheun.

"Well, b'cause I wanted to impress 'er properly an' in a proper place. Besides, David pointed out ta me that even though I can read, I can't write atall. That ought to take a powerful lot of teaching, don't ye think? And Mossie reminded me about addin' sums. An' Artie an' Tick and Harley figger I ain't never gonna learn ta—to—talk proper all the time."

"And what about the girls?" asked Camilla. "Did they not mention anything wrong with you that needs improving?"

"Dancing," grinned Fate. "Seems I remember Jolly an' Grig mentioning as how I need ye to teach me to dance better. I reckon I got enough I don't know to keep ye teaching me for another twenty years at the very least!"

Camilla eyed him sternly but Lilliheun broke into whoops and she could not help but laugh herself. "And if I am to teach you all these things, whenever will I find time to write another book?" she queried at last.

Fate's face grew solemn. "Ye've time ta write a book whenever ye wish ta do so, darlin'."

"And if you cannot think of a story," chuckled Lilliheun, "you've only to let Johnny out of your sight for a day or two and a plot will likely come knocking at your door immediately upon his return."

"Chomping at his heels more like," agreed Camilla gleefully, removing the end of Lilliheun's neckcloth from her son's grasp and taking the child into her own arms. "And afraid though I am of it, I rather think this fellow here will not be loathe to supply his aging mother with a plot or two either."

"Naw," grinned Fate, "not Neddy. Neddy's goin' to be—"

"Going to be what, Jason?"

"Well, I was goin' to say, a perfeck gen'leman, but that don't answer, ye see."

"It does not?" Lilliheun smiled.

"No, 'cause look at you. Ye're a perfeck gen'leman, and I never saw a cove make no bigger muck of things—drivin' around ob—ob—blivious to people tryin' ta kill ye. No, I reckon as how I don't want Neddy bein' quite so perfeck a gen'leman as all that. B'sides—" he added tapping at a closed little fist with one long slim finger.

"Besides what, my lord," prompted Camilla.

"B'sides, I 'spect as how Neddy's got just a bit of the gypsy in him. I reckon it come from yer side of the family, Dendron," he chuckled as the babe's fist opened and Lilliheun's diamond stick pin fell from it into Fate's palm. "Light-fingered, he be," nodded Fate, presenting Lilliheun his jewellery with a grin and a bow, "and that's a fact. Must be your side of the family, darlin'. Ever'one knows my side is above reproach."

WATCH FOR THESE ZEBRA REGENCIES

LADY STEPHANIE   (0-8217-5341-X, $4.50)
by Jeanne Savery
Lady Stephanie Morris has only one true love: the family estate she
has managed ever since her mother died. But then Lord Anthony Rider
arrives on her estate, claiming he has plans for both the land and the
woman. Stephanie soon realizes she's fallen in love with a man whose
sensual caresses will plunge her into a world of peril and intrigue . . . a
man as dangerous as he is irresistible.

BRIGHTON BEAUTY   (0-8217-5340-1, $4.50)
by Marilyn Clay
Chelsea Grant, pretty and poor, naively takes school friend Alayna
Marchmont's place and spends a month in the country. The devastating
man had sailed from Honduras to claim his promised bride, Miss
Marchmont. An affair of the heart may lead to disaster . . . unless a
resourceful Brighton beauty finds a way to stop a masquerade and
keep a lord's love.

LORD DIABLO'S DEMISE   (0-8217-5338-X, $4.50)
by Meg-Lynn Roberts
The sinfully handsome Lord Harry Glendower was a gambler and the
black sheep of his family. About to be forced into a marriage of convenience, the devilish fellow engineered his own demise, never having
dreamed that faking his death would lead him to the heavenly refuge
of spirited heiress Gwyn Morgan, the daughter of a physician.

A PERILOUS ATTRACTION   (0-8217-5339-8, $4.50)
by Dawn Aldridge Poore
Alissa Morgan is stunned when a frantic passenger thrusts her baby
into Alissa's arms and flees, having heard rumors that a notorious
highwayman posed a threat to their coach. Handsome stranger Hugh
Sebastian secretly possesses the treasured necklace the highwayman
seeks and volunteers to pose as Alissa's husband to save her reputation.
With a lost baby and missing necklace in their care, the couple embarks
on a journey into peril—and passion.

*Available wherever paperbacks are sold, or order direct from the
Publisher. Send cover price plus 50¢ per copy for mailing and
handling to Penguin USA, P.O. Box 999, c/o Dept. 17109,
Bergenfield, NJ 07621. Residents of New York and Tennessee must
include sales tax. DO NOT SEND CASH.*

LOOK FOR THESE REGENCY ROMANCES

WATCH FOR THESE REGENCY ROMANCES